A MATTER OF DETAIL

A MATTER OF DETAIL

Maniza Naqvi

Tara Press

A MATTER OF DETAIL

Maniza Naqvi

Tara Press
[Trade Division of India Research Press]
Flat No. 6, Khan Market, New Delhi - 110 003
Ph.: 24694610; Fax : 24618637
www.indiaresearchpress.com
contact@indiaresearchpress.com

2009

ISBN-13 digit : 978-81-8386-083-3
ISBN-10 digit : 81-8386-083-4

Tara Press is an imprint of India Research Press
Printed for *India Research Press* at Focus Impressions, New Delhi.

For Alizay and Sahar

BOOK ONE
A Matter of Detail

BOOK TWO
American Shemerican

BOOK ONE

A Matter of Detail

1

A Matter of Detail

'IT's getting late. Not like him to miss a lesson without letting me know. Not like him at all to go missing like this.' Hajra juts her lips in a pout of disapproval and scolds her own reflection on the gleaming, black, lacquered surface of the console piano. She has now been waiting for Abbas, she is sure, for a good two hours.

She shrugs her tense shoulders. 'Must be an unusually busy evening at the clinic,' she repeats in her husky, nasal voice to her blurred plump image on the piano, which stands against the baby blue of the freshly painted wall of the drawing room. Noting the colour, she recalls her specifications to her husband, 'No, I do not care what Robbialac calls the paint, make sure it's baby blue, Razzak, like the way it always was!' And Razzak had made sure it was just that and that the bedroom was the exact bottle green, like the large glass vats sold in Batli Bazaar she was so fond of and out of which she made many a lamp pedestal for the rooms in 43-G.

Her tiny diamond nose stud catches the candlelight and winks back at her. Hajrabai flexes her fingers, folding them into the palms of her hands and then stretches out her hands, feeling the slight pain of arthritis. She frets, 'What are we to do?' She has lit the candles and if Abbas should ring the bell now they will have to practice in this diminished light. She has been of half a mind to take such liberties as to think that she will still go on with the lesson should he ring the bell now. 'What would have been the point of leaving 43-G and coming here if she was going to do that?' she argues with herself.

She covers her head with the pallu of her cotton sari. She runs her slender, long fingers on the edge of its border and examines the block print of gray and pink tiny geometrical designs. With her other hand, she smoothens her still thick, long, white hair, now gathered in a tight bun at the pale and soft back of her much creased neck.

She has been waiting since the Zohr azaan, Asr has come and gone and soon it will be time for Maghrib. No, this will not do.

She will not answer the doorbell. No point at all if she answers, no point at all. It would all amount to just having made a fuss. To not rest, a terrible thing, but she knows herself and she knows that she will make this concession for him. He is an exception, a brilliant, dear boy and such good company. Surely there can be exceptions?

Well maybe not, but she has never minded the rules. If she had she would not be here today, now would she? Well, not entirely correct. She reminds herself she is back here, in this apartment because after all that has come and gone, she is minding the rules.

'But still! Of course I will answer the door. Of course I will! It would be absurd not to. What? What am I going to do when he comes, stand on this side and not answer? Pretend I'm not here?' she chuckles at the comic image she has conjured up. What is this upholding of tradition now after all that has gone? If her father could have known this? If only her brother could see her now. She will tell her father this when she next visits Mewa Shah. He would have laughed now if he could see her in all her contradictions. But he hadn't laughed then, had he? When she had contradicted him with what he considered to have been her unforgivable transgression. Never saw her face again. Refused to have anything to do with her. Holding such a grudge against the one whom he loved so much. Now she is the one holding grudges against those who love her most. She knows she is doing this. Somehow the pain of it feels sweet. She is bewildered by this.

She goes to see him almost every week. Someone has to. She is doing her duty, she chuckles to herself. Daughters stay, sons leave. She shakes her head, rebuking herself for contorting facts. Meir would have stayed if he could. It was easy for her to have done it. It's best he has gone. Everyone who could leave, did. If it's not one thing, it's another. And her father would have said it was all the same to him, because she left too. She eloped and was banished from her home. She had run away with Razzak one day after college in 1953. She was eighteen and he was no more than that. In those days he was tall and lanky and had towered above her. He had a booming voice. His jet-black hair had been brushed back without a parting, and below a wide forehead, his large olive green eyes, framed by thick eyelashes were mostly downcast due to his shyness. He used to come to their house to learn the piano from her. He didn't learn a thing, but promptly upon setting eyes on a petite, pale young woman with light brown eyes and thick, jet black, wavy hair down to her waist, and a voice so sweet, slightly nasal, husky and as though punctuated with a tinkling bell, Razzak had fallen in love with her thereby causing havoc in her family and in his own, and rupturing a business relationship that had existed for nearly a century. Hajra's father had offered these piano lessons when one day, the thin and stuttering son of his business partner had mentioned his interest in playing the instrument. 'Why, my daughter Hajra is an excellent teacher. Why don't you learn from her?' And that had been that. After the first three lessons which had never gone beyond finding the placement of 'c' on the ivories, they had found many places in Karachi to meet.

Hajrabai has turned off the fan and lit candles and now the room has become oppressive. The evening light coming in from the open doors of the balcony has diminished and the sea breeze has not yet started up. Soon, though not yet. She has dusted a pat of Cuticura talcum powder on the nape of her neck to battle the prickly heat that always bothers her, no matter what the season is. It is late January but in Karachi the heat has already crept back after a short respite. She fans herself with a rolled copy of *The Star*, one of the eveningers brought in by Razzak earlier in the afternoon when he stopped by after Juma prayers to bring her vegetables, fruit and fish. The dhobi left an hour ago, bringing with him ironed and starched linen and her cotton saris, blouses and petticoats. In her ruled copy book, she has carefully noted the number of items he has taken and checked off those he returned against last week's entries. All is in order. She puts a hand on her knee and lifts herself up with a wince. She has spread out considerably over the years. Not the slight chit of a girl she used to be. Not that Razzak is any better. A real giant himself. She chuckles again. How times have changed. He used to be all skin and bones, really single pasli. Yes, girls leave too. Girls get married, they go away to universities, they get jobs and then they only come back in December, or whenever it's convenient for them. The girls have all left, save for Sara. All left for university. It's good that Sara was never interested in an education beyond the bare minimum of a bachelor's degree.

And Kulsum, of course, left with her husband.

She goes out to the balcony, through the wooden slatted teak doors, to the noise of the traffic on Lawrence Road. The evening air was heavy with diesel and petrol fumes from the buses, rickshaws,

trucks, motorcycles and countless cars. She rubs her eyes as they begin to fill up with tears, stung by the fumes. The few plants that she has are withering in the heat. She has forgotten to water them yet again. There is a rubbery palm, a leafy fern and several potted chamelis that continue to yield fragrant white blossoms at dawn. It was different at 43-G where she had a daily morning routine with Zareenabai. With her slippered feet, she pushes a few dead leaves and blossoms, fallen from the branches, that are lying scattered on the pink and yellow tiles of the mosaic floor. She pushes them towards the edge of the balcony and watches their slow spiral descent two floors below to the garden which is bursting with green, thanks to the monsoon rains which came on time this year, back in late July.

The monsoon comes to us from Ethiopia, she remembers how her father used to remind them each year of this. What we consider as being so typically ours, so essential, stuff of song and poetry, originates elsewhere. She looks out over the haze of evening, dust and soot at the darkening treetops across the road in Gandhi Garden where soot and sand coloured kites are circling, coming in to nest only at night. The chattering of birds can be heard above the noise of the traffic. This triggers memory of the Beach Luxury Hotel; she remembers how Razzak and she had picked a table close to the railing near the water's edge. Across the water, the morning mist was rising from the dark and dense mangroves which were alive with the chatter of birds and the flapping of wings. They could see dust coloured kites skulking on branches and beginning to rise, circling upwards, and white sea-gulls that flew low or perched on mangrove branches. Hundreds of tiny, grey sparrows and black and white swallows flew close by, dipping their beaks and wings into the water. White herons glided on to branches and a few pelicans or white cranes dipped their elegant long necks while standing at the water's edge on one foot. Between history and fiction periods at St Joseph's, Hajra managed to meet Razzak for tea at the Beach Luxury Hotel. She had skipped this morning class, the discussion on the parliamentary system in England. It was mid-morning, around ten, the lawns of the waterfront hotel were nearly empty save for the gardeners tending the flowers and grass and the sweepers washing the pathways. As Razzak and Hajra walked towards the outdoor café, a waiter hurried past them, through the garden, up to a room with a tray laden with tea, toast, marmalade and eggs.

She was studying English Literature at St Joseph's and was in her third year at college. A year later Razzak and Hajra had eloped. There had been a scandal, of course. Hajra's father had disowned her, Razzak's father, him. Hajra's father had died of a stroke shortly after. But in Razzak's family, after a brief opposition, his father had reconciled to Hajra being of the Book. This had been 1953. Sara was born in 1954. Then in 1956, Razzak had married again, to his cousin Zareena, thin, tall and graceful in movement with beautiful large eyes, the colour of olives and with thick lashes, just like Razzak's and a complexion to match. Zareena and Razzak had been betrothed from birth and her family wealth made it highly advisable to follow through with the marriage.

After all, in addition to being an obligation and a matter of honour, business was beginning to lag given that the partnership with Hajra's father had been dissolved. It was only in 1968, when Meir decided to leave Karachi, that the business relationship was reestablished. Meir thought it best to rekindle the connection with his brother-in-law. After all, who better to manage the family business while he was away than his own brother-in-law? Such a long time ago all this was. When her brother left, he left all his business holdings to Razzak. Razzak bought out half the business and left the other half in Hajrabai's name. Every month Razzak brings Hajra her share of of the earnings -- 25 per cent. Hajra

wires another 25 per cent to her brother at a London account. Razzak keeps it all clear and worked out in a ledger, a copy book much like her own for the dhobi. He insists on going through the accounts with her every month. What was bought, what was sold, how much and when. And what is left. Whether there is a profit or a loss. He has never reported a loss to her. To Zareenabai, it is almost always a near threat of loss that he talks about. Hajrabai never interferes in these matters. He is not only her husband but is also locked in a business partnership with her family that spans almost 150 years when her grandfather borrowed money from his grandfather to begin trading in cotton. That was in 1862.

'Trouble in America always helped Karachi,' Razzak was fond of pointing out. 'Certainly, it helped us!' And it was true. It was true now and it had been true then. The Civil War in America had done wonders for Hajrabai and Razzak's forefathers; they could only have hoped that such luck would continue. War had always benefitted the city. In 1838, the British afraid of the Russian Empire's expansion to the Arabian Sea, occupied Karachi and the city served as the landing port for their troops for the First Afghan War. In 1843, they annexed Sindh and moved the capital of the province from Hyderabad to Karachi. Then the British made Sindh a district of the Bombay Presidency and Karachi was made the district headquarters. Troops were stationed there and businessmen from all over the country arrived to cater to the needs of the army, an opportunity not to be missed. Karachi started to become a vibrant town, particularly at the confluence of the military barracks and the commercial sector. This area became known as Saddar, the Presidency. Then came the American Civil War in 1861. And with the trouble in America, there was a huge demand for cotton from Sindh. A boom in the cotton trade resulted as Sindhi cotton replaced American cotton as raw material for the British textile industry. Karachi flourished and became a city of commerce, a beautifully planned town complete with parks, libraries and places of worship from mosques to churches, to Parsi and Hindu temples and synagogues. It was a town with piped water and public transportation and a municipal government that collected taxes and kept things running. The Karachi Chamber of Commerce was established and Haji Rueewallah was, of course, a member. The port was improved and steps were taken to develop and market Sindh's agricultural produce to England. Shipping enterprises thrived; there was the Indus Steam Flotilla and the Orient Inland Steam Navigation Company which transported Haji Yunis Rueewallah's purchases of cotton and wheat down the Indus and across Karachi Bay to Karachi Port. As a result of all these developments, a number of British companies opened their offices and warehouses in Karachi and its population increased. By 1868, Karachi was the largest exporter of wheat and cotton in India. Karachi also received a boost with the opening of the Suez Canal in 1869, which made it the nearest port to England in India. By 1872, Haji Yunis Rueewallah's business earnings had increased five-fold in just twelve years.

When Hajra's grandfather, Ibrahimbhai, walked into Razzak's grandfather's shop, Haji Mohammad Yunis Rueewallah was already established in Saddar on Elphinstone Street in a two- storey building. Outside the shop, Ibrahimbhai stopped to drink from the water fountain built into the wall, the inscription on which read, 'Quench your thirst here, and remember the thirst of Hussein.' Haji Rueewallah, like many other traders in the city, was a Shia. He was the main supplier of white cotton muslin to the British military garrisons stationed in Karachi cantonment. War was on in the north in Afghanistan. Hajrabai's grandfather had moved from Calcutta to Karachi to take advantage of the business boom taking place because of the Civil War that had broken out in America. Ibrahimbhai wrote back to relatives in Bombay and Calcutta of the

wide streets lined with palm trees and sandstone buildings, that were interspersed with parks which were sprinkled with water to keep the dust down by water boys carrying mashks, or large leather bags. The daily chirkao, the water sprinkling, also brought down the temperature. He wrote of the wonderful clean sea air, how healthy it was and how beautiful the clear sunlight was against the sandstone façade. His asthma, he wrote, had almost disappeared.

These were letters, much like the ones that Meir wrote a century later from Jerusalem to Hajra. Letters much travelled and much longed for. The hottest news in the business communities in Bombay, Madras and Calcutta revolved around the happy tidings that supplies to the mills in Lancastershire were dwindling and that the British Empire was increasing its production of cotton in the Punjab... And all of it was making its way to England through the Karachi port. Business people were moving to Karachi from Bombay and elsewhere in India. Besides, Karachi was now the capital of Sindh. And business would flourish with the completion of the railways which linked Karachi to the Punjab, northern India and Sindh. On these railways, wheat and cotton production started flowing through Karachi. Oil extraction was moving forward in Sui, and was being exported from Karachi port, and this too was the result of the railway line.

Instead of granting a loan, Haji Rueewallah had proposed a business partnership to Hajra's grandfather: Ibrahimbhai had connections in shipping and cotton in Calcutta and Bombay which would be backed by the financial and real estate clout of Haji Rueewallah, with his numerous godowns in Kharadar and Lea market. Haji Rueewallah would finance the purchasing of cotton wholesale and its storage, and Ibrahimbhai would bring in the distribution sales. The partnership had made them both wealthy men, owners of property with godowns stuffed to the ceiling with cotton waiting to be shipped to mills in England. The flourishing businesses had been passed down to their progeny who, for the most part, had prospered.

In the days before she got married, when Hajra was studying at St Joseph's college which was located in the heart of Saddar, she would ride in a horse-drawn carriage, a Victoria, hired by her father to take her to college and back every day. Burns Road, Preedy Street, Victoria and Elphinstones' in Saddar were the hub of social activities. It was easy to skip classes and slip out to meet at cafés or art galleries. Once, on the pretext of needing to buy cloth for an outfit, she had walked to Bohri Bazaar from her college. She had met Razzak outside a shop and the two of them had walked around in the bazaar as vendors called out to them, hawking their wares of falsa juice, roasted corn, milky tea, paan and cigarettes. It was a bold step to take, to walk together, but they did, though with much trepidation of being seen by relatives.

The pedestrian crowd was enough to keep them unnoticed and Saddar was alive with sounds -- the clanging of tram bells, the calls of tangawallahs and street vendors shouting out to pedestrians, the clippity-clop of the horse-drawn tanga and Victoria carriages, the sound of church bells at noon mingling with azaans from the mosques. Sunlight changed colour on the façade of the buildings, turning them from ochre to rose and to purple in the course of morning, through noon, to early afternoon. Shopkeepers and vendors shouted out the latest items for purchase to passersby—everything, according to them, was up to English standards. There were tinned Capstan cigarettes, silk from China, woollen suits from America, bangles from Hyderabad, refrigerators from Japan and America, copper and nickel pots and pans from Gujranwala, cricket bats from Sialkot. And in this manner, Razzak and Hajra continued to rendezvous at all the venues available to them, the art exhibits for Sadequain at the State Bank and Jamini Roy at the Fyzee Gallery. There was India Coffee House at the corner of Elphi and Preedy Street, and Zelins Café, and Café Grande on Victoria. They would often meet at Thomas and Thomas, the small and much frequented bookstore on Preedy Street. And at Café George and Frederick's Café at the corner of Victoria, places frequented by the city's journalists, writers, actors and unemployed intellectuals. She had gone to the Palm Hotel on Elphinstone Street with her father to see the visiting Shakespeare Company perform plays by Sheridan and Moliére and was once so bold as to let Razzak know beforehand that they were going. Of course, he was there and met them in the foyer and was able to sit with the family to see The School for Scandal. Once they had lunched, miraculously unnoticed, at the very elegant and very crowded Le Gourmet restaurant at the Palace Hotel. The best place to hide is in the open, she had mused.

Now, she is bored. 'Where could Abbas be?' she says to the traffic. She is used to a flurry of activities, one after another. This is how it was at 43-G, people coming and going, never a moment of solitude. Though today she was not alone at all. Zareenabai came by in the morning, then Razzak and right after him, the dhobi. She waits impatiently for Abbas to arrive. She looks as far as she can see to her left, from where he should be coming. She looks to the right just out of habit. As a girl she would have been looking this way from the balcony, leaning forward impatiently, her long, black hair falling about her shoulders and stirring in the breeze as she tried to spot her father, who would ride home on the tram from his shop. And this way, a mile down from here, is where she would have been at this time on a Friday evening in days gone by. At Magain Shalome. That is all gone now. Her father is long gone too, the tram is long gone and that world has all but slipped away. She knows from the few days already spent here, at Lawrence Road that no matter what, with all her airing of the rooms and practicing of rituals, she cannot bring them back.

Practicing rituals won't do that. It would have been possible to practice rituals at 43-G, but here she has been let down. 'Yes, I have! I have been let down!' she says in an annoyed, defiant tone to herself, as though a voice somewhere might have been raised in contradiction. There is no one here but herself. But she needs to remind herself, lest she leave right away for 43-G, right this minute, walking the short distance from Lawrence Road to Patel Park. The evening's advent always puts her into a panic.

Hajrabai comes in from the balcony. She knows that Abbas's clinic is not so far away, at most a mile down the road in Soldier Bazaar. She wonders if she should call him there. She has his number, but for that she would have to go across the hall to the next door or a flight down. And they, her neighbours, both Raymond and Suleiman will mind. They certainly will, given the hour, now past sunset. It would be unacceptable. Wrong. She

has refused to have a cellphone or a landline. Her husband was furious at her obstinacy. Red in the face and short of breath he had blustered, 'Have you completely lost your mind, woman? Are you so bent on removing us from your life?' But she had ignored him and persisted. And to Zareenabai she had said, trying to seem indifferent, 'If you want to talk to me, then you will have to come over.' Finally, after much argument, Razzak and Zareenabai had seen the wisdom of this. It had been Hajrabai's way to make sure that the breach would not widen further and that she would see everyone every day. It was also an excuse to return to 43-G every day. And so they had stopped insisting that she have a phone, or email or a cellphone.

Zareenabai came by early this morning. She had arrived out of breath, having climbed the two flights of stairs too quickly, her plump face, neck and bosom glistening with perspiration, her mustard coloured cotton sari needed to be tied again, having come almost undone as she had trodden accidentally on its hem several times while climbing. She had rebuked, 'Ooff Maulah!' but said nothing more as she arranged her sari and then gathered up her dyed auburn, now thinning hair into a ponytail. Having collected herself and dabbing her neck and face with the end of her sari pallu, she settled next to Hajra on the settee. 'I've brought Hafez with me,' she announced conspiratorially. She had brought with her their much worn and frayed blue canvas cloth bound copy of Divan-e-Hafez. She had told Hajrabai only yesterday that there was a boy in New York, the nephew of a friend of hers, a boy named Zain whom Zareenabai had thought might be a good match for Amina. She was trying to arrange for them to meet. Hajrabai wasn't so sure that this was going to work but she didn't say anything to discourage Zareenabai.

She wanted to see whether or not this boy Zain in New York was worth pursuing for Amina. Hajrabai and Zareenabai always consulted Hafez on important matters which required decisions.

The poet's heartbroken soul had been prayed for and his verses consulted on the marriage of their eldest daughter, Sara, and the verses had spoken of gardens and intoxication, letters arriving and sweet breezes. And sure enough Sara, a spitting image of Razzak and Zareena in their youth, was never happier, never more radiant and content as she was now. Hafez had been consulted on matters of business: whether one deal was too risky or profitable for Razzak to enter into than another.

Hafez had been consulted for Kulsum, their third in line and quiet and serene tempered daughter. Kulsum had been their obedient middle child, pleasing her parents and perhaps making up for Shireen and Sara's independent natures. They had consulted Hafez three times, and each time the verse had been vague, neither promising intoxication nor annihilation. Kulsum, Hajrabai had sighed with dejection, was doomed to boredom. Zareenabai [illegible] had sighed, though with relief. She saw this ambiguity [illegible] a sign that Kulsum would be blessed with stability. Hafez had been consulted after Shireen's marriage as well and the results had been a resounding sound of laughter and joy. This had brought a great deal of comfort to Hajra, Zareena and Razzak after all the trauma that they had gone through with Shireen having married a Hindu boy from Bombay. Amit, a quiet and very graceful man, tall and thin, embodying the stereotype of a professor of political science in New York, had fallen hopelessly in love with the lovely, rosy-cheeked girl from Pakistan, with her olive-coloured eyes, infectious, huge laugh and her light sprinkling of freckles across the bridge of her nose.

Shireen had met him at university where they had been in the same seminar class in their final year. They had informed their parents after their civil marriage at the New York City Hall. What a drama had followed! Amit's parents had temporarily disowned him. Razzak had been furious at Shireen's secrecy. A wedding reception was held later in Karachi. Amit had been understanding enough to go through a nikkah ceremony for Shireen's relatives in Karachi. He had not told his parents about this. Finally, when in a month's time, Amit's mother could not bear the separation from her son and reconciled to the fact that he had married for love, Shireen had completed the pooja and pehras with Amit in Bombay in front of Amit's relatives.

She had not informed her parents of this for years. Resham, the youngest child, and Amina's choice of universities were, according to the verses, to bring them to much taverns and song. Much wine to be spilt there as well. And Zareenabai had consulted the fahl decades ago when making the decision to join Razzak and Hajrabai in marriage. The verse was all she needed to know, 'How beautiful is Shiraz's unparalleled state. God save it from harm and the hands of fate.' The rest of the verse was about gardens filled with fragrance, morning dew, gurgling rivers, laughter and heavenly spirits.

This morning, Zareenabai had also brought with her candles and a canister of imported olive oil as a gesture of participation in Hajra's life. 'Hajrabai, I want you to use these candles this evening. You must forgive me, Hajrabai, you must come home. Come, let's take all your things, pack up and go home. I was wrong, we can do everything. We will do everything. I am younger than you, it is your place to forgive me. You must spit out this anger. Such a small thing, such a small thing I said and you are making it so big.'

Hajrabai felt a lump of sweet grief rising in her throat, her eyes moistened but she had ignored Zareena's entreaties and changed the subject,'So what about this boy, Zain?' It was always easy to distract Zareenabai. 'Tell me about him.' 'Not much to tell you,' said Zareenabai, immediately distracted. 'Except that he and Amina knew each other in New York. They are about the same age and they are in the same profession. So I'm thinking, why not? What's the harm in a little matchmaking?' 'Shall we take out a fahl?'

'Yes!' said Zareena, immediately sitting up. 'Should I?'

'Of course you should, do it right away!' Zareena said the Fateha three times and shut her eyes tight as she formed the question in her mind. Zareena continued to keep her eyes tightly shut as she prayed and then, when done, she opened the book of poetry. She traced her fingers down and counted the verses according to the formula and then stopped at one. She read it out loud:

I said: O fate, when will you awake? The sun is up, it is now dawn-break.

Said fate, you have made many a mistake, Yet keep hope and faith within your breast.

'Oh, what does it mean?' Hajrabai asked. 'Does it mean that this is auspicious, that there is hope, that this time there is hope?' 'I think that's what it means, It seems straightforward enough,' replied Zareenabai. 'What else could it mean?' Hajrabai replied, 'It talks of dawn, a new beginning, of having faith, of keeping an open mind. It talks of hope. It must mean that there is hope in this possibility!'

'Yes, that's what I'm thinking,' agreed Zareenabai. 'Let's think about this some more.'

Zareenabai had forgotten to take the Divan back to 43-G with her this morning. Now Hajrabai sat flipping through its pages.

'Oh, where is that boy!' Hajrabai put the book down and started to walk back and forth in the darkening room. She fingered the black lacquer of the piano and the white crocheted runner upon which she had lit the candles in the menorah. 'It could also mean we should leave well alone,' she said out loud, recalling the verse read earlier that morning by Zareenabai. Hajrabai had lit extra candles to make sure she had the family covered. Sara, Razzak, Zareenabai, Resham, Amina, Shireen, Kulsum, Meir and herself. And one for zachor (to remember) and another for shamor (to observe). She considers the flames and the steady black spirals of smoke rising towards the ceiling. A gust of breeze comes in and the flames sway and waver, burning larger and then steadying themselves. No, she had decided now she would not be able to let Abbas in, nor answer the door should the bell ring.

Was she lonely, she asked herself now. In a way, she always had been since her father disowned her. Was that true, she wondered? No, never quite like this. She felt an uncontrollable anxiety and a sense of helplessness. This candlelight, this silence, conjured up too much. It's true what they say, you can never go back. Razzak visits every day. He was here just now. Came right after the Juma prayers and complained as usual about the stairs. Red in the face and out of breath, he said that the two flights of stairs would be the death of him. 'Hajrabai, what don't I do to reclaim you? Which whims, which nakhras, of yours don't I take up?' She had patted his huge chest and leaned her head against him. He had stroked her hair, took her in his arms, bent down and kissed her mouth tenderly and smoothed her brow with his wide moist palm. 'Are we going to have to organize another wedding, will you make me bring a baraat, have a rukhsati and take you home with me? Is that what this is? You want the whole baraat and rukhsati because the first time around we just ran off?'

Hajrabai had laughed and her husband had continued, 'Because that's exactly what we'll have to do when they all arrive here, and you know they're coming.' Razzak referred to Amina and Resham who were to arrive soon. Hajrabai had laughed. 'Tell them to stay where they are, they cannot bear my fancies, I've already been told that by Sara,' she replied.

Razzak had come laden with groceries and the monthly share from the business earnings. Business, he always tells her, is picking up. She kept most but gave him two thousand rupees for the caretaker at Mewa Shah. Every month she does this, for the upkeep of the graves. 'Tell him, Razzak, that he should wash the gravestones more regularly; there is too much bird shit. Make sure he does that. I will go there next week. I want the graves sparkling at Roshashana.'

Later, when they are done with lunch, he washes his hands in the tiny ceramic sink in the dining room. She is seated at the small, round dining table, spooning sugar into his Ovaltine, stirring it vigorously, and making the spoon clink loudly against the thick, stout glass. She is listening to him talk to her about the apartment in Kharadar. Someone had offered a considerable sum for it. It was falling apart. She knows that. She has told him to get rid of it. Empty for years, room for pigeons and rats. Would she want to sell it?

'What do you think?' she had asked.

'I think it's a good deal,' he had said. 'Sell before we have the headache of a squatter in there. Or worse still, before the government appropriates it. There is much talk nowadays of the KMC taking over historical buildings, and about establishing a cultural zone in the old city. Let's sell now.' She had agreed. And then Razzak said something under his breath, chuckling.

'What's that?' she asked, 'I didn't hear what you said. What are you giggling about, Razzak?'

'Oh nothing, nothing, baba,' Razzak had replied, sipping from the glass she handed to him. 'I was just saying, let's sell it before you get any more bright ideas about moving! Who knows, you may want to move to Kharadar next!' 'Razzak, you know this is important to me!' Hajra protested.

'Why can't you do all this at home?' demanded Razzak. Hajrabai asked, 'Can I?'

'You are the mistress of the house. You are the head of this family. Now don't make a face about that, you know you are! You can do whatever you like! I don't understand what has gotten into you after all these years!' replied Razzak.

'Razzak, I will not listen to your nagging about this now. Let me be. For fifty years I have observed your moharrams, your eids, your rozas, your faqas, your kundas, your barsis of this imam and that. Have I ever said that I want to observe my rozas, my rituals, and my traditions?

Have I ever said that the girls should learn or know? No, don't even answer that. I am not asking you to answer. When I brought it up, Sara and Zareenabai's reaction was enough for me to know that my ways were not acceptable.'

'You know very well, Hajrabai, that you've taken a small slight and made it into a big situation, you haven't even given them a chance to make up to you! You brought this up in front of the most foolish in our household and took their first, thoughtless reaction as their last.'

Hajrabai put her hand up as if to end the conversation, 'Case closed, end of discussion. All I am saying is that I just want to begin to wrap it all up. I want a little part of myself for myself. Is that too much to ask for?'

'Yes it is Hajra, it is too much to ask for. There is no yourself or myself. We are. You are my wife and you belong with me and our children. We are all part of one family. How can you separate yourself from us? You're suddenly getting religious! It is too much to ask for! If you really wanted to observe your traditions, you should have put your foot down. After all you are older, and you would have had your way. What do Zareena or Sara have to do with this? And don't I earn enough for you that you now have to start teaching the piano again?' 'No, you don't make enough! Stop being difficult, Razzak! I do not want to discuss this.'

'Too much sugar in the milk again Hajra, what do you want to do? Give me diabetes? That's it, you are all out to kill me.' 'You didn't have any problems drinking the whole glass down before the sugar occurred to you now, did you? Speaking of money, how much do you think we will get for the apartment in Kharadar?'

'Okay, baba, the girls will deal with you. I will not speak to you about this any more. You are going crazy in your old age!' 'Don't you call me old!'

'Who do you think is calling you old? Your old man is calling you his old lady. Your bhuda is calling you his bhudi. Only someone who is growing old with you!'

'Still.'

'Okay baba. So, you have decided? Do you want to sell?'

'Yes, of course I want to sell. The girls don't want it, yes let's sell. How much do you think we will get for that tiny, godforsaken place?'

Razzak smiled at her and said, 'Just watch. What you are calling tiny and godforsaken is now historical. That's how old we are, we are historical, and everything we throw away is an antique!' He pulled out his cellphone and thumbed in the numbers. After a pause he spoke into the phone, 'Yaqub Bhai, yes, Razzak here, how are you? Alhamdolillah! Yes, I saw you at the Juma but I didn't get a chance to come up and say hello. You had left by the time I was done…Yes, yes! Too many things to ask of God, I got caught up. Too much to give thanks for, you know! Alhamdolillah. Can't complain, can't complain. Anyway, Yaqub Bhai, listen, about the flat in Kharadar, you were inquiring about it the other day…I have a very big party on the other line, they are waiting for my answer, I've put them on hold, and fat-a-fat aaap ka number ghumaya.

I wanted to speak to you first. Aisey hai key, here is how it is, they are in a hurry, and have offered two crore. They are really pestering me, they have been calling me almost on the hour. It seems like they want to settle right away. But I thought I would ask you. Do you want it? I thought I would get your permission to sell before I said yes… No, no time, you have no time to think. Tell me now, yes or no? You know the location… Ideal, no place like it. It's very near your godown…What? Yes, yes, I mean your museum. Bhai, you have to forgive people my age. We only remember what these buildings used to be… What? No question of loss, I simply can't look after it. I don't need it. It's a headache for me… Baba, you can ask your architect later, what is that girl's name? Yes, Rehana.

Very good girl… Yes, my wife likes her very much! Yes, the boy comes for piano lessons regularly… Yes, my wife has taken a real shine to him… How is Rehana's research coming along? She asked my wife a lot of questions about Karachi in the fifties… Yes, I was listening. Took me and my wife back to the good old days. Smart girl, she'll go far… Yes, Sara tells us that the godown is completely transformed… Yes, we will visit. You must come over as well… Very good work, very good work. These things must be preserved... Listen Yaqub Bhai, I can't keep these people waiting. Let me know now. You weren't disappointed with the godown were you? No? Yes?

Good... Yes, without a doubt, without a doubt, beautiful tiles...all over that part of Karachi. Thanks to Nuserwanji, his factory you know... Yes, all gone, all gone now. Very sad. Everyone wants synthetic now, everyone wants wall-to-wall carpeting... Yes, that was very wise of Sara to connect you up to me. I'm glad you bought the place, otherwise it would have been turned into a shopping mall.'

Razzak catches his wife shuddering. 'So, done. It is yours. Mubarak. I'll send over the paperwork right away. I'll have it processed and ready for signature by this evening. Khudahafiz.' He shut off the cellphone and winked at Hajrabai, 'Two crore! I'll email Meir this evening.' He thumbed in another number. 'Atif Beta,' he said to his secretary, 'send the driver to me at Lawrence Road right away to collect a few documents which he has to take to the Kacheri. Tell him to take the papers to the courts right away for notarizing.

Tell the driver to pick up the papers from me and go straight to Major Surjani Sahib at the Sindh Secretariat. I'm calling Surjani right now, he'll be waiting to notarize. Thank you! Khudahafiz, beta. Right away.'

Razzak had called another number, 'Major Sahib ko lagana, Razzak Rueewallah here!' He asks the secretary to connect him. He waits, 'Surjani Bhai? Recognize me? Yes, fine, Alhamdolillah. How are you? Children? Alhamdolillah... Good...good... Mashallah, mashallah...Going to Sussex University? Smart girl. Very good... Mashallah, mashallah... Thank God. Let me know if there is a service I can do in that regard. Any help at all, don't hesitate. Did you get the golf clubs? Very good... No, what borrow-shorro? Keep them, please keep them. I'll borrow them from you when I need them... One small thing, Surjani Bhai, it's like this, my driver is on his way to you, within the hour barring any traffic jam and VIP motorcades... Yes, General Sahib is in town. Again. My man, Surjani Bhai, is coming with a small headache for you, Surjani Bhai. Please take care of it, papers need to be notarized... No, there are no supporting documents at the moment. Just need to notarize, it's an apartment of mine in Kharadar, now in the family for a century, if not more. God knows who would ever have had the papers... Exactly, exactly. Just like the godown in Lea Market. Family people like us, when did we ever think of documents? We are old world people, Surjani Sahib... Exactly... Exactly. Very different times.

But thank God you are there...Yes, selling it off, total headache. Total loss. But better to be in loss than with a migraine... Thank you sir for doing the necessary. Thank you and let me know

if there is any service for you that I may be worthy of.' Razzak turned off the cellphone and smiled at his wife.

'Done, we have a deal. Now let me know should I wire the money to London or do you want to trade land for land here or send it to Resham for investing?'

In all this, Hajrabai had watched her husband with admiration. 'Oh yes, before I forget,' he said, 'there is a group going again for their Ziarats. Kareem Bhai told me today. They'll go to Mashad, Karbala, Najaf, Palestine. He asked me if you wanted to send anything for Meir like the last time. He can pick it up from them in Jerusalem.'

Yes, she will cook Meir's favourite kheer with lots of khoya. Razzak will have it canned. She will go buy Sohni Halva, chilli chips and dalmot; and those tiny, too spicy, samosas from Nimko in Bohri Bazaar that Meir loves so much. She won't buy him the K-2 cigarettes that he likes. She won't encourage that habit. Well, maybe just two packets. And also supari. And, oh yes, a bottle of

Rooh Afza. Surely that won't be too large a package? Kareem Bhai will understand. She'll put the package together for Kareem Bhai who will take it to Jerusalem and give it to Meir with the letters. Oh, and she must get at least six kurtas from the shop of Ghulam Mohammad in Saddar which Meir was always partial to. And photographs, she must remember to send Meir the photos of all the girls.

She knows she's made a mistake with the outburst two months ago when she wanted to move back to Lawrence Road. She misses the house so. She misses Zareenabai, she misses everything.

But she is angry and very hurt. Now that she's taken this step, her stubbornness and pride seem to have made it impossible to reverse her decision. None of the girls understand this move of hers. Resham has been despondent. Called from America every day. Razzak and Zareena tell her this and Hajrabai speaks with the girls on the phone attached to the computer when she visits 43-G.

Resham calls and argues but she will not be persuaded. She cannot understand why Hajrabai has moved away. It makes no sense. She won't be persuaded with the argument that Hajrabai wants to spend some time in her father's home. She will not listen. Shireen alarmed her with a wistful tone in her voice saying she understood the need to return to her father's home. Not like normal jovial, positive and sunny Shireen at all. And Amina had asked, 'Bari-ma, why do you have to stay there? Why can't you do what you always did, go there for a weekend once in a while? Why do you have to live there? Are we going to move in with you?' Amina has been furious. Typical Amina. Kulsum had talked of everything else, never mentioning the move. As though nothing had changed. Typical Kulsum.

Hajrabai goes back to 43-G almost every day, to its breezy, cool, open rooms, her lamps with their bases made from giant glass lab bottles and beaten brass matkas, the Sindhi jhoolas and takhts and all her ajraks framed alongside Sadequains and Jamini Roys. She misses the gleaming, clean tiled floors and the abundance of potted plants in the rooms. She misses the sparkling pots and pans in the kitchen. She misses the scented ritual every evening at 43-G when at dusk Zareena walks through the house, fumigating all of the rooms and perfuming them with the aroma of frankincense and sandalwood smoldering in a small copper pot. This was the ritual of Lobaan which Zareena had adopted from Parsi neighbours many years ago. It purified and perfumed the air and kept away mosquitoes. Every evening at dusk she walked around the house swinging the small copper urn by its chain while the fragrance escaped from its filigree lid.

Zareenabai has done a marvelous job keeping up the house and supervising the servants. But Razzak insists that Hajrabai move back there. She refuses to listen to him on this matter. No, she needs her privacy. She decided two years ago, just before Seder at Passover in 2002, that enough was enough. She wanted to have her own way and life. She had kept up pretenses for too long. Thanked Razzak for all his love and understanding and asked for more. Hajrabai has told Sara about her background. There were, as Hajrabai expected, histrionics. Typical Sara.

Sara had come round eventually. If there was one thing Hajrabai could say for her daughter, it was this—she was the most realistic of the lot. Perhaps the only one who had heeded her advice. Of all of them, Sara was the most pragmatic and flexible in her opinions. What was the phrase the girls used? 'Roll with the punches.' Yes, Sara knew how to roll with the punches. And poor Zareenabai, how she wishes that she could take back what she had said. Razzak has pointed this out to Hajrabai, that she has punished Zareena long enough, it was a grave mistake for Zareena to have objected the way she did, but she hadn't meant any harm and would have never wanted this outcome.

Hajrabai remembered that day when Sara had come rushing upstairs across the black and white tiles; her tall, slim figure tottering on stiletto heels had bumped into the brass pot of the gigantic rubber plant and plopped herself on the jhoola next to the takht. Zareenabai and Hajrabai greeted her as they sat under the whirring ceiling fan, having just said goodbye to several ladies who had been invited over for coffee by Zareenabai. Razia was clearing the coffee table of china cups and left over savories and cakes. 'Oohh, what a day I've had!' declared Sara, rolling her large, lovely eyes as she reached forward to pick up a piece of marzipan pastry and pop it into her mouth. 'That is delicious, I mustn't though, a thousand calories, right there! Razia, please get me a cup of tea! Oh what a day, I'm exhausted.'

'Already?' said Hajrabai. 'It's barely noon.'

'Bari-ma, you have no idea,' Sara said, her hand clasped to her bosom as she tossed her copper tinted hair and ran her slender fingers through it. 'Is that teacup chipped? We must replace it.' Sara reached for the cup but Hajrabai intercepted her with a rap on her hand.

'Yes, it's chipped. It's my favourite set. I won't have it replaced. What have you been doing that you are so exhausted at noon?'

'The blow-dry this morning took ages. I thought I would go play golf, drop the kids to school, go to the beauty parlour and then to my factory. But the blow-dry took forever, there were at least two power cuts and the generator at the parlour took ages to kick in! I told the girl doing my hair that I was really losing my patience, but she completely ignored me!'

'What is it that she's done to your hair?' Hajrabai asked.

'I think it looks beautiful, darling,' Zareenabai said soothingly, quickly coming to Sara's defense, much to Hajrabai's annoyance. 'It goes well with your skin tone! Very coppery!'

'Why don't you like it?' Sara asked. 'Bari-ma, I think it suits me a lot. I think it makes me look young.'

'You are young!'

'Younger!'

'Sara really, you are far too frivolous!' Hajrabai said disapprovingly.

'Okay, anyway, let's change the subject. What were you two talking about?' Sara asked.

'Choti-ma and I were talking about the possibility of my visiting Jerusalem,' replied Hajrabai.

'Jerusalem? Are you going on the ziarat with Kareem Uncle?'

'No. I wanted to go on my own, straight to Jerusalem.'

'Why do you want to do that? Besides, it'll be impossible to get visas to Israel. Bari-ma, you know that!' Sara protested.

Hajrabai replied, 'I want to visit Meir.'

'Who?' Sara had asked, looking from Hajrabai to Zareenabai, who looked very anxious.

'I want to visit my brother.'

Sara had sat there facing her, her head tipped slightly to one side, her heavily kohled eyes narrowing under perfectly plucked, knitted brows. 'I beg your pardon? You never told us you had a brother. I thought you were an only child. That's what you always told us.'

'Meir is my brother who moved to Israel in 1968.'

Sara's voice, nasal and husky like her mother's, rose in alarm. 'I don't understand. Now you tell me you have a brother who is in Israel. It makes no sense at all. I thought only Jews could move to Israel, not Pakistanis.'

'He is a Jew.'

'Your brother is a Jew? How can that be? I mean you were a Parsi and you had converted to Islam when you and Abba married. So your brother converted to Judaism?'

Hajrabai had explained, 'No Sara, my family was part of the B'nai Israel community in Karachi.'

Sara had stood up and walked quickly to the doors to shut them. Now she paced from the doors to the balustrade, back and forth, wringing her hands, pausing to look out over the balcony as if she were afraid that someone below in the lawn could hear them. In the distance she could hear the familiar call of a vendor,

'Gola ganda, faluda, thandah, thandah lailo,' announcing his milk and soya ice cream treats to the neighbourhood children. Hajrabai was talking to her, explaining how she and Razzak had met, how they had eloped, how Hajrabai's father had disowned her, how her brother had left Karachi in 1968. How she had kept in touch with Meir. How Razzak managed her brother's property and sent him his share every month.

Sara had listened but constantly shook her head in disbelief. Panicked, she said, 'But everyone knows that you were Parsi. That is what we were told. That's what you told us. That's what everyone knows. You and Abba met at your house when you were eighteen, you were supposed to teach him the piano. The two of you eloped and your Abba disowned you. That's why we never met any of your family, your relatives. Because they never wanted to have anything to do with us and besides, they migrated to Canada. You told us that. That's what you said. You never told us that you were a Jew, no one has ever said you were a Jew!'

Zareenabai tried to calm her down, 'Sara, times have changed so much that everyone just let things be. There was no need to discuss anything. We all knew and that was enough, we didn't see the point of telling anyone, especially you.' Hajrabai said, 'Everyone then knew my background. If they didn't say anything, it was out of respect for me and my family and respect for your father. Amongst us here in Karachi, us old Karachiites, there was a strong sense of community and caring, there was ravadari. We held together the best we could when the world around us started to fall apart at the seams and change so rapidly. The whole world had gone crazy, the country was slowly going crazy. If everyone thought that I was Parsi, then fine, why change their thinking? Why make an issue out of something that was my own private business?

Those who knew us well, they didn't need to discuss it, there was nothing to discuss and they didn't see any reason to take it outside our homes and our circles. Karachi was a place where people went to jamaat khanas, and temples, and churches, and synagogues and imam bargahs. There were fire temples and towers of silence where bodies were left out in the open for the vultures and at Mangopir, a festival of crocodiles! This was all part of the way of this city. There were processions every Moharram with colourful floats and men on the streets flagellating themselves with chains and knives, with blood flowing down the streets. No one thought anything of it. We were all equally strange, equally queer. There were annual festivals at Bhit Shah and arizas at Netty Jetty and at Nauroz, and huge darshans and deedars when the Syedna visited from Bombay and where the Aga Khan was weighed in gold when he visited from Paris.

There was Christmas mass and Christmas and New Year's balls at restaurants and hotels. All of us here were the same because of our differences. But really, we were just shades apart. It was for outsiders to see that. Why, most people who visited Karachi couldn't tell us apart at all. Bohris, Parsis, Khojas, Memons, Jews, Catholics, Protestants, Ismailis. We were just shades apart. And our last names sounded the same to strangers, named after our trades and not our religious beliefs!! These names were and are on our schools, and hospitals and universities and our orphanages and on everything humane and good in this city. The first mayor of this city was a Parsi, and do you know that there was a Jew, an elected member on his city council, for the Karachi Municipal Corporation? And this was all right. This was the way it should have remained. And no one from the outside looking at all this could tell one from the other. And that was fine. That was all so fine.'

'No, it was never fine! Your Abba disowned you! Don't make it all sound so good. It was never fine! And even if it was not so crazy then it's not fine now. And everyone can tell the difference now. And we should not discuss it further. No one else must ever find out now!' Sara had declared. 'Do you understand, Bari-ma?' 'Everyone else who is concerned will and must find out.'

'Don't you know what that will mean?' Sara wept.

'What will it mean? What did it mean to anyone that I was supposedly Parsi? Shireen is married to a Hindu. And God only knows who Resham and Amina will marry. And Sara, your marriage was never up for questioning!'

Sara was frightened, 'This is different! Don't you know how people will react? Bari-ma, don't you see the madness all around us? The bombs going off in imam bargahs and mosques? It's hard enough for me to be a Shia! Just driving here I saw the truck full of police stationed outside the Mehfil, right around the corner. I mean for God's sake, Jew! That will surely kill us all.' Bari-ma had nodded but had been firm, 'Sara this is not about you. I'm not saying that we should put a billboard outside the house or give interviews to newspapers, but certainly I want your sisters to know as soon as possible!'

Sara had cried and wailed. She had pleaded and insisted that Riaz not be told. Hajrabai had agreed. 'Did Choti-ma always know?' Sara had asked.

'Of course I knew.'

'She has always known. Don't be ridiculous Sara!'

Hajrabai recalled how Sara had wept and wailed. 'It was hard enough being a half sister. It was hard enough being the only one who was your daughter. Everyone else was Choti-ma's!'

'Sara!' Zareenabai had cried. 'No one treated you differently!'

'That's not the point, I always knew, I always felt it!'

Zareenabai's eyes had moistened, a tear rolled down her plump cheek and others followed unchecked. 'That's not true Sara, and you know it. I have loved you more than all the others.' Zareena and Hajra had always marveled how Sara resembled Zareenabai rather than Hajra.

'No, that's not true!' Sara sobbed.

'Not true at all, Resham was always my favourite!' Hajrabai said dryly. Hajrabai could not abide Sara's penchant for theatrics.

But Sara was beyond humour and only sobbed louder. She became more and more distraught and by the time she was calmed down by Zareenabai, she had extracted all the promises from Hajrabai and Zareenabai that her husband Riaz was not to be told and that her sisters would not be told immediately either.

'But now that you do know, we will start celebrating Yom Kippur, Roshashana, Purim, and Passover,' Hajrabai said firmly.

There was with this announcement, an immediate cessation of weeping and consoling between Sara and Zareenabai. Now both looked at Hajrabai, their identical eyes widened, as though confused.

Hajrabai had been surprised by the aloof tone she detected in Zareenabai's voice when Zareenabai had asked, 'What do you mean we will start celebrating? Who will start celebrating, where?'

'Here in our house, we will observe my customs. I have long missed them and I want to make sure that we have these traditions.'

'But Hajrabai, we are Shia and these are not our traditions.'

That was all that Zareenabai had said. No more. Sara had said nothing, she had sat there wide-eyed staring at her mother.

Hajrabai had stood up. 'Very well, then I will go where my traditions can be practiced.' Hajrabai had left for the apartment at Lawrence Road the next day.

When she finally had made her decision to move back to Lawrence Road, she had been gripped with a strange sense of pain, a pain that caused her pleasure. She was harming herself to save herself. But amongst the other emotions welling up in her, of doubt, anxiety and resolution, Hajrabai felt a strong sense of fear; she was afraid of living alone. She had never lived alone her entire life. She had moved to 43-G after her marriage. She was just eighteen then. But she never could have imagined that she would miss it all so much, that she would miss the companionship of Zareenabai. Fifty years of being co-wives and married to the same man. She missed hearing Zareenabai's voice in the rooms around her, she missed the conversations and the small daily irritations. She never imagined that she would miss the day-to-day mundane moments so much; of sharing decisions with Zareenabai, decisions on which rooms were to be swept and what was to be cooked and who was to be invited or left out on which occasion. She missed her position acknowledged every day by an army of people who referred to her as Bari-ma. She was Bari-ma to the entire household and to everyone who visited there.

She was Bari-ma to all the children--Sara, Amina, Kulsum, Resham and Shireen.

Zareenabai was called Choti-ma by them. It seemed that it made no difference to the girls or to Zareenabai or to her, who gave birth to which child. It seemed just a technicality for the purposes of application forms for universities, green cards and certificates. Sara is hers and the rest are Zareenabai's. Hard to believe that Resham is not hers, not of her own womb. It matters not, this technicality, for even more than Sara, Resham is hers. In her voice, in facial expressions, in her temperament, she is Hajrabai. The girls have all turned out all right. Hajrabai was opposed to the girls going to America for their universities. But it seems everything has turned out all right. Well, Shireen married a Hindu, a professor in New York, but the girl seems happy enough. Getting fatter every day, like Razzak and herself. A sure sign of love. She worries about Resham and Amina. Both thin as mosquitoes. Amina is a lawyer and Resham is following her father's footsteps in business. Like their sisters, they are beautiful. Resham is slim and petite with thick black, shiny, shoulder-length hair and dark eyes that sparkle as though they contain crushed diamonds. Amina is taller than Resham and just as slender and graceful, doe-eyed like all her sisters, with long, gleaming, straight hair like Zareenabai used to have. But no eligible man in sight.

Every year, Hajrabai sends Resham a portion of her shares for making investments on the stock market. Kulsum is the farthest away from them as far as she can tell. Razzak should have never married her into a Lahori family. 'So different from our way of living, our ways of *getting up and sitting down*,' Hajrabai had protested in way of counsel when the pros and cons of the proposal were being evaluated. But that too has turned out all right. Thanks

to her special prayers. Kulsum is there as well, near her sisters, and her husband Faraz seems to be civilized enough. Amina has informed her of her plans for December.

The other three don't plan to come till the summer. Hajrabai has decided that she'll move back temporarily to 43-G sometime after Roshashana and Yom Kippur. She'll be there next December when Amina arrives and then she will stay for Moharram. She wishes that the girls had come this winter but they all seemed so busy with work. They'll come next December and perhaps stay on through Moharram. There's much coming and going then and she likes the hallagulla and tamasha. And then Sara will be there every day as well. Hajrabai will return to this apartment on Lawrence Road just a few weeks before Purim and of course, she will be at Lawrence Road for Passover. This schedule will be fine, yes, she'll have Razzak make sure that the apartment is freshly painted before she comes back, this time she'll go a shade bluer in the drawing room and have Sara send all the pots and pans for kalai to Bohri

Bazaar. She'll have Jeevan come to Lawrence Road and wash all the floors, give them a thorough cleaning before Passover. Yes, Sara will take care of the kalai and she will make sure she has hand-ground wheat from the chakki for the matzah and the dried fruit and supplies she needs to make the special dishes. Only from a particular shop in Empress Market. They know her. She'll go herself.

Yes, she'll go and stay at 43-G for a good three months. The two storeyed house, 43-G, as everyone has taken to referring to it, sits solidly within a small grassy compound and is hidden from the road and from the park by tall and gnarly almond and mango trees. Bougainvillea bushes spill over the boundary walls, blossoming in white and magenta flowers. The park in front of the house was used as a parade ground during the Raj and was referred to as Patel Park. The family still refers to it as that but the city has renamed it Nishtar Park. On one end of the park is the Mehfil-e-Shah-e-Khorasan, the imam bargah, an easy stone's throw away from the house and convenient for Razzak's prayers and for all the majlises during Moharram. Majlises held in the park in the evenings and afternoons during Moharram can be heard easily by the family while they are seated on the floor or on the cane furniture and jhoola on the verandah upstairs.

It was a tradition for Zareenabai and the girls to attend the majlis for the ten days of Moharram at the imam bargah around the corner at Mehfil-e-Shah-e-Khorasan. Now of course, only Sara and Zareenabai go every year. It's an easy walk from 43-G to the imam bargah where they sit during Moharram on carpets spread over marble floors under the shamiana which covers the large terrace and is crowded with women. The imam bargah housed a large, shiny, metal filigree mausoleum symbolizing one for Fatima, the daughter of the Prophet. And, as all other imam bargahs in the city and around the world, it housed a special room of miniature replicas of the shrines of all the Shia imams, banners, and alams topped by silver or gold, symbols of hands—the panjathan—which signify the standards and flags of the seventy-two masumeen, the innocents, who were besieged and who died at Karbala.

At 43-G, the girls had grown up playing in the garden, climbing trees, sleeping on the verandah upstairs, or on the rooftop or in the sehan at night during the summers, where Hajrabai or Zareenabai would tell them stories. Hajrabai would recount the times of her life and describe all the interesting people she had known or heard about, spinning tales of their lives—such as Attiya Fyzee—a lady who was a legend in Karachi, whom Hajrabai had heard much of but never actually met. 'What a great lady she was! Marrying that Samuel Fyzee Rahamin and migrating with him from India to Pakistan in 1947 when many like her, and particularly like him, were leaving. But not everyone had a personal invitation, like they did from Jinnah. Attiya must have been about seventy years old at that time. And she thought herself a mere girl. And all of you at your age think you are ancient! She was a singer, a dancer, an author. A great intellectual.

She was fearless and youthful. Always young. What a presence she was. Can you imagine she went to London on a scholarship in 1906? She was a Muslim lady, the princess of Janjeera -- an island off the coast of Malabar. She corresponded and conversed with the likes of Allama Iqbal and Maulana Shibli Nomani. She probably had an affair with Iqbal. And by the sounds of the correspondence between Shibli and her, I think he may have lusted after her as well... I remember her, I saw her at my father's shop. She came in, her head covered, you know, she wore the bohri burqa, her face exposed under her bonnet-like head covering it very much like the hijab girls wear today…as usual, a dozen beaded, long necklaces around her neck. I remember my father asked my brother to accompany her out to her waiting Chevrolet and she had raised her arm up in protest. "Do not come out with me, otherwise there will be a scandal!" she had said. What a delightful person! To have thought herself as a young girl even at her great age! She presided over intellectual gatherings each Thursday evening, for artists and writers and painters at the Burns Club... I wonder what they talked about. I never did attend. I suppose they talked about the possibilities. Those were great days. You know Karachi was the centre of excitement, so vibrant and elegant, so culturally alive.

Can you imagine Attiya had left India to come here! We used to idolize her here in Karachi, all of us young girls back then. But she was not unusual in choosing to come to Pakistan. So had many who need not have come. There was promise here in Karachi, of something new and vibrant and creative. I think it may have been that way for many people who went to Israel in the early days to the Kibbutz. There was so much promise … Don't make a face Resham! What do you think, the mohajirs didn't displace anybody? I remember Attiya when she came to a flower show at Gandhi Garden, such a marvellous woman.'

'It was a sad time too! So many people left Karachi, so many friends you know, so much family. This was heaven, not a place to leave, but people did leave out of fear of what was to come. They should have stayed. It would have all passed over. It would have all been better if everyone had stayed… I know, I know, Razzak, but let me talk, what is the harm of my wishing it were so. You know, people coming from India at that time of Partition were enthralled with Karachi. It was so much more vibrant and beautiful than Delhi, for example. And then it was like being in Europe; there were imported goods that were simply not available in India. Imported cigarettes, wines and whiskies. Books. Imported cars, showrooms for Chevrolets, Cadillacs, air conditioners and refrigerators.

Why, many of those who came from India had never even seen such things! Such things we had… Girls, like Attiya Fyzee.

The kind of woman that people talk about, that wins the hearts of great men and women. Someone who seduces poets and priests. Someone to whom great men are drawn. Scandalising. That is what I wish for you! Find yourselves a Samuel Fyzee Rahamin of your own, a Shibli and Iqbal of your own; write, act, turn a painter into an artist, find galleries, be great and be scandalous. Nothing good comes from being a prude!' Hajrabai thought back to that evening and now chuckled to herself. Three years on, only Sara seemed to have heeded her advice. For all the wrong reasons.

On the phone the other day, Resham had cried and said that her favourite memory of home was waking up at dawn and looking down from her bedroom window on to the lawn and watching Zareenabai and Hajrabai in their morning routines as the dew rose up as mist evaporating off the Dhaka grass. Zareenabai sitting reading the Koran and Hajrabai pacing barefoot on the lawn, checking the plants and blossoms. Resham had threatened to never return to 43-G if Hajrabai did not come back home immediately. 'Well, you haven't been home in two years yourself! So that's not much of a threat, is it?' Hajrabai had laughed. Kulsum's wedding had been held at Patel Park, the shamiana covered most of the large park and there were hundreds of guests, at least fifteen hundred people.

The Lahoris were impressed. And Kulsum. Ah, Kulsum had taken her parent's breath away that day. Kulsum with her classic looks, her wide forehead on a moon-shaped face, large doe-shaped black eyes; her abundance of black hair down to her hips which had been pulled back in a heavy plait and braided with two gold braiding ribbons and flowers had looked enchanting. Dressed as a bride in an olive and purple coloured farshi gharara and six yards of veil, her glowing, golden complexion was set off to perfection. And from here, from 43-G, one by one, the girls' things had been packed into gigantic suitcases strapped with polythene belts to keep mementos of childhood bedrooms from bursting open and spilling out on to conveyor belts at faraway airports. Then the suitcases had been loaded into extra cars for the airport as each left, turn by turn, for America. It was from here that Sara ran away and eloped with a man like Razzak. Sara had picked well. Riaz had a cheerful disposition, he was always meticulously dressed, in suits and ties, his thinning salt and pepper hair closely cropped. And always, he looked at Sara with adoring eyes, through steel rimmed spectacles. Yes, he complemented Sara well. Riaz was a decent man, a good sort, trying his hand at different ideas—sanitary fittings, real estate, import and export. Something was bound to flourish and make him money. Hajrabai and Razzak has suggested that they live at 43-G; after all Sara had a portion large enough for a small family with two children. But Riaz had insisted on living at his own parents' house. Well, no one could argue with that. Like Razzak, Riaz went to Juma prayers every Friday. His mosque was a mile down the road from the Shahe- Khorasan, the large Memon Masjid near Islamia College. Every Ramadan Riaz spent ten days cloistered with men of his Memon community at the large Jamia Masjid near the cloth market. Yes, Riaz was a good Karachi boy, part of the old business community.

At 43-G, Hajrabai's section of the house is maintained for her as though she lives there all the time, her two bedrooms, a drawing room cum dining area and a kitchen. Her drawing room there opens on to the verandah upstairs from where she can see Patel Park. Each of the five girls has a section of her own now, and why not? After all, the house was built for two wives and with the wishful thinking that there would be at least four sons and that they would all live there with their wives and children. The sons were never born. A blessing, thought Hajrabai. There are no daughters-in-law to endure, there was peace in the house, no conflicts at all, which daughters-in-law would bring without a doubt. Instead now there's room enough for five suites for the girls. All sisters, all insiders, all her own. Her beautiful girls. She wishes that Kulsum, Shireen and Sara would all move in with their families. But they don't.

One can and won't, the other two are too far away in New York. Resham, with her good business sense and head for making investments, should come home and handle her father's affairs. He needs help. And so should Amina. But Razzak has never raised this with them. Hajrabai knows that soon enough she will bring it up herself. She thinks about all the talk--her having moved out--there's been enough of that. What they really should talk about is that she wants the girls to move back in.

Why not? They don't seem to be doing anything other than making money over there. And if that's all it is, then they can do that right here at home. As far as she can tell, they don't do anything that is interesting; it's all work, work, and work, from daybreak to night. Dull. Hajrabai recalls a few years ago when they had all been together the last time around, right after Razzak had forgiven Shireen for marrying a Hindu. One evening on the verandah as they were all gathered around her listening to her stories, Hajrabai had said, 'Ah, what dull prudes all of you have turned out to be! You too Shireen, even though you have married against my wishes. In that you did well. That is a plus, but what have you done after that? Be like Attiya Fyzee. We sent you all abroad hoping you would make great scandals but instead we have a lawyer, an investment banker and a real estate agent.'

And here at Lawrence Road, a mile away as the crow flies from 43-G, letters, their envelopes smudged with handling, still continue to arrive, though now sporadically. Letters addressed to Hajra Ibrahimbhai. Most of the senders like her are now too old perhaps to make the effort to write. Many are already gone. Before, the envelopes came more frequently bearing stamps from Turkey, England, US, India, once even from Yugoslavia posted by people travelling there and sent with them by Meir and friends to be posted on to Karachi. Impossible to receive mail directly from Israel. Inside are letters from relatives and friends from Karachi now in Beersheba, Israel.

They used to inquire about her, tell her how homesick they were for Karachi, they complained about the weather and the way they were treated in Israel. It was not so long ago that she decided she would not visit or follow. No that was not for her. There they did not even accept them as one of their own. B'nai Israel is not a tribe they had claimed. No! Why should she go there and be with the goras who consider everyone except themselves kalas. Serves them right. They thought they had divisions here! Now they are finding out for themselves. And no way to return, no way to come back. Why should she go there, better to stay right here, where she knows who she is and keeps to herself. Rejection from one's own? To have someone tell her she isn't? Those who one embraces? No! Never! Let them call her a Jew and reject her here. At least here when she would be rejected it would be a full acknowledgement of who she is.

There they tell her she isn't! There she does not matter at all. But here is what matters to her. Her husband, her daughters. 43-G. This home, this balcony, the proximity to all that once was. The graves are still here. She remembers how good it all used to be. Taking the tram to Magain Sholome which was a mile down the road at the corner of Lawrence Road and Barnes Road. Taking the tram to her father's shop on Preedy Street.

Now there is hardly anyone left to remember, everything is gone. That's what happens when everyone leaves, when 2500 become just 250 and then maybe only 50. When masjids are demolished for shopping malls. Hardly anyone left to mourn this. There is Solomon Dawood, downstairs, and Raymond Abraham across the hall. Rachel is in the hospital at the Aga Khan. Not long for this world.

But the fahl could have been about her! Hajrabai remembers that she was not thinking about Amina in that moment. Hard to imagine that Zareenabai was thinking about Amina as well. Hajrabai remembered that at that moment she was wondering about how good it would have been to be at 43-G. Surely Zareenabai was thinking the same thing too. So what did the verse mean, if this were so. What was it now:

I said: O fate, when will you awake? The sun is up, it is now dawn-break.

Said fate, you have made many a mistake, Yet keep hope and faith within your breast.

Hajrabai went to bed that night with this nagging question on her mind. She awoke in the night thinking she heard the night watchman calling, 'Jagte raho.' It frightened her the way it always had, and she wished she were at 43-G.

It was not until the DAWN was delivered on Sunday that Hajrabai learned of the shooting by unknown assailants of Dr Syed Abbas Zaidi. He had never regained consciousness after being shot in the face point blank and had died on Saturday night. The paper reported that Abbas had been killed execution style just like the eighty other Shia doctors in Karachi before him. 'He should have left, he should have left the country!' she cried out to the walls.

2

Gold-Diggers

HAJRA breathed into the pillow, as she made her bed, expecting her nostrils to be filled with the cool, sweet smell of the freshly changed cover. Instead she wrinkled her nose in disgust to the insidious but unmistakable whiff of rotting fish. 'How many times have I told that wretched man to make sure the starch is completely dried when he irons. Completely dried through with ironing before he folds the clothes and wraps them up into a bundle to bring back over here. How many times have I said if he doesn't do that then the dampness makes them stink! But no, he just won't listen! I don't know how Zareena manages with him. This never happens at 43-G. I certainly cannot make him listen to a word I say!' She threw the pillow back on the bed and proceeded with changing her clothes. She sniffed each garment that had been returned by the dhobi before putting it on. The blouse was fine, the petticoat too, the sari would just have to do.

'Return to 43-G or come with me,' she repeated the sentence out loud and shook her head incredulously. What a week it had been. She could have never imagined that one moment she would have answered the door to let Razzak in, smiled questioningly at him grinning at her, and then in the next moment he would have reached out his arm to the side and have pulled out someone hidden from Hajra's view. Her eyes had not adjusted immediately, her expression, though startled, had shown no immediate recognition. And yet there, standing before her in the doorway that quiet afternoon, was the one person she could have never expected. There he stood, her brother, his gray eyes brimming with emotion, having left Karachi a young man, now elderly, his thick, black hair, now white and thin, his trim figure, portly, his face darkened and lined with creases. There she stood, his younger sister resembling a memory of a mother long gone. 'Meir!' A gasp had escaped her lips and formed his name. She had rushed into his arms and then dragged him into the apartment.

Razzak and Meir had laughed gleefully, pleased at her surprise and masking their own emotional reaction to hers. Time stopped and flew all at once. There he was appearing at her door as suddenly as he had gone. In a single instant they had all arrived back into a moment that was long gone, now here they were and all that was then long ago, preserved in memory, instantly disappeared and was no more. Here they were now, Razzak and Hajra in Karachi and Meir was here with them, though just a visitor. This was not the reunion of twenty years ago in London, nor of ten years ago in Istanbul. No. Now, here was Meir, in Karachi for the first time since he had left. Standing in his home on Lawrence Road, Meir was a visitor to Karachi on a British passport. She had served them lunch, Meir had taken a shower and commented that in Israel too the pressure of water in the shower was weak. He was staying two days and then he would go back to Israel via Istanbul. She had made Razzak a glass of his usual Ovaltine, for Meir she had made a glass of Rooh Afza. She had shown him pictures of the girls. Meir had shown them pictures of his son Emir, a young man, deeply tanned, grinning, his curly head of hair lowered, looking up with his blue eyes at the camera as though embarrassed to be photographed wearing a military uniform, at the start of his service with the Israeli Defense Force. Meir had looked at them apologetically,

'It's mandatory.' Meir had told Hajra and Razzak that he and Emir were planning to be in New York soon. 'Would the girls want to meet me and Emir?' he wondered. 'Of course they would!' Hajra had replied. 'We will arrange it!' Later they would go to 43-G and Sara had been told by Razzak to be there that evening. Razzak had left to go back to his office, telling them he would return in the evening to pick them up and take them to 43-G for dinner, and that Zareenabai and Sara would be waiting. Hajra and Meir had fallen into a silence after Razzak left. Hajra commented on how much Meir smoked, the apartment had steadily filled up with smoke from the pack of cigarettes that he had gone through in less than four hours. She had gotten up to get him a carton of K-2 cigarettes she had at the last moment decided not to add to the package she had sent to Jerusalem with Kareem Bhai. Meir had grabbed them from her appreciatively. He had brought chocolates and perfume from the duty free in London for her, Zareenabai and Sara. The chocolates were for Sara's children.

Finally, Meir told her the reason why he had come to Karachi, 'Hajra, what are you doing? Razzak called me to tell me you have moved here to Lawrence Road and left your own house?'

Hajra had laughed, 'Is that why you are here?'

Meir looked at her as though astonished, 'Why? You ask me why? It's catastrophic! You leaving your husband's home to move here? Alone. In Karachi? No way! You are my only sister, my only family save for Emir! I cannot let you do this!'

Hajra shook her head in wonder, 'It was a foolish reason for you to have come back!'

Meir had taken a deep drag on his cigarette and squinted at her through the smoke. 'Why are you here at Lawrence Road?'

'I'm getting old Meir—we all are. I want my traditions, the traditions I grew up with,' Hajra had protested.

Meir had leaned forward and said slowly, 'And your traditions mean more to you than your husband and family?'

Hajra had looked at him without replying.

'Then you should come back with me,' Meir said after a few moments of silence.

Hajra had said dismissively, 'What? To Israel? Why would I do that? Never!'

Meir had continued in his serious tone, 'Then you should go back to 43-G and to your husband's home. If you will not do that, then you should come with me!'

Hajra had refused, 'No, I will stay right here, at Lawrence

Road in our home here. It will all be fine Meir. You don't have to worry about me. And we are all fine, Razzak is fine, our lives have adjusted to this small change.'

'Hajra you are being foolish,' Meir had said. 'But it was my place to come and talk to you! You will go home and we will sell this place!'

Hajra had stared at her brother as though he had hit her, 'Sell this place? Never!'

Meir shook his head. 'It's my apartment too Hajra, not just yours. If it is causing a breach in your life then I don't want it. Now your home is not here, you are a guest in this apartment. You are a guest and you have stayed here too long already—go home.' Hajra had stopped the conversation, refusing to discuss the issue any further with Meir. The threat from Meir had shaken her. Instead, they had talked about how times had changed, how much Karachi had changed. They had talked about their friends Raymond, Abraham, and Solomon Dawood, and about Rachel who had recently passed away. They had made plans to visit the graves of their parents, grandparents and relatives at Mewa Shah the next day. Hajra had told Meir about all the girls and about Sara. Meir had told Hajra about his amicable divorce after fifteen years of marriage. He had married a young woman from the Ukraine, Tanya, shortly after moving to Israel. Hajra knew this. But the marriage had not worked well though they had tried and had Emir, their beautiful son. He was a good boy. Good looking. Hajra could see from the photograph that he looked just like Meir. Meir told Hajra that he and Tanya didn't have much to talk about. Their cultures were too different and she had left him and gone to live in Coney Island in New York where most of her family had settled after leaving the Ukraine. Emir was a good boy, he had stayed with his father in Israel and he had finished his duty in the military and was now in Boston completing his studies. Emir was studying marine biology. Hajra would meet him soon when she went to visit the girls in New York.

The rest of Meir's visit seemed to have passed in a blur, it was so quick. They had gone to 43-G that evening for dinner. Hajrabai had been anxious about Sara's behaviour but had been astonished at the calmness with which her daughter had met her uncle. She managed to call him Meir Chacha, though Hajra had corrected her and told her that she should call him Meir Mamu, but Sara had continued to call him chacha, addressing him as her father's brother rather than her mother's. Sara had sat up erect at the edge of the sofa, her shoulders straight and her hands folded politely in her lap looking a model of polite discomfort in the presence of a stranger and a guest. Hajra had tried to ignore this precociousness. However, Sara had brought her children to introduce them to Meir. Eleven-year-old Tahir seemed to stare at Meir unblinkingly but was shy and timid, and eight-year-old Zohra, plump, unabashedly sucked her thumb. They had sat for about ten minutes with the grown-ups, munching on the chocolates that Meir had brought for them and then they had run out of the room to go watch TV. Riaz was away in Dubai on business. When time came to go back to Lawrence Road that evening, Meir had announced that he was staying at 43-G. Zareenabai had announced as a matter of fact, avoiding Hajrabai's gaze, that his room had been prepared, she had put his things in Resham's room. It had become clear to Hajrabai that Meir, having arrived in Karachi that morning, had first stopped at 43-G before coming to Lawrence Road. Hajra relented and agreed to stay the night as well.

The next day, Hajra and Meir had gone to Mewa Shah. Meir had driven the car. Razzak had the graves washed and Meir had wept and had been moved by the upkeep of the cemetery. The long route to the cemetery, jammed with traffic, allowed Meir to see how much of the Karachi that he knew from decades ago had changed. What he remembered was in decay and what he didn't was new, ugly and garish. He had pointed to a structure which he remarked was beautiful. 'Isn't that the site of our godown?' He had asked. And Hajra had said it was. 'It has been bought, you remember, and has been converted into a museum and a foundation!' Meir had laughed, 'Why not!' And before she knew it, Meir was standing at the door with Razzak and she was holding on to him, gripping his arms as she sobbed. It was time for him to leave. He had consoled her with the promise to return soon and that they would meet in New York. Yes, the last two days had been as though a dream. The bed made, the tidying done, Hajra turned her head to glance at her silent apartment as though she expected it to speak in protest, beckoning her to stay some more before she walked out the door. A faint smell of cigarettes still hung in the air despite her airing of the rooms, reminding her of Meir's words. There wasn't a sound except for that of the ceiling fan which she had just switched off and was creaking to a stop, and the noise of the traffic outside. She was going to 43-G for a night. She had conceded this much to Meir's efforts. Hajra had thought about Shireen at that moment. There had been a certain forlorn faraway ring in her voice last night when she had called. A dull sound that did not belong to Shireen's vocal cords. Hajra was worried. She would discuss it with Zareena. No, she thought better of it, not Zareena. That would just send Zareena into hysteria. No, Hajra decided she would discuss it with Razzak. Or perhaps it was her imagination. She locked the front door, adjusted her pallu and slowly made her way down the staircase to the driveway where Ilyas the driver was waiting for her with the car.

On the short drive to 43-G, Hajra thought of the recent events as she gazed at the street hawkers selling the eveningers. One alarming headline after the other screamed of death and killings all over the city. The killing of Abbas had unnerved Hajra and frightened her family. She had visited Abbas's family with Rehana. It had been a harrowing experience. She did not know his family, she only knew him. His relationship with her had been confined to her apartment and her teaching him the scale on the piano in the comfort and isolation of her apartment. At his house, the living room had been cleared of furniture for the funeral and condolence visits and was crowded with mourners, family, friends, colleagues, patients, neighbours and onlookers; she and Rehana had difficulty finding space to sit. She found herself clutching Rehana's arm for support in an effort to stave off the claustrophobia of so many strangers pressing against her, wailing and weeping for Abbas. Along with the ceiling fan which was a white blur, churning the hot air in the congested room, a television in the corner remained a flickering source of light, mute and turned on to CNN. Images of nightmares and dreams flickered interchangeably, cars on fire in Baghdad and Gaza, destroyed shrines, protestors on the streets burning banners, American soldiers, President Bush swaggering, waving, winking, and grinning were interspersed with advertisements for holidays in Greece, Turkey and Malaysia and advertisements for cellphones and airlines. Abbas, to her an eager piano student, shy and nervous, was remembered here as the beloved son, full of life and humour, the eldest child, the older brother, the promising young doctor, the pride and the keeper of all hope. He had given his parents a reason for living, and his awful death, without reason—neither of disease nor accident, nor apparent revenge—now gave meaning for a sickness of heart and the wishing of the death of the unseen assailants, and all those out there who had conspired to have him taken from them. She had noticed the presence of official looking young men who seemed to be uninvited guests, incongruent here amongst the family. They were in postures of condolence and persuasion. Abbas's death to them it seemed, was not a family matter now. He had become a rallying point, an asset. She heard fragments of this conversation, 'He belongs to all of us; His death is our death; He will live on into eternity for the sacrifice he has made for his faith.' Innocent Abbas who had been loved by his family, friends and patients alike and who had been devoted to them was suddenly being appropriated in memory and morphing into something else.

The car idled in congested traffic behind a colourfully decorated truck festooned with gold and silver mud guards. Painted on its sides were multiple scenes of landscapes in parrot greens, bright yellows, candy pinks and turquoise blues, culminating in a large mural on the back of the truck which depicted mountains, valleys, birds and lions. A verse at the bottom of the mural depicted the sentiments of the driver: *Hum to dushman ko bhi mohabat ki saza dey tain hain, hath uta tey nahin, nazron sey gira deh tey hain* (We punish our enemies with love. Never raising a hand to avenge; just lowering our gaze and their esteem.) Hajra laughed as she read this out loud to Ilyas. They drove past bustling wayside tea shops nestled alongside mechanics' shops, electronics' shops stocked to their ceilings with the latest merchandise, imported or smuggled from Dubai, medical clinics advertising ultrasound facilities, barber shops promising massages and virility, cloth stores displaying their wares, tailors' shops, car-dealer showrooms, private tutoring schools for English, jewellry shops, and bakeries. On each of the roundabouts there were security checkpoints manned by the army due to the unrest in the city. Hajra thought she had caught a glimpse of a poster plastered on a boundary wall appealing for revenge with Abbas's face on it. 'How many will you kill? We are all Abbas now,' she had read.

The car arrived at the house and Ilyas honked for the front gate leading into the compound to be opened. Hajra stepped out and walked up to the brass plaque inscribed with a simple 43-G that was embedded into the boundary wall. She reached for the edge of her sari pallu and rubbed the plaque to remove a smudge. Then she looked around her quickly and leaned forward and kissed the spot on the stone surface of the boundary wall just below the plaque. She caught Ilyas staring at her, he was scratching his head, shuffling his feet and smiling. 'All the bibis do this, Begum Sahiba, when they get home from the airport!' he said, referring to Resham, Kulsum, Amina and Shireen. She smiled and stepped back. She heard a jubilant voice shouting, 'Salaam Begum Sahiba!' and saw Jeevan, young, gaunt and bony in a pink and green flowery patterned cotton shalwar kameez, waving down to her. Jeevan's sunburnt face shone in a big smile as she cheerfully greeted Hajra from the terrace on the second floor.

As she walked in to the compound, the scent of magnolia blossoms greeted her and the strong aroma of food on the stove, of ginger and garlic, came wafting in from the kitchen. Hajra could hear the chug-a-chug sound of the sewing machine, coming from the downstairs verandah that opened on to the lawn. A helicopter flew by overhead. Iqbal, one of Sara's tailors, sat coughing away on the porch floor on a kilm that was littered with cuttings and scrapes from the bundles and bolts of textiles surrounding him. 'Salaam Begum Sahiba,' he said, scrambling to his feet. 'Sit, sit, Iqbal. How are you? How is your family?' 'Everyone is fine, Begum Sahiba, thanks to your prayers,' Iqbal replied, lolling his henna-dyed, blow-dried head from side to side in a gesture of congeniality which always made Hajra uneasy. She disliked with intensity, this scraping and bowing and unnecessary deference. 'I've almost completed all your blouses and just have to do the falls of two more saris.'

'Good, good. There is no hurry. And what about the clothes for Resham Bibi?' 'Almost done Begum Sahiba,' Iqbal coughed a smoker's cough and cleared his throat. 'I was a bit delayed, I had to go home to Punjab for Christmas.'

'Christmas? That was months ago!'

'Yes Begum Sahiba, but then I got sick over there. Living in Karachi spoils us for the village life!' 'Iqbal, your excuses never end. I'll never get my clothes from you in time, no matter what. If it's not Christmas, it's Easter. If it's not Easter, then its illness, and if it's not that, then worse, a wedding!' Iqbal laughed, coughed and grinned sheepishly, scratched his head and said,'What to do Begum Sahiba, no other way, majburi.'

'Always excuses. Never-ending stream of excuses, Iqbal.'

'What to do Begum Sahiba. Sara Bibi wanted…'

'Ah Sara! I'll talk to Sara then, should I?'

'Oh no, Begum Sahiba,' Iqbal cried out in alarm. 'For God's sake, don't say anything to Sara Bibi, she'll chew me up raw! I'll have finished everything by the end of this week. Kasam sey!' Hajra laughed at how effective the threat was of telling Sara, Iqbal's employer and tyrant boss. She walked past Iqbal and entered the foyer downstairs. Jeevan's sprightly figure came bouncing down the stairs, 'Bari-ma, Bari-ma, how are you? Choti-ma had me clean only your rooms today. She said I wasn't to do any other work.

I was especially careful, Begum Sahiba, with the piano. I cleaned behind it as well. You'll see it's shining. Now we'll hear music in the mornings again! I'm so glad you are here. I was so happy when she told me you were coming home! Bari-ma, come upstairs and check my work. See how nicely I have cleaned everything.' 'Where is she?' Hajra asked.

Jeevan seemed to shrink into herself a little, she scratched her neck and mumbled, 'Sara Bibi and Zareenabai left about an hour ago.'

'Did they say where they were going?'

'I think it had something to do with the digging,' mumbled Jeevan uncertainly.

'What?'

'Digging, Bari-ma.'

'Did you say digging?'

'Yes, Begum Sahiba,' Jeevan shifted her large, kohl-rimmed, black eyes uneasily and managed to sputter through a bit of her dupatta clenched between her teeth the words, 'yes, Bari-ma, digging.'

'Digging? What digging?' Hajra asked, confused. 'I didn't see any digging in the garden outside. Is Zareenabai planting something in the back garden?'

'The dining room, Begum Sahiba, the dining room!' Jeevan said anxiously. Waving her bony arm up and down with the palm open she pointed towards the dining room and backed away to create a bit of distance between herself and Hajrabai. 'The dining room floor, Bari-ma!'

'What about the dining room floor?'

'They had it dug up this morning!'

'What?' shouted Hajra. 'I can't understand a word you are saying!' Hajra hurried across the hall to the dining room, which was now denuded of furnishings. She stopped and her mouth fell open as a groan escaped her. 'Hai ma!' The beautiful mosaic was gone, a huge shallow wall-to-wall gaping mess confronted her instead. Gone was the gleaming red, black and mustard pattern of tiles that formed a simple floral design in the centre and moved out into geometric shapes towards a broad banded border. Instead there was what seemed to be a freshly dug up shallow pit of gravel and dirt.

'Hai ma, what is this? Where is the floor?' Hajra shouted at Jeevan.

'It's lying outside in a big heap in the back garden, Begum Sahiba!'

'Hai ma, what is happening in my house!' wailed Hajra, holding her hands to the sides of her head in disbelief. 'I don't know, Begum Sahiba. I swear I had nothing to do with this! Sara Bibi told Choti-ma yesterday early morning that there, in one of the houses in the neighbourhood, there in the other lane behind us, they had found gold buried under the floor of the dining room. And Sara Bibi and Choti-ma had the floor dug up to check if we had gold here too.'

'Oh my God, what will they do next?' screamed Hajra in disbelief and rage. 'My beautiful floor, my house!' she wailed. 'There was no gold at all under the floor, Begum Sahiba, not even a copper coin!' Jeevan added in distress and disappointment. They heard the gate opening outside and a car coming in. Jeevan hurried to the front door and opened it just as Sara and Zareenabai were stepping out of the car. 'What have you done to my house, Sara?' Hajra shouted in anger from the dining room. Sara and Zareenabai had proceeded in chatting happily to each other, a magazine worthy perfect picture of mother and daughter, matching in eyes and shades of clothing—Zareena wore a light pink and pistachio green sari while Sara wore a light pink tunic over cream colored straight pants. They now stopped dead in their tracks, frightened. 'Now

Bari-ma, I can explain everything,' Sara began soothingly, stepping forward. 'Explain what!' sobbed Hajra.

They had been to the neighbours' earlier in the day before their luncheon at the Boat Club—the neighbours, the ones who had dug up their floors. No gold had been found. It had just been a bad rumour. A rumour about how prosperous and wealthy Hindu owners of the house decades ago had buried gold under the floor before departing Karachi at Partition, in the hope that they would return once events settled down. But Sara and Zareenabai had just learned that the neighbours hadn't even dug up their floors. Their having dug up their floors was a rumour. Sara had tried to explain, but her mother was wailing throughout, 'Hai ma, Hai ma!' Sara continued to repeat her explanation while Jeevan had fled to the garden outside and Zareenabai had gone up to her apartment. The house had gone quiet except for Hajra's shouting and Sara's protests. Only Iqbal had the temerity to come stand at the side of the doorway and peek inside to watch, with a mixture of astonishment and glee, the spectacle of the dressing down of his boss and to see her on the receiving end for once. Sara had caught sight of his lanky frame and caught him staring, and as he ducked back to hide she shouted, 'What are you doing standing there? Get out of my sight!' which had prompted Hajra to shout at her, 'Sara, watch your tongue!' to which Iqbal had replied in a panic, 'Begum Sahiba, I only wanted to ask you for some instructions! I just wanted to know if the armhole should be ten inches or twelve!' But he had run as fast as he could out of the porch and out the front gate where he stood under the shade, calming his nerves by drawing deeply on a K-2 cigarette. Eventually Sara, shaken and chastened, had left for her house. Hajra remained standing in the doorway to the dining room, weeping with rage. She went to her apartment upstairs and sat on her bed in disbelief. Her head hurt, her eyes were swollen. She felt dizzy. Her blood pressure, she felt, was shooting up. She was unsure what to do, whether to go and shout at Zareena some more, or to call Razzak and shout at him. She decided to do both. But as soon as she had resolved to call Razzak, the phone rang. It was Resham. Hajra sobbed a hello. 'Bari-ma! Is that you? Are you there! What's the matter? Are you crying? Is Abba okay, is Choti-ma all right? What's happened?'

'Resham!' Hajra wailed. 'You won't believe what Sara and Choti-ma have done!'

'What!' Resham shouted in a panic. 'What's wrong? Are they okay?'

The sound of Resham's panic-stricken voice had the immediate salutary effect of calming Hajra down. In fact, and mercifully for the culprits involved, it made her start to laugh. 'They're okay.

They've dug up the floor. Can you explain that to me?'

'What?'

'They've dug up the dining room floor!'

'Who?'

'Your sister and Choti-ma, that's who!'

'Why?'

'They're looking for gold!'

'What?'

'Sara heard somewhere that the neighbours had found gold under their dining room floor, and the next thing your Choti-ma was doing was having our floor dug up. It's a mess! My beautiful, lovely floor.'

'Well…'

'What do you mean by that tone, Resham? No, they didn't find any gold!'

'Well, stop them before they dig up the whole house.'

Resham's voice was muffled. Hajra heard a giggle in her voice. For the rest of the day, the house was as silent as a guilty child sent up to its room. Only the sewing machine continued to rattle and chug outside.

In the evening, Razzak had listened to the whole saga, shaking his head from time to time, ducking to hide his mirth or coughing to suppress laughter. 'This is what happens when you leave,' Razzak had said to Hajrabai that night before going to bed. Shrugging his shoulders and chuckling he said, 'Utter and complete madness.' 'Razzak, aren't you at all angry with Sara?'

'Why should I be? If anyone needs to be reprimanded, it's Zareena and you. But not Sara. Not my child. She was looking to increase our fortunes, as far as I can tell! And I admire that! I've raised my children to be entrepreneurial. Don't look at me that way, baba! And don't say it's my favouritism and that I spoil her. I have no favourites. Just firsts.'

Hajra looked at him in frustration and turned her face to hide the smile that she was unable to suppress despite her foul mood, 'Don't flirt with me okay? I'm angry.'

'Okay baba, I'm too old to flirt. Call Rehana in the morning.

I'm sure she can fix everything, she's done a PhD on these tiles hasn't she?' 'What is Rehana going to do for us?'

'Put it back again. What else? She must know whether that old Nuserwanji factory has any supplies lurking about in some dingy, old godforsaken godown somewhere. Or maybe we can have her tear them out of some other old grungy godown. Besides that, your precious floor is all sitting outside in a pile, all is not lost. Just think of it as being temporarily re-arranged—displaced. Now just arrange it back. Don't fret so much Hajra, and stop crying. I know, I know, it won't be exactly the same. Who knows, it may be even better, huh? Welcome home. Let this be a lesson to you.'

The phone rang and Razzak picked it up, 'Resham, yes beta, how are you? Everything okay with you? Yes, everything is under control here.'

Resham said, 'Abba, I've got the others on the line as well.'

Amina, Shireen and Kulsum chimed in with their greetings.

Hajra reached for the phone, 'Is it Resham?' Razzak said, 'It's all of them apparently.'

Hajra reached for the phone, 'Here, let me talk to them.'

Razzak laughed as he held her back and said, 'To what do we owe this group phone call?'

Resham replied, 'I spoke to Bari-ma this morning, she was so upset about the floor.'

Razzak said, 'Well, there's nothing to worry about. Everything will be fixed. Here, talk to her yourself, she's standing over my head trying to get the phone away from me. Baba, hold on a minute, let me talk to them. Okay, okay take the phone.'

Hajra said, 'Hello yes, it's awful, what a mess. It's just unbelievable. But it'll all be fixed. I'll call Rehana tomorrow. Thank God they didn't go ahead and have the rubble removed. It's all there. I think we can save it.'

Amina interjected, 'Well Bari-ma, maybe you should consider this for a moment. I mean, I know how you feel, but maybe change is a good thing, maybe now you should consider a wooden floor. They're all the rage nowadays. Quite classical. I've always liked wooden floors and it'll look beautiful in the dining room. You should see what I've done here in my apartment.'

Hajra replied icily, '43-G is not New York or your apartment. I am not going to put in a wooden floor, I'm going to put in the floor that was here. It was very classical, thank you very much. I don't need New York to tell me what is classical.' Amina said hurriedly, 'I mean it's not like we don't have tiles in the house, all the floors are tiled. Why not have a bit of variety, it would be so sophisticated. Just think about it, wooden slats. They look lovely.' Hajra said curtly, 'No wooden floor.' 'Who is saying wooden floor?' Razzak asked. 'I think you should consider it at least.' Hajra replied, 'Amina is saying that.' 'Well, consider it,' Razzak asserted.

'What's Abba saying?' asked Amina. Hajra answered, 'He's agreeing with you.' 'Well, what about marble?' Shireen chimed in. Hajra responded, 'Well there you go, we have another suggestion. Sheen on top of gold. Now everyone has a brilliant idea.'

'Carpeting?' Razzak suggested. 'No!' said Hajra forcefully, 'Is that what you want? Now Shireen is saying marble.'

'What's Abba saying?' Shireen asked. Hajra replied, 'He thinks carpeting.' Shireen said, 'No. That's awful.'

'What's wrong with marble?' asked Razzak. 'No marble, no wooden floors, no carpeting,' Hajra said. 'I'm going to have Rehana put in the original floor.' Kulsum interjected, 'Bari-ma, I love the original floor but think about other ideas as well.' Razzak asked, 'What are they saying?'

Hajra replied, 'Like you, they're all talking about marble and wood and carpets and cement. I don't care! I'm putting back the floor that was there!' Resham said soothingly, 'Bari-ma, I agree with you. But will you be able to do that? Where will you get the tiles? I mean, the factory doesn't even exist any longer, does it?'

'We'll use the same tiles,' said Hajra. 'They are damaged but I don't care. I'm sure Rehana will know what to do. I'm sure she can even place an order somewhere for us. She must know how to do these things.'

The next morning Hajra woke up early and went down to the lawn where Zareenabai sat reading from her Koran. Zareena looked up meekly when she saw Hajra. 'Hajrabai listen, I was thinking we could now put in a new floor, you know the marble tiles or Sara was suggesting a wooden floor. She said she knows a Malaysian firm that makes wooden floors. It'll take two days only. What do you think?'

Hajrabai took a deep breath and said softly, 'Quiet! No, Zareenabai, we will not put in a marble floor or a wooden floor. We will put back the floor exactly as it was. That's what I told the girls and Razzak last night and that's what I'm telling you. Open your ears wide and listen.'

'But Hajrabai, I went to see some samples with Sara yesterday…' Hajra glared and walked away and left Zareena staring at her Koran.

It was just after three in the afternoon when Sara and Hajra arrived at the limestone building of the godown which had been restored and converted into the museum and the foundation offices. They had come to enlist Rehana's help in restoring the dining room floor. Sara had insisted that she accompany her mother, for after all, she reasoned, Rehana had been introduced to Hajra by Sara during the time that Rehana was completing her research on old buildings in the city. 'Now Bari-ma, there's no need to mention how the floor got dug up, is there? I mean, it will just make me look stupid in front of people who have a lot of respect for me!'

Sara had prompted her mother outside the foundation building. Hajra had lifted her sunglasses off her face and pushed them to the top of her gray head and considered her daughter's remark.

'You don't need my help in that department Sara,' she had replied caustically. And, ignoring Sara's crestfallen expression, she had continued, 'But don't worry, I'll tell her that we had thought of having a wooden floor put in and then we had realized our stupidity and upstartish ideas and had changed our minds.' And with that remark, she swept forward, hitching up her sari slightly with one hand and climbing up the steps into the main hall of Yaqub's foundation and museum, with Sara skulking in behind her, stinging from the remark. The large hall was bathed in sunshine, its walls, an earthy clay colour, seemed to cast a rose hue across the cavernous space. Sunlight poured in from a skylight in the centre on to the reflecting pond. The trickling sound of water which overflowed from the brim of the gigantic earthen bowl in the centre of the pond gave the room its beauty. Water awash in light cast patterns on to the surrounding walls which seemed to shimmer and glow. Sara looked around and said to her mother, 'We could do this.' Hajra looked at her with irritation, 'What? Now you want to blow off the ceiling to let in the light and excavate a pond in the dining room? Shall we ask your father to bring home a gigantic nihari pot to place in the centre of the dining room?'

'It's a nice idea, Bari-ma, for a house.' 'For a house maybe, but not for a home. But Sara, go ahead do whatever you want to in your husband's house, that's your home now.'

'You don't seem to think your husband's house is your home,' Sara said under her breath.

'What's that?' Hajra asked. 'Nothing, Bari-ma, I was just thinking out loud. I mean, Resham is having a gigantic bathtub installed in her apartment. A huge copper tub. I mean, as far as I understand, that's the main feature of her new apartment. You didn't find anything wrong with that.'

'It is in her bathroom—it's a bathtub!'

'Sounds like her bathroom is so huge that it is her main room! And besides, we have a sink in the dining room. Why not think about that. Perhaps we can make the sink like a wall fountain. Wouldn't that be lovely?'

'Sara, I don't care what Resham does in her house, whether she turns it into a hamam or a swimming pool or a toilet. And I don't care what you do in yours, be my guest. That is your house. But I will decide what happens in mine. No wall fountains!' The sound of the water splashing in the pond reverberated gently in an echo all around the large space. At the far end, Hajra noticed a blonde woman, the receptionist, who sat behind a marble-top desk, sleepily watching them. As they walked over to her, she asked her if she could be of assistance. Sara asked to see Yaqub. The receptionist picked up a white intercom phone and spoke into it. Hajra noticed that when she mentioned Yaqub's name, it was in a hushed almost reverent tone.

'Please Madam, kindly take a seat,' the receptionist said. 'My name is Noor Afshan. Ms Rehana will be with you right away.' Hajra looked around her and saw a single wrought iron bench arranged near the water. She went to it and sat down. Sara sat down next to her. Sunshine encased them in this spot. Looking up towards the skylight through the dust particles shining like foolsgold in the stream of sunshine, Hajra saw that they were seated inside a covered courtyard and that the three floors above had balconies running all the way around, overlooking the courtyard and benefiting from the skylight. The atmosphere of serenity was overpowering. For a public museum, Hajra mused there was hardly anyone around. In fact, no one except for herself, her daughter and the receptionist. Sara, still smarting from her mother's rebuke and sarcasm, sat next to her mother and cast about a gaze of a patron saint's look of satisfaction. After all, this would never have transpired had it not been for Sara's vision. She considered herself the source of this wonderful success that Yaqub and Rehana had achieved.

Sara always felt that everyone in her family never saw her for the visionary that she was and instead thought she was selfish, greedy, manipulative, ambitious and untrustworthy. 'You may not think my ideas are worth noting Bari-ma, but all of this is because of me!' She sniffed. 'I'm sure it is, Sara, I'm sure it is!'

Sara thought that except for her father and Choti-ma, no one appreciated her. They can say what they want, she thought, Barima can act as sarcastic as she wants to. But Sara had never cared a bit for what anyone had thought, she had always done what she wanted to do. She was Sara Aziz, she did as she pleased. Without caution, without care, without anyone's ridiculous control over her! So Amina and Resham thought that they could shout at her over the phone about the floor, and about this and that, whenever they felt like it? Sara felt that her intentions were good, and that she never meant any harm. It didn't matter if no one else saw it that way. What did she care, anyway, she was a good girl. She prayed five times a day like her father and Choti-ma. And God knew. So then why should she care what anyone else thought? If she started caring about what others felt or what they thought about her, she knew she would never have gotten as far as she did. She looked around her at what had been a hopeless, damp, dark, run down godown which had been infested with rats and pigeons and had been transformed into this delightful work of art and light. No, she would not have gotten to where she had if she had paid heed to all the admonishing. She never listened to them, never, she was always right. She had vision. She was creative. Creative people didn't care what others thought, she thought to herself. I never had any illusions about that. Delusions about that! I never took advantage of my father the way that my sisters have. I made my way here, myself, by staying right here while they took the easy way out. Leaving for America. And look at me today, I am more settled, more established, wealthier, better known and more beautiful and desirable than any of them. I didn't have to leave my country to become someone. I love Karachi for this, it's so forgiving and is able to forget and enable you to make it here if you're rich. I adore it. I became who I am here, right here. I am known. Who are they? Nobodies! Nobodies in a foreign land. In places where they are forever talking of leaving and coming back here, in places that I only visit for shopping, and where I can spend the kind of money that makes their jaws drop. I have what they can never have: I am home. I do what I want and I always have and that's because I trust only one thing, one entity. God. I am answerable only to God. I pray five times a day and I have done that all my life. Those sisters of mine who are forever criticizing me haven't ever said a single day's worth of prayers unless under duress. Does anyone think God will not forgive me for my small transgressions? I have only been human. He will never forgive them. In their efforts to remain saints, they have not lived and they have not prayed. They have never failed, they have never fallen. They don't know the meaning of asking for forgiveness, the meaning of praying for redemption, the meaning of struggle. If only Bari-ma would see them for what they are: simpering, self-loathing, self-satisfied ninnies. Sara thought of all the times they sat in unfair judgement over her. Telling her what was right and wrong, lecturing her on ethics, democracy and morality. It made her laugh, and at times she cried with pity for them. They wouldn't survive a day sitting in a room with all those people, those poor people, for whose welfare they are always professing to inquire about with all their phone calls every time there is an explosion in this city. Not even two hours would any of them last with the people they say they care about! Sara never argued with her sisters, she would keep quiet. She tolerated them. She would only show them that she loved them and she did, they were her sisters, they had grown up together. Sara thought, 'I do it all for Choti-ma's sake. Bless my dear Choti-ma, she has always appreciated me, encouraged me, always. Always praised me and never said no to anything I wanted to do. But Bari-ma does nothing but criticize me.'

Sara recounted to herself how she had always wanted to sing, Bari-ma always said Sara didn't have a voice for it. And Bari-ma only focused on Resham—on how lovely Resham's voice was. It was. No doubt about it. Sara thought it was lovely too. But she thought hers was lovely as well. But no, not for Bari-ma. Only Choti-ma said that Sara should have her voice trained by an ustaad. And Sara did, she trained it, she got herself a teacher, she practiced every day. I can sing. I sing beautifully, everyone wants Sara Aziz to sing at their parties and events. I am always the centre of attraction. I wanted to learn how to dance. Choti-ma said I must get a maestro to teach me. I did. I dance, I took dancing lessons, kathak. This I do for myself. But everyone knows that I take dancing lessons. And yoga, every day. I have a body so beautiful, so flexible, so pliable, I'll be young forever. While the rest of them only got an education I did all that and more. When I enter a room, I bring in life and joy. Choti-ma tells me so. Abba tells me so. That's me. Everyone loves me, Sara Aziz. And everyone loves to hate me as well. That's the way to go. It would be dreadful to come into a room and for no one to take notice! It would be dreadful to be considered, that nice Sara Aziz! No baba not for me! I'll leave that to my sisters. That unlived life of Amina and Resham! No, not for me. And Sara painted. She smiled to herself and then quickly changed her expression, afraid that Bari-ma would know that something was going on in her head and start interrogating her. Indeed, Sara did paint. Bari-ma had shown her a brochure that she had saved of an exhibition that had taken place decades ago, and particularly the painting of a room in their old house in the old city.

Sara had been mesmerized. Bari-ma had told her that the painting was lost, either painted over or destroyed, and that she had been searching for the painting quietly and was obsessed with it. There and then, Sara had decided that she would do something about it. The day after, Sara had visited and snuck the brochure into her bag just before she left. Bari-ma never even noticed. That was about two years ago. Since then, Sara had set to work. It took her about a month to get the painting done. She had no idea what the colours were in the original painting but she realized that neither did Bari-ma. The brochure was black and white. So that wasn't going to be a problem. No one who would have known the colours was alive now to tell her. So no one who knew what the colours were would dispute it. Not the artist, nor the subject. The artist was dead, the house destroyed. It was all in Sara's hands. How perfect. Memory, Sara had learned, is what we make it. Facts in front of our eyes, trump the reality of the past. One just has to outlive those who remember and then memory and the past belong to you. Sara consoled herself that her intentions were good. Her plan was noble. She was going to give this as a birthday present to Bari-ma. It was going to be her huge winning-over of Bari-ma's affection. She was going to spin a tale about how she had bought the painting from an art dealer who had sworn her to secrecy. She had made sure that the canvas looked convincingly old and battered. Sara allowed the paint to weather for a while. It was unmistakably the same painting as in the brochure. Bari-ma wouldn't know the difference. What was the harm? Why not? And then, along came Yaqub. What a project he was for Sara. A full time hobby. He still was. Someone Sara could completely relate to. Yaqub, the very wealthy, very simple-minded, very earnest, very much the full-time-in-need-of-rescue by Sara project, wanting-to-be- refined Yaqub. Who better than Sara to introduce him to society and take him under her wing? Sara didn't think there were many in the city like Yaqub with his kind of unfettered wealth. Riaz always said to her that she knew how to spot a diamond in the rough. No one really knew who Yaqub was in terms of his background, beyond his recent arrival in Karachi, not even Sara. Yet she knew from the moment he walked into the charity ball that night ages ago, she knew that he was someone with potential. Someone who Riaz and she should cultivate. She had observed Yaqub across the room, standing in the entrance to the ballroom at the hotel, undistinguished in his appearance, wearing an ill-fitted and out-dated three piece, brown polyester suit. And yet, he was noticeable in his demeanour and carriage, which displayed a quiet self-assurance though at this moment, at the edge of this crowd, he seemed to falter and looked anxious. He had broad shoulders, a trim physique, a head held high and salt and pepper hair like Riaz, though in greater quantity by a small margin. Yes, he had potential. Sara knew that he needed her. She agreed, she knew diamonds. Really, she thought if she hadn't found

Riaz, God give him health and life, Yaqub would've been just the man for her. Anyway, that was neither here nor there, she knew that her current prominent place in society as a leading party-giver, the hostess to know, the benefactor and organizer of many a charity ball, was completely due to Riaz. Her glittering image in the Karachi social scene was because she had her wonderful, respectable and rich husband. Smart, beautiful and brilliant women were a dime a dozen in this city. But they were nothing without husbands, especially rich husbands. Sara knew that well.

As soon as Sara had set eyes on Yaqub, she knew he was in need of her protection. She had given him ten minutes to feel alone enough in that crowd and to feel the chill of being ignored before she had made her solicitous way to him. He was standing there, just inside the door, tapping the invitation card with one hand on the palm of his other hand, seeming to weigh whether he should stay or turn around and run out of there. All around him, gyrating to techno-rock and fusion music were the throngs of party-goers who considered themselves the beautiful people of the city. Swaying and sliding on the dance floor were dozens of women in low-cut, strapless, slinky ball gowns, and halter top blouses over mini skirts, there were women in backless blouses over trousers or saris. The men were dressed in suits and tuxedoes. Cigar and cigarette smoke filled the air. Champagne, wine and whiskey flowed freely. Anyone would think that a man visiting from abroad would feel at home in all this, Sara thought. Within half an hour she knew that this man, Yaqub Kishtiwalla, had lived a very quiet and a rather conservative life abroad and had more money than Riaz and Sara could ever imagine having. She managed to extract this information from him without him even realizing that he was being assessed. He was a guest in the hotel and had been there for a week. Just newly arrived in Karachi.

He was planning to return home to Karachi permanently after spending twenty years in Dubai and Italy or somewhere. He considered Karachi home, though it was not clear why since he did not have any family in the city. Abroad, in Dubai and Italy, he had made pots and pots of money but didn't manage to get an education or learn English properly. Here, in this party, he was completely and utterly socially lost. It was quite clear to Sara: give him a shop and a cash register, or give him the docks or godowns filled with sugar, timber, paper and spice, and he would be fine. Or at a local mosque in the south end of London or in Queens. But throw him into this setting of cigars, halter tops and all the hoi polloi of Karachi, rubbing shoulders here with all their relatives and friends from abroad, home for the holidays, and he was nowhere. Or even worse, he was like a scared child in a shopping mall in Dubai who had been abandoned by his parents. Riaz and Sara insisted he come home with them for coffee that evening. And there in the comfort and safety of their home, Yaqub told them about his plans to establish himself in Karachi after being away for so long, since he was a child, apparently. He confessed to them that he was unable to write without difficulty. His reading was better but speaking in English was still difficult for him. 'Thank God for computers,' he said, 'at least I can read the names and prices of stocks!' Riaz had laughed congenially and said, 'And that's all that matters!' Riaz had insisted that Yaqub move into their guest annex. 'No point in staying at the hotel,' said he. Yaqub was taken aback and said he couldn't possibly do that, it would be too much. Sara insisted, 'Riaz and I will simply not hear a no from you.' When it came to social interests coinciding with business instincts, Riaz and Sara were a formidable team.

It was about five in the morning and they were sitting in their cozy lounge, talking with this odd and very intriguing man. 'Right,' said Riaz. 'We are going back to the hotel right now to collect your things. That's it.' Poor Yaqub spluttered and his eyes were as big as his wide open mouth. But the kind couple simply didn't give Yaqub a chance to refuse or even say a word. Yaqub was completely overcome with emotion by their generosity and friendliness which they seemed to dismiss—Yaqub they felt had been away too long and had forgetten Karachi hospitality. Off they sped to the hotel with Yaqub in the front with Riaz who drove the car and Sara nodding off in the back. They stopped on the way for Sara to get a supari paan and then they were back at home by seven in the morning. It was Sunday morning and the household was asleep. Sara woke up the children's ayah who stuck a mosquito repellent into the wall plug of the guest bedroom, made sure that there were towels and a new soap and asked him what time he wanted his morning tea. That day Yaqub, like Sara and Riaz, woke up in the late afternoon, more relaxed and much happier. And with that, Yaqub was installed in the guest annex for a year. Sara had found herself another cause. Yaqub was under her wing. Riaz would have his business venture. Sara proceeded to educate Yaqub. She had discreetly hired a tutor for English for him. The best she could find. She spoke to the children's headmistress who recommended an old retiree based in Murree, an Anglo-Indian lady, a Mrs Richards, who had been the headmistress of a girl's convent and whose grandfather had been stationed in Murree in the British Indian Army in the early 1900s and had stayed on in the country after the Raj had ended. He and his family had seen no reason to return to the discomforts of England having lived in great luxury in the Empire. Mrs Richards's father had, in turn, married an Indian woman and had been a school master in Lahore.

Mrs Richards had been sent to Murree convent when she was eight and had stayed on years later after she finished school to become a teacher and finally the headmistress there in the pine and cloud covered hills that she loved so much. Now retired, she was leading a quiet life in the Murree hills, occasionally providing tuition to the convent students. Sara, through her friends who were alumni of Murree convent, had been able to persuade her to come to Karachi and to come and live with her for about six months or so. Mrs Richards helped the children with their studies but really Sara had hired her for the tutoring of Yaqub which she did every day for several hours. Within three months, his English was better than Riaz's. Within six months, he could read and write. Mrs Richards was simply marvellous. Sara and Riaz introduced Yaqub to everyone. To Abba, Bari-ma, Choti-ma and all their friends. They advised him on who he should invite, who he should meet with and who he should associate with. To Sara's bemusement, Yaqub had said that Sara reminded him of his mother. She was very pious. Sara had thought to herself, 'Why not? Yaqub was very rich. No harm in being a bit like his mother, no?

Can't be anything else at this stage. Allah toba, toba, toba. God forgive me. I'm so well settled, mashallah, and so happy with Riaz. Mashallah, mashallah. Khuda ka shookar hai.' And Riaz thought it all so funny, Sara taking Yaqub on as a project. But really it had spiced up their life considerably. They were getting a bit bored really with their hectic but usual routine. When Yaqub arrived it was like they had a new child. As though Yaqub was their long lost son whom they had found or who had been returned to them after he had made his way alone in the world.

Only difference, because in this case Yaqub was grown up and extremely wealthy and now all that they, Sara and Riaz had to do was to groom him in everything to make him perfectly presentable. And it was something like that for Yaqub as well because he treated Riaz and Sara with such affection and deference as though they were his parents and not his peers. In return, Sara and Riaz were thrilled with all his achievements. They were over the moon to see his transformation. Sara smiled with pride when he said *very* instead of *wery*, and noted with satisfaction the change in his accent which was steadily becoming the Irish laced English of the Murree Convent.

Summer came and Riaz and Sara had their usual plans to go abroad, this time to Europe. They insisted that Yaqub accompany them. Paris, London, Rome, Florence, Venice, Prague. They took him everywhere. He drove them through Rome, Venice, Florence and Sienna, teaching them both a thing or two about how to get along in Italy with very little money. But they didn't have to worry about money. Yaqub paid for everything. It was marvellous. And yet, he kept thanking Riaz and Sara, which was even more marvellous, Sara thought. It was all too sad as well, for as Sara discovered—the man had not seen the Uffizi, or the Vatican, or the Sistine Chapel, nor had his photograph taken at the Spanish steps. No photos at all! It was so sad, Sara thought, it really broke her heart. Well, she would take care of all that. And Sara had done so and made sure that there would be lots of lovely photographs to show for their trip. There they were, Riaz and Sara with Yaqub between them on the Charles Bridge, at the bookshop which Kafka visited often, Sara posing with a book looking satirically studious. There they were at the feet of David, and looking bored in front of the Uffizi, Buckingham Palace, at the Louvre, Eiffel Tower and Notre Dame. And yes, doing the stereotypical pose—leaning, at the tower of Pisa. Snap, snap, snap. And so many, many photographs at well known cafés and restaurants in every city they visited. Sara forgot which ones were in which country. It didn't matter, it was just important to have the photographs. Photographs at landmarks. There were no photographs off the beaten track charming alley ways that they found themselves in when they were lost.

Why that was just a waste of a good photograph. They took him to the sights and to the museums that he had never had time for before. They went to the theatre in London, opera in Verona, nightclubs in Paris. Concerts in Prague. Sara hated the opera but she thought it would do Yaqub good. Good to have that in his ears. It was supposed to make a person European, like the azaan in your ear at birth makes you Muslim! What a giggle, she thought. She loved theatre, so they went especially to the musicals. She hated plays. So boring. 'No play-shay for me,' she said when Riaz so much as suggested it. It was all marvellous, fabulous, absolutely fabulous, in her words.

Riaz and Yaqub shopped together and that was part of the transformation of Yaqub's outer appearance. London didn't do him the world of good that Sara had hoped it would. He got by with speaking in Urdu and Punjabi everywhere. And Sara knew that the best chance for him to improve his English was back at home and with Mrs Richards. From the night of the charity ball onwards, Yaqub had stayed with Sara and Riaz for a year. And in that year, his spoken English as well as his reading and writing had improved to manageable levels. Sara's children too had done well, both got first class grades in school as well. She was so proud of all of them. Thanks to Mrs Richards. God bless Mrs Richards, thought Sara Aziz. And then Yaqub had this idea about renovating an old godown into a home. Must be the effects of his business background, trucks, ships, wholesale storage. The mango doesn't fall far from the tree as they say, Sara had thought ruefully. Godowns were probably where he felt at home. Fine, she thought, baba who am I to interfere with people's personal choices. And Sara introduced him to the architect that she considered the most promising for restoration work.

Then one day Yaqub told Sara about his art gallery idea. That was when she had an idea too. One afternoon, when they were having tea together, as had become Yaqub's habit, to come over to meet Sara for tea at about four, just when she was wrapping things up at her boutique for the day, and about half an hour before Riaz got home. Sara's 'atelier', as she was fond of calling her office and tailoring workshop, was in her house and was a separate two storied structure which she had had constructed at one of the far corners of the large front garden. Sara occupied the first floor so that her office opened on to the garden while the workshop with its eight artisans and one master cutter and the machines was located on the second floor. Tea with Sara and then afterwards when Riaz would get home, he and Yaqub would go off to the club for a round of squash or golf or a swim.

Riaz was trying so hard to get Yaqub to go into a partnership with him, but whatever it was that Riaz was telling him, it didn't seem to be working. Yaqub would listen intently for hours but wouldn't offer to invest or go into a partnership with Riaz. But it had to happen, Sara thought in exasperation and optimism. Her husband just didn't have the kind of money for this type of venture, and Riaz needed to get Yaqub involved. Sara knew what she had to do! Whenever Riaz was talking business with Yaqub, Sara only came in and out to serve tea or sherbet or snacks and to insist that they only speak in English. It was rather sweet. Just like she insisted with the children every day. 'Speak in English only. What's the matter with you? Speaking like the servants-shervants!' And then she would leave, saying as she went that she didn't want any part of this business talk. Her interest, she had declared and demonstrated through her actions, was simply to see Yaqub thrive in Karachi.

One afternoon when Yaqub was sitting with her while she was drawing designs for her summer collection, all soft voiles and Egyptian cottons, Sara asked him if he could keep a secret. She made him swear on her life that he would have to keep the secret. Sara told him that she had bailed out a friend of hers, who was in deep financial crisis but who was also, as she put it, 'An art dealer-sheeler.' She told Yaqub that she had bought his entire painting collection. Sara said that the collection was impeccable. She told him that Riaz didn't know about it at all. He would be very upset if he found out, Sara said, because she had managed to nearly wipe out her own personal savings in order to bail out her dear friend.

No one knew that she had the paintings, and the art dealer friend had died of something shortly afterwards. 'Something sudden, I think it was a heart attack-shartattack!' Sara had explained to Yaqub as she showed him the paintings, which were all stacked up in her workshop. She told Yaqub that he would be doing her a great favour if he would take the collection from her and hang it up in his gallery once it was completed. She told him that he should consider them as his own and that doing so would be a favour to her. He agreed immediately but insisted on paying Sara for them. Sara absolutely refused to accept his money.

'Baba, you're like a son to me!' she had declared in a mock taking of offense and with a hand to her heart while keeping a straight face in front of Yaqub, who was at least fifteen years older than her. And to herself she reasoned, 'But I'm married, no? And he's single. So, I'm the mother in this.' She told him that it would give her the greatest pleasure to see these paintings displayed and open to the public. Sara declared that she would want nothing more. She lived for art and beauty. And with this, she rose further in Yaqub's esteem. She made him swear that he wouldn't ever tell anyone that these had come from her. Instead, he was to say that these paintings were his, collected by him over decades. This she insisted would add to his stature. Naturally, as in all advice cultural and social, he listened to Sara.

Now through her musings, seated with her mother in the space which she had helped create, she heard the crisp sound of feminine advance, of high heels clippity-cloppiting and turned to see Rehana's slender form, wearing a pale blue cotton shalwar kameez, her head covered as usual in a colourful hijab. Sara waved to her. Rehana hurried to Hajrabai and took her outstretched hands. 'How are you?' she asked. 'I'm fine, beta,' Hajrabai replied. 'How is Abbas's mother? I can't think of anything else.' Rehana shook her head sadly and heaved a sigh. 'She's not well at all. She hasn't stopped crying. She is on sedatives and it is all so awful. It was so good of you to come to the chaleesvan with me.' Hajra replied, 'It was the least I could do. I miss him so much. And I hardly knew him. His poor mother.' They stood looking at each other in silence for a moment and then Sara impatiently intervened by clearing her throat noisily. Sara said, 'We came today to visit and to talk to you…' Rehana turned towards Sara and smiled broadly, her large sparkling eyes shone, 'How are you Sara?'

Sara smiled back warmly, 'I'm very well. How is the PhD coming along?'

'Thanks to you Sara. It's completed!' I'm really grateful to you for all you've done for me!'

Sara waved her hand dismissively, but with a pleased expression on her face. She said, 'Really, you deserve to be working here with Yaqub—he needs your talent! After he read your thesis and after he saw the design of my workshop, he was completely impressed. By the way, you should come and see your creation! All my clients love the workshop and are constantly asking me to give them the name of the architect! I think I will have to put up a plaque with your name on it outside—designed by Rehana!' Rehana laughed happily, 'Thank you so much! And the interviews with your mother and father really helped me understand old Karachi.'

Sara said, 'And just look at this place, it's marvellous! You are really a genius Rehana.' Rehana took Sara's hand and squeezed it warmly, 'Welcome to the Foundation. I'd like to show you around. May I take you for a quick tour of our art gallery?'

Sara said, 'Yes. That would be nice.'

Rehana showed the way and the two of them walked towards the staircase on the side. Hajra noticed an elevator near the staircase. Rehana explained that it only went up to the top floor. 'The top floor is closed to the public and it is the residence of Mr Kishtiwalla.'

Climbing the steps, they arrived at the first floor, the length of which was a large room whose walls were covered with paintings. Rehana handed each of them a slim brochure from a pile on a marble table-top.

Rehana turned to Hajra asked, 'Would you like me to accompany you or would you prefer to view these on your own?' Hajra said, 'Please don't worry about me. I'm happy to look around on my own. But we really came over here to ask for your help with our house. It's a tile floor that we want you to help us restore.' Rehana looked at her quizzically but said that it would not be a problem at all. 'I'll sit here while you look, and then we can discuss the floor,' she replied. Sara moved away and proceeded to walk around the room, looking at the art work. Hajra too walked around, looking closely at each painting.

Sara ventured, 'You know Rehana, I was just thinking that perhaps you should consider adding a bookshop and a café to the museum.'

Rehana agreed, 'That's a very good idea. But I don't know what Mr Kishtiwalla would say to that. Wouldn't that make everything commercial and non-serious?' Sara said, 'Art galleries and museums should be fun! This place is empty. Isn't it open to the public? It seems to be closed to the public.'

Rehana replied, 'Well no, it isn't closed. But it isn't exactly open either.'

Sara asked, 'What do you mean?' Rehana replied, 'We're still sort of operating on the basis of *By Invitation Only*. Only VIPS allowed at this time. Such as very important guests like you.'

Hajra, who had been listening, interjected, 'Well, that's too bad. It should be open to the public. Museums all over the world, art galleries and things like that always try to attract more people and one of the ways to earn an income for themselves is to have a bookstore, a gift shop and a café.'

Sara watched her mother moving closer to a particular painting. Hajra gasped. There it was, on the closest wall right before her eyes, the painting of the old house—the old home in the old city. Rehana was replying to Sara, 'Mr Kishtiwalla doesn't need to earn an income.'

Sara kept an eye on her mother as she moved closer to the painting and stood gazing at it in disbelief, and as though in joy. 'Everyone needs to earn an income,' Sara said casually. She saw the look on her mother's face and came up next to her and said innocently, 'What is it Bari-ma?' Shaking her head in disbelief, Hajra managed to say, 'This painting!'

'Which painting?' Sara asked innocently. Then, coming closer to her mother, she peered at the painting and exclaimed, 'Unbelievable! Isn't that the one in the brochure that you showed me, Bari-ma?'

Hajra looked at Sara, 'Yes, the very one.'

Sara swung around and asked Rehana, 'Are these for sale?'

'I am not sure. I don't think so,' Rehana said, 'But you will have to speak to Mr Kishtiwalla.'

They heard footsteps coming up the stairs. Yaqub appeared. Sara noticed Rehana straightening up. She turned to look at him. He looked different here. He wore a light, charcoal wool suit over a pale, blue shirt with a bright, yellow tie with tiny gray flowers woven into it. Sara remembered that Riaz had picked it for Yaqub. Here, today Yaqub seemed in control and sure of himself. Powerful. Not a trace of anxiety or nervousness around him.

Yaqub moved towards them cheerfully, pleased at their presence, 'Welcome! We're honored you're here. I am so sorry to have kept you waiting. I must apologize. I was just on the phone. It seems that there was a bomb blast down at the docks.'

'Another one?' Sara asked. Yaqub shrugged and replied, 'It's an everyday thing now.' He turned to Hajra and asked kindly, 'Have you already seen the full collection? Shall we go to my office and have tea? We can all talk over there.'

Hajra said, 'Thank you. No, we haven't finished seeing the collection. This is quite incredible, really. I'm very surprised.'

'Well, I'm flattered,' Yaqub replied. 'That's a big compliment.'

'Yes,' murmured Hajra, 'It is, isn't it? This painting—I wondered where you got this. How did you get it? Where did you get it?'

Yaqub reddened and looked at Sara and remembered his promise. 'Well,' he said, 'I've owned it for so long that I can't even remember now. It's been in storage till very recently.'

'Has it?' Hajra asked. 'You didn't purchase this abroad?'

Yaqub looked confused, 'Why abroad?'

'From anyone or an art gallery abroad?' Hajra inquired.

Yaqub laughed, 'Oh no, it's a painting from Karachi. It was

purchased here, decades ago. No, no it's been here in Karachi, in storage all along.'

Hajra smiled, 'Well, it's quite a coincidence. Quite a coincidence indeed. You see, it's the portrait of our old family home. But here it is. I'm amazed to see it here. Quite astonished really!' Yaqub and Sara exchanged glances. Yaqub said, 'Please let's go to my office and sit down.'

Hajra remembered why they had come and said, 'I'd like to come back here afterwards and look at this painting again, if I may.' 'Of course,' said Yaqub. 'Stay as long as you want, come as often as you want, consider this your home! Tell us what you think of this building.'

Hajra replied, 'This building has transformed. It has become so beautiful. I could have never imagined that this space would be so lovely. It's hard to believe that this was a godown.'

Yaqub ushered them towards his office where, once they had settled down, and the tea and coffee ordered, brought in and served, Hajra made her request. She explained to Rehana and Yaqub that there had been a misunderstanding and the flooring at 43-G in the dining room had been dug up. Rehana's assistance was required in restoring the floor. Rehana promised to come to 43-G with them that very afternoon and see what could be done.

3

Rehana

HOLDING the edge of her hijab to cover her mouth and nose, Rehana pushed open the door and entered the sehan, coughing. She called out to her mother, 'Amma, I'm home!' The air was murky with smoke and soot, her eyes watered from the sting of it. 'Not again!'

Her mother came out into the sehan, her hair covered in a black paste of hair dye, a towel spread around her shoulders. 'There's no controlling them,' she said in exasperation. 'How many times have we complained to the KMC, that useless municipal office! I think someone should go to the police. I came home after six and you should have seen the smoke at that time. It's better now.'

Rehana replied angrily, 'This is ridiculous! One of these days that fire over there is going to get out of control and this whole neighbourhood will be destroyed! But in the meantime we're all going to get cancer from this smoke.'

A nearby garbage dump had once again been set on fire by scavengers. By burning the garbage, scavengers were able to separate the lucrative metal waste more easily to sell to recycling businesses.

The courtyard of their house was small, just enough room for a clothesline, several potted plants of tomato, lemon and green chilli; and a bird cage filled with yellow, red, blue and green lovebirds, asleep for the night and stirred and twittered as Rehana entered. The sehan floor had been recently tiled in terracotta tiles interspersed with blue tiles from Hala. This was of course, Rehana's idea and her modest and affordable exercise of her talents. The shalwar kameez she had worn yesterday, now dripping with water, was hanging on the line to dry. A sign that they had finally had running water this afternoon after a two day absence. Her mother must've just done the washing and hung it out. They always did their washing at night, the sun was too strong in the daytime and faded away the colours. And outfits needed to last for at least two seasons. The searing heat of the tiled sehan floor was evaporating the puddle of water under the washing almost as soon as it was formed.

Rehana coughed and rubbed her eyes: 'Why did you do the washing? I could have done it tonight. You don't have to do everything yourself.' Amma was coughing as well.

'I know, I shouldn't have done anything, I'm so tired today, the children in the afternoon shift were so rowdy. Very difficult for me to control. Anyway, why are you so late today, beta? Rehana said, 'I think it's too much work for you to teach the morning and afternoon shifts. Can't you ask them to reduce your duties?'

Amma replied, 'No, the workload is fine. I'm just tired today. Why are you so late?'

'I had to stay late this evening to finish up on some work. In the afternoon, I went over to Begum Rueewallah's house. You know Sara Aziz's mother—I interviewed her for my research and I also introduced her to Abbas. She was teaching Abbas how to play the piano.'

Amma: Why did you go there? To talk about Abbas? She must be very upset. It was good that she came to his parents' house for condolence.

Rehana: Of course she would come for that! Yes—she is very upset of course. No I had gone there to advise her about some work, she needs done at her house—Amma you should see their house, it is amazingly beautiful—really an old Karachi house—tiled floors— huge verandahs—old trees—right in front of Nishtar Park. I stayed there till about six and then I went back to work.

Amma: How did you come? Did Yaqub Sahib arrange for a ride back home? At this time of the night, it isn't safe.

Rehana replied: No, I caught the bus. It was okay.

Amma complained: I worry. He should take better care of his staff.

Rehana reassured her: Don't worry. I have my mobile with me. You can call me. And I think soon enough there will be an office car to pick up and drop us home!

Amma said: An office car would be so good. But I think you should demand more, Rehana. After all, everything he seems to be doing now is due to your hard work over years. Ask for a salary increase, a car, better working hours!

Rehana said: Amma you don't understand these things. I'm very lucky to be working for him. And he respects me a lot. I'm so grateful to Sara Aziz for introducing me to Yaqub Sahib. That piece of work that I did for her—designing her workshop—really was my big break. I really put my heart into it. I knew it was just a small job but I made the most of it—I really used the elements of my thesis—I could never have imagined that it would lead to so much. And now I can influence so many things. Anything that I say, Yaqub Sahib does. Look at all the projects that he is investing in. All my ideas. It's as though my thesis is coming alive. What more could I ask for?

Amma said: An office pick and drop—that's what you should ask for and a lot more! Maybe you should ask Sara to do that for you! Rehana was irritated: I just told you that that's going to happen very soon! Look at my feet! Oh no, I knew I shouldn't have worn these chappals to work today! They're ruined! The naala outside is overflowing again and I wasn't paying attention. I have to go wash my feet. Is there any water left?

Amma said: Here give them to me, I'll wash them carefully, you'll ruin them! Yes. Water came on at 3.00 p.m. today so we have a full tankie. Now I'm going to go take a bath before dinner and wash my hair. Anyway, I worry.

Rehana asked: Did you take your medicine on time today?

Amma replied: Yes I did. Here take this mug of tea with you and give me your chappals.

Rehana said: You know what the doctor said. We can't go for your final tests until you have completed this course of medicine.

Amma replied: Yes, yes. But taking it makes me sick. I feel so bad; it was so expensive. I feel so guilty.

Rehana: Don't be ridiculous. You always manage to see the wrong side of everything.

Amma: All your salary goes for this, my medicine, your brother's books, the house.

Rehana asked: What else should it be spent on?

Amma said: Your dowry!

Rehana laughed: Do you really mean that? Is that really what you are still thinking?

Amma laughed as well: No. It's silly of me. I thought I should at least say what is expected from a mother of a young daughter.

Rehana asked: When have you ever done what was expected? They laughed.

Amma smiled: You look so beautiful in your new shalwar kameez.

Rehana replied: Of course I do! You made it!

Amma replied with a gentle rebuke: I just wish you wouldn't cover your head that way. Such beautiful hair and no one ever gets to see it.

Rehana's mother was in her late fifties. She never interfered in her children's aspirations. She was widowed when her kids were teenagers. She taught at a school in the city in the morning and afternoon shifts for which she got up at 6 a.m. and was picked up by a hired Suzuki van for work every morning along with other teachers at her school. She took in sewing from neighbours and tailoring shops which she worked at on weekends to earn extra money. Having forgotten many a times to cover her head when she heard the azaan, she could not understand why Rehana wore the hijab.

Rehana frowned and raised a hand in protest as though to stop the conversation: Amma please, we've been through that before as well. This is much easier. This makes coming home on the bus at night much easier.

Amma said: Well you know better. My time was so different. So will you take it off once the office car is arranged.

Rehana replied: No. Let's not talk about this right now, okay. The tea is perfect today. Just what I needed.

Amma sighed and said sadly: I went over to Zaidi Sahib's home this afternoon. Rehana: I'll go tomorrow.

Amma continued: What a tragedy. How will they live without Abbas? His mother is completely sedated. They said she went half out of her mind when he died.

Rehana agreed: It's just awful.

Amma: Yes, yes. And no one can point any fingers at who did it—they say a man just walked into his clinic and shot him and walked out. Just disappeared. This is so frightening. So many boys, all of them doctors, have been killed so far. Dozens it seems. Maybe a hundred, maybe more. All Shia boys.

Rehana said: God only knows what's going on.

Amma snorted and shook her head: It has nothing to do with God.

Rehana: Poor Abbas. He should have left the country when he had the chance. I thought he was going to migrate to Canada.

Amma replied: He was going to but then he changed his mind.

Rehana said: Who knows what this is all about. Maybe he had some mafia dealings?

Amma was dismissive: That is ridiculous.

Rehana said apologetically: I know. I don't even know why I said that.

Amma said: Anyway, why don't you put your things down and go change your clothes.

Rehana hurried into her bedroom. She had the same tiled floor as that in the sehan. A takht served as her bed and a slim desk on which was propped a shelf stacked with books stood in one corner of the room. A computer sat on the desk along with a lamp. A tin canister camouflaged by a bright flowered wrapping paper sat on the floor nearby and held rolled up architectural plans and maps. An architectural detail on sepia colored paper of a museum that Rehana had designed as part of her doctoral thesis was framed as a poster and hung above the takht. There were drawers under the takht which contained her shoes, and a large wooden armoire to one side of the room stored her clothes. A low large table carved in black lacquered wood was placed in front of the takht next to which was a matching settee whose back and seat were woven with jute twine. A large fern sat near the window. Blue and green pottery interspersed with copper bowls and jugs were placed on the large table and near the plant. Rehana put her bag on the takht and sat down. She took off the hijab and shook out her shoulder length thick black hair. She rested her palms on either side of her on the takht and stretched out her spine and looked at her image in the mirror across the room. Her face looked pale against the darkness of her hair, she seemed thin and her shoulders seemed bony to her.

She noticed that her large eyes seemed larger when she wore the hijab. She took off her soiled shoes and felt the cool tiled floor against the soles of her feet. It felt good. She looked at her pale feet and light pink painted toenails. She wriggled her toes. She needed to wash her feet. She finished drinking her tea and went back out into the sehan. She turned on the tap at a floor level basin near the entrance of the sehan and washed her feet and dried them with the frayed and not so clean towel hanging on a peg on the wall nearby. She climbed up the stairs to her sister-in-law's room on the second floor of their narrow house just as the azaan began at the nearby mosque. Her mother called out after her, 'I'm putting on dinner. There's a new play on at 10.00 p.m. on VTV.' Rehana thumped her open palm against a white door and let herself in. The bedroom was cluttered with the items that her sister-in- law had brought with her when she married Rehana's brother two years ago.

The room was a shrine to Saima's dowry. Contained within this room was a wall-to-wall red carpet overlaid with two Persian rugs and furniture meant for an entire apartment. A sofa and two matching armchairs in soft pistachio and pink upholstery sat cheek to jowl with a king size bed, a large armoire, a china cabinet, a sideboard and six dining chairs. A large television set and stereo player sat covered in plastic on top of the sideboard while a small fridge held a large microwave oven on top. A china cabinet to one side was filled with two tea sets and dinner sets. A vanity with an oval mirror was crammed full of make-up items alongwith a golden framed wedding picture of Saima. Rehana's mother had insisted that all these things remain in the room which Saima occupied until such time that the newly-weds had a house of their own or until a third floor apartment was added to the house.

Saima reclined on her bed, with its elaborately carved headboard with a centre medallion upholstered in red velvet. She lay on her side, propped up by one arm with her hand cupped on the side of her head. Rehana was reminded of an image of a film star on the tin canisters of talcum powder; curvaceous, sweet faced, dewy eyed and lying in bed made up as though she were about to go to a party, her kajal was perfectly applied to her eyes as was the bright red lipstick that glossed her bow shaped lips. A tiny diamond nose stud, caught the lamplight and glistened, giving Saima the final touch of newly-wed perfection. She had been reading an *Urdu Digest* and listening to the FM station on the radio. The FM station was playing an advertisement for Luxury soap, a brand which was sponsoring the 30 minute segment of songs. 'People ask me my age and wonder if I'm still in school,' crooned a female voice over the radio and then, with a titter, it went on, 'I tell them that's the miracle of Luxury.

Try the Luxury test and see your skin grow radiant and young in just seven days.' Then a loud, male voice repeated urgently, 'Just seven days, you too can be as beautiful as the world renowned Lena.' No last name, just world renowned Lena. Saima reached over and turned the radio off. A large framed photograph of Saima and Rehana's brother at their wedding was on the wall above her head. Saima was very young, not more than twenty-three. She loved being married and loved her in-laws especially her mother-in-law who pampered her and allowed her to do whatever she wanted, which as it turned out, since she had been married, was to do nothing except spend her days lazing around, sleeping and reading magazines. Saima had just taken her final exams at university in literature and was treating this time as vacation time until the results came out. Like her mother-in-law she planned to teach but in a private school. But Saima had heard that there were interviews being held for 'call girls' by companies who provided support to large corporations in America through answering services based in Karachi. Someone sitting in New York who needed information about a computer or his telephone bill would call a number in

America which would be connected to a number in Karachi and someone like Saima would answer with a cheerful, 'Hello this is Sammy, how can I help you today?'

If Saima could get one of these jobs as a call girl, she would earn far more than Rehana or her mother-in-law or even her husband. Saima said, 'Anyway, we'll see what happens.' She sat up and stretched out her arms as she smiled at Rehana who plunked herself down at the end of the bed. Saima picked up the magazine she had been reading, 'This short story that I'm reading is so good. Rehana, you must read it! It's about a professional woman like yourself and all the problems she faces at work! And then when she comes home her in-laws are no support whatsoever, even though she is earning all the money to support them.'

'I have no in-laws,' Rehana responded.

'I'm your in-law,' Saima rebutted.

'But you're not my mother-in-law!' protested Rehana.

Saima responded, 'Well, read the story anyway, it is very interesting. Are you done with that tea? Shall I make you some more? I have some chilli chips here, want some? I'm going to apply for that job as a call girl.'

'Call girl?' asked Rehana. 'What a name! It sounds odd—but yes, it would be so good if you got that job! I'm done with the tea, yes. And give me the magazine when you've finished reading it.'

Saima got up and opened a drawer in the china cabinet from which she pulled out a bag of wafer thin potato chips covered in red chili powder, tea-bags, and a bottle of powdered milk. She turned on the electric kettle which sat on the sideboard. She brought out two flower patterned white mugs from the china cabinet. 'So how is your Yaqub Sahib?' She asked with an impish grin on her face.

She opened the bag of chips and placed it in front of Rehana while she busied herself with making tea. Rehana ignored the look on Saima's face and replied: 'He's fine.'

Saima: 'Just fine?'

Rehana munched on the chips: 'Very fine!'

Saima: 'So does he have any idea how you worship him?'

Rehana protested: 'I don't worship him! I can't help it if he's such an angel.

Saima: So now he's an angel? Angel! Well, well.

Rehana: Let's go.

Saima laughed and handed Rehana a mug of tea and took a sip from her own mug: Well your angel kept you late as usual! The clinic probably will be closed now. Anyway finish your tea, have some more chips. Do you want some chocolate? I have some chocolate as well. My mother came over this morning to visit and she brought me some Kit Kat. She said especially that I was to share it with you.

Rehana said: Keep it for me. I don't want any now maybe later after dinner. Saima picked up a DVD and waved it at Rehana: My mother brought me this from one of the call centers. I saw it this morning. It's part of a training program for nurses from India who are going to the United States. It's supposed to be useful for the call girls as well. You want to see it? It's very short. 'Sure!' said Rehana, and as Saima removed the plastic covering over the DVD and TV set and slipped the DVD into the player, a woman came on the screen.

'This country where you've come to work to make a life or to earn and go back is blessed because it has you. You make it work better; because of you, it is a kinder and gentler place. Everything about you makes it richer, more colorful and more interesting. There isn't a thing you need to change. You are perfect. But everything and every person is perfect in a time and context, outside of that, while certain attributes are timeless and contextless, change is always a good thing. Remember, that you are not the only one changing; those who are coming in contact with you are also changing. Change is constant and a good thing, change transforms all of us. Makes us better. Imagine if you're a nurse from say Kerala and you walk into the room of a patient in the US who has just come out of his anesthesia induced stupor, and who asks you, 'Nurse, am I going to make it?' You know of course that making it means he's asking you whether he's going to live. You then give a huge smile and say nothing as you squeeze his hand and move your head reassuringly. You see the panic in his eyes and to your horror and utter confusion he wails,

'Oh no!!!' Oh no? Why, you ask, you've just told him yes, of course he's going to survive. Your eyes said so, you nodded your head. The problem is you moved it from side to side, which means 'No' in the West and definitely, most definitely, YES back home. So say 'Yes' and nod your head up and down, this means yes. And that whole eye thing, if you need to say something, say it. Saying it with your eyes won't be understood. Over here, they aren't in the whole eye language thing. Words, use words. First use words. Use simple words. Speak slowly and clearly, we are used to speaking very fast in our languages. In English you must speak slowly. Also if you need something you're going to have to ask for it. Don't expect anyone to look out for you or know what you need or what you are thinking. If you've done something that you think is very good and deserves notice, point it out to your supervisor, don't expect them to know. Silence is not rewarded in the US.

Also leaving the least and worst for yourself and giving the first place and the best to a friend or colleague or a total stranger isn't seen as kindness or good behavior. It's seen as having low self-esteem. Still, continue to stand up for old people and pregnant ladies when traveling in a bus. Help them with their luggage, etc. Help others always. Also, try not to attach a 'no' at the end of a sentence when you you're looking for a yes. 'You are okay now, no?' 'Feeling better, no?' Adding a 'no' at the end of the sentence does not mean 'yes', here. It means 'no'. And that letter 'M' is pronounced Em. Not YEM. Same thing about 'w' and 'v'. It's not wery, it's v-ve-very. People like their 'space' in America, they have a different sense of distance and space than we do. Don't stand too close to anyone when you speak to them. Keep a distance of at least two feet between yourself and the other person. Don't touch anyone else's child without asking for permission. Never hug or kiss a stranger's child, people might think you're a child molester! Body odor is something Americans are really sensitive to.

They don't like it. At all. So plan on using deodorant after a shower. Take lots of showers, there's plenty of water all the time. Our spices cling to our clothes, people don't like the smell of that either. That's your call, if you can't do without that in your cooking then plan on having your winter coat laundered a lot. Okay, the next couple of things are totally up to you and maybe you will take offense, but think about it. I apologize in advance. The sindoor—they'll think you're bleeding from the head. And the bindi—unless you really want to look 'exotic' don't use it. Same thing for the nose ring or stud. Use these things on the weekend when you are among friends or walking around and you don't care what people think, I know a lot of teenage girls in America are now using these things, but they aren't doing professional work and people don't consider them as serious people. You are going to be a nurse and people need to be able to have confidence in you. Try not to wear too much gold jewelry on the street, you might get mugged. Oh, and even though we are really dark skinned, we seem to think it's okay to make negative comments about dark skin, even our own. DON'T DO THAT. People will think (rightly so) that you are a racist if you call someone 'fair' when describing them as being beautiful. On the other hand, they may not get the word 'fair' because over here that means being just, and not white.

If someone is getting fresh with you at work, that's not cute and that's not acceptable. If you really don't want them to continue, you can report it. There is nothing to be ashamed of. If they are junior to you or your boss you can report it to the administration. There is always someone in the office who deals with these issues. First, let the person who is misbehaving with you know that you are not interested. Be very frank and straightforward. Eating with your hands, rice, etc., is considered really rude and impolite here. Don't chew paan, don't spit anywhere, and especially not beetle juice. People will think you have the plague or something and are bleeding from your mouth.

Try to make sure your mouth and teeth are not stained with paan. And oil in your hair, they think your hair is oily and therefore dirty and slimy, not shiny and healthy. Also these people you may have noticed can be really, really fat. It's not just because they eat a lot. They eat really bad food. It may taste okay and bland but its full of hormones and chemicals that make you fat. The meat here, if you eat meat, can be injected with hormones. Something like that. Try to get your groceries from places where food isn't injected with hormones. And fast food, while back home that's considered cool and very expensive, it's the cheapest food here and its very bad for you. It's full of fat, carbohydrates and chemicals. Try not to eat it. Stick to your daal chawal. There are plenty of Indian, Pakistani and Ethiopian stores around which have all the ingredients we cook with.

When the tape was over, Saima turned to Rehana and said, 'Interesting, no? I mean, this is for people who are going there to live but still it's interesting for call girls as well.' Rehana said, 'Amazing, that's really something, huh? I guess it's important to know these things. Ethiopians have the same spices as us? Will they give you training on how to speak in American?'

Saima nodded enthusiastically, 'Yes, if I get selected then I have to have at least two weeks of speech training. "Hi, my name is Sam!"' She mimicked an American accent. They burst out laughing. Rehana said, 'Maybe the whole world can just become a call girl for American companies! How about that? C'mon let's go, we have time, it's open till midnight, I called them earlier.' 'But if we go now we'll miss the TV program! It starts at 10.00. And at least finish your tea.' 'Listen Sam! Do you want to go or not? It's up to you. We can go tomorrow.'

Saima laughed, 'Okay Renny, let's go! We shouldn't waste any time. I need to find out right away. I'm not going to take any chances. It has to be a boy!' 'Then let's go.'

Saima took another sip of tea and frowned with indecision, 'But should we have dinner first, I cooked nihari for you. Rehana exclaimed, 'Nihari! Well maybe we should eat. No, let's go. We can have dinner without hurrying through it when we come back.'

Saima agreed, 'Yes, maybe it's better to do this on an empty stomach.'

'Why? Rehana asked.'

'I don't know maybe its clearer when there isn't food in there.'

Rehana frowned, 'I don't know, but I think those are two separate places in the body, no? Let's go.'

'What will we tell Amma? I don't want to tell her. But I definitely want a boy.'

'We don't have to tell her anything. We can say we're going to the bookstore to pick up a few snacks, more chilli chips to have while we watch the program tonight. Let's go.' They made their way downstairs and told Amma that they were going to the shop in the next lane.

Amma responded, 'Bring back something sweet as well. Try to come back as quickly as possible I want to make sure that we're done with dinner before the play starts. It's supposed to be very good.'

Rehana and Saima stepped out into the lane and walked to the clinic which was a two-room office on the second floor of a building whose ground floor was occupied by the 'Top Class' travel agency, the 'Good Luck' milk shop and the 'Mercury' photo shop.

They climbed the stairs to the clinic and waited for their turn on a brown wooden bench. On the wall behind them, a tube light made a whirring electrical sound and cast its blue-white glow on the room. Neutralizing everything, like a mug shot.

4

Success

STANDING before the elevator, Yaqub examined his hands, palm down and palm up. His sunburnt hands, the palms darkened with hard labour, his fingers gnarled and a mangled heap of skin in place of the nail on his right thumb. He had been lucky that day, twenty-five years ago when the heavy machinery that he had been operating hadn't sliced off his whole hand. That was a long time ago. It had been a long and difficult journey from the docks in Keamari back to this godown less than a mile away, a journey of one mile that had taken thousands of miles and three decades of constantly and steadily reinventing biography.

He traced with his fingers the hardened calluses on his palms—hard earned, hard healed, and then with his thumb he pressed in the code for the elevator—the doors opened and he stepped in as the doors shut behind him. He pressed another two-digit code and the elevator moved up and stopped at the top floor of the building. The doors re-opened and he stepped out and into his home and switched on the lights—a foyer area led to a large open living area sparsely furnished—a sleek kitchen gleamed at one end; a door on the other end led to a small corridor and the two bedrooms beyond. He walked over to a white upholstered three-sided wide sectional sofa and plopped himself on it. He shut his eyes and threw back his head—then he reached for the remote and pressed a button— the painting on the wall in front of him slid to the left and revealed a large flat screen TV. He leaned back slouching into the couch, switched the TV on and flipped through the channels. He stopped at CNN—which was showing a rerun of a documentary on the planes hitting the World Trade Center. Yaqub snorted in disgust,

'Nineteen Saudis, nineteen Saudis! They want us to believe that! If it were nineteen Filipina maids working for the Saudis, I would have believed it. Saudis are too lazy to wipe their own backsides, let alone fly planes. Filipinas yes, Bangladeshis yes! Pakistani workers, yes. Saudis? No way! Precision military flying? No way! Bunch of lies!' He turned off the sound. He watched the images with the mute button on. Images of Abu Ghraib—an American soldier—a cigarette dangling, from her mouth abusing naked Iraqi prisoners. Hooded prisoners—frightened prisoners backing into prison bars as dogs with bared fangs strained on leashes towards them, Iraqi cities being bombed, tanks, soldiers, children bleeding, women shrieking and pulling at their hair; Bush grinning. Enough said. It was past midnight, his stomach growled and he remembered that he hadn't eaten since morning.

He got up and walked to one of the many large floor-to-ceiling windows and looked out. All around him there were buildings in the old city—old and decrepit dimly lit apartment balconies strung with laundry. He could see into those apartments and rooms that were at his floor level across the street where the lights were still on and people moved about. He could look out at them but they couldn't look in and see him, his windows were all a one-way view—a luxury he could afford. He walked across the room to the other side and opened the floor to ceiling glass French windows that opened out on to the balcony overlooking the inner courtyard. He stepped out on to the balcony and looked down at the beauty of the reflecting pond.

The sound of the fountain was soothing and his alone to hear. He felt an immense sense of security and comfort. Yaqub breathed in deeply and walked back inside. He went over to the counter in his kitchen and moved the cursor on his computer keyboard—the screen saver disappeared and the Bloomberg stock market screen flickered on. He stood staring at the graphs and moving the cursor to turn the pages to his saved sites. He noted down how different stocks were doing on a paper pad on the counter. Then he turned and used another remote to switch on the radio. The sound of his favourite station FM 105.3 filled the room through surround-sound stereos.

He moved to the kitchen, opened the refrigerator and stood looking into fluorescent light and the cold mist rising from inside—he contemplated his choices. He drummed his fingers on the refrigerator door, then considered the pasta filled large glass jar on the kitchen counter. He thought about boiling some pasta and mixing it with chopped garlic fried in olive oil and some dried basil and diced fresh tomatoes. That would be fast and easy. He reached inside and grabbed three eggs and a Coke. He opened an overhead cabinet and took out a glass and poured the Coke. Then he pulled out a mixing bowl—a chopping-board and a knife. He opened the refrigerator again and pulled out a tomato, green chilies, and fresh coriander. He picked up an onion from a bowl on the counter and a clove of garlic. He chopped up the onion, tomato, chilies, coriander and garlic. He cracked the eggs into the mixing bowl and beat them with a fork and added all that he had chopped into it. He reached for the red chili pepper from his spice-rack on the wall—added it in with cumin powder and salt. He reached for the turmeric and added in a pinch. He found a small frying pan—poured in a little olive oil and the egg mixture. He grabbed a plate from another cabinet. He opened the freezer and pulled out a frozen paratha. He flipped the omelet over, turned off the stove, put the paratha over the omelet and covered the frying pan with the lid to warm it up with the heat from the omelet. The talk show host said on the radio, 'Listeners, if you have anything on your mind this evening, or a song you want to hear, call me.' She gave a phone number. Yaqub reached for his phone, punched in the first three numbers, stopped, shook his head and laughed and then put the phone down. 'Pathetic,' he said. He removed the lid from the frying pan and lifted up the omelet and paratha on to his plate. He picked up his glass of Coke, grabbed a fork and moved back to the couch. He switched the TV channel to BBC and ate his dinner. Ten minutes later he went back to the kitchen, opened the refrigerator and pulled out a Pyrex container of nihari. He put the nihari in the microwave and going back to the refrigerator took out two naans. He turned the oven up high and put them in. Ten minutes later, he was back in front of the TV, watching the news on mute, listening to his FM station and polishing off the nihari. He wiped his fingers with a napkin, picked up the glass of Coke and took a long gulp, and then leaned back against the sofa and burped softly and contentedly. A few minutes later he was asleep.

5

Monkey Business: Tamasha

REHANA's pale yellow silk hijab rustled in the breeze as she shaded her eyes against the sun with her hand and squinting, looked out towards the sea. Her architect's gaze roamed appreciatively over the vast permanence of unconstrained space. She breathed in deeply—these ever changing never changing colours, a constant play of shadows and light, of cobalt and mercury shimmering white on water. Here was that one space at the edge of the city that was unencumbered by encroachments and was in no apparent danger of destruction. She stopped her thought process—she was standing on land reclaimed from the sea and her back was turned to all the ugly developments rising on it—and in the near distance just over there to the right of her vision in the water not too far out, was the hull of the cracked oil tanker, sunk and grounded. It was just past noon and there were a few people, mostly couples who sat along the seafront or strolled on the beach. Most of the tea kiosks were closed since it was too early in the day. Business would begin for them in the evening as people from all over the city crowded to the beach front for cool air and for the same sensation of openness and freedom that Rehana felt. It was an afternoon of clear blue skies and the air felt clean without the smell of cars and bus fumes or dust. Nearby on the beach, a family was chasing the sea as the waves lazily came in and went out. Nearer still, Mr Chaloo rapped his colourful wooden stick on the pavement, adjusted the baseball cap on his head and brought the audience to attention. He sat surrounded by children squatting around him in a large circle. Rehana and Noor Afshan sat on the beach wall and watched these proceedings. They munched on roasted corn on the cob, flavoured with lime juice, salt and red chilies, purchased from a hawker who squatted nearby and who watched them as they licked their chilli burnt lips with their tongues while marshaling their wind-blown hair with one hand and holding the corn with the other. Noor Afshan compared to Rehana was sexy and glamorous in a Bollywood movie sort of way. Her face was heavily made up and she wore dark lipstick in a shade of congealed blood. Her eyes were treated in heavy mascara and blue eyeliner. Her hair was blow-dried and tinted to appear absurdly blonde. In comparison, Rehana seated next to her in her hijab with a scrubbed clean face seemed dignified and timid as though she were Noor Afshan's badge of honour. Noor Afshan considered Rehana to be her closest friend. She admired Rehana's contentment with life—a sentiment she herself did not share. She wanted all the things that well-to-do women had. She wanted to be one of those women whom she saw breezing in and out of expensive shops and driving expensive powerful cars. She wanted glamorous sunglasses and the latest cellphone. She was the sole earner in her family and hankered for luxury but money was so tight. She felt it was due to her and she intended to go to quite an extent to get what she wanted.

Mr Chaloo, shook the daug-daugi, the small drum that he held in one hand. It made a rattling sound. 'Well my dear bandar, monkey, Mr Monkey, what are you doing? What? What did you say? Mr Chaloo put his hand to his ear to listen carefully and then motioned to the assembled crowd, 'Attention bhai, attention! Everyone stand up. Mr Bandar is coming into the room. A-tenshawn!!!' The monkey walked around moving his head from side to side. 'Look at Mr Monkey walking in to the room wearing a suit. How does Mr Bandar wear his suit? Show the children, shaabaash!' The monkey lifted his paws and hooked them on either side of his jacket.

'What did you say, hain bhai Mr Bandar, you are giving a speech. No? What did you say Mr Bandar? It isn't at the United Nations? Not this time. What is it? It's a press conference. Bhai wah bhai wah. Bandar Sahib is giving a speech. How does Mr Bandar give a speech? Oh yes, very good, what is Bandar Sahib saying? He is saying, I am very, very powerful! Shaabaash! Show your muscles monkey.'

The monkey grinned and bared his teeth and flexed his arms. 'How does monkey do his morning exercises?' The monkey raised his arms above his head and bent his knees and then straightened up, once, twice, three times. 'Wah bhai wah, Pehlwan Sahib. How does monkey take over the world?'

The monkey screeched, stomped his feet, jumped up and down, bared his teeth in a grin and walked around, stomping.. 'Shaabaash, Mr Bandar, stomp on the earth, stamp out the ants, like this, like that, Monkey Sahib. Stomp out the earth. I am going to take over the world. I am going to bring freedom and democracy: Jumhooriat or Azaadi! Wah bhai wah! Wonderful, wonderful! Shake your finger, monkey, Mr Bandar, show your disapproval. Very good. That's the way uh, huh, uh huh, I like it ah huh, ah huh. What did you say Mr Monkey? What's that? The enemy is very, very bad. He is not good. There is an enemy of democracy; we will fight that enemy. Show the children how you fight the enemy, pick up the gun, march, HALT, aim, fire. Well, well, well, now how does Mr Bandar answer questions? Wah bhai wah, look at Mr Bandar looking at journalists raising their hands. How does Mr Monkey look at journalists? Yes, shaabaash, shade your eyes with your hand. Very good. Point. Look at Mr Bandar squinting his eyes pointing his finger at a journalist. How does Mr Bandar point to a journalist like that yes, pick up your hand, point a finger, very good. Squint, Mr Bandar. Shaabaash. How does Mr Bandar squint? Like this, yes.' The monkey squinted and covered his eyes and grinned.

'What is the journalist asking? What did Mr Bandar say? Shrug your shoulders, monkey. Very good. That's the way. Show how you shrug your shoulders. What does Mr Bandar say to the journalist? Oh bathameez journalist! No manners, impudent journalist! The journalist is asking, why should we believe you? Well Mr Bandar what can you say?'

'Oh look at Mr Bandar, he is hopping back and forth, he is angry, now he is thinking. Thinking, shinking, thinking shinking. Good, Mr Monkey, think. Shaabaash, Mr Monkey, show the children

how you are thinking. Yes, pacing back and forth, arms behind his back, head down. Shaabaash. Oh yes! Very difficult, very hard, lots of thinking! Thinking requires work. A serious face. Shaabaash, Monkey Bhai, show the children your serious face. Oh, what is that? Look what Mr Bandar has found. What is that? A tape. What is on the tape? Mr Bandar must listen to the tape. Show the children how you listen to the tape. Where is your cassette recorder, hain jee? What, no cassette recorder? Stop screeching Mr Monkey! Monkey is insulted. Where is your walkman? Stop monkey, why so angry? Oh where is your CD player? Okay, okay, monkey, what, what? What did you say? Okay where is your iPod??? Very good. Wah bhai wah. Mr Monkey is listening to the tape. Wearing walkman. Is it music? No, look how surprised Mr Monkey is. Oh, Oh. OH. Hands on his head. What, what does the tape say Mr Bandar? What did you say? It's the evil one, the enemy. He is saying on the tape, exactly what you just said in your press conference, that he is the enemy. Wah bhai wah, Mr Bandar. But the bathameez journalist, he doesn't believe you. Now look at everyone, everyone is scared, after hearing the tape, everyone is shaking. Now, Mr Bandar. Everyone believes you. Yes there is an enemy. He keeps sending tapes. Shaabaash, have press conference, then have tape, have speech, then have tape. Wah, wah, Mr Bandar. Take over the world.

Rehana and Noor Afshan sat on the beach wall and watched the bandarwallah make the monkey do his antics. Rehana sighed, 'It was a good idea to come for lunch to Clifton beach. I never get a chance to come here.'

Noor Afshan turned to her and arched her eyebrows inquisitively, 'Why not? Why don't you ask Yaqub Sahib to bring you here?'

Rehana was irritated, 'Yaqub Sahib? Why would he bring me here? Why would I ask him?'

Noor Afshan smiled slyly, 'You know…' 'What nonsense! Why would he come here with me? We don't have any projects on the beach!' Noor Afshan said in mock disgust, 'You are really stupid.' 'I'm not stupid. You are being very stupid. Okay stop this talk, it's very silly.'

Noor Afshan shook her head sadly, 'He'll never know what a devoted admirer he has in you.'

Rehana was getting more and more flustered, 'No, he won't!'

Noor Afshan continued, 'Oh well. His loss! Let's see how much I've got in the loot from today. Thank God it was finally my turn for the committee. I've been counting the days.' Noor Afshan opened her purse and pulled out a clutch of thousand rupee notes. She licked her index finger and began counting and leafing through the notes. She counted carefully. She shook her head and said, crestfallen, 'This still won't cover everything.'

Rehana exclaimed, 'But this is a lot of money! And please put it back in your purse! It's not safe to take it out here! We're going to get mugged! Please put it back!'

Noor Afshan stared at her, 'Relax! Is it a lot of money? For what? Not for my purposes! I have my cellphone bill and I have to pay for my own and my family's clothes, shoes, school fees, medical expenses, the installments for the new TV and DVD player, the car, the credit card payment, the electricity bill, the water bill, the groceries.'

Rehana was surprised by the long list. 'Can't some of the expenses wait?'

'No, they can't. I won't be young forever. I want to enjoy my life.'

Rehana was surprised, 'I don't know what to say.'

Noor Afshan said, 'But I know how to make ends meet.'

Rehana asked, 'Have you got another committee or can you get another job?'

Noor Afshan said mysteriously, 'You can say I do have another job.'

Rehana excitedly, 'You do? You mean you have two jobs? I'm very impressed. You didn't even tell me. How? Where?'

Noor Afshan said, 'Take a look around you. See all the cars parked at this time of the day. See the couples?'

'Yes?' Rehana prompted.

Noor Afshan said, 'Well, they're not husbands and wives or sisters with brothers!'

Rehana said impatiently, 'Well, of course they're not. They're out on dates. So what?'

Noor Afshan said scornfully, 'Dates? My dear, most of them are out on paid dates.'

Rehana said incredulously, 'What?'

Noor Afshan continued, 'Of course, paid dates! That's my second job.'

'What are you saying?' Rehana asked.

Noor Afshan said, 'Look, it's fun and it pays. So what?

They're lonely or bored or neither. Looking for fun. I'm

alone, free, independent, educated, intelligent, well-groomed, good to talk to and good for other things too. They have the money and the car. I have the time. Don't look at me that way, Rehana.'

Rehana said uncomfortably, 'We should go back to the office.' Noor Afshan was nonchalant, 'Suit yourself. I'm collecting enough money to send my brother to Australia and joining a committee just won't do it. And my monthly salary certainly won't do it. Inshallah, by next month I'll have enough money to arrange for his safe passage. After that, once he gets there and starts to earn, the rest of us will be taken care of. This is a tough city. Do you know what I saw two nights ago?'

Rehana asked, 'What?' Noor Afshan smiled, 'You'll never believe me.' 'What?' Rehana repeated. Noor Afshan obliged, 'I was going home very late at night, I was driving by myself. It must have been at about three in the morning.'

'Three in the morning?' Rehana asked. 'What were you doing out by yourself at that time?'

'That's not the point of my story,' Noor Afshan said. Rehana said, 'Okay, go on.'

'I was driving when suddenly I saw a man jump out on to the road and he was waving for me to stop.'

Rehana looked at Noor Afshan, 'I hope you kept driving.' Noor Afshan said, 'No, I couldn't. He had stepped in front of my car, I had to stop.'

'What?' Rehana asked. Noor Afshan explained, 'He wanted a lift.' Rehana exclaimed, 'That is so dangerous!'

'He was completely naked.'

'You're making this up!'

'No I'm not. I swear on the Koran. He was completely naked. He had a beautiful body. He was white. I thought he was a ghost.'

'Who was he?' Rehana said breathlessly. 'This is frightening. Okay, are you going to tell that old worn out story about the ghost on the bridge?'

Noor Afshan said firmly. 'No. No. He was real. He was not Pakistani. He was from Uzbekistan, or somewhere like that. Very young, a teenager. He was crying.'

Rehana was shocked, 'Why was he naked? Why was he crying? What happened to him?'

Noor Afshan said, 'He could speak some Urdu and some English. He came to Karachi looking for work. He couldn't earn enough money and then he met someone who gave him a job earning real money. He became a stripper! Can you believe it?'

Rehana put her hands on her ears as if she didn't want to Hear this, 'Oh my God! No, I can't believe it. How horrible!'

Noor Afshan said, 'Can you believe it? He was a stripper. He

had been hired to dance at a party. A wedding party. Incredible.' 'You mean a mojra?'

'Exactly.'

Rehana mused, 'So now men want young beautiful men?'

'Why not?' Noor Afshan challenged. 'Mojras are not uncommon. Why not a man?'

'I guess you're right,' Rehana admitted.

'But that's not all.'

Rehana asked, 'Oh God. What was it?'

Noor Afshan continued, 'It was a mojra for women. It had been a bride's party! All women! Here in Karachi!'

'I don't believe that!' Rehana exclaimed.

'Believe it,' Noor Afshan said. 'That's what happens in these Defense and Clifton houses.'

Rehana said, 'Are you saying that the bride's side had a mojra for the bride's friends?'

Noor Afshan smiled, 'Not just a mojra, but a naked mojra.'

Rehana continued to cover her ears and her mouth alternatively, 'God forgive us. God forgive us. But what was he doing at 3 a.m. naked on the street?'

Noor Afshan tossed her head in the direction of the houses, 'These people who are rich, who live over there in those big rich houses are heartless.' 'Tell me! What happened? Did he forget his clothes at the party?'

Noor Afshan continued, 'At the end of the party, when it came time to be paid, they refused him the amount he had wanted! An argument started. The boy said he wouldn't leave until he was properly paid, as had been agreed in advance. The servants threw him out, a bunch of them, according to this boy, raped him and left him on the street without his clothes and without his earnings!' Rehana had her hands over her ears, then she clasped one hand over her mouth and uttered, 'Oh my God. Oh my God. Is this what we've become?'

'You mean they've become,' Noor Afshan emphasized. 'Not we. This is what they always were!'

Rehana held her stomach and bent over. 'I feel sick,' she said.

'That's what these rich bitches are,' Noor Afshan said bitterly, 'and they look down on us.'

Rehana asked urgently, 'Where did you take him?'

Noor Afshan said, 'I had a whole bundle of my clothes in the back seat. I gave him a kurta and pajama and I made him put it on. I gave him some money. I gave him every rupee that I had in my purse. Luckily, I didn't have too much money with me. I would have given him everything I had if I had more and then I would have had nothing with which to pay all the bills at home. Anyway, I was so sad. Then I dropped him at a bus stop.' Rehana and Noor Afshan sat in silence. The bandarwallah had finished his antics and had moved on. The lunch hour was over and cars were beginning to leave the beach front. Finally, Rehana said, 'Let's go back. Please let's go back. It's getting late.'

6

Restoring the Floor

FOR the next month Hajra, Rehana, and five day labourers who worked with Rehana on her restoration project for the godown, spent their days on their hands and knees painstakingly sorting out those mosaic chips which were retrievable and then placing them back together like a giant crossword puzzle under Rehana's supervision and instructions. Rehana had sifted through the pile of rubble and rescued each salvageable piece of tile. Then she had separated them by color and shape. She then drew the floor design and the plan to scale to show how the tiles would be placed and fitted in. Then began the slow process by trial and error of laying, adjusting and restoring the tiles back to their places.

Every day Sara would come by and watch the proceedings from the doorway. She was careful not to say a word. She watched Hajra and Rehana on their knees, or squatting or sitting, peering at the floor and piecing it together alongside the Afghan, Pathan, and Kashmiri day labourers. Her mother, with her gray hair gathered in a tight bun, was completely engrossed in her task. Occasionally she would stop and lift her bent head to wipe the sweat from her brow with her sari pallu. Rehana, wearing a hijab over her shalwar kameez and sneakers, measured and adjusted tiles and consulted her draft papers. The labourers in shalwar kameezes did the heavy lifting bringing in wheelbarrow loads of wet cement and tiles and worked alongside the two women. A radio was tuned to an FM station that played pop songs and relayed the cricket commentary. Rehana had managed to convince Hajrabai of a few changes. She had suggested that from the walls inwards, a border of wood slates of about one foot in width should be added at the edges like a picture frame. This would give the tiles a richer appearance and would allow Hajra and Rehana a larger number of undamaged mosaic tiles from the rubble to choose from for the restoration of the middle section of the floor.

Hajra had resisted but succumbed to the pressure when the labourers had sided with Rehana and pleaded with Hajra to at least give the idea a try. Hajra had agreed to try this approach, and when Rehana had reconstructed a corner of the dining room using the wooden slate border, Hajra had agreed that it did in fact look remarkable. Later as they worked, Hajra had suggested that they also add wood chips instead of tiles as a ring round the large central medallion which consisted of a large ten-pointed star, interspersed with a floral pattern. This had slowed down the work considerably. Rehana had to have the wood chips cut to a precise dimension in order to create the circular ring. It was a process of trial and error and took up to an entire month of adding and removing chips. Zareenabai had been pleased with the addition of wooden slates and felt that it was Hajra's way of forgiving her by acknowledging the wooden floor and incorporating it as an important detail. During this time, Hajrabai carried on a steady conversation with Rehana about Abbas. She wanted to learn more about him and she asked Rehana questions while she placed the tiny pieces of mosaic chips into place.

'He was crazy about music!' Rehana said.

'Yes,' Hajrabai said, 'I could see the passion in him.'

'He played the harmonium. You know, we always had sessions at our house or at his. He would play and we would all sing along. My brother, myself, Abbas, his sisters and brothers and other neighbours in the mohalla. It was our favourite way of spending Friday evenings. We miss him terribly. It's hard to believe that he's gone.'

'I can imagine. I miss him, and I hardly knew him,' Hajra replied.

'He wanted to be a doctor ever since he was a kid in shorts playing cricket in the alley way. He studied hard; he got first division marks and second position in all of Karachi. When he got admission at Dow Medical, I remember how happy he was. He took us all for a treat to the Chinese restaurant at Clifton beach. We had to hire three Suzuki vans to be able to take all our mohalla friends. He borrowed money from me to be able to do that. I told him it was my treat, I was so happy for him. And that night, we had a long musical session at his house, in the same place where we read the Koran for his soul.' 'It is so awful,' Hajra said, shaking her head. 'He loved nihari and tikka kebabs, he knew all the best locations in the bazaar for the best maghaz, or nihari, or bihari kebabs or parathas, you name it. He always brought us something good to eat at least once a week and definitely always for our music sessions!'

'Generous boy!'

'We started joking with him when he started to take piano lessons! We thought he was going to abandon us and medicine for the films!' Rehana laughed. Hajra laughed too. She and Rehana would end up with tears in their eyes after each of these snippets of conversation. Hajra had said one afternoon, 'I feel I must do something, I cannot let him go this way.' Rehana had looked questioningly, she understood that this was the ongoing conversation about Abbas, 'I want to do something as well, but I don't know what to do. I go and spend time with his mother and father but I feel so sad. There is such a silence there. I wish I could remove the silence and get him back, somehow.' Hajra had nodded, 'Yes, I feel that way too, somehow I want to be able to bring him back. It's absurd, I feel so hopeless, helpless. I don't know, but there must be some way to make this less senseless.'

Their attention would be diverted when their conversation was interrupted by one of the workers and they would go back to placing the chips back into the floor. Sara had watched her mother and Rehana work together in harmony and was feeling quite envious of how easily her mother agreed to Rehana's suggestions. It seemed to Sara that her mother at times took on Rehana's suggestions as though they had been her own, such as the central wooden ring. One day, Sara came in just as Rehana was wiping the perspiration off her mother's forehead. Her mother was leaning forward, her arms outstretched, her hands covered in cementing mixtures or some such gook as far as Sara could tell. Sara had felt a sudden pang of envy shoot through her. Never had she done or been asked to do any such thing by Bari-ma, this smallest of gestures made by a perfect stranger, who had achieved such a closeness to her own mother. One afternoon Razzak joined Sara at the doorway and looked in at the labour of love underway in the dining room. He had put his arm on Sara's shrinking shoulder, aware that she was expecting a dressing-down from him. 'Good work, beta,' he said. 'Well done. Here she is.' And Sara had turned to him with a broad grin. The conversation with Shireen, Kulsum, Amina and Resham about why Hajrabai had left Lawrence Road had been surprisingly easy. Hajrabai had called each of the girls separately, and explained to them her background and her need to practice her own traditions.

All four had asked many questions and had sounded intrigued and quite amused, but saw no reason for Hajrabai to live at

Lawrence Road. Hajrabai had been surprised by the nonreaction to her revelation that she was a Jew. Living in New York had made them view things quite differently. Perhaps if they had been living in Karachi, they too would have reacted as Sara had done, thought Hajrabai. Shireen immediately suggested a trip to Jerusalem. Typical Shireen. Resham was appalled by the idea that Emir had been in the IDF and was not sure she wanted to meet him in New York. Kulsum, Amina and Shireen had told her to keep politics out of what they were talking about. Hajrabai had told them that none of them were under any pressure to meet Emir, but that she would be delighted if they did. On the phone with Resham and the others one morning, after hearing the tirade of accusations from the other side about tearing up the dining room floor, Sara had laughed and said, 'Listen to me all of you, do you remember what Bari-ma said when she left? Well, I don't know what she said to you, but I remember what she said to me. She said it wouldn't make any difference. She said "So what if I go and live at Lawrence Road, the house won't fall apart if I don't live here." I just proved her wrong. She's back, isn't she? What more do you want? Honestly, the things I have to do! Frankly, I think all of you should thank me! I'm the only one who understands the ground reality! I keep things together by constantly making them fall apart.'

7

Nothing Defeats Like A Tube Light's Blue

NOOR AFSHAN paced back and forth, avoiding Amjad's attempts to reach out and embrace her as he sat before her on the edge of the bed. What was she doing in this hotel room, she asked herself. She noted the arrow on the wall for guests to orient themselves towards the direction of Qibla for prayers. Somewhere in the room, perhaps in the drawer at the side-table by the bed, there would also be a copy of the Koran. She caught a glimpse of herself in the mirror above the bed and was momentarily distracted by the pleasure that she got from seeing the blonde tint in her hair catch the light from the overhead lamp. She had gotten it done along with a blow-dry at the beauty parlor near her office just that afternoon. She enjoyed the way her heavy head of hair swung and shone because of the blow-dry. She looked at Amjad, who was leaning back on his hands, her eyes drifted to the front of his trousers and glanced over the bulge at the crotch. She looked away embarrassed. His gaze she noticed was aligned with her breasts. He sat there suppressing his impatience while she continued to pace back and forth. Why had she agreed to meet him here?

She said in an outburst, 'I simply can't do this, can't go ahead with this. My family thinks I'm staying late at the office for work. They never even once asked how I've been able to buy the DVD player, the television, the air conditioner, or how the bills get paid.'

Amjad leaned forward and crossed his legs, 'My wife never asks me how the bills get paid.'

'Mmmmmmm,' Noor Afshan murmured as she walked over to the side-table and pulled open the drawer. Yes, there it was. A copy of the Koran, and a tazbeeh as well. She pushed the drawer shut and straightened the lampshade. 'My father never asks. He lives in his own defeated world. Ever since he was laid off, I mean retired, from the cement factory, it's as though my salary is really his pension. The pension he expected. That's what I think. What does he think? That all that we have is because of all of his good deeds? That God is just being benevolent and sending us gifts which I bring home?'

Amjad said gloomily, 'No one asks me how we have such an expensive car and the house we live in. An income tax officer's salary can't bring in that kind of money.' Noor Afshan looked at him and asked, 'You know what I hate?'

'What?'

She ran her fingers through her hair and straightened her shoulders, and Amjad noticed that this posture made her breasts seem even larger.

He bit his lower lip and asked again, 'What do you hate?' Noor Afshan pouted as she considered the lamps on the sidetables with their green onyx bases and their grimy cloth shades with tasseled fringes. 'I hate the light in our house when I get home.' Amjad coughed, cleared his throat and uncrossed his legs, 'The light?'

'Yes. I hate the tube lights that we have to put up in our house instead of lamps and bulbs. We have these ugly lights because they are cheaper to run and use less electricity. I hate tube lights. They make everyone look dead, colourless. And they make a constant whirring sound. It's a silent maddening sound. It depresses me so.'

Amjad said, 'I hate the sound of the television when I get home.'

Noor Afshan continued, 'You know nothing defeats me like the blue colour of the tube light. I am going to buy lamps. That's the next thing. I'm going to buy lamps. My family thinks I'm at work right now. Can you believe it?' Amjad laughed, 'At this time of the night?' Noor Afshan snorted in ridicule, 'Just imagine. A receptionist! They never question it. They never ask. They never question me because we need my job to keep all the bills paid! To keep defeat at bay.'

Amjad said soothingly, 'I've told you so many times, I'm going to keep helping you with that.'

'For how long?'

'I don't know, but I will.'

Noor Afshan tilted her head, 'You are good to me. But you'll see. You'll change.'

A toilet flushed in the room next door. They both listened to the swoosh and the sound of a door banging shut.

Amjad shook his head vehemently this time, 'No, I won't.' 'No, you won't what?'

'Change!' said Amjad emphatically.

Noor Afshan sighed deeply and shook her head, 'When money is involved, change is necessary!'

Amjad laughed, 'Is that some kind of a joke or a filmy dialogue?'

Noor Afshan smiled as well, 'Perhaps it's both. I just thought of it now. Do you think they can hear us talking in this room? I mean we can hear everything in the other room. I can hear the water tap dripping in the bathroom.' They both fell silent, staring at each other and listened to the drip-drip-drip emanating from the open doorway of the bathroom. Outside, the azaan had just begun.

Amjad reached out for her, 'Why are you worried about that?

Come here. I love talking to you. You are so witty. So clever. I don't have that with anyone else.'

Noor Afshan kept standing, 'Even so, you can't keep helping me. I really do appreciate it though. Especially the perfume you got me.'

Amjad smiled at her, 'You are welcome. I hope it was what you wanted.'

'It was exactly the one I wanted, though it was not as large a bottle as I thought it would be.'

Amjad laughed, 'Next time. Finish this and I'll get you more.'

Noor Afshan lowered her voice to a husky, purring tone, 'And thank you for the red leather bag you got me last time we went out for lunch. It matches with so many of my outfits.'

Amjad laughed with pleasure, 'It gives me so much pleasure to see you happy.'

'And it gives me so much pleasure to make you happy,' she said sweetly.

Amjad was serious, 'You cannot even begin to understand how happy you do make me.'

Noor Afshan's tone was childlike, 'And you make me very happy too.'

'Let's make a deal.'

'What kind of a deal?'

Amjad's eyes were shining and his brow was beginning to sweat with excitement, 'Let's agree that when we are alone together, we'll behave like everything is perfect, as though we have no worries in the world.'

'As though we live inside a beautiful place.'

'Yes.'

Noor Afshan said, 'It's a deal. We'll behave like we live inside a beautiful film. A film where the hero and heroine are very beautiful, very rich and very much in love.'

'Exactly. That's exactly how I want it. And we can even listen to songs while we are here. That way our film will be complete.'

'Our time here should be like a box-office hit!' She was excited. Amjad said softly. 'Yes.'

'That would be wonderful for me too. But all I'm saying is that I can't think clearly right now. I'm under so much pressure,' she sighed.

'I realize that.'

Noor Afshan balled her hands into fists and shrugged her shoulders and stamped her foot and pouted. 'It's not fair. I'm beautiful.'

Amjad looked at her with desire, 'So very beautiful.'

'I'm educated. I should have everything.'

'Let's pretend in this room that you and I have everything.'

She frowned, 'We can do that for a few hours at most. But I have so many responsibilities. My brother can't help my family, can't help us at all. He's sick.'

'What's wrong with him?'

Noor Afshan replied despondently, 'He has become a heroin addict. We didn't know what it was at first but now we know.' Amjad shook his head. 'That is terrible. So many people are becoming addicts nowadays.'

Noor Afshan continued, 'My younger brother and sister are in college, I have to pay their medical college fees. At least they'll both become doctors. And my mother's school teacher salary is not good enough to even cover our grocery bills. But what will become of me?' 'You'll be fine. You are beautiful and you have your job and you will be fine,' he reassured her.

'Just look at me. Look where we are today. In a hotel room. This isn't just a drive to the beach or a dinner at a restaurant anymore.'

Amjad sighed, 'Right, I understand, it's your call. I wasn't thinking. I just wanted so much to...'

Noor Afshan said quickly, 'I know. So did I. I'm not blaming you. My actions are solely my responsibility.'

Amjad noted the flurry of hands and arms, eyebrows in movement, breasts heaving, eyes wide open, hands constantly pushing back her hair from her face. He swallowed and nodded understandingly, and reached for her again. She avoided him and moved a bit further out of his reach.

Amjad said in a lowered voice, 'I love it when you do that.'

'Do what?'

'Push your hair back like that.'

Noor Afshan was annoyed, 'Pay attention, Amjad! I'm serious. Much as I want to act on impulse and throw all caution aside, I know I'll be very ashamed of myself if I go on in this way. In fact, it's not going on anyway. It's like, well, it can just be characterized like... like...'

Amjad suggested, 'Like an addiction.'

'Exactly. Like being a heroin addict or an alcoholic getting a hit. First, it was a drive to the beach, then a dinner at a restaurant, then a few walks, then now here we are in a hotel room. It's more and more.'

Amjad asked, 'But you want to, don't you?'

Noor Afshan said in despair, 'For the sake of a few hours, I'm going to mess up too much.'

Amjad said sadly, 'I understand. A few hours of pleasure...'

Noor Afshan's tone was sad as well, 'Yes, pleasure.'

'And that's what life is about, isn't it? Living it to the fullest pleasurably.'

'Yes.'

'And like the song says, such moments don't come back. They're rare.'

Noor Afshan was conflicted, 'But shouldn't all my actions be actions that I can live with, at least justify to myself, and especially those actions that are meant for the sake of making me feel good?'

Amjad agreed, 'It's up to you. I understand.'

'This is not having a feel-good effect,' Noor Afshan shook her head.

Amjad looked at her, trying to gauge her mood, 'It isn't?'

'Absolutely the opposite effect. This makes me feel ashamed of myself. Ashamed of my behavior, my thinking, my actions. I cannot afford to lose self-respect and self-esteem.'

'I would never want that to happen. For either of us,' Amjad said quietly.

Noor Afshan continued, 'At the very minimum, self-respect is a need, not a want. I cannot afford to lose what I need. At the very minimum, I have my self esteem intact, that's all I have! It's the sum total of my existence, that is what makes me content and confident. I can't throw that away.' 'Life is like that, wrong place, wrong time, right place, wrong time.'

'I think I'm at that point, I'm standing at that point in my life now. Somewhere along the line, I'll be in the right place at the right time. You, Amjad, in your life, I think are in the right place, right time, right everything, although, you're in the wrong frame of mind. Though that'll work out, if only you'd let it.'

Amjad said, 'Yeah, I know.'

Noor Afshan continued, 'If only you would let yourself

be this way with your wife and not just me. God has given you everything.

Be happy and know that is happiness.'

Amjad replied, 'But I want you.'

'Wanting and needing are two separate things.'

'Are they?'

'And I shouldn't be encouraging you in this wrong frame of mind. I would, if I could, help you get back into your real life or help you see all the good things that surround you; or help you gather the kindling required to get the fire going again in your marriage, your most important relationship.'

Amjad said, 'Kindling? Okay. Would you, would you do that. I'd like that. I need that.'

Noor Afshan explained, 'But it's quite simple, it's not me that you are concerned about, it's you in your life and your marriage. I am for you, just a means of valuing and cherishing and understanding, giving renewed meaning and interest to your marriage.'

Amjad protested, 'You sound like a maulvi!'

She raised her voice, 'Amjad! I'm serious.'

'There is nothing to renew. There was never anything there. It was an obligation. An arranged marriage and that's all. It is an obligation and a responsibility. And I am fulfilling both,' he replied.

'You have to make it more than that.'

'Okay. I think you're absolutely right, I agree with you completely. But Noor Afshan, you're really wound up. What we are doing right now is not a big deal, it happens every day, every second of the day. Everyone's doing it.'

'I'm not everyone!'

'I know that,' murmured Amjad.

'It's a big deal to me,' she continued.

Amjad said, 'I know, I know.'

'It is a big deal Amjad,' Noor Afshan said. 'I don't do this all the time. I don't do this. I'm above this.'

Amjad said, 'Sorry, you know I didn't mean it in that way. I was just trying to relax you a bit.'

Noor Afshan said tersely, 'Well, I'm not relaxed. I'm panicking!'

Amjad said softly, 'Okay, shush, come here. Sit down.'

'Okay. No! I can't. I just can't,' she protested. Amjad said, 'Here, just sit down will you, sit down now, just relax okay. Just sit down for a moment. Catch your breath. Nothing happened. Nothing is going to happen. You are right.'

Noor Afshan sat down next to him. He placed his hand on the nape of her neck and kneaded it gently and then he stroked her back. She murmured in approval and arched her back, 'So then, what is this about? What are we doing here?'

Amjad's tone was soothing and hushed, 'I don't know. It just happened. Well, we're just two people needing each other in an isolated space in time. That's all. Two people who fit together.

That's all.' Noor Afshan sounded like a child, 'Nothing more?'

Amjad interjected, 'I wouldn't put it like that!'

'Then how would you put it?'

'Why do we need to put it in some way? We are two people who want the same thing.'

Noor Afshan persisted, 'What is that?'

'Pleasure.'

'And nothing else,' she finished.

Amjad looked at her, 'Anything else leads to pain.'

'Yes,' she agreed.

Amjad said resolutely, 'But let's face it, there can't be anything more.'

Noor Afshan jumped up and began pacing again. 'Right.

Right? Right. And all it is…really… I mean we are just human, and in many ways like everyone else, vulnerable, unable to live up to incredible expectations. I'm no angel and neither are you.'

Amjad reached out to grab her arm but she moved away.

'Right. The sooner we stop trying to be angels, the sooner we'll be happy,' he said.

'All I'm saying is that...' she started. Amjad grew impatient, 'I understand completely. Shall we go? Let's get out of here. Should we go out for dinner? Shall we do that instead?'

Noor Afshan was agitated, 'I'm sorry for this. But that's just the way it is. I cannot. I'm sorry. What makes me feel good, and will continue to make me feel good is that I can look at myself in the mirror and not squirm, and that you think well of me as well.'

She placed both her hands over her breasts and pressed her fingers into the cleavage as a manner of speaking from her heart.

'Enough! For me, that is enough!' Amjad found it hard to breathe, he stood up and mumbled, 'Uh huh.'

Noor Afshan shut her eyes tightly and then opened them. They were shining brightly, 'Fine. I am going to do the right thing here and so please respect that.'

Amjad said, 'Fine. Of course, Noor Afshan, I do respect you. Shall we go?'

Noor Afshan stood in front of him, staring at him.

Amjad said, 'Noor Afshan? I know you're worried. What is it that you need? Tell me.'

Noor Afshan said, 'I'm so worried about the bill I have to pay for electricity. It's so big.'

Amjad replied, 'I'll take care of it. Here take this. It's about two thousand rupees. Will that cover the bill?'

She didn't respond, but took the money. As she reached out for her bag, Amjad grabbed her hand and said, 'No, not there.' She smiled at him and pouted her mouth and then her tongue parted her lips slightly as she rolled up the two currency notes and tucked them into her cleavage. She stared at him, her eyes brighter still. He moved forward and took the money out again, put it in her hands and watched her put it in her purse. Then he reached out for her, kissed her mouth, stroked her hair, her neck. She pushed against him, causing them both to tumble onto the bed. Later on in the evening, Noor Afshan dressed hurriedly while he stayed in bed, lying on his stomach and watching her. 'I'm going to buy you some beautiful lacy underthings, something silky in black and red.'

Noor Afshan said, 'I'll get them, just give me the cash.'

Amjad said, 'Wear something red next time. Okay?'

'Okay.'

'We were fantastic.'

'It's really quite simple,' said Noor Afshan. 'It's basic human instinct.'

Amjad pulled on a serious face, 'I hear you!'

'I don't get it. Well, I do. But still. You have a good, solid life, a good rooted life, nothing there will change. Will it? That's what's important for me to know, that it's not bad for you, your life. Is it?'

Amjad said, 'Yes.'

Noor Afshan held her head in her hands, 'What am I doing?

What am I doing? Oh God, Oh God! I'm someone who should and needs to urgently move towards having the sort of things you have. The things that normal people have. I need to move out of the weird and abnormal life I have put myself into.'

Amjad played along, 'It's something to think about Noor Afshan. I wish I could be of some help. I'd like to be able to help you.'

'I'm just under so much pressure,' she exclaimed.

'I know. Look, let me help you.'

'I need about two thousand more in cash right away,' demanded Noor Afshan.

Amjad murmured, 'Look, I have at least three thousand more in my wallet and it's yours.'

Noor Afshan breathed, 'Thank you! You're a good man. You are a good example to model yself on. You know, someone who is settled, comfortable, totally rooted.'

'Noor Afshan, please. It's okay, you don't have to…'

'No, no really. You are a partner in my good and bad times You are so close to me and you do care. You care a lot. You work at it. Strange as that sounds, it seems to me that you do work at it, even with your wife and family. You're a good man,' she said softly.

'It's not easy.'

Noor Afshan said, 'No, I am sure it is not easy. But only someone as good as you can take care of everyone. Take it from someone who knows well what it means to have to take care of everybody. You and I are so much alike.'

'Yes, we are,' agreed Amjad. 'Thanks, you really are wonderful. Please never change. Go buy yourself something beautiful to wear. I always want to see you looking beautiful.'

8

Profit and Loss

TO Razzak, this peaceful time of night, on the last Friday of every month after prayers and dinner, and just before bed, was his most sacred time alone. He would sequester himself in his study with its dark wood shelves lining the walls and where the scent of frankincense lingered on from dusk when Zareena would walk through the house with lobaan. The bookshelves were filled with business folders holding records of his business transactions and files full of newspapers cuttings. Collecting newspaper cuttings was his hobby and he would carefully cut newspaper articles that were of interest to him from the *Business Recorder or DAWN* and store them up for reference. These were articles that would catch his attention and ranged from announcements of company stock issues, annual reports, obituaries, announcements of conferences, sale of properties, new government policies and laws in business and real estate, changes in laws, deficits or surpluses in wheat, cotton, or rice crop harvests. They included references to the import quantities of pipe fittings, price rises of ghee and milk, port legislations and duties, national budgets and taxation rates, changes in civil service and business positions, appointments for government cabinets at national or provincial levels, announcements for road diversions and closures due to municipal repairs and construction, schedules for DDT sprays for mosquitoes during the winter months, schedules for train and airplane arrivals and departures, timings for water and electricity supply being turned on and off in different locations of the city as well as timings for iftar and sehri during Ramadan and the announcement each year for the route of the Moharram procession on Ashura.

A cloth dust cover with a pattern of flowers and birds embroidered by Kulsum when she was about fourteen was draped over the fax machine. In the middle of the room sprawled a large desk in heavy teak wood behind which there was a much weathered and faded leather upholstered chair upon which Razzak now sat, drumming his fingertips on the frayed cardboard cover of the lined copy book, his accounts ledger. It was in these hours at the closing of each month that he meticulously entered by hand and in pencil, the month's earnings, losses, debits, credits, accrued interests, and debts owed and money to be collected. It was his time to enter how much each of his responsibilities and wards had earned due to his endeavours, what they were owed and what was theirs by right and by the law of the land and by that of God, and by his own opinion and ethics. In the event that he should pass away, nothing would be left to dispute or to question. It was all here.

Clearly marked. He had entered by line the names of Hajra, Zareena, Sara, Amina, Shireen, Kulsum and Resham. His two married sisters who were the daughters of his father's third wife; his trusted accountant; the staff at his shops, the servants in the house; the caretaker of his godowns, all were entered by name. The names of his grandchildren, Sara's two, Tahir and Zohra; Shireen's two, Kiren and Rahul; and Kulsum's Zainab and Sakina were entered here. Meir's name was entered here as well. Everything and everybody was accounted for. The cash in national and foreign banks, the capital invested in shares on the Karachi Stock

Exchange, the capital Resham was managing in the New York Stock Exchange, the house 43-G, the properties around the city, the shops in Saddar, the godowns in Kharadar and Keamari, the lands in phase 8, 9, 10 and 11 in the Defense Housing Authority, the building in Bath Island; the property in F-7 in Islamabad and the four shops in Anarkali in Lahore. Now into this ledger, he had entered the recent sale of the godown in Kharadar. What was bought, what was sold, what was borrowed, what was owed—all were entered here. Hajra had come to him earlier in the evening, agitated about that boy who had been shot. She wanted to do something. She didn't know what but Razzak was sure it would involve money. He tapped the point of the pencil against the line item he had just entered—the money from the sale of the property in Kharadar. He shook his head and sighed.

Razzak frowned and took a white envelope from the ledger. He sat drumming his thumbs on it, contemplating it. Then he picked it up and removed a single sheet of paper from it. He sat staring at the paper, his brow furrowed in deep creases. He let it drop on to the ledger and rubbed his tired and strained eyes and passed the palms of both his hands over his worried face. When Hajra looked in on him a few moments later, he was sitting hunched over his desk with his hands over his face. She recoiled in alarm and then moved towards him. His hunched shoulders, his face covered by his hands frightened her. 'Razzak,' she whispered. Her husband jolted forward,

'Hajra, you frightened me, woman! Frightened me half to death. For God's sake!'

'What's the matter?' she asked, coming into the room quickly. She stood in front of him, she saw him turn the page in the ledger to cover a sheet of paper.

'What's that?' she asked.

'Nothing. Nothing that concerns you.'

'Well it concerns you, and I can see that you are worried, so it concerns me. What is it?'

'Nothing,' Razzak said gently. 'It's nothing. Just business.'

'Razzak, what is it? Show me, tell me what business it is?'

'Nothing!' Razzak shouted. 'Now go, go to sleep, I have work to do! Can't a man get any peace in his own house?'

Hajra stood staring at him, considering his outburst. She said, 'No, you can't. Show it to me. Razzak, show it to me, or I will leave for Lawrence Road immediately!'

Razzak moaned in frustration and raised his voice again, 'What kind of threats have you taken to lately, Hajrabai? Why do you keep on doing this? Are you getting demented in your old age? Look where this has brought us!'

Hajra reached over and lifted the sheet of paper from the ledger. She stood reading it and slowly sank into the chair in front of the desk, her hand on her heart. 'Hai Ma!' She uttered in a hushed voice. There were three sentences. 'Shia hunood, wedded to Yahood, death is yours unless you repent! You will be told when, where and how to pay your exemption tax by the end of the month.'

'Oh Razzak, how could this have happened?'

'I don't know Hajrabai, I don't know. You should have stayed here. Why did you go to Lawrence Road? I don't know what this is. God knows who this is. It could be anyone! But don't worry.

This is not the first time I've been threatened or blackmailed. This is just another ploy.'

'What are we going to do?' Hajra asked weakly.

'Nothing. We are not going to do anything. At the most, maybe we will all go away for a holiday for a while, go visit the girls. We will see. In the meantime, I've spoken to Haji Kareem and he has already posted plain-clothed guards in the vicinity of the house. No one can enter our mohalla or leave without their knowing. So don't worry.'

Hajra said quietly, 'We must let Zareenabai know immediately and Sara. We must inform all the girls immediately.'

'No! I don't want to spread any panic. Now calm down!'

'Razzak, I have to tell Sara and Zareenabai. They are here and they could be in danger. We must tell them.'

Razzak considered this. 'Yes,' he said after a pause, 'yes, we must tell Zareena and Sara. But don't tell the rest. Not yet. But Zareena and Sara should be aware of this.'

The next day Hajrabai told Zareenabai and Sara amidst a much expected scene of hysteria. 'I knew it! I knew this would happen, it had to. How could it not? I warned you!' Sara had wailed and sobbed.

The month came to an end and no other letter arrived, though it was nervously expected every day. One afternoon, Hajra asked Rehana if she would accompany her to the clinic where Abbas worked.

'It's closed,' Rehana had replied. 'We could go there but it no longer functions. He was the only one there.'

'I want to see the place,' Hajra had said. 'Do you have a car here with you? I don't want Ilyas, my driver, to take us there.'

Rehana said that she didn't have a car but she could call her colleague at work. 'Can we go now?' Hajra had insisted. Rehana had called Noor Afshan, who arrived half an hour later to pick them up. Hajra had sat in the back seat while Noor Afshan and Rehana sat in front. Rehana gave the directions and they made their way to the address in Soldier Bazaar, a short drive from 43-G and where Abbas had set up his clinic. It had been a rented shop.

The shutters were down and padlocked. Hajra had sat in the car which Noor Afshan had parked right in front of the clinic. The two young women had stepped out and had gone to speak with the owner of the car repair shop next door. Hajra nervously peered out after them as a couple of men loitering about gathered to watch the two women and talk amongst themselves. Hajra instinctively raised the pallu of her sari and covered her head. Razzak would be furious if he found out. Coming here this way and parking right in front of the clinic. He would be apoplectic if he found out and Hajra knew that he would not be wrong. Anything could be assumed by anyone who might be keeping a look out. Surely Abbas's assassins would have spies! It wasn't just a random killing. She had been right not to bring her own car. Hajra felt her pulse beginning to throb in the side of her temple. She had rolled up the car window and she was beginning to sweat. Her gaze alighted on a shimmering black mass, a small mound on the ground in front of a butcher shop. A man passed by and suddenly she saw that it was offal that was pullulating with flies and was exposed when disturbed. The flies rose up in the air, lifting upwards as though in unison and then settled down again. She imagined the flies licking and sucking the

blood out of the discarded intestines of a slaughtered animal, now lying exposed on the street. The sight made Hajra nauseous. Noor Afshan and Rehana returned a few minutes later and got back in. 'Are you all right?' Noor Afshan asked anxiously; she too was nervous. Hajra nodded and managed a feeble smile. She patted Noor Afshan's shoulder.

Rehana said, 'That man says that this location is for sale or for rent. It seems that it will become a video shop. He wanted to know who we were'

'I told him I was a fashion designer looking for a workshop for my tailors,' Noor Afshan giggled and watched Hajra's face through the rear-view mirror. 'What a terrible pity, all of this is. Awful. That man said that Dr Abbas Zaidi had a long line of patients waiting for him every evening, all people who couldn't make it to the hospital or couldn't afford expensive fees of the doctors nowadays. My brother and sister will become doctors soon. They're both studying. Just one more year for my brother and two more for my sister.' Hajra had remained silent. Someone knocked on Rehana's window and they all jolted and shrieked. The man, taken aback, leaped backwards. Rehana quickly lowered the window and shouted, 'What kind of behaviour is this. Who are you?

What is it that you want?'

The man seemed confused and scared, 'I just wanted to know if you are related to Abbas Bhai.'

'Who is Abbas Bhai?' Rehana continued to shout. 'Can't three women stop to find out if they can rent a boutique?'

Noor Afshan started the car, and in her nervous haste managed to press the accelerator and brake at the same time.

The engine choked and the car lurched forward and stopped. She started it again and eased it back into the traffic. The man stood scratching his head and watched the car disappear into the traffic.

Noor Afshan drove Hajra to 43-G and she and Rehana made their way back to the Foundation. She noticed that her knees were shaking as she drove.

Hajra went straight up to Zareenabai's rooms and picked up the *Divan-e-Hafez*, then went to the balcony where Zareenabai was dozing off. 'Zareenabai wake up,' Hajra said breathlessly. 'I have something to tell you.'

Zareenabai woke up with a fright. 'What is it? Is everything all right? What happened?'

'Everything is fine, it's going to be fine. Zareenabai, can you take out a fahl for me?'

'Hajrabai, you scared me half to death! I thought there was another letter that had arrived, or worse! Really, it's too much!'

'I'm sorry! I'm sorry Zareenabai! But can you read out a fahl for me?'

'Of course I can, but what is it?'

'I'll tell you afterwards. No, don't worry, it's not about the letter.'

Zareena said the Fateha, told Hajra to concentrate and think of her question.

Then Zareena opened the *Divan* and traced her fingers down to a verse and said, 'These are the lines my eyes have rested upon. Listen...'

The messenger who arrived from the land of my friend Brought a charm, fragrant, and in the hand of my friend.
Hafez, fear no foes who reprimand my friend
Thank God, I am not ashamed of me and of my friend.

Zareena looked up and asked, 'Hajrabai, does this mean anything to you? It sounds like its alluding to the letter!'

Hajra had tears in her eyes, 'Yes Zareenabai, perhaps it is. I could conclude that too! But it means everything. It must be done then!'

'What must be done?' Zareena asked, bewildered. 'What are you thinking?'

'I know what I have to do, Zareenabai. I am going to set up a waqf, a trust, in Abbas's name! This fahl is telling me to do so. That was my question whether I should purchase the shop which Abbas had used as his clinic in Soldier Bazaar and set up a trust from the money from the sale of the apartment in Kharadar!'

Zareena looked at Hajrabai's joyful face and read the verse again.

Hafez, fear no foes who reprimand my friend
Thank God, I am not ashamed of me and of my friend.

Then she said, 'Hajrabai, what a good thing, what a good thing. You must talk to Amina about how to do that, she will know. Of course, so will Razzak! And Sara, she would know. How about Yaqub or Rehana?'

'So you approve?' Hajra took Zareenabai's hands in her own.

'Of course I do. Who wouldn't?'

That evening Hajra made her way to Razzak's study and sat down in the seat in front of his desk. He looked up and said 'So?'

'Razzak, the shop that Abbas used for his clinic is for sale.'

'So?'

'Can you find out how much it's for?'

'Why?'

'You know why.'

'You want to buy it and start a clinic in his name?'

'Yes, I want you to set up a waqf, a trust, in his name with the money from the Kharadar property. The clinic, its equipment and the salary and cost of medicines will be part of the trust.' It was a month later, in the middle of the day that Razzak unexpectedly arrived home and started shouting for Zareenabai and Hajrabai from the moment he entered the house. He made his way up to the second floor balcony where the two women were encamped for the afternoon, as usual. 'I have some important news,' he said, plonking himself on a cushioned seat. 'Kareem Bhai came to my office this afternoon. He brought me copies of letters that have been received by twenty businessmen who've contacted him for security. All the letters have exactly the same message but different dates. I saw them all. And that's not all! Even Kareem Bhai has received exactly the same letter. We are in good company. It's just a threat, the usual ordinary threat, full of slurs! We have nothing to fear that is in any way different from the others!' He wiped his brow, 'Just the usual, drive-by shootings, kidnappings, assassinations! Nothing different. We have nothing different to fear. Khuda ka shukar hai.'

Hajrabai sat gripping the sides of her armchair. Zareena stood up and came over to her and they hugged each other. Then Hajra began to cry. And there they sat, the three of them, vulnerable and graying, tears streaming down their cheeks. 'Maula tera lakhlakh shukar hai,' Zareenabai said, raising her palms up and gazing up at the sky, giving her thanks to God a hundred thousand fold and reciting duas, prayers of thanks and protection, blowing them in Hajrabai and Razzak's direction and blowing them back on to herself and the whole house.

9

Transformations

'BARI-MA, Choti-ma, where are you? Where are you? I have only five minutes and then I must run!'

Sara had arrived. Her voice was filled with cheer and urgency and rang through the house, reaching them upstairs. This was Sara, rushing into the house in her typical manner of a driving wind, leaving everything in its wake slightly stunned and off kilter. In she came with a flurry of color, wafting perfume and relinquishing from her arms, her many parcels and bags to anyone who came in her way, which at this moment included Jeevan, Razia and the cook. She entered the terrace where Zareenabai and Hajrabai were seated. Hajrabai sat on the takht. A pile of newspapers and magazines were lying beside her. There was the *DAWN, The Friday Times, Nawa-i-Waqt; Daily Times,* and *The News*, all of which Hajra and Zareenabai read through the day, saving articles of interest for Razzak. In a large wicker basket to her side were the week's newspapers as well as the monthly magazines published in Karachi; *Herald* and *Newsline*. Several outdated magazine copies of *The Economist, Life, Times* and *National Geographic* were amongst the papers. Zareenabai sat in a high backed wicker chair. A Sindhi jhoola, a wooden swing carved and inlaid with bits of ivory, colored enamel and tiny mirrors, was placed at one end of the terrace. On either side of it were large leafy palms potted in huge deep red clay earthen urns. A wicker chaise longue, an ottoman and several wicker chairs were arranged around a large low square coffee-table. Hajrabai had just finished reading an editorial written by a political pundit now living abroad. She shook her head and laughed, 'I do enjoy reading Adil Azimi. What a transformation this man has gone through! What a chameleon, from being the spokesman for the Jamaat-e-Islami to that of military regimes to becoming a minister and a spokesman for the elected governments, then changing sides when the opposition came into power. And still he is considered credible! The fact is he is quite a spokesman, quite outspoken and quite eloquent! I do like to read what he says, infuriating as it is, these changing of colors, he makes sense!'

'Are you discussing Adil Azimi's editorial?' Sara asked as she

flopped down on the chaise longue. 'A true Karachiite! Changes with the times! Pragmatic man. Feet on the ground. I love reading him! Oof Allah, Choti-ma, Bari-ma, what a day I've had! I've been on my feet since 6 a.m.!'

Sara adjusted the silk scarf on her shoulders and draped it casually over her head. 'I've brought the dishes you wanted me to bake,' Sara said. She had baked a cheese casserole and a lemon meringue pie on Bari-ma's request for the dinner party at 43- G that evening. Razzak had invited a visiting group of Chinese businessmen from Shanghai, who were looking for someone to represent their interests in Pakistan. Razzak intended to introduce them to Sara's husband Riaz this evening as their man. 'I peeped into the drawing room, the flowers are beautiful and the ones in the foyer are very nice too. I could get some of those lilies that you liked so much at my last dinner party.'

'No,' Zareenabai said, 'they are too expensive, we don't need imported flowers from Dubai. Our gladioli are just fine.'

'Do you need my help in setting up the buffet table?' Sara asked.

'No, I'll take care of that myself later in the afternoon,' Hajra replied. 'You can look in later and see if anything is missing.' The girls had always been responsible for the parties at 43-G, for laying the table, baking the desserts and serving the tea and drinks. Sara had kept up the tradition.

'How many people tonight?' Sara asked. 'I'll come earlier just to help out. Riaz will come a bit later.'

'I think there should be about fifteen,' Hajrabai replied. Sara sighed, 'Well, that's very manageable. I tell you, it's just too much. I am so overworked. I'm just glad the wedding season is over. December is the end of me. I need a vacation, I need a massage, I need to sleep! Oof Allah, it's been such a hectic day. What can I tell you? First I got up to say goodbye to the children, they left for school at about seven, then off to the golf course. I played nine holes today. Choti-ma, it was wonderful. Then back home for riyaz, my ustaad said that my voice is superb now, comparable to Sorayia Multanikar. He says I'm much better than her. Listen to this Choti-ma.' And Sara launched into a raag. 'Bari-ma, look at me, have I gained weight?'

'Why have you covered your head?' Hajra asked suspiciously.

'Are you cold?'

'Why no, not at all, I'm just experimenting with a new look.

How do I look with my head covered, Bari-ma?'

'Like a grandmother.'

'No, I don't! I think I look rather nice.'

'What has gotten in to you?' Hajrabai asked in an annoyed tone.

'Nothing!'

'Well Sara, I can never tell with you. You're sitting there with your head covered, it's not the azaan and there isn't a wind blowing!' Hajrabai said sarcastically.

'Do you say that to Rehana?'

'Rehana? What does Rehana have to do with the scarf on your head?'

Sara whined, 'You don't seem to have a problem with her hijab.'

'Her hijab? Is that what's on your head? Is that a hijab? Hai Ma!'

'Well, I'm just seeing how it looks. And you don't seem to mind Rehana's hijab.'

'She's not my daughter!'

'Well, it's hard to tell when she's around whether she is or not!'

Hajra raised her arms in exasperation, 'Sara, you are beyond my understanding.'

Sara ignored her mother, slipped the scarf off her head and inquired, 'Choti-ma, do you think I've gained weight?'

'Don't be ridiculous, Sara! You're too thin. You need to eat. Here, let me have the cook bring you lunch!' Zareenabai said.

'No Choti-ma, please! I'm on a very strict diet! I've had my soya milkshake already!'

'Sara, you are going to make yourself sick!' Zareenabai admonished.

'I'm fine! Now what was I saying?' Sara took up where she had left off on recounting her busy day. 'Oh yes! After the riyaz, a few instructions to the servants and then on to the bazaars. Hai Allah, look Choti-ma, Bari-ma, aren't these just catastrophically beautiful, aren't they just catastrophically pretty? My jeweler finally delivered them last night.' She thrust forward her arm and waved her wrist and showed off her new pair of diamond bracelets.

'I'm going to wear them to the charity ball. It will just kill the other women, don't you think? Here Choti-ma, I've brought you the incense you liked so much, khas ka ittar, right? There, let me dab some on for you!'

Zareenabai ducked out of the way of Sara's arm jabbing out at her. 'Stop attacking me with that, I've got perfume on already, but you are a gem, live my dear, live forever. Jeeti raho.' 'Bari-ma, Choti-ma, I just had an idea. Do you want me to make my Lo Mein and the stir-fry crispy beef chillies that I always make so well? You know how good that is! It would be perfect for this evening!'

'Yes, you're right,' Hajrabai said.

'Ok! Done. I'll come early, it'll take me half an hour, it's all so quick. I'll bring the noodles and the beef. What's the menu for tonight?'

'There's going to be Bombay biryani, shami kebab, korma and roast chicken,' Choti-ma said.

'That's perfect!' Sara said.

'Razia! Come quickly! Where are you?' Zareenabai called out.

'Come at once. Bring Sara Bibi tea and lunch. Sara, there is some good news that we must tell you at once! Remember the letter that your father received? The threat?'

'Yes?' Sara said, sitting up in anticipation, her eyes wide and round with fear.

'Well, it's all fine. We found out through Haji Kareem that the same letter went out to at least twenty other businessmen, including Kareem Bhai himself!'

Sara breathed a deep sigh of relief, 'Thank God!'

Hajrabai agreed.

Sara said, 'I was so frightened.'

'So was I. We all were. I couldn't sleep a wink until your father told us yesterday,' said Zareenabai.

'I'm going to immediately give a sadqa. A goat. Tomorrow morning—no, this afternoon. And I'll have it sent to the orphanage near our house. Anyway, we should try to be a bit more careful this Moharram. Riaz was telling me that the authorities are expecting a lot of trouble this year,' Sara said.

'There's trouble every year in Moharram, nothing new about that. And don't waste your money on goats,' Zareenabai said. 'Get some medicine and send it to the Civil Hospital. And maybe you can forget about the scarf. I agree with Bari-ma dear, don't think about covering your head, it looks so ugly, that ridiculous scarf.'

'Well, I don't think so. I think it looks very pious. All my friends are doing it,' Sara said.

'What has happened to everyone, is everyone going mad?' Zareenabai asked.

'Why Choti-ma? Wanting to wear a hijab doesn't mean I'm mad.'

'No, Sara, it means you are up to something. Now out with it, what are you up to now?' Hajrabai said dryly.

'Hai Bari-ma, what do you mean? I'm absolutely up to nothing except being good. I've found my spirituality that's all.'

'Humph,' said Hajrabai.

Zareenabai intervened, 'Anyway Sara, you are always so busy.

Please tell me if you are going to be here next December.'

'Why? Is there going to be some event?'

'I don't know yet, but just tell me what your plans are.'

'Well let me see. We didn't go for Hajj this year and of course I'll go nowhere in Moharram next month. But in the summer, most probably to America and Canada but just for four weeks baba. I can't handle it there, too much work. We'll take the kids to Disneyland, I'll do some shopping whopping, we'll stay with Kulsum this time. She's been insisting that she feels we never go to her. But Riaz doesn't want to go, he thinks we should only go where we won't feel uncomfortable. He wants to go to Shanghai or Dubai or Kuala Lumpur. We'll go to Thailand this year in Ramadan, which will be November, then back for Eid. Of course, we will be here in December for the shaadi season, Christmas charity balls, then for New Year's we'll go to Malaysia, or maybe Goa, then next year for sure *we'll go for Hajj. We'll all go and then perhaps an Umrah in there somewhere*. Ooof Choti-ma, my feet are killing me!'

And with that, she extricated her feet from the magenta silk slippers which were hand embroidered in gold thread at her own workshop and perfectly matched her magenta tunic and blue culottes.

'Poor thing! I have just the remedy!' Zareenabai said. She shouted for Razia, who came running. 'Razia, bring the silver basin from my bathroom. Fill it with warm water and bring me my vial of khas ka ittar.'

The silver basin arrived and Zareenabai sprinkled generous drops of ittar on the warm water, then Sara's feet were gently lowered into the basin by Razia, who knelt on the floor beside her, while Sara remained half inclined on the chaise longue, her arm thrown across her forehead. The scent of wet hay floated around them like a cool breeze. After a few mmmmms, ooohs and other sounds of satisfaction, Sara asked, 'Anyway, Choti-ma, what's happening in December? Hai Razia, janni, please can you massage the soles of my feet? I'm totally wrecked after the day on the golf course. You know, I can't continue to work so hard!' Razia sat by the silver basin at Sara's feet and massaged the soles of her feet, kneading them gently. Each ripple of the warm water seemed to release the scent of khas into the air, filling it with drowsy coolness.

'Oh, that feels so good. Right there! That spot, exactly Razia. Knead! Knead! Ooooh Yes!'

'I was planning that Zain and Amina would get married,' said Zareenabai.

'Hai, how wonderful Choti-ma! Not so hard, Razia! Is it all settled then? Has Amina agreed, has Zain agreed? No one tells me anything.'

'No, no, no my dear, not yet. I think they are only just about to meet each other in New York. You know, because of Faiza and me. She's arranging it. For now, nothing is certain or set. Sara, my dearest girl. Jaani, my little chanda, you must take this important task of mine in your hands. You must do this for me, dear child, you must make this happen.'

'Hai Choti-ma, who more than me could want Amina to settle down and be occupied with something really worthwhile?

Of course I'll do this. Of course she'll be married. Just leave it to me.'

'Bless you, Sara, bless you, live, keep living, live forever.'

The phone rang and Zareenabai picked it up, 'Yes, oh hello, Samina! How are you? Yes. Of course I will my dear…just phone me on the morning of the 8th of Moharram… of course I will my dear! Don't I always? You have nothing to worry about.' Zareenabai talked to her friend, who had called for her yearly request, for a few minutes. Every year before Moharram, she called to confirm that Zareenabai would make a wish on her behalf on the 8th of Moharram at the shrine in Kharadar. Zareenabai received dozens of such requests from her Sunni relatives and friends before Moharram. Resham said it was like a stockbroker receiving purchase orders for shares or a bookie taking bets on horses. New wishes were made every year and Zareenabai brought back silver and brass rings from the shrines around Karachi for her friends to wear for as long as they waited for their wishes to come true. Then if the wishes did come true, the following year they would resolve to bring back the ring, with food and silver rings for others to pick up, and money for the shrine. This was the tradition. Believers offered what they promised to do if their prayers came true. Give alms to the poor, donate blood, build a school or a hospital, go on pilgrimage, or simply be good; maybe sacrifice a sheep or two. Zareenabai handled all the logistics for these requests as a go-between for the shrines and her friends who wanted their desires to be fulfilled but preferred not to acknowledge intercession through praying at shrines. So all the going to the shrines and the dispensing of food and money once the wishes were completed was Zareenabai's responsibility. It kept her busy around the year. Located in Kharadar, which was part of the gated city nearest the sea in old Karachi, Hazrat Abbas's dargah was the oldest imam bargah of Karachi.

It was dedicated to Abbas the standard-bearer at Karbala, the half-brother of Hussein, the loyal kinsman and uncle who died trying to bring water from the Euphrates to his thirsty niece, Sakina. The shrine revered Abbas and his attempt to quench the thirst of a child from a river embargoed and blockaded by an enemy coalition force of overwhelming strength. Black banners on poles in each alley way around the imam bargah, as tall as the nearby four-storey buildings signified Abbas's banner in battle. The faithful held on to the pole, kissed it fervently and said prayers and made wishes. Tiny candle-lit shrines dotted every corner—decorated with papier mâché horses, swords, banners; flowers and sweets on trays. Dirges blasted over loudspeakers implored and rebuked the Euphrates and the heavens for the pain of Abbas. Colourful banners and fairy lights criss-crossed over the heads of the crowds in the alleys.

Thousands of people visited the shrine during Moharram and throughout the year to pray, be blessed and to ask for all their dreams and aspirations to come true. The loyalty and valor of Abbas was an endearing feature that served to make him a channel for praying for God's mercy. Many a school test or quiz or college exam successfully passed, an engagement or marriage, the threat of a husband's affair or second marriage averted, or impotence corrected, a birth, a promotion, an illness overcome, a healing, a success in Karachi were attributed to this dargah. Throughout the ten days and nights of Moharram, this area and its narrow alley ways were lit up with celebratory fairy lights and large searchlights. There were banners and black flags everywhere. Believers of all stripes, men women and children, poor and not so poor, sick and healthy, contented and not so much, lit candles at makeshift shrines at every turn and corner.

These replicas signified the shrines in Karbala, Najaf, Mecca and Medina and were festooned with the battle colours and banners of the Imam and his followers. Pathos, poetry, politics, story-telling, theater, tragedy, and street parties—all became proxies for prayer and for politics. Each space around a shrine, the neighbourhood and street leading to it, each park and open space for a congregation were transformed in the minds of the mourners into encampments and the territory of the ahyle bayt, the Prophet's household, at Karbala.

For Zareenabai, each Moharram, Karachi remapped itself as the home of the righteous, the faithful, the lovers of God, the besieged, and for her, its nooks and alley ways became sacred and full of mystical quality, symbolizing the possibility of miracles.When they were children, Sara, along with her sisters, had attended majlises with Zareenabai and Razzak during the first ten days of Moharram. Now, it was just Sara and her parents who attended from their household in Karachi. In New York, once in a while Shireen, Amina, Resham and Kulsum attended a majlis in the suburbs, either going to New Jersey to an imam bargah in Edison or to someone's house.

But the effort needed to coordinate and schedule attending a majlis, jostled with soccer mom duties and corporate schedules. Resham claimed each year that she would start holding at least one majlis at her apartment, where she would recite nowhas. And Amina had said that she would write an essay on the Prophet's grand-daughter Zainab, whose speech at the court of Yezid was, to Amina, an important early document on laying out a case for war crimes and was an account of crimes against humanity. Amina had always wanted to write an essay on this and had told Resham that she would read it at the majlis when Resham organized it. But neither Resham nor Amina actually carried out this plan, though it was passionately and resolutely discussed after each majlis that they attended and from which they returned inevitably frustrated and disappointed because of the lack of prowess on the part of the zakir to narrate the events or provide the theological, historical and intellectual context that made it relevant. The majlises they had attended in Karachi had been presided over by renowned speakers who pulled in huge crowds because of the force of their oratory.

They came away feeling that the significance and relevance of Moharram had been overshadowed by shaky fundamentalist theology and Bollywood histrionics of questionable zakirs that, in no manner, were comparable to the intellect and historical references that they had been exposed to as children in the majlises in Karachi when the likes of Allama Rashid Turabi and then his son Akeel Turabi had graced the congregations. Now the speakers seemed to be emphasizing the retrogressive aspects which were not at all the discourse which the girls had grown up with. And, as far as Zareenabai and Sara were concerned, these were all excuses. Moharram, for the girls in the States, had from all sign of their activities, been reduced to just a phone conversation with 43-G or Sara holding up the cellphone during the procession in Karachi for them to hear, just for the flavor of it in New York. But for Sara in Karachi, these ten days each year were marked by a stoppage of work and an acceleration of pathos, piety and festivities. To her, it was truly a miracle, a mojiza, that a city as chaotic and seemingly disorganized as Karachi, as sprawling and disconnected as it appeared every day, seamlessly and effortlessly came together passionately for ten nights and put together a massive event of street theater complete with costumes, lights, action and food. Observers of Moharram claimed the streets of Karachi and its open parks and maidans by festooning them with banners and panjathans, their presence resembling the encampments of the besieged at Karbala. For her, it was a nonstop, ten day event of public trial hearings in song and speeches, political rallying, group crying and socializing. Sara closed her shop and had a full, pre-planned schedule and routine of attending her Moharram activities with the fervor that others elsewhere around the world might devote to a lecture series at a university or to the Mardi Gras or a jazz or film festival. She picked and chose and jostled and juggled options for attending majlises based on a few important factors: the reputation of the person who was delivering the majlis, the zakir's knowledge and intellect, the force of his or her oratory both of which was evidenced by the crowd that came to listen and on the location in terms of tradition, convenience and timings. Sara ecstatically reveled in this season of Moharram, and was rejuvenated by it.

Every evening in the ten days of Moharram, the Shias of Karachi who had vehicles congregated in their cars at the brightly lit building of Khalikdina Hall on M. A. Jinnah road for a majlis at 9.00 p.m. The location was in the old part of the city and its business district which hustled and bustled with activity during the day, and which on ordinary nights was desolate and silent, save for the vagrants and drug addicts lying in the shadows of shuttered shops entrances. The wide avenue here was lined by limestone buildings whose elegant façades were marred by billboards and decay and which were built during the time of Sara's great-grandfather, many of which would have been their places of doing business and their godowns—buildings that housed the wholesale market of Karachi, from commodities such as raw cotton, to textiles, to spices and sanitary fittings. Narrow side streets opened on to M.A. Jinnah road. During the ten days of Moharram, the entire road was blocked off to regular traffic from 8:30 to 10 o'clock in the night and transformed into a giant parking lot or a drive-in theater as cars, buses, jeeps, and small pick-up trucks drove and parked in orderly columns. Women sat in the cars while men stood alongside or sat on the ground beside the cars or on the hoods. The atmosphere permeated the throngs as though they were in the tents under siege at Karbala. It was as though here, on an avenue in Karachi, they had been transported and encamped and under siege at Karbala. Victimization, besiegement, and righteousness reigned here.

Shops lining the street were closed and their shutters were down. Paan shops were open and so were kiosks which sold water, soft drinks and snacks. Teenage boys in uniforms, the Hussaini scouts guided cars, controlled the crowd and distributed naans, kebabs and parathas as tabaruk, the food consecrated and offered to the believers in the name of the victims of Karbala. Perhaps like taking communion. And those partaking of the offerings in abundance were always amazed at how ordinary food such as this had never tasted better and could only taste like this on the ten nights of Moharram. The one hour sermon of the zakir was relayed over loudspeakers to everyone. The sea breeze which usually started to blow in the early evening cooled the crowd and carried the zakir's voice across the neighborhoods in the area. Sara had a majlis at her house on the seventh and then Zareenabai had one at 43-G on the eighth of Moharram. The girls had all helped out with the preparations when they lived in Karachi and Resham had always recited nowhas and marsiyas at the majlis at 43-G, and Sara at her majlis after the sermon which was delivered by a female speaker. With Choti-ma, Sara went for ziarat or pilgrimage of the major imam bargahs in the city and in the old city of Kharadar. These shrines were lit up with fairy lights and were festooned with the ubiquitous black and green banners splattered in red dye, the alams and the silver panjathans depicting a hand to symbolize the ahyle bayt, the

Prophet, Ali, Fatima, Hasan and Hussein. The shrines in Kharadar and other parts of old Karachi had been established mainly by the Khoja community—who were descendants of migrants to India's western coast—the Kwajas from Iran, who had settled in Gujrat and in Bombay and Karachi—much like the Bohri communities.

They visited the newer suburbs of the ever expanding and sprawling city, and went to neighborhoods in North Nazimabad such as Hyderi, Ancholi and a residential area referred to as Terha Number, named for its zoning number, thirteen. Here majlises were held in large parks with huge screens set up for people to see the zakir speaking. There were shrines here set up by the bara sadaat, the immigrants from north India who were Shia and who traced their family lineages to the twelve imams. The atmosphere in these neighborhoods was festive and lively throughout the night, with heart-wrenching marsiyas and nowhas being played from boom boxes and loudspeakers as though they were disco music. Dirges eulogized the majesty of Imam Hussein, his valor and his courage. About how the Euphrates wept at his plight, how the desert between Karbala and Kufa trembled witnessing his siege, how the angels sobbed, how the heavens hid their face in shame with the veil of the night.

There were a multitude of dirges sung about Abbas's valor, his strength, his steadfastness, his love for Hussein and his family. There were dirges about Zainab, the daughter of Fatima and of Imam Ali, the sister of Imam Hussein, left alone as the head of the family when her brother was martyred, how she walked to Damascus in chains and faced the tyrant Yezid. How she saved and protected the only living son of Imam Hussein so that he could be the next Imam. How her courage and her words shook the court of Damascus. How she had narrated and preserved the events of Karbala in spite of her difficulties and her humiliation. Her dignity, her courage and the martyrdom of her kinsmen that she alone narrated and saved for posterity. Dirges about Imam Hussein's eight year old daughter Sakina's thirst, her imprisonment, her bewilderment at their plight, her love for her father, her search for him in the darkness of the night at the end of the battle. People wept and beat their breasts for the pathos of it, the poetry of it, for the tragedy and the triumph of it. People related their own everyday trials and tribulations to that of Zainab, alone in the desert, the head of the Prophet's household, alone defending the true faith and facing down tyranny. Story-telling here was a heightened form of group psychoanalysis and catharsis. People thronged the streets and visited imam bargahs set up in different houses.

Bright-eyed, giggling young girls, their heads covered in black dupattas, or chadors or hijabs, wearing black shalwar kameezes, walked around in groups, chattering excitedly, moving without a care from alley to alley and house to house, visiting makeshift shrines set up in people's homes along the way. Equally bright-eyed boys, ostensibly relatives, swaggered behind, following them or alongside them in escort. There was an atmosphere of street fiestas throughout the ten nights. Houses were lit up with fairy lights and stalls of food were lined along the streets at intervals, there was an abundance of free food to eat. There were cauldrons full of haleem, mountains of kebabs, piles of sheermal, parathas and an assortment of halwas and suji. And milk flowed from vats in the form of the traditional pink colored milky sherbet. All the food was in honor of and thanksgiving for prayers which had been answered and had borne results.

Amidst a raucous din of drums, cymbals, dirges and color, almost 700 different processions began at night on the ninth of Moharram from neighborhoods and communities all over the city, and meandered through the city to converge at dawn on Ashura outside the Shah-e-Khorasan for the main Ashura procession on M.A. Jinnah Road. DAWN each year published the schedule and route of the procession: 'The route of the procession will be Nishtar Park, Sir Shah Nawaz Bhutto Road, Father Jaminis Road, Mehfile-Shah-e-Khorasan, Mohammad Ali Jinnah Road, Bolton Market Road, Bombay Bazaar, Kharadar and Nawab Mohabat Khanji Road.' Of the 700 processions from all over the city's neighborhoods, about 400 were of Sunni dastas (associations) while 300 or so were of Shia associations. The Sunni processions on the eve of Ashura celebrated the victory of Islam through the sacrifice of Imam Hussein, claiming that Islam was renewed at each Karbala. Beating drums and blowing on trumpets, their processions moved just on the outskirts of Kharadar into the huge playground, soccer field and the site of many a historical political rally, the park called Kakri grounds. Here the events of Karbala were celebrated noisily and boisterously, complete with floats depicting the battleground and sword swallowing and fire breathing acrobats. Banners were held high with the words, 'Islam comes alive after each Karbala.'

Parents dressed their children in paper hats, in green and red colors and cardboard swords bought from roadside kiosks while the Shia processions readied themselves for mourning the massacre of the Prophet's household on Ashura.

Zareena turned to Razia who was massaging Sara's feet, 'Razia, where's the lunch for Sara Bibi?'

Razia protested and pointed out, 'Begum Sahiba, you asked me to come and massage Bibi's feet.'

Zareenabai retorted sternly, 'Don't answer back! Yunis! Yunis! Where is that man? Go Razia quickly, tell him to bring lunch and come back and massage Sara Bibi's feet.' Sara moaned happily, 'Hai Choti-ma, this is heaven.' Hajrabai shook her head in irritation and went back to reading the paper. From the street below came the call of the kalaiwallah. 'Kalaiwallah! Sheen man's here! Get your nickel coating done, shine your pots and pans. Make them new!'

BOOK TWO

American Shemerican

10

Let's Roll

IN her apartment at Crosby Street in Soho, New York, Amina wakes up with a jolt to the sound of the morning edition on National Public Radio. She turns over to hit the snooze button on the radio alarm clock. Still half asleep, she listens to the news and groans, 'I need to start listening to Democracy Now. And I need a new occupation!' At that exact time, at just past four in the afternoon in Karachi, Rahim, aged eight, shoeless, his shalwar kameez soaked through with sweat, calls it a day and stabs and spears with a sharp stick his last black polypropylene bag that clings to a thorny bush adding it to his bulging sack of scavenged garbage, found on the outskirts of a luxury apartment complex at the edge of the Arabian Sea. The air conditioners in the surrounding buildings hiss heatedly, raising the already high temperature around him. His attention is caught by a box of Fauji cornflakeslying next to an unfurled and bloodied sanitary pad. Inside the cereal box he finds a plastic bag half full of flakes and ants. He shakes out the bag and stuffs it in his pocket. His meal for the afternoon, this infested snack, wrested from the ants.

In the near distance on the waters, the Greek tanker, the Tasman Spirit, cracked down its middle, looms like a small new island, having bled its cargo of oil into the waters. And a few miles away Iqbal, his head aching from the long day at the sewing machine across the city, raises his fist at the SUV that narrowly misses him as he criss-crosses traffic and clambers on to a bus that is already full of human and petrol odours, muttering, 'That Sara Aziz!' His body jammed against others, his toes trodden, eyes blurred from sweat meandering down a furrowed brow, he is heading for Malir with a busload of equal resentments. Just then Rehana, on the same bus in the ladies section up front, wipes her brow and clutches the shopping bag full of groceries and medicines for her mother. She wonders if she'll make it home in time to see Aishwarya Rai on the Zee TV special to be aired tonight.

She has to go to the clinic before with her pregnant sister-in-law, who is expecting a son. Her hand pats the bulge of her handbag, because along with her month's pay, she has her share of

this month's committee safely tucked in there. She moves her hand up to readjust her hijab, she's feeling very mod-squad, the term her sister-in-law often uses as she teases her when their paths cross in the evening, with Saima going to work and Rehana returning. Saima, her sister-in-law, has just started a new job at a call centre; she answers phone calls during the night when it's day in the USA. 'Hi, this is Sam. Can I help you?' With the committee loan, Rehana is going to have an extra room built for herself on top of their upwardly moving narrow house which squats much like all the houses around it on 250 square feet of city land.

Its first floor outer walls are whitewashed while the second storey is still exposed concrete and cement blocks. Just at that very moment on the Upper West Side, Zain turns off his halogen lamp left on from last night, and kisses his lover, awake, hard, tender, wet. Just then, exactly then in fact, a bright green parrot alights on the balcony railing and peers at Zareenabai seated on the verandah at 43-G, American Shemerican overlooking Patel Park in Karachi as she opens her mouth and stuffs a paan into her left cheek, and heaves a sigh. She misses the girls -- Amina, Kulsum, Shireen and Resham. She waddles away from supervising the cleaning woman who is on her knees, mopping the living room floor. Jeevan looks up and sticks out her long, pink tongue at Zareenabai's retreating backside. And just then Yaqub Kishtiwalla, rubbing the scars on his thumb with his forefinger, eyes a photograph in an evening newspaper with satisfaction. In the picture, Rehana, Sara, Riaz, Razzak and Hajrabai look on as Yaqub Kishtiwalla steps back on the terracotta tiled floor and out of the flashing camera lights to watch the Provincial Governor cut the ribbon for the opening of the new art gallery, whose origins lie in his fortunes; a one time dock labourer, now a multi- millionaire denominated in dollars and registered in the Seychelles.

And in Texas, Brigadier General Henry (Hank) Brown, retired, age 54, peers into the computer screen, the tanned skin at the corners of his blue eyes creasing as he considers a job as a military consultant to MSVBC. He checks his inbox from dating.com and responds to a few interesting prospects, then quietly lets his lean muscled self out of the front door to begin the task at hand, of shaking off the memory of his wife of 32 years, high school sweetheart, the lovely Gloria nee Hansen, as sweet as a Maltese dog in a Burberry raincoat, now resting in peace and dearly beloved. He surveys the route ahead and mutters under his breath, 'Well, let's kick that can down the road,' and begins his early morning jog. 'Revving up the engines as they say. Let's roll!'

11

The Pursuit of Happiness

REGARDEZ! Comme la main de Fatima, non?' giggled a woman, pointing towards the Don't Walk sign. The man standing next to her thrust out his lips and shrugged. 'Comme le souvenir au Grande Bazaar, non? Tu te souviens?' Amina, standing next to them, licked her lemon gelato cone contentedly and squinted at the blinking red lit hand, the symbol for the Don't Walk sign. Shetilted her head and shrugged as well. It could be a panjathan she thought. It did look like the hand of Fatima or a Hamsa. Amina balanced her sandaled feet on the edge of the sidewalk, rocking back and forth while she waited for the sign to change. She was running last minute errands before the party: dessert, wine, flowers, candles. 'Fatima!!' She had forgotten to invite Fatima!! She pulled out her cellphone from her large limp bag slung over her shoulder. Relieved that she had reached the voicemail and wouldn't actually have to have a conversation, she said breezily, 'Hi Fatima, Amina here, listen having an impromptu party this evening, starts whenever you arrive. Would love to see you. Totally informal. Bring Tim. Do come. Sorry for the short notice! See you!' So much more convenient than actually having to talk to her on the other end.

A passing bus created a swoosh of breeze, rustling her ankle-length, white cotton skirt. The light changed, she crossed over and thought about her party. It was a celebration. Amina had become a citizen. She had gone for her oath-taking at City Hall just the day before yesterday. All these years of paying taxes, now finally she was able, eligible, and entitled, to vote in a couple of months on that all-important date of 2 November. She started to review the list of guests that she had invited for the evening. About twenty people. Her experience from the past had shown that at least thirty would show up so she had prepared for double that number. She was trying something new tonight. She had invited people without paying any attention to whether or not the guests were compatible. She hadn't given any thought to that at all. Well, actually she had given it a lot of thought. She had called everyone she could think of; the theme for the party was -- the 'crammed to the gills scene'. Standing room only. Her rule of thumb last week had been that if people called her first, before she got to them, they got invited. An updated 'A' list based on who had thought of her in the past seven days.

Tonight, if everyone turned up there could be a dozen lawyers, most from her firm. If Fatima came then that would add a human rights lawyer or two to the corporate eight or so others, that is if Tim came along. It would make for interesting conversation to have a few good souls around instead of the usual money making corporate junkies. Of course she'd invited her sisters. Kulsum couldn't make it because her in-laws were visiting and her coming would mean that all of them would come along in tow, resulting in discomfort for everyone. The in-laws would not approve of Amina's friends, or of the wine being served by their daughter-in-law's sister. Shireen would be there with her husband Amit. Amit was humorous and kind, and could always be counted on to keep the party on a steady even keel and in an eclectic intellectual stream.

Resham was sure to bring along several friends, most of whom worked in the investment banking business.

Then there would be several doctors; a psychotherapist or two, a pediatrician and at least one cardiologist. There would be at least one wholesaler, distributor of leather jackets, a caterer for birthday cakes, a designer of windshield wipers for an electric car prototype and several aspiring writers and actors. There could be a professor or two in the house especially if Ana, her yoga teacher and friend, showed up with her partner and his friends.

Amina thought that there should be enough Sufis, saints, sinners, socialists, capitalists, poets and generic pains in the ass there tonight to give everyone a hang-over tomorrow. She grinned at her reflection in a shop window. Her eyes followed the svelte figure of a young girl swaying ahead of her on the sidewalk, with a guy at her side who had his thumb hooked in her back pocket. Amina looked at the tattooed lower back of the woman walking in front of her. She couldn't tell whether the tattoo was of a cross or a sword, it could be either. Maybe she, Amina, should get a tattoo? No, she thought hurriedly, she could never bear the sight of the needles or bare her midriff that way. Wistfully, she thought it would be nice though to have a guy—especially the delicious looking young man up ahead, walking beside one with his thumb attached to one's bum. In her day-dreaming, Amina bumped into an oncoming man with a poodle in his arms. They both said 'sorry' in unison as they continued walking, passing by each other to move on in different directions. She rubbed her shoulder and hoped she wouldn't bruise, she was planning to wear a stunning number tonight that would show off her well toned upper arms and lovely neck. Her cellphone rang. She stopped and rummaged around in her bag while it trilled insistently. Her hands fumbled around a hairbrush, her wallet, several lipsticks, her blackberry, a lost dangly earring now found, keys, and oddly, an eraser labeled

Liberty, and finally, as the ringing stopped her fingers found the phone. She had missed the call. She looked at the number; it was unfamiliar. The message tone went off. It was an unfamiliar voice with a thick Pakistani accent. 'Halo, Halo, Amina? Yaqub Kishtiwalla here.' She noticed he pronounced here as hair. 'I'm a friend of your sister, Sara. I'm in New York and wanted wery much to come by to see you. Sara has sent a small package far you. Please call me back when you get this message. Okay.' There was a pause. 'Well, okay. Hope to hair from you soon.' Amina stood tapping her foot, weighing the phone in her hand while considering what she should do. She called back. Yaqub answered right away. 'Thanks for calling back so quickly,' he said.

Amina replied cheerfully, 'No problem. Are you visiting from Karachi?'

Yaqub answered, 'Yes.'

Amina asked, 'Are you in town for a couple of days?'

'I've been here for four days on business and am leaving for Toronto tomorrow and then back to Karachi next week. Sara has sent something for you. Is it possible to give it to you today?'

Amina thought for a moment. 'Ummmm… Well, I'm busy today. Let me see. Are you doing anything this evening? The thing is that I'm having a dinner party at my home this evening. You are most welcome to join us.'

Yaqub replied cheerfully, 'That would be my pleasure. What time?'

Amina said, 'Whatever time is good for you.'

'Excellent! I'll be there,' Yaqub said.

She shrugged her shoulders. Why not? It fit in with her party plan, he had called and he was invited. She had given him the address: 114 and a half Crosby Street. The more the merrier, she said to herself and continued to walk and think about the party that evening. She was looking forward to it. She had ordered food yesterday and it was to be delivered at 4 p.m. this afternoon. A cab driver who was a regular at the café across the street had agreed to pick up her order in Queens and bring it over when he came by for his tea. Amina figured that people would start arriving at around 7:30. She had asked Rosario to come at four to vacuum the place and to bring in the last minute groceries and take the delivery of the food. And Resham had said she'd come by seven at the latest. Amina was walking down the street on her way to pick up the desserts that she'd ordered from the delicatessen a few blocks down on Mercer, which made the most sinfully delicious chocolate mousse cake with a marzipan icing, layered with raspberry sauce. She had a small list of things she had to pick up. Napkins, candles, wine, dessert and flowers. But the question was, what kind of flowers? Calais lilies? Ordinary lilies? Roses? Sunflowers? Sunflowers.

That's it. Sunflowers were what she wanted for tonight. Though Calais lilies were definitely more poised. They signaled that she had grace. Sunflowers said she had none. No, she changed her mind, she wanted sunflowers. She was in a sunflower kind of mood for today. She had decided on coloured roses earlier this morning. Now, at near noon, roses didn't at all feel right—too hot and they seemed to say blah. Calais lilies, though subtle and elegant, said she was doing what was done by everyone. Sunflowers on the other hand, said blah, done, but still fabulous, they spoke volumes. Sunflowers it would be. Sunflowers said that she could if she wanted, get a tattoo or two. Sunflowers said she may even have a few hidden away already. Done! Three abundantly filled vases of sunflowers. One to be placed on the wrought iron console in the small foyer and the other on the high marble top side-table which lived next to the chaise longue in the living room. She knew from experience that people would bring flowers too so it was best to keep a few vases empty and waiting. She stood at the corner of

Bleeker and Broadway, waiting for the light to turn and examined her fingernails and then her feet, turning them this way and that to see what shape her nails were in. No, she thought critically, that wouldn't do at all. She immediately decided that she had to go for a pedicure and manicure. Should've had that thought earlier she said irritably to herself. A pedicure and manicure would take at least an hour. But it was only noon now. If she did do her nails first then there was no way she would be able carry all the stuff she needed to get without ruining the polish. She could first go pick up the stuff and then have her nails done. Or alternatively, she would order everything now and have Rosario pick it up for her. She could call Rosario on her cellphone now and ask her to pick up the cakes and the wine. Or she could pick up the cakes, the candles and the flowers first, order the wine, have it delivered at four and then go for the pedicure and manicure. She stood at the corner in complete indecision, tapping her foot. The light changed several times before she finally crossed. She called Resham, 'Do you want to meet me for a manicure now?'

'No, I can't. Sorry,' Resham replied. 'See you in the evening. Do you need anything else?'

'No, I'm all set,' Amina put the phone away and stepped into the liquor store and ordered six bottles of Pinot Noir, a few Merlots and Chardonnays and a couple of Zinfandels. That would do. The shop owner assured her that the wines would be delivered by five. Rosario would get the juices. Then on to the speciality candle store, but first turning back and into the liquor store to add on a bottle of Kasasha rum to her order. Then she retraced her steps towards the candle store where, after much deliberation, she settled on a dozen long stem candles in pink. Which she rethought and changed to green to match the stalks of her sunflowers. She stopped at the Korean store and examined the flower stall with the Mexican salesman. The sunflowers were glorious this August.

Just the type she liked, the ones with a green eye instead of black. The candles would look spectacular. There was something to be said about bio-genetically modified plants, they were gigantic and preposterous. And indestructible, it seemed. She took a dozen. She checked candles and flowers off her mental list. Done! She stopped at the corner of Prince and Broadway, almost home. The flowers were beginning to weigh her down. She felt like a giant multi-headed sunflower stalk prowling down the street. She imagined someone reporting her: 'Officer, there's a giant stalk stalking down the street,' she giggled. 'Ma'am you're under arrest for obstructing the sidewalk!' She joked to herself. She mused that perhaps she should have a sunflower tattooed on her back. Not enough time and besides, she would need to get over her fear of needles. People were looking at her. She was attracting attention. She smiled as she passed a small construction site and the workers there shouted a few appreciative and explicit remarks her way. 'I would,' she replied hurrying on, 'but I have to get my nails done!' A party does change the pace of things, she thought. She could do this full time, she mused. For a moment she thought of Sara in Karachi, who did this almost every day. What a life. Amina decided she definitely needed a break. She was tired of all the business traveling and the long hours at work. She needed something new to do. Something new to occupy her. A new occupation that could promise happiness.

Or at least ample leisure time. Perhaps she could throw a party every week. That would make it quite a chore. And carrying these sunflowers for two blocks was already proving to be one. Why did even leisure seem like work? Why did everything in the city become work, requiring perfect planning and precision execution? But that was not the point, the point was that she needed to focuson finding something to do which made her happy. It would take a little pursuing and oh, just a bit of misconstruing. She peered around her sunflowers to look at the Prada store front on the corner of Prince and Broadway. She thought to herself that the manne-quins displayed in the Prada windows looked like a new breed of bio-genetically modified clones drafted and pressed into service as army troops. All lined up row after row, as though waiting for a military review or a march past. Their tiny nipples taut as though with the excitement of war. Dressed in military colours, accessorized by dabka and kamdani embroidered brooches and belts and shoes. Television sets inside the shop showed clones running and jumping as though in escape, and a large cage made of iron that held manne- quins, as though imprisoned. That was the motif for the season, or seasons to come: capturing the East, war and imprisonment. A few blocks away near Bleeker and Lafayette, the play Guantanamo had just opened at a theatre, with tickets set at a mere fifty dollars a seat. War, it appeared, was on display as an expensive trend that seemed to appeal to all. And Brahms mixed with fusion Middle Eastern, Bollywood and Sufi music provided white noise in restaurants, boutiques and cafés. It was the season of barricades and cages. Of barbed wire and wealth. Of Barbies and brocade. It was the season of conventions.

The Republican National Convention was about to get underway at the Madison Square Garden tomorrow. Women, it seemed, could not get enough of khaki camouflage, much like the leopard pattern of years earlier. From theatre shows to handbags and hairbands, a bit of war was de rigueur. The war raged on in Iraq and Afghanistan, and Bollywood was big on Broadway. Amina made her way back to her apartment which hadn't much to recommend except for its gorgeous view of the art deco iron building across the street, its hop-skip and a jump access to subways for the R, N, W and D, B and 6 and 4 trains. The Lahore Café, with the best tea and samosas in New York and with a steady stream of cabs parked outside it as the drivers ducked in for a quick bite, was just across the street. Her apartment was a renovated loft, early twentieth century on a cobbled street. She had recently moved from a one bedroom pre-war building (World War II that is, she was keen on staying) on the Upper West Side and she missed the greetings and banter with the doorman there. She made up for that by popping into the Lahore Café to pick up her tea every day on her way back from work and exchanging a few greetings with the cabbies who happened to be there. Here at her apartment building, she was on her own as far as opening doors was concerned. It was essentially a four-storey walk up though the building did have an industrial-size, rickety, old elevator that threatened to stall, or worse yet, held the risk of plummeting downwards. But that was part of the charm. The building had mosaic tiles in the corridors and in the apartment. Yesterday's cruel sweatshops were today's lofts and prized possessions. She had had the place remodeled so that the loft no longer was a large open space. Instead, it resembled a conventional apartment, only with tall ceilings and very large windows. And according to Resham, she had reduced the resale value of the property by inadvertently destroying the arty appeal of the loft. The kitchen no longer opened in to the living room, it was now a separate room.

A small foyer now provided an unnecessary Victorian formality at the entrance leading into the living room. An arched doorway divided the dining room from the living room from where yet another door opened into a small bedroom. The windows in the apartment were all located in the living room and dining room area. Amina placed the sunflowers in the sink in the kitchen and filled it up with water. They would go into vases later. She turned on the electric kettle and made herself a cup of tea. Then she carried the mug of tea to the bathroom turned on the cold water tap in the bath, took off her sandals and soaked her feet for a few minutes. She had forgotten the cakes. She called Rosario and left her a message to pick up the cakes on the way to the apartment.

Cooled and refreshed, she went out again for her leisurely manicure and pedicure. Looking over the Fall issue of Vogue as the Chinese woman who was unable to speak English and who was bent over Amina's feet, massaging her toes, It was a perfect day. The doorbell rang at 6:30 p.m.. Amina had just finished drying her hair. Rosario answered the door and came to tell her, it was Yaqub. Damn! She should have specified the time, told him 9 p.m.! What kind of a Karachiite was he anyway, arriving so early for a party? She hurried out and found him seated in the dining room. He stood up as she came in, they said hello and he handed her a package of clothes from Sara. Yaqub had also brought her a box of mangoes from Pakistan. 'What an extravagance! You really shouldn't have gone through such trouble,' Amina said. Yaqub hesitated before replying, 'Why not? It was the least I could do.'

Amina said appreciatively, 'A whole crate of mangoes!!'

Yaqub responded after a pause, 'I thought it would remind you of home.'

Amina said hurriedly, 'It certainly does! But how did you get them past customs here?'

Amina noticed that Yaqub paused before replying, as though he was formulating his sentences in his head before he spoke.

Yaqub grinned, 'Well, I have my ways.'

Amina said, 'I'm very impressed.'

Yaqub replied, 'Well I hope you enjoy them. No real good mangoes here in this country.'

Amina responded, 'I agree. Nothing like our mangoes from Pakistan.'

Amina felt sorry for the man seated across from her in her apartment as they waited for Rosario to bring in tea. She thought he was ill at ease as he sat there rubbing his thumb with his finger, obviously nervous, picking on the cufflink at his wrist or drumming his fingertips softly on the tabletop. He had told her that he had come straight from his last meeting and wore a tan coloured linen business suit with a white shirt and a brown tie. His brow was slightly furro ed below his receding, graying hairline. She attributed this to his shyness in her presence. She smiled a self-satisfied smile. Yaqub sitting across from her caught the expression on her face and thought instantly that she had an inflated sense of self and was considerably conceited about the impression that she had made on him. And he wasn't wrong. Amina thought to herself, 'He's trying so hard to please me, poor man. He's had to come a long way to see and woo me.' She was sure that he had been sent by Sara for a viewing of her. Amina was flattered and aware of the slightly uneasy feeling this gave her. She thought to herself, amused, 'Woo and view!'

Yaqub said, 'A place without mangoes is a difficult place to live in.'

Amina chortled, 'Well that's a bit extreme! Mangoes are seasonal in Pakistan, are they not? And here they're available all year round. Only they are a bit different in taste and texture. Mostly from Haiti and Mexico, I think.'

Yaqub wagged a finger at her and shook his head in disagreement, 'Very different, not at all like our mangoes from Pakistan.'

Amina tried to suppress the sarcasm that she was feeling, 'Got it. Understood. Different completely.' Yaqub gestured towards the window and the city outside.

'Those things at the fruit stalls here can hardly be called mangoes.'

Amina replied, 'Though I must say, one gets used to them.'

Yaqub shook his head, 'Difficult to see how people live here!'

Amina raised her eyebrows in astonishment, 'C'mon! Just because of the absence of mangoes?'

Yaqub sounded serious, 'No, of course not. But I can't see what the attraction is about this place.'

Unwilling to understand what he meant, Amina asked innocently, 'This place? You mean my apartment? The attraction of my apartment? Well, I like it! It's my home!'

Yaqub looked alarmed, 'Oh no, I didn't mean your apartment. This is very nice. Very nice indeed. Very tastefully done. You've really done it up very nicely.'

Amina was gracious, 'Well, thank you.'

Yaqub continued trying to make it up to Amina, 'And these sunflowers are quite unique.'

Amina explained, 'Yes, with the green centres. Bio-genetically modified, I think.'

Yaqub looked at her, confused but said after a moment, 'Very nice. Your sister Sara is also very talented in interior decoration.'

Amina agreed, 'Yes, she is.'

Yaqub asked appreciatively, 'When do you have the time to do all this Amina? Have a dinner party without servants?'

Amina was flattered, 'Well, I've got help, especially tonight.

And then almost everything tonight is really take-away.'

Yaqub nodded, 'Yes, very convenient. There are many conveniences here. But it seems like life here is so hectic that there's no time to enjoy anything. I can't imagine living here. I've lived abroad for a long time, but now the thought of it—I can't imagine it.'

Amina said defensively, 'There's plenty of time to enjoy things.

Well, I love this place. New York is my home. I can't imagine being anywhere else. And then there is the Lahore Café across the street!'

Yaqub slowly caressed his thumb with his forefinger and said, 'But you don't matter here. It doesn't need you.'

Amina, taken aback, thought for a moment before she ventured, 'Perhaps. No, I'm sure that's true. But it matters to me.I may not matter here, but it matters to me. It's the only place on earth I feel at home outside the house. Here, I feel at home on the streets. On the outside and inside. It's a good place to be.' She grinned at this self revelation.

Yaqub persisted, 'You work here. This is not your original place.'

Amina insisted, 'I live here.'

Yaqub asked, 'What about Pakistan, what about Karachi or Lahore?'

Amina shook her head and shrugged, 'I don't know. If you want the honest answer, that's a loved one, like a family, you're born to them and so you love them. This is choice. This is the great, huge, love affair.' She swept her hand over a speck of dust that she had spotted on the table. 'It requires a bit of Pledge.'

Yaqub was confused, 'Pledge?'

Amina said, 'Polish. I need to polish this table with Pledge. It's furniture polish.'

Yaqub laughed, 'Oh. Well your commitment to living here is nice.'

Amina laughed and said, 'And to polish!'

Yaqub was confused and then said, 'Ah yes, hah! But your commitment to living here, it does exclude any other options!

Doesn't it?' He had reached over and picked an apple out of the silver fruit bowl on the table between them. He sat sideways, his legs crossed, an arm slung over the back of the chair. With his left hand he tossed the apple into the air. He looked at her as he continued to toss and catch.

Amina watched him and said in an amused tone, 'I guess it does. I really can't imagine living anywhere else.'

Yaqub threw her a sidelong glance, 'America is like this apple, no?'

Amina was getting bored, 'I know what you mean. Healthy

and flawless? Everyone who wants to criticize America always uses the apples here as an example!'

Yaqub replied, 'Understandably so, no? Gleaming and shiny.

Its gleam is all wax.' He sniffed the apple. 'No fragrance.' Then he took a large bite out of it. 'No taste.' He spat it out into the palm of his hand.

Amina leaned back and crossed her arms and countered coolly, 'It's a matter of sensibilities.' She thought to herself, how distasteful, spitting into his hand, how crude. Who does he think he is talking to me that way?

Yaqub shrugged and went on, 'Perhaps it is sensibilities. Mine have been dulled by reality. No, I can't live here, not for more than a few days at a time. I'm going home.'

Amina said, 'That's refreshing. Good for you. Most people who come here want to stay and never go back.'

Yaqub said, 'People who are nothing at home go abroad to become something.'

Amina said sarcastically before she could stop herself, 'I'm sure my father would like to hear your opinion about that! And you've already lived abroad and done that as far as I understand, so you've become something!'

Yaqub laughed, 'I'm sorry, I didn't mean any offence. That sounded terrible. I meant the opposite for you, you and your family are so well established in Karachi, it's just hard for me to understand the charm of being here. But yes. I am done with that. Everyone knows me and recognizes me at home. I'll stay there!'

Amina thought to herself, 'What an upstart.' She said out loud, 'And I'll stay here! I'm not particularly fond of mangoes.'

Yaqub smiled, 'Ah well, perhaps next time I'll send you a crate of apples from Hunza. I leave tomorrow. I hope I'll see you when you come to Karachi.'

Amina glanced at her watch, 'Oh, I'm sure of that! It's inevitable! Now if you'll excuse me for five minutes, I'll just go and change for the party.'

Yaqub jumped from his chair, 'Oh, I'm terribly sorry. I've come too early.'

'No, not at all,'

Amina said graciously as she got up and headed for her bedroom, waving her hand at him reassuringly. 'You're fine.

That's fine. Make yourself at home. Please just excuse me for a moment. Oh, and here are some candles. See the candle-holders in this room? Can you stick these in? There's one in the foyer as well.'

With that she left Yaqub holding a bundle of green candles. Yaqub watched her hurry towards her bedroom and he smiled to himself.

He could tell that Amina was quick to judge and impulsive in all her decisions even though she tended to seem indecisive. He could see a bit of Sara in her. He was sure that like her sister, Amina too had a quickness of opinion and jumped to conclusions, which probably often coloured her perceptions of others and their motivations. 'I'm only here to deliver the package, you silly girl, don't get carried away,' he thought.

He walked about the living room, dining room and foyer sticking the candles into their holders. 'I bet she matched these with the flowers,' he thought. Runs in the family. His chore done, he moved around the living room looking at photographs and paintings. A large mustard Bakhtiari with patterns of blossoming trees in shades of red, blue and green was spread on the wood tiled floor and set a tone of warmth. He sat down near the large coffee-table which had several lit candles upon it, and all the requisite props for intellectuals; a pile of big picture books. There was a black and white coffee- table book of photographs called Crosby

Street, which was placed on top of Sebastiao Salgado's Migrations and his book, Workers. There was the big book on Lahore's Old City, then one on Karachi and one with a picture of K-2 on the cover and which mainly had pictures of the Northern Areas, full of snowcapped mountains and green eyed, fair people. Another picture book was entitled 'The Warrior Race'.

Yaqub pulled towards himself the heavy Salgado book. He flipped through the pages and then stood up when Rosario came in with a tray of tea for him. He poured himself a cup and walked over to the bookshelf in the foyer and peered at the titles. There was the complete works of Faiz Ahmed Faiz and Culture and Imperialism by Edward Said, Country Without a Post Office, Shahid Ali Agha's work, Indus Saga by Aitzaz Ahsan, Orientalism by Edward Said, If I am Assassinated and The Great Tragedy by Z. A. Bhutto, Sumantra Bose's Kashmir, The Sole Spokesman

by Ayesha Jalal, The Oxford History of India, and Can Pakistan Survive by Tariq Ali. Oscar Wilde, Complete Works of Shakespeare, and all the books in the series great books from the Folio Society. And of course, but of course, there were several—if not dozens—of books by Noam Chomsky. Yaqub read out the names of various other authors under his breath; Mehmood Mamdani, Chris Hedges, Karen Armstrong.

A few minutes later, the doorbell rang and Yaqub looked around. He turned to the door just behind him in the foyer and opened it. 'Come in, come in,' Yaqub said and seeing the surprised expressions on the faces of the two people, 'I'm one of the guests. I arrived too early, the hostess is changing.'

'Fatima, Tim, hi, look at those flowers, oh my!' Amina came rushing out of her bedroom. Yaqub turned around to look at her. She was tall in high heels and dressed in a body hugging black sleeveless dress. 'Look at you!' breathed Fatima. 'Is that a Donna Karan? And just look at that necklace!' Amina wore a black wraparound dress and stunning diamond choker worked in the Hyderabadi style of jewelry, an heirloom from Bari-ma, which encircled her delicate throat. Amina laughed and complimented in return Fatima's miniskirt that flounced around her in turquoise organza, and was covered with tiny orange flowers. A pale slate shahtoosh was carelessly draped on one shoulder.

Fatima flung her slim arms around Amina. 'Anyway my dear, you look lovely. And I'm glad we're not the first ones here!' she said.

Amina reassured her, 'No, no, it's great you're just on time.

Come on through to the living room. And Tim, how are you? This is Yaqub; he's visiting from Pakistan and is a friend of my sister's.

Tim, Fatima, Yaqub.'

Fatima said warmly. 'Pleased to meet you. Glad you can join us for the celebration.'

Yaqub looked questioningly at Amina, 'Oh? A celebration?'

Fatima interjected, 'Yes! Amina just became a citizen this week. Congratulations dear on your new voting status. You've been paying taxes long enough!'

Amina responded with a bored drawl, 'Citizenship, it's rather meaningless, isn't it? What does it mean really other than to travel without hassle through major airports?'

And Fatima responded in an equal carefree manner, 'Yes, for real!'

Yaqub was amused by Amina's nonchalance. 'Then why throw a party if it's so unimportant?'

Amina dismissed him cheerfully, 'As an excuse to have a party, of course!'

'Ah,' said Yaqub. 'We have charity balls in Pakistan as excuses for parties! And weddings too!'

Tim laughed, 'That's a good one! If you look at the divorce rate here, you could say we do the same, have weddings just for the party. And we have charities to protect our money from alimonies!

Anyway, Amina you look stunning.'

Amina blushed. She looked away from Yaqub who was staring at her and said, 'I hope the tea wasn't tasteless like the apple?'

Yaqub smiled and said it was fine.

Amina turned to Fatima, 'We're having such lovely cool weather this summer, it certainly allows for a better dressed evening.'

Yaqub cleared his throat, 'Yes, it's quite chilly for me.'

'It has been an unusually cool season, too bad we're almost at its end,' Tim said.

Fatima laughed, 'Cool enough to pull out the extravagant shawls and stoles. Who knows, maybe we'll have a sweltering winter. By the way, did you have the walls painted recently, Amina?

I love this color! What is it? Sage?'

'Yes it's sage, but its called autumn mist for some reason.'

'Lovely, really brings out the Sadequain paintings,' Fatima said appreciatively. 'What a collection!'

'Yes, doesn't it? I think so.' Amina murmured.

'It's a lovely transition from the deep ruby red of the foyer.'

Amina laughed, 'Darling we no longer transition, we segue!'

'Ah yes! That we do! Like we're segueing from democracy into fascism!' They all laughed.

Later more guests arrived complaining about how they were late because of the roadblocks caused by the security blockades set up to harness in the demonstrators on the streets who had spent the week protesting against the Republican Convention about to get underway in New York. Amina glanced back into the foyer with satisfaction. The large arrangement of sunflowers, lit up by the glow of the multi-tiered candelabra holding the green candles, set against the deep, dark red walls, was exactly the dramatic effect she had wanted.

Yaqub too stood surveying the room with his serious eyes and an anxious look of unease as he thought about whether he should take his leave or stay a while longer. He had come here as an obligation to his friend Sara who had insisted that he meet Amina. Yaqub looked across the room at the two Pakistani men standing near the windows and made his way to them. Speaking in Urdu he greeted the slim, young man with an olive toned complexion and short black hair.

'Sorry,' said Alejandro, 'I can't understand what you just said.

I'm a Latino, from Mexico! But I get this all the time, don't look so embarrassed. Man, it's okay!'

'Oh, I am terribly sorry,' Yaqub replied. 'I thought you were Pakistani—you look just like a Pakistani.' Someone tapped him on the shoulder. 'Zain, here! Reporting for duty! I'm from Naya York, here via Karachi and can speak Urdu.'

Yaqub turned to stare into the face of a pony-tailed, olive skinned, Latin looking guy. 'You must be Yaqub,' Zain said with a twinkle in his laughing eyes which seemed permanently creased on the edges because of smile lines. 'Amina just told me to look after you and to keep you company. I see you've already met Alejandro.'

Yaqub looked from Zain to Alejandro. He shook his head and grinned. 'Well, both of you look like the same nationality to me. Very desi!' The two men grinned back, looked at each other and nodded.

Yaqub asked Zain, 'So what brings you to New York? What do you do?'

'Well, I'm an investment banker,' Zain replied. 'Smith and Brown.'

'I'm a lawyer,' Alejandro offered. 'Prudential. And what do you do, Yaqub? Don't tell me you are here to attend the Republican Convention! Representing the coalition of the willing!'

'No!' Yaqub laughed. 'No, I'm just an ordinary businessman. Shipping, that's my main area of business.'

Alejandro asked, 'Are you based here?'

Yaqub said, 'Oh no. I'm visiting from Karachi. I'm based in Karachi. I had a few meetings in New York this week. I go back tomorrow.'

A little later, Amina looked across at Yaqub who was standing near the window and half hidden behind the sunflowers, and in deep conversation with Zain and Alejandro. Amina pulled her face into a mock frown. 'What are you all shouting about over there? Really, Zain, you seem fairly apoplectic!'

'Of course I am apoplectic. Why shouldn't I be?' replied Zain, twisting his body around to face her, with one hand on his hip, the other holding a cigar, his eyes stretched wide open. 'It's amazing that I haven't had an aneurysm! I mean, doesn't anyone

see the hypocrisy of it? The New York Times reports corporate media as saying that the reason the pre-convention protests against the Republican Convention haven't been covered so far in the media is because they aren't violent. Can you believe it? So then why does the same media preach to the Palestinians for a passive resistance!!!?'

Amina didn't understand what he meant, 'Why are you smoking? And a cigar of all things!'

Zain put up a mock apology, 'Ooops, you don't mind me smoking in your apartment, do you?'

Amina laughed, 'Well of course I do, but you've already lit up so go ahead.'

Resham had just arrived and, having not shown up earlier as planned, was now sheepishly seated cross-legged on the floor. 'My God, are we in Pakistan?' she said mockingly, referring to the huge contingent of police on the streets of New York, there to protect the Republican Convention from trouble makers. She was dressed in a pair of hip hugging jeans which were slightly stained and over which she wore a hot pink T-shirt that said 'I'm a Muslim, Don't Panic' across the chest. Resham was a petite woman with thick, shoulder length, silky, black hair. She was an investment banker. She was, like most people in the room, in her late thirties. She exuded a sense of self-confidence. She lived comfortably and was financially secure and independent. Resham was considered by her sisters and friends as clear headed, rational and practical and, above all, frank. Shireen, her sister, sat near her husband Amit as he reclined on the chaise. 'No, but is a military takeover here so unthinkable?'

Amina said dismissively, 'Yes, of course it is!'

Amit raised his head slightly and asked Amina, 'Really, is it? Why? They've discussed canceling the elections if there's an emergency situation!'

Shireen shuddered, 'Invoking emergency! God help us!'

Zain came closer, 'My dear over here, down there in Washington at the Pentagon, the patrons of our Generals back in Pakistan, past and present, are just dusting off the advice they've been giving Pakistan for the last fifty-six years and now they are using it here! Surely something, if not a lot, was bound to rub off.

That's called pigeons coming home to roost. That's the real blow back—the stuff they've been blowing out at other countries all these years is blowing right back in. Of course a military takeover here is possible. A coup already has taken place—just look at the last elections. The pigeons have come home to roost.'

Resham laughed, 'More like vultures!'

Amina added, 'More like cancer!'

Shireen said, 'More like fascism!'

Amit looked at the three sisters and grinned, 'Enough! Pour me some red, will you? No, not that one, the Zinfandel.'

Zain said gloomily, 'And as for occupation and repression, we are all part of that enterprise!'

'Enterprise!' Yaqub said. 'Well that's the right term. Over there at home, we have the Fauji Foundation, the Bahria Foundation, the Defense Housing Authorities, the cantonments, the Shaheen Foundation... Everything is owned by the military. And here it's Halliburton, Root Brown, Total Information Assessment and whatever it's called, DynCorp and the mercenary armies in Afghanistan and Iraq!'

'What?' Amina asked, 'What do you mean we are all part of the enterprise? What do you mean by that? I certainly am not! I'm not part of that, I protest. I'm doing my bit, I'm socially conscious, I'm out there protesting at every demonstration against the war!'

'Here, here,' Resham shouted, waving a fist in the air. 'Let's drink to the protests!'

Zain retorted, 'Sure, but you're living on occupied land!'

Amina laughed, 'Excuse me? I'm living in Soho.'

Zain said theatrically, 'Yes but who did this belong to?'

Amina gave him a playful push, 'This apartment? The previous owner, you schmuck!'

Zain responded, 'A-huh, really?'

Amina groaned, 'Oh God, you're going to do the whole native American thing...how we shouldn't do the whole Turkey thing, etc...'

Zain began, 'Well...'

Amina interrupted him, 'Well, then next time I do Thanksgiving, I'll make sure I keep your sensibilities in mind!'

Zain grinned, 'Okay, someone pass me the Zinfandel...this is going to be a long night! Go ahead bring it on, talk to me about occupation, Zinn me!'

Yaqub came up to Amina, 'Quite a large group of friends you have here!'

Zain answered, 'She certainly does. It's the same bunch that we can be sure to find here on a regular basis, a group of would-be poets, revolutionaries and saints.'

Yaqub sounded interested, 'Really?'

Zain smiled at him benevolently, 'Well of course. What else do you expect of refugees? They're all the consequences of having their former residences getting in the way of trading routes and oil pipelines.'

Yaqub looked around him appreciatively. 'Is that what they are?'

Zain explained, 'Of course! Their day jobs are, as day jobs go: doctors, lawyers, engineers, traders and diplomats. That's what refugees are nowadays; don't let anyone tell you otherwise, my dear. All of them claiming America as a residence and homelands as Pakistan, India, Ireland, Russia, Italy, Lebanon, England, Sri Lanka, France, Lithuania, Bosnia, and Germany. New York must be the largest ever refugee camp in the world!'

Yaqub said, 'Ah, I see. I really had a completely different notion of refugees and refugee camps.'

Cupping his mouth, Zain whispered theatrically, 'And for your information, most of the people who are getting so heatedly involved in the political debate this evening about the elections and George W. Bush aren't even voters. They aren't citizens!'

Yaqub said, 'Well, that isn't surprising. That's usually the case, isn't it? That those who have the most to say don't even vote?

Anyway, I really should be going.'

Zain grabbed his arm, 'Stay: No really, stay. Tell us your notions. Stay for dinner and we're going to watch the Jon Stewart show about the RNC. You might as well watch it with us and be a part of this voyeuristic passive generation.'

'Jon Steward?' Yaqub asked.

'Stewart. Jon Stewart,' Zain explained. 'Yeah, he's a comedian.

He tells us the truth, that's what we're down to—truth is a joke in this country. We laugh about everything, war, lies, death! It's really fun. So stay! Laugh with us.'

Yaqub laughed and patted Zain on the shoulder appreciatively, 'I like your way of putting things. You are very perceptive.'

Zain said, 'Thank you. My perception is that you're a bit nervous.'

Yaqub was surprised. 'No, not nervous, just a bit out of place perhaps. I don't know anyone here.'

Zain said, 'Well you know Amina. And now you know me and Alejandro. Don't worry, I won't leave your side, you have nothing to worry about, you're with me, you need no other introduction. Drawing rooms, like border crossings, look more formidable than they really are. But you have nothing to worry,

I'm by your side.'

Yaqub laughed, 'Like border crossings! You're very poetic!'

Zain grinned and winked, 'I try! Stay for the show.'

Amina said, 'It'll be fun. Stay!'

Yaqub replied, 'Well thank you.'

Suddenly Shireen had started up a chant, 'Song, song, c'mon Resham, give us a song!' Almost everyone in the room took it up and Resham rose up like a reed from the pool of guests that she had been seated amongst on the floor. Shireen shouted, 'Sing Faiz, Resham, oh please sing one from Faiz Sahib.' The conversation died down and the room quietened down into a hush, save for the few coughs and giggles as Resham casually put her weight on her left leg, jutted out her hip, hooked her thumbs into the back pockets of her jeans and cleared her throat. She began humming in a deep, low tone which rose and fell as she warmed up. She tossed back her curly head of hair and shut her eyes. Someone shouted, 'C'mon Resham, get started. The convention will begin soon. Haven't got all night, mate!' Resham flipped her middle finger at him and grinned, masking her shyness with an air of bravado. Her eyes still shut, her eyelashes casting a shadow on her flushed cheekbones, she caught her flow by humming. Her shoulders moved as though navigating harmony and keeping time with the rhythm of her humming. Then she parted her lips and threw back her head and began singing. The sound was soulful as though she was getting ready to sing the blues, her tone rising and falling in half notes, her shoulders moving forward and back, keeping time and rhythm, she sang:

Jab dukh ki nadiya mein hum ne
(when in sorrows stream we had)
Jeevan ki na'o dali thi
(pushed out our boat of life)
Tha kitna kasbal bahon mein
(in our arms there was such strength)
Lahoo mein kitni lali thi
(in our blood there was such red)
Yon lagtha tha, do hath lagey
(it did seem that just with two strokes)
Or na'o pooram par lagi
(our boat would cross to the other shore)
Aisa na hoa
(but this did not come to pass)
Har gharey mein
(in each current)
Koch undeykihi manje dharein thein
(there were some unseen whirlpools of strife)
Koch manji tey unjan bohath
(and the boatmen untested green and inexperienced)
Koch bey parkhee pathwaren thein
(so were their oars)

Aab jo bhi chaho chaan karo
(now criticize as much as you want)
Abh jithney chaho dosh dharo
(now blame as much as you want)
Nadiya to vohee hai na'o vohee
(it's the same stream and the same boat)
Ab tom hee kaho kya karna hey
(now you tell us what is to be done)
Ab kesey par utharna hey
(now how do we get to the other side)
Jab apni chati mein hum ne
(when within our own breasts)
Is desh key ghao dehkey tey
(we saw the open wounds of this land)
Tha Vedon pey vishwas bohat
(we had such faith in its sages and medicine men)
Or yaad bohathsey nuskey tehey
(and memorized so many pages of cures)
Yoon lagta tha bus kuch din mein
(it seemed that in just a few days)
Sari bipta kat jaeey gee
(all these troubles would pass)
Or sab ghao bhur jaen gey
(and all the open wounds would be healed)
Aisey na hoa
(but it didn't come to pass like this)
Key rog apney kuch itney dehr pooraney tey
(because the ailments were so many and so old)
Ved on kee to ko pa na sakey
(the healers couldn't figure them out)
Or totkey saab bekar ga-ae
(and so remiss were all their cures)

Ab jo bhi chao chan karo
(now figure it out as you want)
Ab jithney chaho dosh dharo
(now blame as much as you want)
Chati to vohee hey
(it's the same breast)
Ghao vohee
(the same wound)
Ab tum hee kaho kya karna hey
(now you tell me what's to be done)
Yey ghao kesey bharna hey
(how do we fill these open wounds.)

The room burst into raucous clapping and whistling. 'More! More!' people shouted but Resham sat down, her eyes glistening with tears, she laughed. Shireen walked over to her and gave her a hug and kissed her on her head and whispered in her ear, 'Why so worried, kid? She's back home, na. It's all fine!' Resham nodded. A few days earlier they had all assembled here in Amina's apartment to meet their Meir Chacha and his son Emir. It could have been an uneventful occasion and only dramatic in that they were meeting such an important member of their family for the first time. But then Resham had taken issue with Israel's occupation of Palestine and with Emir on having served in the IDF. An argument had ensued. Emir, who hadn't said much at all, had suddenly fired back at Resham, 'How does the Pakistani army behave? And do you not have any family or relations in India? I believe your country has fought three wars with India and none with my country yet.'

Shireen had calmed Resham and Emir with, 'Welcome to the family Emir, there's never a dull moment. We are all great arguers and I see you are too!' Emir had replied, 'Well, as I understand

Resham, you and I are not blood relatives. Even if we were, you have no reason to meet me. I will go if that is better for you!'

Kulsum who had been quiet till then, had intervened, 'No, no, no!

I think we should all calm down!' Meir had smiled at her gratefully.

Shireen had gathered them together for a digital group photograph to send to Karachi and everyone except Emir had promised to stay in touch. The visit had lasted no more than two hours.

Amina had thought about inviting Emir, their new-found cousin with his startling blue eyes and jet black, curly head of hair.

Too bad he was a cousin, she had joked to an unamused Resham.

And then she had forgotten to phone him and it was too late when it finally occurred to her again. The guests continued to pour in. Amina stationed herself in the foyer for the first part of the evening, greeting people as they came in. She kissed everyone on both cheeks and from time to time, admired herself in the large, gilt mirror which stood almost floor to ceiling on one side of the room. People moved into her drawing room and arranged themselves on the carpet, the chairs and the black upholstered chaise longue, which obligingly seemed to show off all their outfits to perfection. The colours this evening seemed to resemble those of a wedding party in Delhi or Karachi. Zain chattered away with everyone while Yaqub looked on, taking in the scene.

Zain muttered to Yaqub, 'Angst alert!'

Yaqub looked confused, 'I beg your pardon?'

Zain said, 'Just watch and listen. Here we go, without this proverbial perennial angst, this crowd is totally lost.'

Yaqub asked. 'And please, what is that?'

Zain said, 'What is the angst they have?'

Yaqub said, 'No, I mean, what does angst mean?'

Zain looked quizzically at Yaqub.

Alejandro, 'I know what you mean. I never get these words either. But I think angst is just the state of anguish.'

'Oh I see, anguish!' Yaqub said gratefully. 'Thank you.'

Zain smiled kindly, 'Yes, angst. And the angst in this case is this conversation which is always present when we are gathered together, about how awful the place we've left is. The state of affairs, the martial law, the ruin of religion!'

'It seems sort of like the way older English ladies like to discuss the weather,' Yaqub offered.

Zain laughed appreciatively, 'Precisely. Well put. Pakistanis angst like the English discussing the weather. For a minute you had me going when you asked what angst meant. Like old English ladies talking about the weather—that's good! Or like we New Yorkers talking about subway breakdowns!'

In Amina's drawing room, the party was much like many nights before this one. Many years worth of nights before this it was the same old politics as conversation filler, much like the state of play in the weather: chatter about the state of the state of the stateless. White noise on all that was wrong in the country that had been left, the country that they refused to return to, but pined for.

With the consistency of white noise this was conversation that could be tapped into almost everywhere in the room each time the volume was lowered on the fusion music of Latino, Hindustani, Celtic and Algerian singers.

'It's about institutions!'

'What do you mean by institutions? The army is an institution! Is that what you want?'

'There can be no institutions in the absence of politics!'

'Of course there can be!'

'No, there can't be. It's over. Game over!'

'Oh please. Enough already!'

And in another corner, people were talking about the same old, same old: all about religion.

'Who decides what is our faith, what is it that we believe in?' asked a woman.

'Well, if you're a Muslim, what you must believe in is quite clear, with no ifs, buts and maybes!'

'Well, I'm on the first part of the syllogism: There is no god but God. I'm still on the first part that there is no god. I think I'll spend the rest of the years deciding on the last part.'

'Very clever and cute. But that's not good enough!'

'Well, I'm half a believer! That's got to count for something!'

'That's like being half pregnant. No such thing. No half believers either. That was not the message!'

'Message? Really? How fascinating! And you would have received the authentic message?' A squabble naturally ensued.

'What is the message? And what is important—the message or the messenger?'

'The message is in the comprehension of the receiver, not the initial deliverer.'

'What? The messenger is unimportant? The message is interpretable?' someone shouted.

'Please, no sermons! Haven't we heard enough on television tonight?'

Zain said to Yaqub, 'It seems to be a never-ending debate and we are all grateful for it, this conversation will continue. There is no end to it. This is our collective, group angst. And mercifully, there is plenty of champagne and that divine Buehler from Napa Valley!'

Someone lightened the mood with an observation on how neither Islam, nor poverty or revolution could be discussed with any gusto or robustness without the presence of emptied wine and champagne goblets, and copious amounts of Bombay style biryani and gulab jamuns, warmed in the microwave throughout the evening.

Amina said, 'Thank God for Kebab King in Queens. An easy trip on the N or the 7. The best part is that I have a fabulous system going. I can always get one of the regulars at the tea house across the street, one of the cab drivers, to pick up my order for me in his cab. These guys are so sweet.'

The guests munched, drank, talked, shouted and some danced. Occasionally yelps went up in unison and a few people feigned delight as someone not met in over a week walked in. 'I know! Our schedules are crazy! We keep crazy hours.'

Amina said, 'I'm never around! I mean, do we really live a block away from each other?'

'This is really unacceptable!'

Shireen lovingly looked across the room at her sisters' beautiful faces. She wished Kulsum could have come as well.

She thought about Sara and looked across at Yaqub talking to Zain. And in all this the night passed, the party moved from the living room cramming into the bedroom, where the oversized flat television on the wall beamed in analysis of the convention events, and related jokes and stories. The party moved back to the living room for more angst.

'A total failure of reason and rationality!' said a man with abundant white hair who smoked a cigar and was seated in a comfortable, leather upholstered chair and who was quickly identified as Ana's friend. He appeared to be holding court since at his feet and arranged around him were a group of some ten women and two or three men. He was a professor at a nearby university, Amina hadn't picked up on his name. The professor seemed to have absent-mindedly reached his hand towards Ana's head to stroke her golden hair. She must ask Ana what his name was. She looked at Ana, whose belly was beginning to show. Ana was lucky, Amina thought. She was doing what she wanted to do, have a child. She hadn't disclosed the identity of the father, but Amina was taking a guess. Resham came up to Amina and said, looking in Ana's direction, 'Yup, if you're thinking what I'm thinking, I'd have to say she's a lucky gal! But he's a dead bore if you ask me. Do we really need this bloody lecture?'

'She's assured herself good genes.'

'If not tenure,' Resham said dryly. Amina laughed.

'But he's a lucky man!' Amina replied.

'But a dead bore.'

After a sip of his caiparinia the professor continued, 'Failure of reason is a must for the justification of occupation of land and oil, and water.'

'And for the re-entry of God!' said Ana who was dressed in a sequined tank top tonight, and sat cross-legged leaning back against the professor's feet, like a very beautiful devotee.

Resham turned to Amina and rolled her eyes, 'Snore!' she whispered.

The professor said, 'Precisely. God (bless him!) has always flourished with the rise of mercantilism and adventurism. Humanness is suppressed in order to justify this control, and God has risen.'

'Ditto for this whole issue of identity!' another woman piped up.

'Indeed!' said the lovely professor with the hair. 'The prevalence of this thing called identity beyond being just human, and sharing the same blood plasma and DNA, is a necessary condition, a necessary dividing mechanism, for the occupation of land, division of land, control of freedom of movement, and control of other economically valuable resources.'

Ana said, 'Well, as Susan Sontag says, identity transcends universal values and DNA and is another form of extremism and fundamentalism.'

'Absolutely,' said the professor approvingly, stroking Ana's hair.

'And these polarizing, divisive positions of identity and religion are necessary conditions to justify the inequitable control and access to scarce resources. And to justify war. So in the Middle East for example, three resources are of great value. One of these that is in abundance, namely oil, is most valuable to outsiders. The other resources are scarcer and are more necessary to the region itself, and are land and water. The unquestionable control of resources, and the suppression of dissent, requires an asymmetrical notion of goodness and fairness which, of course, is religion. God.'

A woman listening enraptured said, 'You should have your own blog!'

'Ah blogs,' sighed the professor. 'Blogs are the new drugs, the LSD and the hashish and communes of this generation. It's escapism from the realities of war!'

Resham shouted, 'Makes sense!' and to Amina she whispered, 'God, what a dead bore! He should have a blog called Fuckingbore.com!' Amina giggled.

The professor was warming up to the subject and smiling appreciatively at his captive audience. 'The reason that an Israeli can justify the consumption of four times as much water as a Palestinian living incarcerated in the West Bank and Gaza is because God says so. The reason a Palestinian can be pushed off the land and incarcerated is because God promised it be so.'

Ana laughed, 'And the reason that a Texan can drive an SUV and say, "What is your sand doing on top of our oil" is because God blesses America and our way of life.'

'See how we've solved the most pressing problems, right here in this gracious home!' The professor looked around in search of his hostess, to whom he hadn't been introduced yet.

Zain said, 'As usual!'

The woman in the sequined dress commented cheerfully, 'The mark of a good party!'

The professor continued, 'And the reason why the rage on the other side gets crazier is because God wills it. The guys justifying their actions through God need the other side to go crazy through God too. Irrationality is a necessary condition to justify war and the continuous need for security and weapons. It's the only way to keep the order of things. Otherwise, the order of things, of control by a few, breaks down. The control of scarce and valuable resources in unjustifiably inequitable ways engenders the absolute necessity for an irrational discourse of justifications, which transcends reason, i.e., religion and identity, as we see in the speeches and dialogue of all concerned—a liberal peppering of God, evil, good, righteousness and an utter and complete disregard of reason and human sameness. Therefore, the abandoning of reason is fundamental to war, control and occupation.'

'Is irrationality predicated on the illusion of chaos?' asked a woman whose face glittered with her dyed and highlighted blonde hair and faux, dangling, diamond earrings.

Resham leaned over to Amina and whispered, 'What a fucking bore!' Resham mimicked her in a mincing, sweet voice. 'Is irrationality predicated on the illusion of chaos?'

Amina giggled and whispered back, 'Surely you have another sentence in you!'

Resham laughed, 'At the moment, none!'

Meanwhile the professor was saying, 'Chaos is a must for reason and rationality!'

Resham said, 'Okay, this is way too much for me to absorb!'

And in all this, the night passed and by this time with enough food and drink consumed, everyone was contently discontented and amiably convinced that they were all misunderstood, misfits and mavericks and just that much more special than those with whom they rubbed shoulders tonight. A World War was inevitable, fascism was on the rise. Everyone agreed cheerfully and dismally that the end was nigh.

Ana held up her glass of tomato juice to toast, 'We have entered into the age of women. No matter what's going on now, we can be sure that it is going to be a gentler kinder century.'

'Yes,' said the professor, his tone laced with sarcasm. 'We are told that is what feminine is. This notion alone should keep us occupied.'

Zain whispered to Yaqub 'God help us and not lead us to our own demise on either end of the spectrum, we are in the hands of Madams Clinton and Rice.'

Yaqub laughed, 'You're a poet!'

Amina walked around the room, filling people's glasses and serving hors-d'oeuvres. She noticed Yaqub rescue a glass that was sitting dangerously close to the edge of the marble table from its eminent tumble. Everyone seemed to be having a great time. But Amina felt uneasy. Most of the conversation this evening seemed to be about war and surveillance and yet people were celebrating. She was celebrating. And she was doing nothing to change anything, or to get involved with any protests in any meaningful way. Everyone was talking about what could be done. What was to be done? But no one was saying what they were doing. Except for wearing provocative T-shirts with slogans on them. Resham had her slogan on and another woman wore a 'Code Pink' shirt, someone had a Che Guevara shirt. What could be done? She didn't have any answers either. Pro bono work at the law firm for people who were fighting deportation—she did that. How soon before the cases coming in would be about illegal wire-tappings and surveillances? Would there even be such cases? She couldn't come up with any ideas that she could follow through with.

She could advise people. But could not do anything herself. She moved away and made her way to the other side of the room. If she peered into the sky through the living room window, there it was, that Fuji blimp that had been rented by Homeland Security, floating above them outside. Whirring and clicking, zooming in and cross-checking information. This too was added into the conversation, along with everything else. She shrugged her shoulders to shake off the pesky thought of being observed and spied on. She looked down on the street where cabs were parked for picking up their tea. Most of those guys were probably under so much stress, being from Pakistan.

She followed Rosario into the kitchen carrying a tray of empty wine and champagne goblets and flutes. Amina put down the tray on the granite counter and turned to Rosario, 'Don't forget to eat, huh?'

Rosario turned on the tap to wash out a few glasses. 'Don't worry Amina, I've been eating all night,' she said.

Amina replied, 'Yes, but eat properly now. There's haleem heating in the microwave. I'm going to have some now. Do you want some? There's no more coffee so add that to the list of groceries that you have to get tomorrow.'

Rosario turned off the tap. 'Amina thank you so much for this job!'

Amina grimaced dismissively, 'What do you mean? Thank you! You're such a big help to me!'

Rosario's tired face was filled with gladness and her large brown eyes overflowed with kindness. 'I know that you've hired me only because I asked you to when I came to clean your office at night.'

Amina said, 'Why else would I have hired you? You had to ask, no? You showed initiative. We like that in America. And you always brought me something good to eat on those late nights I was pulling. We also like that in America. We've all got to help each other out, no?'

Rosario replied, 'Yeah. Thanks so much! So many people, this is the biggest party you have had so far, no?'

Amina looked into the living room, 'Yes, I think so!'

Rosario said to her, 'Very nice people.'

Amina shrugged, 'Not bad.'

Rosario said, 'I like that man.'

Amina looked at her surprised, 'Who?'

Rosario smiled, 'The one who came too early, mango man.'

Amina laughed, 'Mango man. I like that! He's alright. Kind of serious and boring.'

Rosario asked, 'Is he married?'

Amina said, 'I'm not sure. But I think not.'

Rosario said, 'He would be a good husband.'

Amina laughed, 'Ah huh. And you know this because…'

Rosario said with a sly smile, 'I noticed how he was looking at you all night long.'

Amina said, 'Well forget about it. You may have noticed that I wasn't looking at him.'

Rosario replied, 'Okay. Your friends here, they have parties like you?'

'Yes, they do,' said Amina.

Rosario asked, 'Where do they get the food?'

Amina said, 'Probably same places I do. They cook, they get some things catered.'

Rosario asked, 'Catering from restaurants?'

Amina said, 'Yes, but some times there are people who cook the food for them.'

Rosario asked, 'Like a small business?'

Amina said, 'Yes, Rosario, exactly like a very small business.'

Rosario changed the subject and said, 'You know, you call me

Rosario but my neighbors call me Talibana!'

Amina said, 'What?'

Rosario said, 'Yes, they call me Talibana. Yesterday, when I walked into the beauty parlor, Melinda the owner called me a Talibana.'

Amina replied, 'I'm sorry, I don't get it. Why do they call you that?'

Rosario asked, 'Talibana? Because I am married to a Bangladeshi. Everyone in the neighborhood calls me a Talibana. Then her Chinese helper started calling me a Talibana too. I said, look, I don't call you a Cheunga, you better not call me a Talibana.'

Amina was perplexed, 'They probably say that affectionately.'

Rosario agreed, 'Well, yes. I know, but I don't like it, no?'

Amina agreed, 'No, of course not. Oh well. That's very sad.

But look at your beautiful earrings, they look very Pakistani, very desi to me.'

Rosario smiled proudly, 'Yes, my husband he buy with his first profit, for me from the gold jewelry shops in Jackson Heights.'

Amina asked, 'Did your friends in the neighborhood who call you a Talibana see them?'

Rosario laughed, 'Yes, they did.'

Amina asked, 'Any comments?'

Rosario laughed again and mimicked them, 'Your Taliban he love you very much. Yes I said, my Taliban he love me, no fight, no drink, no hit me. Yes, they say, you right. But he marry you for Green Card, no? No, I say, if he marry me for Green Card, why he stay now for more than six years with me? Why?'

Amina asked, 'What do they say to that?'

Rosario shrugged and made a face, 'Nothing. They can say nothing. I ask them, tell me where is your husband today? Nobody in the room saying nothing to me then. I know, because nobody have husband at home. All leave and go find another woman. Go find somebody else. But not my man. He work hard, night and day, for me and my children. He buy me things, he take care of us. He buy candy and hot dogs for children in the neighborhood.

He good man. Everybody know that.'

Amina said, 'I think everyone is just being affectionate to you.

They don't mean any harm.'

Rosario replied, 'I know, Amina, I know, but still some day we get out of that neighborhood, go live somewhere else. Someday he will own his own shop and then I'll see who will call me what.

And I will help him. Amina, I want to start my own business.'

Amina said, 'Sure, what do you want to do?'

Rosario said, 'I was thinking about catering. You have parties all the time and your friends too. I can supply the food.'

Amina said, 'That's a good idea. But you know many times I have biryani and haleem at my parties. But you can't start a business just with me as your client!'

Rosario said excitedly, 'Yes, I know, I can make food for all your friends and their friends when they have parties, no? I can make empanadas and other things for your party but I can also make haleem and biryani.'

Amina was surprised, 'You can?'

Rosario said, 'Yes. My husband, he teach me. I know. What I don't know, I can learn. You teach me.'

Amina laughed, 'Done. Okay, put everything down. Put down those dishes. Don't wash them now. Come eat. I can't teach you but I can ask my sister Kulsum to teach you. Okay?'

Rosario insisted, 'When?'

Amina said, 'Whenever you want.'

Rosario asked, 'Tomorrow?'

Amina laughed, 'No, not tomorrow Rosario, but this week. Okay? I'll have to talk to Kulsum first.'

Rosario was grateful, 'Thank you.'

Amina smiled, 'You are welcome, Talibana.'

A few minutes later out on the street, Yaqub stood at the curb, waiting for a cab. He watched the dump trucks on their rounds of the streets, the clanging and banging and ruckus of the men collecting garbage, who were swinging heavy bags and cans of trash over their heads and into the trucks, mixed with the occasional sounds of police car sirens. Beneath him, the ground rumbled and reverberated as a subway train passed underground.

Stray sheets of newspaper and brown bags flew about on the pavement and into the cobble stoned street, giving it a feel of desolation despite the din. He walked up to Houston Street where there was a steady stream of people on the sidewalks, coming in and out of the subway nearby, on their way to their night-shifts or coming out of cafés and nightclubs. The city seemed lonely at this time of the night though still awake, loud and active. Yaqub spotted an available cab and waved as it eased out of Crosby Street. Settled in for the long ride back to The Pierre Hotel in midtown, he shook his head and laughed to himself, 'These Americans!'

12

Citizen Amina

'BUSH lies. Thousands die! Bush lies! Thousands die! Get out of Najaf! Get out of Karbala!' Thousands of protesters chanted slogans as they marched up from Union Square up Broadway to 34th Street at Madison Square Garden where the Republican National Convention was underway, looped around it and then marched back to Union Square on 14th Street.

Amina stood watching the march as it returned to Union Square. She stood on the sidewalk where a Russian man was selling sunglasses. Nearby, a group of protesters distributed socialist manifestos. It was a beautiful, sunny, clear summer morning the day after Amina's successful party. Amina had stepped out for a walk and had made her way to Union Square from Soho. Amina had taken part in almost every protest march against the war in Iraq. More than a year ago, on a freezing February morning in 2003, 15 February to be exact, Amina and her sisters and one million other people had made their way slowly up the avenue on the East Side and then down again on First Avenue. They were going towards the UN building as the mercury continued to drop. It seemed like the job of the cops that day had been to discourage the marchers and to disperse the crowds, because almost every street leading into First Avenue had been barricaded by police who were not letting people through, unless they could prove that they lived on that block. The cops were on foot and, more menacingly, also on horseback. From time to time, the cops on horseback tried the tactic of charging into the dense, tightly-packed crowd. But that was a tactic that they quickly had to abandon—the crowd was too large to move and such a stunt would have only accomplished a stampede had it not been for the demonstrators warning each other. And the organizers telling the crowd over loudspeakers to hold their ground and to be aware of the possibility of a stampede. People stayed and waited it out, they were going to get seen and they were going to get counted. And Amina and her sisters had huddled together that day in winter's most savage month and stayed put like everyone else.

Helicopters belonging to the media and to the police whirred above. That day, people weren't going to be deterred, they were so determined and confident that they could stop the war by the sheer power and persuasion of their numbers out on the streets.

A sense of euphoric triumph, camaraderie and neighborliness seemed to catch the crowd as people looked around themselves and felt that they were part of a huge community; a slow mass movement of people whose sole purpose that day on 15 February 2003 was to be out there on the streets to stop a war. Out in the freezing cold, recruiting their bodies in sub-zero temperatures into the numbers trying to stop the unspeakable violence about to be unleashed in the world. It was on that day that Amina felt like a citizen, a citizen belonging with everyone on that street around her. She felt like a part of them and as the news came through of the numbers sitting in the streets all over the world in different time zones; as night approached in Europe and in Asia the march in New York was getting started. She was a citizen of the world—she didn't need a passport to identify her. She identified here, with these people. And they with her. The marchers could hear the loudspeaker announcements by the march organizers and the radio announcements from independent media broadcasters who were reporting that all around the world that day, more than fifteen million people had marched to protest the war. In Berlin, in Munich, in London, in Sidney, in Prague, in Budapest, in Sarajevo, in Karachi, in San Francisco, in LA, in Madrid, in Moscow and in hundreds of other places people were shouting no to war. 'NO to War!' No to a war which hadn't even begun yet, while in the UN building that day Colin Powell was acting out the embarrassing charade for a case for invading Iraq. Shireen and Kulsum had taken a train in from the suburbs.

They had said that the trains had been over-crowded with people coming in from all over the North East for the demonstration. Metro-North had added on more train services and the platforms at each stop along the way were crowded with demonstrators waiting to get on the trains coming into the city. Other people told them that it was the same story at Penn Station and at the bus station at Port Authority. Holland and Lincoln tunnels were clogged with buses loaded with demonstrators from all over the country who were making their way into the city. Having checked the weather report before leaving her house and thinking ahead to the day out on the streets, Shireen had put on a pair of ski boots and was wearing a fur coat and a hat, much to the envy of her sisters who hadn't planned on being barricaded for over six hours on the streets of New York by the police. Shireen had looked around her at the crowds huddled together and said warmly, 'Honestly, I needed this. I need this for myself. I need to prove to myself, I need proof from America that it gives a damn. That it feels something. Just look at all these people: grandmas, grandpas, kids, parents, sisters and brothers—everyone saying no to war!'

Resham was so exhilarated and excited she shouted out all the anti-war chants far too loudly and was now hoarse. 'I love this country! Just look around you, the streets have spoken, the streets say no to war! No war!' But the invasion of Iraq had happened anyway. The people in the streets had been ignored. The facts had been ignored.

Now here in late August 2004, a few months before the Presidential elections and more than a year after the invasion and occupation of Iraq had started, it was time to try to oust the warring President and his party from the White House. If Amina hadn't stepped into the crowd today, it was because she had lost hope. Demonstrations didn't stop anything and she was sick at heart after all the incessant and shrill hysteria for war in the newspapers and on television, and all the noise against Muslims and Arabs in the media every day. After all the numerous, heartbreaking arguments she had gotten into with people who she had thought would have thought differently about war and about religion. Amina had been most shocked when Stanley Owen, a guy that she had recently started dating, and who was a lawyer like herself, and who had seemed very caring and thoughtful had very casually pointed out that the Middle East needed civilizing and that embedded in the region's culture was a religion that preached violence. Amina had broken off the relationship immediately. That was about two weeks ago. It seemed as though that had been a relief to Stanley because they had increasingly been talking about nothing except politics, religion and war. Stanley had felt he was being lectured to and Amina had felt there was no way to have a conversation with someone who didn't even know the basic facts about history. No, Amina was not convinced that these demonstrations mattered.

They only created an illusion for the rest of the world that there were people in America who cared about them. Yes, the people in the marches cared, but that was a million at most and mainstream Americans probably did not identify with the hippies of yesteryears and the anarchists of today. In fact, Amina noticed that most of the people who were marching were white Americans. Immigrants were not here, and the African-American community was hardly present in the crowds. Yes, there was a spokesperson or two at the head of the march, but not in the march as ordinary people. Shireen had been wrong, this was not heartwarming and this was not going to make a damn difference. The 15 February 2003 march had not stopped the war. Watching the demonstration today, Amina felt that Americans cared too much about having large grocery stores where they could buy food in bulk, they cared too much about plasma TVs, humvees, cheap gas at pump stations and whether or not Britney Spears was having a baby. And perhaps so did she, after all, she had a huge party at her place last night when there was such an awful war going on.

Two protestors marched by carrying a billboard that read, 'War Criminals and War Mongers,' and listed, 'Kenneth Pollack, Donald Rumsfeld, Paul Wolfowitz, Douglas Feith, Richard Perle, Dick Cheney, George W. Bush, Condoleezza Rice, John Negroponte, Paul Bremmer, Colin Powell, Thomas Friedman, Alberto Gonzalez, John Ashcroft, John McCain, Billy Graham, Ted Haggard, Pat Robertson, Joe Lieberman, Jerry Falwell, Judith Miller, most if not all of the editors and journalists of the *New York Times*, the *Wall Street Journal*, *USA Today*, and almost every newspaper in the country, Christopher Hitchens, Bill O'Reilly, Dennis Miller, Daniel Pipes, Bernard Lewis. Another poster accused the American Physicians Association for having advised and condoned interrogations and torture. Amina wondered if they would ever be tried for their war-mongering? They had managed to defy the will of millions who had stood in the streets to protest against their lies. A few people had made the difference with an army of 140,000 volunteer soldiers, willingly joining up for the war. So then only a few people had counted and had mattered much more than the millions who had marched against them.

How was this possible? How could this be possible? Amina felt it was because the silent majority, those that didn't speak and didn't march one way or the other, were actually with the war mongers.

The shop windows with their displays of military fashions showed this, they reflected consumer sentiments. They weren't draped in peace signs. People were buying war.

As Amina watched the demonstrators that August morning a year after the war had begun, her heart was filled with confusing and conflicting thoughts of alienation and resentment towards the marches, but also with a sense of solidarity.

Amina's eyes filled with tears, she turned off her iPod and pushed her sunglasses off her face to the top of her head as 972 flag draped coffins made of cardboard were carried on the shoulders of the marchers, and then held aloft over their heads in a mock funeral procession. This was the public funeral that the 972 dead soldiers so far in the war on Iraq had never gotten. An expanse of coffins stretched across two New York blocks. People clapped and cheered. Amina's hand went to her heart. Her hand gently beat time on her chest in rhythm with the chants, just as she would have done in Moharram in Karachi when the tabooths, the mock coffins of martyrs at Karbala, went by. In her other hand she held a copy of the American Constitution, a pamphlet passed out by a human rights group protesting in this demonstration. 'Know your rights!' they had shouted. She wanted to somehow feel resentment towards the coffins, draped in the American flag, and she wanted to shout out to the marchers, 'What about the coffins of all those people, men, women and children, who these soldiers had killed?' But she could not. She didn't have the heart for it. It was stupid, and she knew it.

'Fuckin' tragedy! All of it!' a gruff male voice that was oddly familiar said to no one in particular.

'Yeah,' she nodded without looking back.

She watched the last of the marchers make their way to Union Square and thought about making her own way back to her apartment. The Fuji blimp that was being used by the FBI for surveillance hovered overhead. A few cops appeared around her.

One smiled at her as she wiped her eyes. Then there seemed to be a sudden movement of people around her, shouting and protesting, and before she could turn around to see what was going on, a giant, orange net trapped her like an insect, and she found herself wrapped in plastic mesh with dozens of others. The police were cordoning off the socialist group that she had been standing next to. The socialist group, their manifestos, Amina, her iPod, her cellphone, her handbag and the constitution she was clutching in her fist were wrapped up in orange mesh.

This couldn't be happening Amina thought. No, this could not be happening. 'Hey,' she shouted to the cops, struggling with the guy who was trying to drag her to a police bus. 'Let us go!

This is America! This is our right! Freedom of speech, freedom of movement, freedom to protest, to congregate! What the hell are you doing?' But her voice was drowned by the protests of all the others caught with her and not a single coherent voice could be heard. Everyone had their own, separate rage against the cops.

'Move on! You're blocking the sidewalk, you don't have a permit to demonstrate. You're under arrest,' she heard a cop shouting on a megaphone.

Amina realized that what was meant to have been a lovely morning in the summer sun was going to end up as a nightmare. Ahead was a long night at a makeshift holding center for the arrested demonstrators in a cold and dimly lit three-storeyed, cavernous building, which was a former bus garage at Pier 57 on the Hudson River across from the Westside Highway. The cops were using this as the holding center before those who had been arrested would be taken for processing at the Central Booking at 100 Central Street. Amina waited to enter the building and, like everyone else in line, had her hands behind her back, handcuffed with transparent plastic handcuffs. Cops kept shouting, 'Keep moving! Stop! Spread your legs, keep your hands behind your back!' When Amina's turn came to register, she gave them her name and her address and her driver's license. Thank God she was a citizen, she thought, thank God she was there with hundreds of other people, otherwise this could be a real nightmare. She thought about all the men incarcerated secretly and not so secretly for being from Pakistan, or for being Muslim or being Arab, even though they were American citizens. Fingerprinted, photographed. I-D'd. Disappeared and missing. Then the cop asked her if she was an American citizen.

They hadn't asked the kid with the hair dyed orange and purple and a metal stud pierced in her lip who was in line right in front of her whether she was American or not. Amina was upset, as a lawyer she knew that the cop was out of line asking her this, but she thought better not to point this out. She remained silent. The purple haired girl turned around and said, 'You can't ask her that. That's against the law! Know your law, know your rights.' Amina smiled at her gratefully and said to the cops, 'You know you guys are going to be in a whole lot of trouble on all kinds of charges, for the targeting and surveillance of innocent people, the crackdown on criticism and dissent, the unfair questioning and unlawful detention and treatment of persons held by the United States in detention facilities…' She was interrupted by the cop, 'Can it, lady and keep moving!' Amina moved on and shouted back, 'Hey, only doing my duty. If you see something, say something, right?' Around her people cheered and clapped. Amina had repeated the slogan on the ubiquitous posters put up by Homeland Security all over the city as a citizen's self-surveillance measure. Amina pulled out her cellphone and called her friend Fatima and left her a voicemail. 'Hey, come down to Pier 57 and start doing your thing. Lots of civil liberties being violated right now. In case you want to know where I am, I've been arrested while standing on the sidewalk watching the demonstration go by at Union Square. I'd say there are about a thousand people in here who've been arrested so far. Probably a lot more coming. Call me!'

Then she called Tim and left him a similar message. She moved around the crowd giving people Tim and Fatima's phone numbers.

Along with hundreds of other frightened and irate detainees, she stood around in the crowded holding pen and when she finally got tired, she sat on the bare cement floor still marked with yellow lines to indicate parking spots for buses. The floor was spotted with bus diesel and oil and the air still smelled of chemical fumes. Like many others she had managed to take off the plastic handcuffs, while some still had them on. The heat and the smell were making her eyes itch. She looked around her and saw old signs from the days when this place was a repair facility for buses. There were signs that sounded like chemical formulae, and in fact, some signs said, 'Chemical Storage Area'. No wonder her eyes were itching. She was getting scared.

It was hard to imagine that right outside this makeshift prison was a boisterous, noisy, fast moving city on a bright crisp sunny day at the end of August. She watched the detainees, most of whom were in T-shirts and shorts and in sneakers or sandals. Like her, they were shocked, angry and frustrated for having been hauled in while they were simply walking by, or were watching the demonstration from the sidewalks. Others seemed to be living their expectations for the day by having been arrested; some held on to the protest signs and the labels of their organizations that they had carried in the March, 'United for Peace and Justice', 'War is not the Answer', 'Code Pink' and 'Still We Rise'. Some were having a good time, continuing with the party atmosphere of the demonstrations, confident that they would be out soon enough, while others looked tearful and frightened. Most of them were very young. Some who had managed to keep their cellphones, like Amina, were on the phone with their parents or friends, telling them excitedly about being arrested and talking about the police state, Guantanamo Bay and Abu Ghraib. Amina had been frightened by the arrest but the camaraderie inside the warehouse was making her less anxious. Amina had seized on this as an opportunity to reconnect with Stanley. He had answered his phone after the first ring and she had told him giddily that she was in trouble and had been arrested at the demonstration. She had told him where the warehouse was.

She had asked him to come over and get her out. There had been a silence on the other end and finally Stanley had said, 'I think you should call one of your own people, call your sisters. I can't help you.' Stanley had hung up. Amina had been so ashamed of her phone call that she hadn't been able to bring herself to call her sisters till another two hours had passed and it didn't seem like the police were about to let the detainees go. She called Resham and got her voicemail. Next she called Shireen who answered instantly.

They could barely hear each other, on either end of the line there was so much noise from the crowds of people. Shireen and her husband had been in the protest march and were now making their way back to Grand Central station to catch a train to go home.

Amina told her what had happened. Shireen said she would come to the Pier immediately. About twenty minutes later Resham called Amina. Shireen had called her and gotten through. She was on her way as well. Kulsum was very upset and was going to drive in with her husband as soon as she had arranged for a babysitter. 'Don't use up the cellphone, Amina!' Resham had said, her voice strained with panic. 'Let's plan to call you in about another hour, okay? Turn off your phone till then. Shireen and I will call you in an hour, turn on your phone in an hour.' Amina did as she was told, she was relieved that she was working according to a plan that Resham was putting into place. Shireen and Resham would get her out. Thank God her citizenship had come through just four days ago! Otherwise, this could be a real mess. She could have jeopardized her citizenship if this had happened a week ago! She shuddered. She was sure she was going to be okay. She leaned against the wall and looked around her at the now despondent faces—the excitement had died down and people were beginning to look scared. Amina told herself that it would all work out and she would just have to wait patiently.

Night passed and Amina chatted with her fellow detainees. She felt a sense of kinship with her fellow prisoners but then she caught sight of a woman wearing a T-shirt that said, 'My cunt could do a better job than Dick Cheney.' Next to her was another woman who was completely naked and had a 'No War' slogan painted on her body—'Make Love Not War.' Amina felt a sense of revulsion and walked up to them and asked the woman with the T-shirt, 'Do you think demeaning yourself this way in public is going to change anything, or do you think it simply strengthens the resolve of people who think all of us in here are weirdos?' The woman looked at Amina and said, 'Aren't you in the wrong place? The RNC is a few blocks down, baby!' They laughed. Amina said, 'Lemme ask you, do you think your doing this, your being naked, and your wearing this T-shirt, is for the Iraqis or is it just for yourself? Because I can assume that very few people in this country or that country can identify with you. What you're doing is making sure that you confuse the message on real serious issues like people dying with your own selfish need to be sensational and get noticed!'

Amina moved away before the women could answer but she heard a 'Go screw yourself, cunt. Fucking Republican.' Amina shook her head, 'Here's a prediction—the guy is going to win again. People like you make people like him win again and again!' She thought of the time a few months after 11 September 2001 when she was returning from a business trip to Dubai and had been detained at JFK airport. The immigration officers had asked her to step into a room where there were several other people, mostly men from South Asia and the Middle East who had gotten off the same flight she had been on. The officers wanted to know why she had gone on the trip, they wanted evidence of her being a lawyer and, most importantly, they wanted to know why she had also visited

Karachi on the same trip. She had been frightened and instead of the usual anger that she would have shown in such circumstances, she had shown them her laptop and files in it. She had shown them her business papers and cards. She had answered their questions in detail, she had called her voicemail at work for them to hear her messages on her office answering machine.

They had let her go after an hour. But as she left, she couldn't stop herself from turning round and saying sarcastically, 'Next time I'll wear a shirt that says, 'Flying while Muslim'. Everyone waiting along with her in the room had laughed. She was still shaking with nervousness when she picked up her luggage which had been stacked on the side of the now empty arrival area. She was unsure whether she was still under surveillance, and if it would remain that way. She had taken a cab home and told the Pakistani cabbie what had happened. He had sympathized and told her a few more stories similar to hers. Now, here she was, almost two years later, at the end of summer, detained inside an abandoned bus garage, contained within the city that was her home. Borders were shifting, now she was detained with mostly white American teenagers and who appeared to be well-off middle class kids, or even trust funded by rich parents. Discrimination, it seemed, was progressively becoming less discriminating. No longer defined by race and religion but rather by politics and thoughts. Think differently from us? Think again! Protest against us and we will imprison you! A dictatorship seemed to be warming up and getting underway in a bus garage in Manhattan.

Shireen and Resham called her in exactly one hour, the phone rang as soon as she turned it on. They were outside the Pier, across the street on Westside Highway. The police had cordoned off the area and, unless they wanted to get arrested, they had to stay put. That's what one of the cops had said to them. He had looked at Resham and said, 'What's a nice girl like you doing here in this crowd?' And Resham said, 'Trying to be better.' The cop had laughed and said, 'I hear you. Boy, do I hear you! See that thing up there?' He pointed to the Blimp. 'It's taking pictures right now and the heck if I know what they're going to do with them.

Do you know that's not the NYPD? It's Homeland Security and something called Total Information Awareness! It's a whole new ball game!Totally different from anything we did before. They're calling all the shots here. We're the nice guys. I've been on my feet for the last 36 hours ladies, and I've had it with locking up New Yorkers!' Shireen had replied coldly, 'Then don't lock them up, do your job and uphold the constitution!' Shireen repeated what Amina had told her. She had said, 'If you see something, say something.' The cop had laughed, he shook his head and said, 'I hear you! Lady, didn't you hear me. Didn't I just tell you something that I see?'

The jailers called out Amina's name at about 10 a.m. the next morning—Ameena Roeweella. She walked over to the door and got into the bus. They were going to the Criminal Courthouse at 100 Center Street. Amina could never have imagined this for herself. Years of living diligently and abiding by the law, paying bills on time, before time, now four days after becoming a citizen she was about to be booked for standing on the sidewalk! She turned on her cellphone and let her sisters know.

At the Courthouse, Amina answered every question just as she had done at the airport, she filled out forms, got fingerprinted, had her photograph taken. She was told that she had been uncooperative for not letting her arresting officer know that she was an American citizen when he had asked her. 'What difference would that have made?' she asked, tears rolling down her face. 'We've got enough complications on our hands without your needing to be a smart ass!' came the curt response. And then, more gently, 'You're helping the terrorists when you don't give us straight answers lady. You're clogging up the system, making it harder than it has to be! You're stopping us from doing our job.'

Amina asked frostily, 'Which is?'

'To protect you!' Amina stared at the court-worker in disbelief. She was too exhausted, too itchy, and too frightened to argue. And with that, Amina walked out into the summer sun with hundreds of twenty-something protestors. She had been let out. There weren't any charges. Her head ached from the smell of oil, diesel and chemical fumes. She was free. Her sisters, Amit and Faraz were waiting for her across the street.

13

That Sara Aziz!

AMINA was seated at a sidewalk café, sipping her latte with magazines scattered on the table in front of her, text messaging on her cellphone. It was a crisp, clear September morning. In a high-rise building on Wall Street, Resham sat at her desk, pushed back her hair from falling into her eyes and peered into the screen in front of her as she emailed. In the suburbs of Westchester County, their sister Kulsum was in her kitchen contemplating her chores for the day ahead. She was in her late thirties and was the mother of two small girls. Kulsum was considered by her sisters as someone who was wise, quiet and conservative and who had a misplaced, strong hankering for home, more specifically, for 43-G, for a loyalty to tradition. She wore her long hair in a single, thick braid down her back and preferred to wear shalwar kameezes as often as she could. Kulsum was still at the stage in her life where she wished for the luxuries back home in Karachi. Her sister Shireen had passed that stage and had transitioned into a soccer mom who was concerned about where her kids would go to college. Seated behind the wheel in her mini-van hybrid SUV, Shireen had recently discovered success as a real estate agent. She was the second eldest after Sara and was rosy cheeked, plump and good humored. Shireen was married and was the mother of two teenagers and blended in with trolley-pushing home-makers in sweats and sneakers, in suburbia's supermarkets. Shireen sat in her car; stuck in traffic on the Triboro Bridge, and was attached to her cellphone via an earphone.

Kulsum in her kitchen was mixing coriander, gram flour, salt, chili, pepper, cumin and onions into a batter in a blue colored bowl.

She finished mixing the batter, washed her hands, and stood looking out of the window, drumming her fingers on the kitchen counter. She went to pick up the cordless phone, dialed a number and went over to the stove and turned on one of the burners when the phone rang. Then she reached in the cabinet for a frying pan. Resham reached for the phone on her desk as it rang.

Kulsum: Hi Resham, are you very busy?

Resham: Hello, my dear! Never too busy to talk to you. What's up?

Kulsum: Oh nothing much, the usual. You know. It's so quiet now that all the in-laws have gone home. It's amazing how quickly the summer has gone. Faraz is off on a business trip to California, and will be back next week. The kids are out with the nanny. So finally, I have a moment to myself.

Resham: Well, I hope you're taking it easy. Don't do anything. Just sit back and relax.

Kulsum: Yes, relax, that's a good idea. No, yaar they're all very nice, they helped out and everything. Everyone realizes this is not back home; you have to do things yourself over here. They are good sports, they said they actually had fun cooking-shooking, cleaning-sheening.

Resham: Still, yaar, so many people, just relax.

Kulsum: Noooo. Oh, what so many people? If we were back

home, I'd be living with them, no? So once in a while if they come over, I like it very much…

Resham: You don't always have to be such a goodie-goodie.

Kulsum: I'm not being a goodie-goodie, I mean it. It's so quiet now that they're gone, no one to talk to, no one to eat with. I mean, it's just so different here alone. The kids are missing everyone too. You know, the grandparents and the uncles and aunts...

Resham: Well, you're going to Lahore for the winter holidays… Anyway, how are the little favorite munchkins of mine?

Kulsum: Fine, just beginning to sound a bit too American for my liking. At three and five, it's becoming why mom this, and why mom that, on everything! And whining about everything.

Resham: Well, that's going to happen, they were born here. Though try to keep the attitude to a minimum.

Kulsum: I keep telling Faraz we should go back. We have two daughters, I mean, I don't want to raise them here. We should go back for a couple of years.

Resham: You're sounding like a total jaahil. What are you trying to say anyway?

Kulsum: Don't get me wrong. I want them to do all the things, get educated, work, everything, but growing up here, I feel worried.

Resham: What are you worried about, for God's sake?

Kulsum: I mean they are growing up alone, no relatives, no idea of sharing, and no values.

Resham: That's bull, they'll have your values and whatever else you want to teach them.

Kulsum: I can't teach them everything. The culture…

Resham: Trust me on this one, whatever you don't teach them, they don't need to learn.

Kulsum: I don't know yaar, I'm beginning to worry.

Resham: You have nothing to worry about.

Kulsum: No honestly, yaar. Look, we weren't raised here. I want them to have our upbringing!

Resham: I know. I know what you mean.

Kulsum: I don't want them to lose out on that. That's all. Listen, why don't you come over? Yaar, it's been weeks since we've gotten together, shouldn't we all get together? Why not come over for dinner?

Resham: Tonight?

Kulsum: Yes, tonight. Just catch the train and I'll pick you up at the station. Why don't you take the 7.05, it'll get you here at about 7.45. I'll meet you at the station. I'll cook biryani and there's tons of haleem and kebabs in the freezer.

Resham: Can't tonight, how about tomorrow?

Kulsum: (Sighs) Fine.

Resham: Don't sound so sad! We'll do dinner tomorrow. Kulsum, what's wrong?

Kulsum: Nothing's wrong.

Resham: Then why the deep sigh?

Kulsum: It's just so quiet here.

Resham: You're just having the post 'guests-from-back-home' blues.

Kulsum: Guess so.

Resham: You're not still depressed about Bari-ma, are you? I mean, she's back home now.

Kulsum: No, I'm not. But still I can't help worry.

Resham: Worry about what? Nothing to worry about. They all sound so cheerful whenever we call. So nothing to worry about. We always make a big deal about every small hiccup back home. And they move on and forget about it, meanwhile we're stuck worrying. Anyway, we'll talk up a storm tomorrow night, and I'll stay over, go straight to work from your place, okay?

Kulsum sighed: Sounds good! Tomorrow is fine.

Resham: Great. Stop sighing.

Kulsum: Let's ask Amina and Shireen too.

Resham: Okay.

Kulsum: Hold on, let me get Amina. Amina?

Amina: Hi Kulsum!

Resham: Hi, I'm here too.

Amina: Oh hi, Resham. Whatup?

Kulsum: Oh please Amina, just because you were arrested doesn't mean that you should start talking like a hoodlum.

Amina: Oh sorry dear, adaab, how are you? Is that okay for your newly acquired Lahori sensibilities?

Kulsum: Yes, much better. Now you're reflecting your Karachi background.

Amina: Hey Kulsum, before I forget, can you teach Rosario, my housekeeper, to cook biryani, haleem, chicken karahi, karri and kebabs, your style?

Kulsum: Sure. Why, are you hiring her to cook as well?

Amina: No, she wants to get into the catering business for us desis.

Kulsum: Won't be easy to get into that market.

Amina: Yeah, but we can help out.

Kulsum: Okay, well I'll teach her everything. When does she want to start? Tell her just to come over to my place. Take the train, I'll pick her up at the station.

Amina: Thanks Kulsum, you're such a sweetheart. Okay, she'll probably come tomorrow. So what's up. What's going on?

Kulsum: Dinner. Tomorrow night dinner at my place.

Amina: Sorry, Kulsum, I can't. How about the day after?

Kulsum: Another quick trip?

Amina: No, I'm meeting Zain and Alejandro for dinner tomorrow night.

Resham: What about that guy who was at your party? The

one that Riaz and Sara sent over for you to meet?

Amina: What about him?

Kulsum: Why aren't you having dinner with him?

Amina: Excuse me?

Kulsum: I heard from Resham and Shireen that he was rather nice.

Amina: He was nice. That's it. He wasn't sent over to meet me. He was delivering a package from Sara. Beautiful clothes she's made for me. Absolutely stunning shalwar, kameez. Anyway, when he called I just invited him over that night for my party.

Kulsum: So, wasn't he a possibility?

Amina: No. And he's gone back to Karachi.

Kulsum: Too bad.

Amina: You're out of control. He's just a rich guy, a total upstart from Karachi. Shipping and real estate and God only knows what.

He needed some advice on legal issues on real estate. Offered me a job in Karachi.

Kulsum: A job? Not marriage?

Amina: Paleeese! I can't even imagine it.

Kulsum: Why not?

Amina: Not every single male that I remotely mention having come into contact with is marriage material, Kulsum! For heaven's sake!

Kulsum: Why not?

Resham: You have to admire her persistence. Kulsum, you're incorrigible.

Kulsum: Girls, I'm only being ambitious, aggressive and strategic. Isn't that what the two of you are always talking about?

Resham: Yeah, but about mergers, stocks, acquisitions.

Kulsum: So you get my point. Try using some of that for this.

Resham: Good one!

Amina: Point well taken. By the way, we're not girls. And he was not a boy. This guy was grey, wimpy, nervous and totally uncool.

Wore a brown tie with a tie-pin. And a designer suit. Ew, ew, ew!

A tie pin, for God's sake! And that awful brown tie with diagonal dark brown stripes. If he'd made a pass at me, I swear I'd have passed out with revulsion!

Resham: Don't be so cruel! He looked very nice to me.

Amina: Sure, whatever! I'm not cruel, just honest. That's what I am, Resham. Honest.

Kulsum: Okay, so no proposal once again.

Resham: Well, a job offer isn't bad… For what?

Amina: Some restoration thing, to head a foundation that would raise funds to set up a museum and library. The guy is into distribution, ships, trucks, storage space, real estate.

Kulsum: It sounds worthwhile. A worthy cause. Could be just the thing for you.

Amina: I'm not going to have second thoughts about him Kulsum, if that's what you're thinking.

Kulsum: No, honestly, an opportunity like this might be just what you need.

Amina: No way.

Resham: Well, think about it at least.

Amina: What's the matter with you guys…?

Kulsum: You're the one who's tired of corporate mergers. This could be your great sabbatical back to Pakistan.

Amina: Okay, case closed. Can we discuss dinner?

Kulsum: Okay, well then the day after tomorrow we'll meet.

Resham: Fine by me.

Kulsum: Okay.

Resham: Kulsum, should I get Shireen on the line.

Kulsum: Would you? Thanks.

Shireen: Hello!

Resham, Amina and Kulsum: Hi Shireen.

Shireen: Oh good, my favorite three, what's up?

Kulsum: Dinner day after tomorrow, my place, Kulsum and Amina can make it.

Shireen: Darlings! I'd love to. But what to do, can't, it's my group meeting, we're doing posters for the march on Sunday. But my yoga class got cancelled for tonight. So I'm free tonight or tomorrow.

Resham: Can't. I have a blind date tonight.

Amina: Can't tomorrow night, I have my book group and then I have to rush for my tango class.

Kulsum: C'mon yaars, can't we ever get together?

Resham: Next week is all clear for me.

Amina: Can do Tuesday next week.

Shireen: Me too.

Resham: Me three.

Kulsum: So dinner next week Tuesday for all of us, we're on, my place. But Resham, you're coming over tomorrow, too.

Resham: Done. Ciao. Maniyana.

Amina: Adios.

Shireen: By the way, are you all going to the protest on Sunday?

Kulsum: No way. They say that the authorities are going to be very harsh with the protestors and especially people like us. So I'm going to stay put. And so should you!

Shireen: People like us? What's that supposed to mean? We're American, it's our right!

Kulsum: Pakistani-American. And we're Muslim. So be very careful Shireen.

Amina: I'm not so sure after what happened to me just a few days ago.

Kulsum: Protests don't achieve anything. Didn't stop the war in Iraq, did you? And protest marches and demonstrations only makes them look good. It gives them a façade of freedom like there is really democracy here.

Shireen: Ooof Kulsum, I can't even get started on this right now, I simply cannot.

Resham: Ummm, I think I agree with Kulsum.

Shireen: Well I'm going. We can't lose hope like this. Bye for now.

Kulsum: Khudahafiz.

Resham turned to her computer and began reading her emails. As she read her emails, she said, 'Fuck! I can't believe it! What the hell? This is unbelievable. She's really done it this time, the dumb ditz!' She picked up the phone and punched in the numbers. The phone rang and Kulsum took the frying pan off the fire and went to pick up the phone and walked back to the stove.

Kulsum: Hello. Siddiqi residence.

Resham: It's me again.

Kulsum: Look Resham, I don't want to hear of any change of plans and scheduling conflicts about how you can't come over tomorrow!

Resham: No, not to worry, that's not why I'm calling. Guess what? You are not going to believe this!

Kulsum: He asked you and you're getting married.

Resham: What? Don't you ever have anything else on your mind?

Kulsum: No, not where you're concerned, no. What else am I supposed to think about?

Resham: Anyway, before you really get me angry, do you want to know what I called you for?

Kulsum: What? Tell me, I hope it's good gossip.

Resham: Oh yeah, oooh yeah, this is a good one. And it ain't gossip.

Kulsum: Okay yaar, I can't take the suspense.

Resham: Guess what dear Sara is doing?

Kulsum: She's moved on to pulling down the entire house?

Resham: Oh no, much better than that. Much, much better. She's really done it this time. Are you ready?

Kulsum: Do I have to sit down for this, because I'm doing dangerous work right now, I don't want to hurt myself with the shock.

Resham: Yeah, sit down. Are you ready? Dear, stupid, hypocritical, dizzy Sara has gone into…

Kulsum: Labor, coma, business with the drug mafia, exile, convulsions, what, what?

Resham: Hijab.

Kulsum: What?

Resham: Hijab.

Kulsum: What?

Resham: Exactly.

Kulsum: What? Where did you get that?

Resham: Just got an email from Tehmina who saw her at a party last night. Dear, dear Sara, our own flesh and blood, walked in covered in a hijab. And Tehmina said that she hadn't believed it either when people had told her because a lot of women had seen her around, you know picking up the kids at Grammar School, etc., but last night at the fund-raiser for the Heart Center, there she was, in hijab! Tehmina wanted to know if I could explain my sister's transformation.

Kulsum: So what?

Resham: What do you mean, so what? It's ridiculous!

Kulsum: But many girls wear hijabs here, don't they? And in France and Germany and England.

Resham: Yes, here. But not Pakistan, it's not our thing! It's not our culture. I mean, it doesn't go with what we wear! It's western, for God's sake!

Kulsum: Malaysian and Indonesian women wear it.

Resham: For God's sake, they're western, compared to us.

Kulsum: You're losing it.

Resham: You're being stupid, and you know it.

Kulsum: Well, you're just being silly.

Resham: We're talking Sara here.

Kulsum: So many other women in Pakistan are doing this now.

Resham: She's not them!

Kulsum: Look Resham, women need to wear the hijab because they're going out more and more to find jobs, working in offices, factories, and are taking public transportation. It's just a way of security for them and acceptance of their stepping out in the domain of men. Oh wait, I have another call coming in. Hello, haan, Amina, I've got Resham on the line; you are not going to believe what she just told me. Hang-up, I'll call you right back.

Resham, are you there?

Resham: Yes.

Kulsum: I'm going to get Amina on the phone with us. Hold on. Amina?

Amina: Hi!

Resham: Hi again, Amina!

Amina: Hi Resham!

Resham: Where are you?

Amina: Bus yaar, finally an afternoon off! I decided to just take in the sun. I've had it with the deposition work, I hate the hours, I hate my bosses, I hate being on the partner track, I want to drop this whole thing, I'm telling you, it's just too much. I just got back from bloody Tokyo over the weekend only to find out I had to go for a one-day meeting to London, I just got back last night. I cannot understand why these things cannot be done through teleconferencing, I mean, it's totally ridiculous. Okay, so one does chalk up the frequent flier miles, but frankly, one doesn't need them. A: because one can never take a vacation and B: because one has enough money to buy one's own tickets, thank you very much. And C: again, because one never has the time to take vacations anyway! Then the first thing that happens this morning is that my client tells me he's having a panic attack, can't go through with the damn merger, and I'm saying go take a Prozac, calm down, do yoga, whatever, but I am not going to listen to not going through with the merger after I've sacrificed six months of my days and nights, slaving over the bloody price earning ratios parity bullshit. I'm really thinking about…

Resham: Join dating.com.

Amina: What?

Kulsum: What?

Resham: Dating.com. My blind date tonight, that's where he's from. I'm telling you, it's the best thing.

Kulsum: You're going to get killed by an axe-murderer!

Amina: She's right, Resham.

Resham: Calm down! It's totally the thing. Since you're doing the 'whatup' thing, you might as well do the dating.com thing as well.

Amina: Seriously Resham…Call me as soon as you get home tonight just to let me know you got in safely.

Kulsum: Amina, shut up. Acha, shut up, we've got news for you.

Amina: (bored) What?

Resham: You're going to love it.

Amina: What?

Kulsum: Sara was sighted last night at a charity ball in Karachi.

Amina: So? So what's the big deal. I thought news would be if Sara wasn't sighted at a charity ball in Karachi. Sort of like man bites dog.

Kulsum: In a hijab.

Amina: Excuse me?

Resham: Sighted at the ball in a HIJAB!

Amina: I'm assuming it was a fancy dress ball and she was going as the Saudi Princess off to have her head chopped off, or the love interest of Mullah Omar.

Resham: Good, very good. That was funny.

Amina: What the hell is she doing in a hijab?

Resham: This is just too good, let's get Shireen on the line. Hold on, everyone. Resham dialed the number.

Shireen: Hello.

Resham: Hi Shireen, I've got Amina and Kulsum on the line as well.

Kulsum: Hi!

Amina: Hi!

Shireen: Hi, hi! Traffic is hell on the Triboro.

Resham: What the hell are you doing on the Triboro at this time?

Shireen: Trying to get home to pick up the kids, yaar, had a property I was showing in mid-town. Why the hell did I get into the real estate business? I'm going crazy with the driving and the traffic.

Resham: Well a good girl from our family should definitely be dabbling in property.

Shireen: Of course, it's in the blood, my dear. It's in the blood. Acha Resham, are you still interested in that loft in Tribeca, because you really need to let me know pretty soon.

Resham: Next week for sure, okay?

Shireen: Is that a pukka okay?

Resham: Yes, okay, next week, definitely.

Shireen: Fine.

Amina: How's the real estate market doing?

Shireen: You tell me! You guys are the ones on Wall Street! I don't get it. It seems like people are just made of money, they don't know what to do with it. I just showed someone a place on West 72nd which can only be referred to as a walk-in closet, and the guy is putting down 750 for it. What is going on?

Resham: What can I say, it's the stock market. It's the about-toblow. com. It's crazy and it's about to blow.

Kulsum: You say that every day Resham. It hasn't blown yet.

Shireen: Well, until it blows I'm sure making beautiful commissions and that's fine for me, baba. It's going to put the kids through college, yaar. So don't say stuff that's going to jinx things, or get the gods upset.

Amina: Shireen, we've got some juicy stuff for you.

Shireen: Prada has a new design out in shoes in your neighborhood?

Amina: Well, not as good as that.

Resham: Well, almost as good.

Shireen: Dirt?

Amina: Oh yeah!

Resham: Second that motion.

Shireen: It better be good dirt.

Resham: Oh yeah, babe, like how!

Kulsum: Well, it isn't dirt.

Amina: Oh yeah it is, it's about Sara, not Mother Teresa.

Shireen: She's not marrying again! I can't take that. I don't think any of us can.

Resham: Nope.

Amina: That's not dirt, that's mongo!

Kulsum: It's mango?

Amina: Not mango, mongo. Recycled waste.

Kulsum: Whatever that means.

Resham: Yeah Amina, what does that mean?

Amina: Don't know, just thought I'd say it.

Shireen: Okay, get with the program. Not an affair-shafair or anything?

Resham: No such wimpy stuff.

Shireen: Oh my. This is going to be good. What is it? Naked again?

Resham: Keep guessing, Shireen.

Shireen: Give up!

Amina: Hijabing it.

Shireen: Hijabing it? What's that? Some kind of drug thing?

Kulsum laughed: No! She's gone into hijab.

Resham: She's gone nowhere, she's going everywhere as usual only she's wearing a hijab.

Shireen: Sara's in hijab?

Resham: Yup.

Shireen: Hijab?

Amina: Yup.

Shireen: Unbelievable.

Resham: Why? It fits in with all her other craziness.

Kulsum: It's not even part of our culture.

Resham: Exactly.

Shireen: I mean, what's happened to the place since we left? It used to be normal when we were there. Never heard of the hijab.

Kulsum: Of course dupattas…

Shireen: And chadors, and really, if one was from the old city, then burqas. But what's with the hijab action?

Resham: It's totally Saudi, and our dear Sara is doing that hijab thing!

Shireen: Yet another one of Sara's fads!

Amina: Only this one's in our faces, this one is really making me throw up and get angry. How dare she do everything, break every rule and then throw this morality in our faces? She's such a hypocrite!

Kulsum: Hold on, she isn't doing this to you.

Amina: Oh yes, she is. For her two days worth of whimsical trendiness, copycating somebody else, I'm sure, she is causing such a lot of harm.

Kulsum: Well…

Amina: Don't say she isn't! You know she's not capable of an iota of original thinking. I bet some social butterfly out there that she hangs around with has suddenly decided to take the hijab and so Sara Begum decides to don it as well.

Kulsum: Maybe it's more than that.

Resham: Why should it be? How many transformations have we seen, the remaking, the recreation of Sara Rueewallah—I mean Sara Aziz. She went from long hair to short, from fat to thin, from brown eyes to green contact lenses, from brown hair to blonde.

From well off to filthy rich. I mean, there is just nothing about her that you can say is consistent or constant.

Kulsum: That would make for an interesting person.

Amina: Or an extremely vacuous one.

Kulsum: Or perhaps there's some Mullah Omar in her life, she seems to attract men…

Amina: Ooofh! For God's sake!!

Resham: She thinks she can suddenly go into hijab after all that she has done and suddenly become Ms Saint.

Kulsum: Well, it's been known to happen.

Shireen: Well, I think it's just in keeping with her frame of mind. Frankly, I think she's anorexic. Did you see how thin she was last time she was here? And she ate absolutely nothing and she was on the treadmill all the time. A spoon of Ben and Jerry's, God forbid, and she would spend the entire night on the treadmill at my place. Honestly baba, she drove me crazy. Tauba!!

Amina: Ben and Jerry was acquired by Unilever.

Resham: Yes!

Shireen: Oh no! Does that mean my kids are going to make me boycott it? I mean years of not eating Haagen Dazs remember, because they invested in South Africa, now this! A big corporation takes over sweet eco-friendly, anti-war, ice cream…

Resham: It's history, Shireen. Long, long time ago. I don't know why I even brought that up. It's all about big, ugly corporations now. Get with the agenda. Anyway, coming back to the point and about Sara, she's just selfish.

Shireen: Or you know what?

Kulsum: What?

Shireen: I think it may be she's getting older, and you know how obsessed she is about being young.

Amina: And the hijab covers the thinning hair the sagging skin around the jowls and the neck?

Resham: For God's sake, she's only forty-three!

Kulsum: But Sara stopped at twenty-nine. So she's twenty-nine.

Hijab is so much healthier than botox!!!!!!!

Resham: Oh yeah, we're really eleven years older than her. Give me a break!

Kulsum: This year we are, but next year, darling, we'll be twelve years older than her.

Shireen: No, I think you are absolutely right, I was going to say the same thing, you know. I think she is really afraid of getting old and this is a good way to cover it up. But I think she's anorexic also. And then you know she really got a scare this year with the heart attack that Riaz had.

Resham: Give me a break. Scare? My ass! It took her exactly one week after that to start planning her next trip to Europe.

Kulsum: What does that have to do with anything? Doesn't mean it didn't affect her.

Shireen: I think she really took it to heart. You know she really loves him.

Amina: Sara only loves herself and anyone who remotely likes her!

Kulsum: That is not very fair, is it?

Resham: Amina, really, it isn't.

Amina: It's my opinion.

Shireen: Poor Sara.

Amina: Why poor Sara? She's a bloody hypocrite. Nau sau choohay kha key billie kerney challi hajj. The cat snarfs down 900 mice and heads off to perform Hajj.

Resham: Hajj! That's it. She went for her Hajj, didn't she? Maybe all the trips for Umra and Hajj have done this.

Amina: Give me a break, Hajj and Umra. You know I don't buy that at all. She only goes there to buy gold. It's the best place to buy gold, y'know!

Kulsum: Don't be cruel. That's really unfair. She has always been religious. She has always done these things.

Shireen: That's true, that is one thing she has always done since she was a child. She has always prayed five times a day.

Amina: Well, you know what: I wish she hadn't. Because all her life she has done whatever she pleased, broken every rule in the book, lied through her teeth and made sure she absolved herself five times a day. So don't give me that shit.

Kulsum: I don't think we should sit in judgment of her that way. She feels she's had a rough time of it, being the first child and all.

Amina: Hard life, hard life? What hard life has she had? She lives like a queen! Done only as she pleased, got her way in everything, and never given a damn about anyone.

Resham: I second that motion!

Amina: How dare she! How dare she, under the circumstances in the country, do this!

Kulsum: What?

Amina: What do you mean what Kulsum?

Kulsum: What circumstances are you talking about?

Amina: This situation in the country!

Kulsum: What do you mean?

Amina: There is so much sectarian violence, Kulsum. So much violence in the name of religion. Just look at what happened to that Dr Zaidi who Bari-ma was giving lessons to. And Kulsum, women are being killed in the name of honor!

Kulsum: What does this have to do with Sara?!

Amina: You can't be serious! Everything! Women are being killed in the name of honor for demanding a divorce or wanting to exercise their choice in marriage! All in the name of honor and chaar-divari.

Women there work, just like they do here. They need to be able to move around, interact with other people. And she, she of all people of all the people, Sara, should have the audacity to take this up as a badge. To actually become a part of that. Now that she has all she wants by doing exactly whatever she wanted all her life, she wants to take that away from everyone else.

Kulsum: She's doing it to herself, she's not inflicting it on anyone else.

Amina: Oh yeah, if she walks into a room with all of us, and she is in a hijab while the rest of us aren't, what does that say for us?

Kulsum: Why should it be about you or us? It's about her. Why are you reacting this way?

Amina: Don't you dare call me a reactionary to that bloody hypocrite. Don't you know what happened next door with the Taliban. Don't you read anything ever Kulsum?

Kulsum: Well, I do know my geography darling, it's not next door, next door is Scarsdale, quite frankly.

Amina: Do be serious!

Kulsum: Why don't you be less so? Do you really think I don't know what's happening in Pakistan or the world? But around you, I swear, I really feel like just giving it all a rest.

Shireen: Bibiyon! Bhainon! Hazrat!! Women! Sisters! People! Girls! Kids! Dolls! For God's sakes!

Amina: No, I can't let this just go, I can't let it rest. It has to matter.

There is a country of women who are being buried alive in their houses, behind chadors, even their footsteps cannot be heard.

They are dying of suffocation. And Sara thinks she can fool around with the hijab because of whatever.

Resham: Well, I think there's a bit of exaggeration there. And I'm not ready to condemn the Taliban, they at least controlled most of the country and if they could have stopped the fighting and the killing, and let the women be in chador for peace, so be it. And it couldn't have lasted forever, it was only a phase. For peace, it was worth it. Now look at the mess.

Amina: Oh my God I cannot believe what I'm hearing! Are you crazy? What's happening to everyone? It's all about the drug trade, the pipeline for oil. And women and children are paying the price.

Kulsum: Frankly Amina, I don't think you want to hear anyone except yourself.

Amina: Frankly, Kulsum, I have something worth saying, it's hard to hear someone prattling on, asking silly questions about who, what, why all the time!

Kulsum: Well, excuse me!

Shireen: Time out!

Amina: Why time out? Why should we try to even explain Sara's behavior? We know what she is all about, suddenly this hijab should make her worthy of being above-board, deserving of our respect.

Kulsum: No one said that.

Amina: Sure, they did, maybe its anorexia, maybe its Riaz's heart attack. Bullshit. She is thin because she thinks she can attract the next fat cat with her sexy body and frankly, should someone richer come along, Riaz dropping dead would only facilitate the matter.

Shireen: Don't be stupid, Amina, watch your mouth. God forbid.

Kulsum: Really, Amina. Tauba. God forbid.

Resham: Amina, cool it. Okay?

Amina: Fine. God forbid anything should happen to Riaz Bhai.

Kulsum: I mean, if Sara, who has always been inclined towards religion all her life should chose to do this, why is it such a terrible thing?

Shireen: I mean we don't seem to have a problem with women wearing long skirts one day and short skirts in another season when the magazines dictate it so, so why be so overcome with anger over a hijab? If tomorrow a gori woman walks down the street in a hijab or a Prada mannequin on Prince Street is wearing one, then I'm sure you'll see things very differently!

Amina protested: No, I won't!

Resham: C'mon guys, Sara has to manage her garment business. She does travel to the inner city areas, where people are probably conservative, all her workers are men and they are, I'm sure, pretty conservative. She probably earns a lot of their respect by dressing that way and it probably allows her to stay around them for longer periods of time without question and without hassle.

Amina: I just cannot believe this shit. I cannot believe you guys.

Kulsum: And if you are going to follow the words in the Koran then…

Amina: Don't you dare say what you're going to say.

Kulsum: It's in the Koran.

Amina: It is not, it is not, this is exactly what absolute ignoramuses like yourself will say. You've never bothered to read anything…

Shireen: Amina, watch it!

Kulsum: Are you telling me that it isn't in the Koran?

Amina: I am telling you that the Koran has one reference, my dear.

'O Prophet, tell your wives and daughters and the women of the faithful to draw their wraps a little over them. They will thus be recognized and no harm will come to them.' That's it. In a state of war, it's in a contextual frame. Think about it, in a war, when men are animals…

Kulsum: Are you sure that's the only reference?

Amina: As far as I understand it. Yes.

Kulsum: Wow Amina, I didn't realize you were such an 'Islamic'.

Amina: See! For you, that's an exogenous feature, I have to be something to do that. To me, reading the Koran is not a big deal! And in any case I have to, to be able to ward off fools like you!

Kulsum: Wow, I'm very proud of you. But are you sure? Can I quote you?

Amina: Of course I'm sure. I'm not you! And you're not quoting me, it's the Koran.

Resham: Amina, I'm not so sure. Yaar, it's all over the place.

Amina: Where is it? Show me, tell me? Where?

Resham and Shireen: In Sura-e-Nisa.

Amina: I knew it! I knew it. You guys are so damn predictable. Women, in the section labeled women. You bloody affirmative raction freak heads! Turns out gals, no. Not a word about any hijab, a whole lot though about sowing fields and guess who them fields are...us, us being the fields, but not a word about the hijab action. And, by the way, while I'm at it, that business about two women equal to one man, that is also bullshit. One reference only in the Koran under a business transaction only, again contextual because women didn't deal with financial matters in those days.

Kulsum: Oh no, you don't! Caught you! The Prophet's wife, Khadija was a business woman!

Resham: Yeah, but she did hire him to take care of her financial matters? Okay, so we've come a long way, baby.

Amina: Exactly and again contextual. Although I wish we could be more like her. A forty year-old marrying a twenty-nine year old and doing the proposing as well. Talk about a woman of the twenty-first century.

Kulsum: Resham, learn something!

Resham: If she were here, she'd be one of us. And Kulsum, do you think she was in a hijab when she did that? If she were here, I tell you, she'd be like us!

Shireen: Stuck in traffic on the Triboro, after closing a fabulous deal.

Amina: I think she'd be sitting here, sipping a café latte with me. She'd be the head of some corporation.

Kulsum: Tauba, tauba, tauba... God forbid...

Amina: And she would be telling Kulsum to shut up while dialing Sara to tell her to get a life!

Resham: Any second now, we're all going to be struck down by lightning, I can feel it.

Kulsum: Please don't blaspheme, Amina!

Shireen: Haan baba, please watch it, I think lightning travels and I certainly don't want to be zapped while stuck in a traffic jam, for you having a mouth on you.

Amina: Honestly. You guys are too much. Sara and her vacuousness seems like holy devotion to you while what I say is blasphemy!

Kulsum: She prays.

Amina: How the hell do you know what I do?

Resham: Yeah Kulsum, Sara is not the only one who prays, you know. She may be the only one who manages to be such a conspicuous performer.

Shireen: You know just like the maestro sang it: I think of you all the time—people remember you just five times a day.

Amina: Good point—Nusrat Fateh Ali Khan sang it like it is.

Kulsum: Amina, how come you don't have a problem with Abba having two wives?

Amina: That's totally, totally different. And do you now have a problem with Choti-ma and Bari-ma? I mean, are you seriously drawing parallels between our parents and Sara's actions?

Kulsum: Just a thought.

Amina: Well lose the thought.

Resham: Guys! Please, we are really going nuts here. Let's talk when everyone calms down.

Kulsum: Okay, everyone, bye.

Resham: Ciao.

Shireen: Later.

Amina: Hasta Lavista, babes.

Resham: Don't hang up Amina. I want to talk to you.

Amina: Okay. Look, I'll call you right back, okay? Bye everyone.

Resham: Okay. Bye everyone.

Amina: Hi, it's me.

Resham: You sound much better. Are you?

Amina: Yeah, I guess I'm much better. You haven't told anyone, have you?

Resham: No of course I haven't. But are you okay? I mean after you told me what Stanley had to say when you called him after your arrest, I was really angry. But I'm glad that happened. Now you know what a jerk he is.

Amina: Americans are so…

Resham: Don't go there. We're American. Stanley is Stanley. One guy. You can't superimpose and generalize his behavior onto everyone.

Amina: You're right. Yes. I place bets with myself that I'll hear from him the moment the weekend ends and he gets back to work. And so far I'm winning my own bet. I'm just one of his bad travel habits of cigarettes, quick gulps of Bloody Marys, surfing cable channels mindlessly.

Resham: You don't get it do you? Amina, listen to me, you can't possibly be thinking of continuing this. There is nothing in this for you, what are you trying to do Amina? Why are you bent on hurting yourself like this? Amina, what's the point?

Amina: I just don't get this. What an asshole. What a user!

Resham: Look, leave it for what it was.

Amina: To not be acknowledged, that's what hurts. I've got to at least say this to him.

Resham: No! Let go please. You've had two weeks of a break and then you called him when you really needed his help. He was a jerk and that was it.

Amina: No surprise there. I tested the hypothesis, and it tested positive. Pursuit, conquer, demolish, move on. All this is so pointless. POINTLESS!

Resham: No. You needed to get that out of your system, it's done. Not pointless for that purpose. Pointless if you do anything more. Amina, all you are doing is validating all the worst notions about you to yourself. Thinking his thoughts for him. Thinking everyone's thoughts for them. Validating your suspicions.

Amina: I get that from my shrink, I don't need it from you too!

Resham: Amina, it's true. This is one more reason for you to continue to be angry with yourself and with everyone! To remain angry and cynical. He acted as you always worried that he would. And you acted as you feared you would.

Amina: And your point is?

Resham: Break this cycle you're in. Amina, is this helping at all?

Promise me you are not going to call him again.

Amina: It's over. Don't worry. I'm done.

Resham: Your 'done' extends to a very long time. I know from past experience.

Amina: This time I am done. I'm there at the end of the long time. This time I'm really done.

Resham: Promise?

Amina: Khuda ki Kasam. I promise! Okay?

Resham: Okay, Amina, okay.

Amina: I have to admit though, Riaz Bhai married Sara, she's lucky. And she's his second wife too. And Abba and Bari-ma and Choti-ma, first and second wives. But they are happy and they are married.

Resham: Amina!

Amina: You have to admit they're happy.

Resham: You're sounding totally ridiculous.

Amina: Perhaps.

Resham: Trust me. Dating.com. Try it.

Amina: Don't be ridiculous!

14

Frankly Hank

HANK Brown adjusted his sunglasses and began his morning run and his daily assessment of the dating game that he had entered into when he posted his profile on the matchmaking website: 'I'm easy going. Love the outdoors, love to sail, ski, hike, bike, run. Would love to explore the theatre. Am a widower. Not looking for a commitment at the moment. Would like to start living again.' The part he didn't post on the website went something like this: Every morning the same routine, the struggle to tame the beast, keep it at bay. I can hardly stand the smell of myself, the look of myself, the graying hair, the swollen face, the sagging parts. The shower, the shave, the electric toothbrush.

Two aspirins right away to manage the hangover, to take down the swelling, and to keep the arteries pumping. Later, after the black coffee enters the blood- stream, wheat germ, soy milk and the gingko, ginseng, essential fish oils concoction, and shit if I'm so lucky, and that too taken to the dulcet sounds of Ms Petula Clark on the piped in music system I've installed in the john. And of course the extra two Advils before the five mile run. All this before the beast begins to retreat. This including the dating game because at all costs, I am and will be young at heart and in appearance. And so you, my dear, whoever you are, you must be so too. Got it? Because whatever I am not able to hold back, keep at bay, fix, smoothen, tighten in me, you must surrogate for me, be its proxy for me. Guys look at the other guy's car, and the other guy's girl. And darlin' goddammit, you must be tanned, I am. Be athletic, be thin, be tight, be funny, be young, be free, and laugh, laugh a lot. I like that. Turn heads, make those guys stare at you. Make them stare at you when you're with me. Yeah, I like that. No downers, here okay? I'm taking four pain-killers as it is. Be Gloria, be that, take me back to the glory days. No, be more than that, be Petula Clark, be Doris Day, be all of them all at once, all in one night. Don't give me shit! Don't lecture me about men like me. I don't need the feminist bullshit of all the boobless, juiceless, gray haired, love-our-wrinkles, flat sensible-shoed, shrill shriekers. I'm evolved, okay? Okay, so I drink too much and smoke one pack too many. But I could still outrun ya, outlive ya.

I'm built to last. And I've had ten years of therapy. This is what I learned from it, I was born a racist, stayed confirmed as a racist. I took a 180 degree turn on that, hey, I don't cross the street anymore to the other side when I see one of 'em coming... Okay, so cut me some slack… I've been through the war, no draft-dodger me. Been part of a street gang, seen the mean streets of Detroit, dropped out of high school, had my arm broken, had my heart broken, got a girl pregnant, lived nine lives before you even had one, went through two wives, got myself a kid, a grandkid, made my way to the top of the heap regardless... Been there, done that. That was then, this is now. But still at the end of the day, these are the things that matter, the car, the girl, and the ability to get it up and give it good.

I'm Hank. To me, that's who I am. To the world I am Brig. General Hank Brown. A good guy. I have lived an exemplary life.

I have been an exemplary man. Let me rephrase that, because we are after all in a different age, completely. I have been an exemplary person. I don't care what the facts are, the facts are just that, facts, and therefore meaningless, without feeling and without any grounding whatsoever in reality. For example, it is a fact that you breathe, your heart beats, your lungs work and you are termed as physically and mentally fit. Does that mean you live? Or that you are fit? Not in my book, you aren't. In my opinion, it means that your heart beats, your lungs work and you breathe and you have control over your muscular and nervous systems. That is all. Got it? It does not mean that you are alive, that you live. That you're workin' it. It is the difference of body and soul, of letter and spirit. If you ain't workin' it, you ain't got it. And you sure as shit aren't living it.

And then Rita showed up for Hank as an ad. He had been scrolling through the possibilities on the website of dating.com in the parameters that he'd set. Age group 25–42, eyes any color, physically fit, didn't care about religion, etc., and he couldn't say preference of skin colours. The system didn't allow for skin color preferences. So there was Hank wading through and squinting at more than a hundred and fifty photographs and profiles, when he clicked and there she was. Her photograph didn't give much away, her downcast eyes gave away long lashes, the shape of her eyelids promised large eyes. Her lips were beautiful and in a half smile, she had high cheekbones and her hair was dark. It was a black and white photograph. Hank didn't give much thought to that. But he was distracted by what she had written as a way of introduction.

Something about her style had him hooked.

It said: 'So I'm sitting on the beach on Memorial Day weekend, on the Jersey shore, having an extended conversation with the main Man. And I'm basically saying, would it be too much to ask for if a simple good guy finally made his appearance and was focused ENTIRELY on me? THIS time, I promise, I SWEAR, I would not be arrogant, I would recognize his worth, not consider him a wimp just because again here was someone paying attention to me. God, I continued, warming to my plea, I'm not asking for a rocket scientist, a brain surgeon, an anthropologist, or a raving intel- lectual communist poet freedom fighter (any more), or some kind of a warrior, commando crack trooper or something. It'll be okay if he's, 'um, well even say…um, ah…a carpenter, a goat herder (since God seems to like that type); a car mechanic, for God's sake, I mean Your sake, a truck driver would be fine, the point is he's got to not make my toes curl with boredom or alternatively, fear! And I promise just because he likes me, I won't despise him. PROMISE. He doesn't have to be from Jersey City or NYC or Karachi. He could be, for all I care, from Alaska! I've learned my lesson. Alright? Okay?' So Hank responds to this, 'Okay! That's alright with me!'

She writes back, 'Who are you?'

'God,' he wrote.

'Uh huh,' she wrote back.

'Okay, not God. So did you hear from him? What did he say?'

'I did indeed,' she wrote back.

'And?'

A long answer comes back, much to Hank's amusement: 'So this conversation I'm having, with the Big Guy in the sky as I watch a kid chase waves and shriek as they chase her back, and then suddenly five dolphins appear. Dolphins, for God's sake, friggin' Flipper. It's too perfect. So I'm thinking, now in 20–20 hindsight, obviously that the portals of heaven were open, and God was doing some serious listening time. He was actually listening!' 'Was He? Sure could've fooled me!' Hank wrote. 'Doesn't He listen to you?'

'Nope.'

'Well He was in my case,' she wrote.

'And you know this because...'

'This I know, I gather, surmise as they say, the day before yesterday as I'm walking home, musing about carpenters and such, get home, and sure enough there's this postcard in the mail for me, from Alaska, with three moose on it. I swear to God, I kid you not!'

'Hmmmm,' he wrote back. 'Shouldn't it be meese?' A few hours later came the reply: 'Turns out, no. I learn there and then, that the plural of Moose is not Meese or Mooses, because the caption above their antlers reads: "Mother and Baby Moose enjoying the Alaskan Summer." All two days of it. I say back. Can't help it, I got a mouth on me. I'm talking to a postcard, I'm being a wise-guy to a postcard. Anyway. The postcard is from a high school boyfriend, back from back home days. He's from Alaska.'
'Uh huh,' Hank wrote.

'I swear to God, I'm not making this up.'

'What?'

'Yea, he was always from Alaska, back then too. Bonafide Alaskan, or something. Oh yeah, played the guitar too. Very good with his hands which, as we know, now in later life, is an important talent in men. Who knew! You've got to understand, back then I was a good girl, and us good girls, we didn't know.'

'I like this!' he wrote back. And she continues, 'So I'm reading this postcard, and he refers to me in his postcard, get this, me, as, "The most excellent bike passenger". Only he's forgotten the 'c', and so its most exellent. But since I'm trying to practice non-arrogance after my surrender on the beach on Memorial Day, I'm thinking this is a man of the future, with vision, exploding paradigms, dispensing unnecessary redundancies, a minimalist, a pioneer. Why indeed would an X ever require a follow up c?'

'Why indeed?' Hank wrote back. 'That's my question every morning when I look at myself in the mirror.'

'Why indeed,' she responded. 'No need at all. So now I'm thinking James Joyce and Jimmy Dean all in one. As usual of course, I'm getting carried away at this point.'

'Hey, no problem. Knock yourself out,' he said. 'The postcard provides a phone number with an area code at the frontier of digits, never dialed before by me Of course, it's Alaska I'm callin'. So he picks up. Hi, it's me…wow…you. Yadi Yadi Yada. I'm laughing. We have a great chat, and as his accent gets thicker and harder for me to understand, mine does too. He's the new kid in school from Alaska and I'm the class president from school way back when, suddenly, again. I must uphold the drawing room's drawl, you must understand, very refined, la-di-dah n' all that.'

'Class President, huh? I'm impressed.'

'Yeah. Is that good or is that bad?'

'Its good,' Hank wrote back quickly. 'Why?'

'Okay, it's bad. And the la-di-dah stuff… What does that even mean? Some New England, East Coast thing? Is that where you're from? Let me guess. Connecticut, Westport?'

'Never mind. We reminisce about the night way back then, when he and I were almost flying, or when we were fleeing.'

'Fleeing?'

'Yeah, fleeing. On a trail bike. He's riding it and I'm hanging on in the back, clutching on to him for dear life, and a car load of scary, rich boys with far too much unspent testosterone, chasing us. And this Alaskan kid and me, a kid too, getting away after an hour or more of a harrowing car chase.'

'Kid and I.'

'What?'

'Kid and I.'

'Kid and me, kid and I, what's the difference? You got the point, didn't ya? I can't even begin to imagine what would have happened if they had caught up with us.'

'What could've happened?' he asked. 'It's not like they were the Taliban or something!'

'Geez, do you really believe that? Nothing goes on here that's bad between men and women in this country? Women here are as oppressed and maltreated like everywhere else. It's all the good old fashioned way.'

'Geez Louise! Oppression…are you some kind of feminist?'

'Give it a rest.'

'Right. But this isn't exactly Osama country.'

'Osama, yo mama! This is the only Osama country! Ever been anywhere down south or out of a big city? Those guys out there, especially the dumb guys with the drink and the pick-up trucks, the tattoos and the military haircuts, am I going to have to give a lecture in sociology? Where were you when feminism one-Oh-one was being taught??? Women, property, honor! Remember? Any woman, out there outside her family's protection is of little value except for one thing. Get it? Okay, so there we were. Seventeen. It was an open invitation for the hunters that hunting season was on, and everything was fair game. But they didn't catch us, came close, but couldn't because we were cool, way too cool, and way too fast, and way too good. That's cool with a capital K-E-W-L. Most exellent passenger! Yeah. Because even back then, I knew how to go with the flow, merge with the rider, become one with his machine. Ahem.'

'I like that.' Hank wrote back. He really did like it.

'So all these years later, all the way back from far away from home, there's a postcard from Alaska. I've come full circle. I'm thinking, it's a boy from Alaska, from back home. Then, of course, I run through my CV and he tells me about the oil pipeline, good money and the mechanic shop. He runs a car mechanic business,

I'm a lawyer. After all that, I ask him if he ever got to drive the eighteen wheeler that he wanted to drive cross-country. Can't remember he says. Brain's too fried. Hmmm, I say. Remembering. That explains the slow easy drawl as well. He asks me if I got married.'

'Did ya?'

'Nope, never got round to it. So anyway, he tells me about his partner, something about dating.com and a search in the five mile radius of Umiat or some place, and now they are about to adopt two kids.'

'Partner?'

'Yeah?'

'So he's gay?'

'What? How'd you figure that?'

'You said partner so I figure, the guy's with a guy and they're adopting kids!'

'Well I don't care. Do you?'

'Let's not go there, okay? Keep going on with the story.'

'Okay. Anyway, as soon as he had said he had a partner I felt I was saved! I tell him I might adopt one as well some day. I can't stop laughing. He must think I'm on dope or something. So now I'm tipping my metaphorical La Resistance beret (black) at the Big Guy and saying that was good, very good. Poetic, poignant, a touch of irony, a brush of poetic justice... Nicely done, I like YOUR style, Darlin'. That's good, a guy from Alaska, from back home.

There's a certain sweet aesthetic in there. There's a story in there somewhere. You're getting close, very close, keep them coming, next time though, I said with a smile, make him single okay? And straight. I could almost hear him chuckling back. And so it goes.

I think he has a huge crush on me.'

'That's cute!'

'Like it?'

'Yeah. Very sassy.'

'A bit of this, a bit of that—I try.'

And with that, Hank was hooked. He had to meet her. So they emailed back and forth some more, keeping the exchange short, sweet, quick and plentiful. A rat-tat steady exchange of rapid friendly fire. They finally decided to meet. She said she was going to be in New York to take in a few museums and shows over the weekend, visiting from Toronto. Hank replied, what a coincidence because he was going to be there too, coming up from Houston. And they agreed to meet at this restaurant, her choice, up on the East Side, somewhere between 1st and 2nd on 82nd. She was staying at the Stanhope next to the Metropolitan Museum and Hank was a bit further down, on the West Side at a Double Tree. She showed up at the restaurant at the appointed and agreed hour.

She was definitely not what Hank was expecting. 'Na uh. No sir, no way. No sirreee.' But there she was. And so Hank was thinking, what in hell would be the quickest way to get out of this total fuck-up. Panicked that he would have to spend a couple of hours of his precious time with this totally-not-what-the-advertising- had-promised he came up with the idea that he should talk about something that he knew a lot about, and, judging by the way she looked, she wouldn't know a damn thing about. He was thinking, C'mon Hank, pal, make this short. The idea is to bore her, have a quick lunch and get the hell out a there. A sort of awe and shock strategy, a quick in and out. Hank was thinking, 'Move on, move on. And before long.' Hank thought he'd totally lost it. But he was thinking about how he could cut his losses and move on. He needed to be a gentleman, a WestPoint man to the finish. Hank had set up another couple of dates, breakfast, lunch, coffee, drinks, dinner and a nightcap for the next day, so he wasn't exactly upset that this one was a total washout even before they'd said hello.

Hank wanted to kick himself. He had put in the parameters, all that stuff he wanted in a woman and yet, after all that, after all the specifics, the Universe coughed up Rita!

When she showed up, Hank could not have been more frustrated or angry with the system and with himself. Hank was so disappointed. 'So fucking A damned disappointed! Disappointed with the system. Wouldn't ya believe it. Goes to show. Profiling can't be about simple parameters. I should have worked the recce on this one better before walkin' into this fuckin' ambush.' She was not what he had ordered. Completely wrong! Wrong wrapping paper! Oh sure, the statistics he wanted were there, all there and then some, but the product just came in the wrong packaging. Hank kept a straight face and went along with it. After all, he considered himself a gentleman.

He might be a bigot. But goddammit, he was still a guy who could take a gal to the prom in style. She had mentioned something about being back home. Hank had mistaken that to mean Westport. Not Bag-Fuckin'-dad. Or wherever the heck Sri Lanka was. First generation Canadian. Shit, goddamnit. But dammit, there was just that something about her that made Hank stick around. Her photograph had been a knockout, a real princess, goddammit, he realized that he should've focused on the fact that it was in black and white. Hank had figured that she'd be Italian or, worst come to worst, Jewish. And her ad had been funny. What really got Hank was that whole black beret and motorbike thing and all that talk about God. But when she walked in he thought, 'What pretty peepers and wow! Take a load of those hooters, sure would've liked to have those against my raw hide on a motorbike, getting chased by rich boys, heck the Taliban from New Jersey or wherever the heck she grew up, anybody would've made it worthwhile.' And while she was there with him, for a couple of hours right there, he felt like he was in high school again, God bless her!

But after they had settled down at their table, Hank stayed with the shock and awe strategy, trying his best to get rid of her as fast as he could. So he started off with, 'Like baseball?' And she was already drumming her fingernails on the table. Bright red polish, tap dancing on white cloth and she said, 'Is that like, "Got milk".'

'No, it more like, do you follow the game?'

'Oh,' she said. 'No.'

Hank puffed out his chest, 'Well, that's my game. Baseball.'

She shrugged her shoulders, 'Doesn't interest me.'

'Does me! I got a feeling that this is the season for the little guy, the real hero, home-grown, with passion and a love for the game, ignored because he didn't cost enough and didn't bring in the big bucks. All this guy knows is how to play ball. This year is going to be the year of the guy who knows how to play ball. But I see you're bored.'

And coming in, right on the money, just as Hank had figured it, she was annoyed. 'Yeah,' and then she said, 'The Twins stand a chance. We'll see. But, like I just told you baseball isn't my game. Cricket is.'

And Hank was thinking, 'She knows who is playing? How come she knows that?' But instead he said, 'Cricket's for pansies.' Case closed. He could see the ethnic shutters closing down for business. 'No, it isn't for pansies, whatever that means. A billion people watch it. I guess it's a culture thing.'

'What the hell does culture have to do with it?'

'Well, it isn't your culture to watch cricket. You watch baseball.'

'Yeah lady, we watch games where there's an outcome, people win!'

'The point for all American games is to win, while for us in cricket, the point is to play the best game possible.'

'Bullshit! That's a load of crap. The usual America hating crap!' Hank fumed.

'Well, that's the difference of cultures!'

'Define culture. Does that mean; those who hate Americans and those that don't?'

'I really don't think I'm going to even answer that!'

'No, I'd really like to be educated on what culture means. So tell me,' Hank had said.

'Okay. Though I don't see why we're doing this. Culture is the unwritten code or terms of engagement and conduct that everyone understands and recognizes within a society.'

'Uh-Huh. Sure, like the marine code,' Hank offered.

'The marine code?' she had asked.

'Yeah, the marine code. Everyone knows where they are and how they'll react given any situation, without needing to verbally communicate.'

'Uh-huh. Right.'

'Okay. But some of that culture is screwed up! Like over there where women are covered from head to toe. Like in I-ran, I-raq and Saudi Arabia,' Hank said.

'It's E-ran, E-raq, by the way! Why can't you think of that as Canada or over here in the winter?'

'What?'

'Well, everyone here has to cover up from head to toe to step out in the winter and un-peel when they go indoors. Same thing.'

'You don't believe that, do you?' Hank said.

'Nope.'

'Ok, so we have some agreement.'

'Perhaps. Not sure, but perhaps.'

'So we can have a civilized dinner date?'

'Yes.'

'Ever been married?'

'Nope.'

'Whoa. Now hold on there! Whoops, that's lethal!' Hank snorted.

'Why?'

'A woman not married is a bitter thing!' Hank laughed.

'You're one charming man, you know that? You know what, this isn't working out at all!'

'No, wait a minute. Okay, I apologize. That was rude. I admit. I was raised better than that. You could be an exception to that rule! Do you want to get married?'

'Are you proposing?'

'You are funny. Nope. I'm not proposing. But I'm asking. Do you want to get married?'

'Yes, I want to start a family.' She looked embarrassed.

'My ad specifically said I was done with that, and I was looking for just meeting people.'

'God this is so embarrassing! I think we should say goodbye,' she said, half getting up.

Hank said hurriedly, 'Sit down, I'm only pointing out that you didn't read my ad carefully enough.'

She said, 'Yes, but I did read that you live in New York, which you don't! You live in some place in Texas.'

'In Houston,' Hank corrected her. 'And you're not from here either. But just meeting people, that was the bottom line.'

'If that was the bottom line, then why did you have to give such a long description about yourself, why complicate it?'

Hank said, 'The service said we had to write about ourselves. Yours wasn't exactly a settling down kind of a message either. Black berets and motorbikes? Thats pretty racy, not exactly Miss Domesticity. Though pretty good, pretty funny.'

She smiled, flattered. 'Thanks, but you're wrong. Mine said everything about the fact that I was looking for the right guy to settle down with. Why didn't you just say that all you wanted was to meet people and not get involved.'

'I thought that was what I said.'

'That's not what I understood,' she said.

'You need to learn to read, lady.'

'I'm quite able at that. Thank you! And you need to know where you're located!'

'Quite? Quite able at that? How quaint! Quite. And as for where you're located, you don't live here either!'

'Well, I want to live in New York!'

'Wanting and reality, baby, are two separate things!'

She stood up, 'Okay, then we're really done here.'

Then she gave Hank this look, the look that said, 'You're so beneath me.' It reminded him of that look that Gloria had given him the first time he had set eyes on her. Thirty years ago, Hank

the farm boy, showing at the Student Council Board members meeting back at college, wanting to join up. That knocked their noses out of joint. Wrong kind walking into their club. Hank had decided that minute that he was going to show Gloria. Who the hell was she giving him that look? And Hank did, he showed her.

She was begging him to marry her a year later. Got her good and pregnant. Sure did, Ms Gloria Hansen, class president, debutante belle of the ball. Anyway, in the here and now, at the restaurant, this opposite of blonde chick, doing the Gloria thing, had gotten up, she was about to walk out on Hank and they had just ordered dinner.

No way was she going to walk out on him. 'Hey we just ordered dinner! Sit down.'

'Let's cancel,' she said, but she sat down again.

'It's only been five minutes and this is not exactly cheap!'

'Well, let me pay for it, but I'm outta here,' she said. She was already reaching into her pocketbook and pulling out her credit card. Hank hated it when broads did that. These new age broads were just out of control.

'Hold on! Why do that? It's not like we're being chased by anyone!' Hank grinned, trying to look sheepish.

She had smiled. Hank thought, 'There we had that to share.'

Hank went on, 'We can eat, can't we? I mean, we need to eat!

Let's break bread okay, before we go our separate ways. I mean, if things haven't gone according to script, at least we're still working with the plan.'

'Excuse me? You sound like Donald Rumsfeld.'

Hank said, 'You're funny. What I mean is that we're here to have a nice evening. So let's try to do that.'

'In silence?'

'Here we go again! We haven't been silent since you got here, have we?'

'Well, we have nothing to say to each other. I don't play or watch baseball. So unless you're a monk, I don't think we can have a nice evening in silence.'

'I'm not a monk by the way. And I'm not Rumsfeld either. Just in case you need to know that,' Hank said.

She was smiling. Hank could see that in her eyes and her cheekbones even though she had set her mouth on 'stern'.

'Well, glad to know that. But let's try to just get through dinner. Okay?'

'Okay. Let's eat and get it over with,' she sighed.

'We could talk? I mean, for two people who have nothing to say to each other, we've said a lot.'

'Well, most of it has been that we've got nothing to say to each other,' she said with a laugh. 'And I don't know anything about baseball. Is that going to be our conversation? You're going to bring up baseball and I'm going to keep saying I don't know anything about it.'

'We could pick on another subject.'

'Just told you, I don't know anything about basketball or football. American football, that is.'

'There's more to life than sports,' Hank said.

She eyed him. 'Hmmm, if not sports, what? War?'

Hank thought, 'Bitch' but controlled his anger. 'More to life than war.'

'Politics? The Republican convention was in town. The protest demos?'

'Nope, none of that! Let's talk about something pleasant and neutral.'

'What's neutral? The stars, the moon?'

'Well, we own the moon. We got our flag up there. Thanks

to Nixon. God Bless him. But yeah, now you're talking, there you go. See, that wasn't so hard, Let's talk about the moon. The moon over Texas.'

'Like Texas, Texas? The moon over Texas?'

'Poetic. Now there's an idea, let's mix the two. Texas and NASA. We could talk about the moon landing,' Hank said, trying to be funny, and feeling very dumb.

'What?' she said looking irritated and confused.

'I don't know, help me out. I'm tryin' to make intelligent conversation here. The landing on the moon in 1970.'

'What about it?' She was getting fed up.

'It never happened, y'know.'

'What?' She looked at him incredulously.

Hank warmed up. 'See what I'm thinking is how come they only went there once and never again? Huh, why's that? How come we didn't, like, go and set up a space station on the moon?

How come the Russians never went to the moon? I mean,

they got their sputnik up and around first, didn't they? So how come, huh? What's that about?'

She had her arms folded in front of her. 'And now you're going to tell me you believe in aliens?'

He opened his eyes real wide, 'Don't you?'

'Why don't we talk about the war?'

'Nope, don't want to.'

'Why not?'

'Nothing to talk about? We were attacked and the President is doing what he needs to do and that's it.'

'See that's it, you're probably not willing to believe that the government is responsible for acts of war in other countries, and is up to no good here, but you are willing to believe in aliens!'

Hank grinned, 'You've got gazpacho dribble on your chin.

I'm an ex-General, I don't believe in acts of war.'

'What?'

Hank wiped the grin off his face and looked real serious and said real slow, 'Listen to me carefully, we only go in to save, rescue, liberate. No acts of war, war criminals, bullshit. Okay?'

She shook her head, 'I am so done here! An ex-General? Did

I tell you I was a lawyer?'

'So?'

'I care about human rights and stuff, y'know?'

'Lady, you gotta lighten up. What I wanted to say was you should come to Texas sometime and check out the full moon, its real pretty in the desert. Especially after it rains. Red, gold, bronze.

As a matter of fact, a lot like you. Flowers everywhere. I'd pick you some. Okay? Isn't that sweet. C'mon, I can see you liked that. Can we leave human rights out of it? Now sit down.'

For some reason she sat down. She looked totally bewildered.

Hank didn't know what it was but she was just staring at him, undecided and confused. It made him nervous but he liked it, he thought she was responding to the authority in his voice. He liked that. He liked that a lot. And, she had a knock-out body. Had to say, he thought, she had a knock-out body. When recalling the evening later on, Hank figured that the short itty bitty dress that she had on was the exact blue of Gloria's eyes. The color of the Texas blue bell. She had looked around her at the other people.

She had stared out of the window, she had ordered tea for herself and Hank a beer, she had tapped her fingers on the table. Red. Hank thought she was going to really come back at him with some hugely political, human rights, save the whales, blah, blah, blah. The waiter arrived with tea, beer and menus. Hank drank his beer. He watched her as she undid the red paper wrapper and withdrew the teabag from it. She dipped the teabag into the white teacup filled to the brim with hot water. She shook her head in disapproval and said, 'Tea should never be made this way, in hot water. It needs boiling water poured over it. This is so bad, but what to do? It's wrong to order tea in this land of tea-less people.'

She laughed. Some private joke in her head, he guessed. She said, 'Glad I'm Canadian.'

Then she totally threw him off by saying, 'Look, I don't think I'm the right person for you. You seem like someone, someone who's…who's…um…more blonde. More Fox News! And I just don't fit those categories!' There was absolutely no sarcasm in her voice at all. Fox News? Hank was amused and touched. She was so sincere and so nervous. Sort of breathless. Hank couldn't believe what he was hearing. He had this all wrong. This was a self-deprecating beauty, not Gloria at all. He was older now, and this tone and sweetness of hers sounded darn right attractive. More Fox News? Darn it! She said the sweetest things. And he had never mingled with the natives when he'd been there in 'Nam or in

Desert Storm, well now here was his chance to bone up. It would be good background stuff to have to being savvy about the ground reality and stuff. Good for getting contracts out there. And who knew, the way the war planning had gone it seemed to Hank that they would be recalling retired guys like him pretty damn soon. She was from somewhere over there, that's for sure. Hank couldn't believe it, he was actually trying to keep her there instead of getting her to leave.

He liked the way she listened to him. Her eyes were soft, kind of kind and the expression on her face changed with his tone.

Like sunlight on a West Virginia meadow when there are clouds in the sky, he thought. He could really tell her stuff and he talked and talked. It felt so good. And three hours later when their supposed five minute dinner ended, Hank suggested that they go take a walk.

She looked anxious, almost afraid. Hank said he didn't know
the city much, it was a nice night, so why not? She laughed and said she didn't know the city much either. He told her he only knew the route from his hotel to this restaurant, about a mile. 'Okay,' she had agreed. 'Let's walk in that direction and then I'll take a cab back up to my hotel.' Hank suggested that they could walk to her hotel, but she said it was only a couple of blocks away and it wouldn't be much of a walk. Hank was amused that she really thought they were going for a walk. 'Okay,' Hank almost whispered softly. There was something real gentle about her, unsure and fragile. For a grown woman, it was strange, but somehow attractive.

She looked like she needed protecting. Hank held her hand while they walked. Like the way he used to with Gloria, her arm tucked under his, holding her hand with his other hand. Sort of snug, real close. Old fashioned, like his Dad would've done with his mom. But Hank felt Rita was uncomfortable with that. Shy. So after a while, he just held her hand. He asked her a few questions, mainly about her community in Toronto. She said she was from Sri Lanka.

They were walking down Broadway. 'Sri Lanka, hell, I don't know the place. This is my chance to catch up on some geography. I mean the theatres I'd been in were the Gulf in 1990 and Vietnam. Never been to Sri Lanka. The motorbike ride n' stuff? That's not in Sri Lanka is it?'

'Nope. That was about Canada and of course I wrote about the New Jersey shore as well.'

'So it's kind of a flight of imagination thing?' Hank asked appreciatively.

'Yes. Quite.'

'Right, right, I get it. Quite.' Quaint, the way she talked.

Hank liked it. 'Sri Lanka, huh? Wasn't there some kind of war down there?' he asked.

'Oh yes,' she said, 'a civil war.'

Hank had asked her which side she was on. She said she was always on the losing side. They had laughed. That was a thaw maker. Hank could feel a meltdown. This was all taking him by surprise, he was the one feeling a meltdown. He felt like they were getting someplace. Getting close. Real close. Like they understood each other. It was special. It was special alright he decided, he was going to treat her right. What the heck. She was a lady. A real fine lady. Hank could see that. Fox News! She was wrong about that.

He was wrong about that whole 'Beneath me thing'. He had that dead wrong. He decided to work on her real good on the walk back to the hotel. There was no way she was going to take a cab back to her hotel once they got there. That was his goal and he was taskin' it. Hank figured that she was just kind of nervous, scared. It was a cultural thing. She was just kind of shy and that was kind of nice. She was probably used to the unfeeling, macho guys from over there. They're like that over there. Burnin' women and stuff. Yeah, he'd read that stuff. Seen it on TV all the time. *USA Today* did a big feature article once, if he remembered right. She probably had gotten in on an asylum plea or something in Canada. He'd have to ask her later. Hank decided that when he got home he was going to go Google this good. But tonight Hank Brown was going to show her what a real man was like. He was going to blow her away. Hank liked to think, that he had. He thought he had a real gift with the gals. 'The star tattooed on my chest ain't for nothin.' Days later, Hank couldn't seem to shake that image: the dog tags and cross dangling on a chain around his neck, tangling with some sort of a tiny religious gold medallion around hers. There she was dancing before his eyes, naked, leaping off the bed, swishing that huge, hotel bed sheet around her like a silk banner. All lime green swishes and swirls and red painted nails, blowing Hank away.

15

Clinical Clarity

THE doctor had said everything was fine when she had come in last time. He had said she was going to be just fine. There was nothing to worry about. She was a strong, healthy woman, in the prime of her life. She could do this.

Everything would work out. Nothing to be nervous about. Now she would just have to wait and see. Another couple of weeks and she would know. Amina sat in the waiting-room looking around her at all the other women who were praying, hoping, trying so desperately to do what seemed to come so naturally to others. The pain, the needles, the seemingly endless tests and experiments. What women go through, she thought to herself. It seemed so unfair.

She walked out into the street and into a bright day. It was a perfect October day, blue skies, sunshine, and crisp air. She walked over to the hot dog vendor, music in Arabic played from a small radio perched on his kiosk. She ordered a hot dog, spicy and juicy.

He asked her where she was from. Downtown she said, Soho. He smiled.

She winked at him and walked away.

16

Bath of Roses

RESHAM walked about her apartment, twisting a curl of dark hair and winding it around her finger as she spoke with her father on the phone. She let go of her hair, reached out with her index finger and wiped the dust off the edge of small mirror on the wall as she considered her own nodding reflection. It was ten in the morning on Saturday, New York time, evening in Karachi. She interrupted her father on the other end of the line, 'Abba, I'm repeating myself. Don't worry, leave this to me. They're up one day, the next day they're down... I know what I'm doing!' Her gaze moved on to a painting on the wall and she moved over to it and peered at it with satisfaction. It was the miniature that she had bought from a friend in need of selling about five years ago. It was now a collector's item, the artist, Shahzia Sikander, had become a much celebrated presence in the international art scene. And Resham was proud of her own astute purchase. 'I'd really advise you not to look at how the stocks are doing every day... Yes...exactly...you should just focus on the performance of the entire portfolio...I want you to look at that on a quarterly basis.' She rubbed the glass on the painting with the sleeve of her blouse to remove a smudge that she had noticed. This miniature took the viewer into a world onto itself which was anything but miniature, and was, in fact, immense, once the eye was drawn in to the astonishingly detailed overlay of images, each signifying a narrative of its own.

The more she looked at the tiny canvas and its intensely and intimately worked space, the more it emerged as huge, noisy and intricate. 'Abba, really, just leave it to me... Look at how we're doing annually...You saw that right? Exactly! I mean we've had a 12.4 per cent growth in our portfolio compared to a market average, which is pretty flat...we're doing really, really well. Yes, thanks to Google!' Resham noticed a tiny detail that had slipped her attention earlier and she peered closer at the painting.

She listened to her father talking while continuing to inspect her acquisition. She thought appreciatively that it was indeed a remarkable act of making tradition modern. Adhering to a

technique and a form, while slipping away from its beginnings as a genre of romantic repose and a view of the world held by the elite. Here it was, the same technique, depicting an explosion of movement and change. A tradition that used to reflect only the opinion of the rulers, an opinion that was defined by the vocabulary of the rulers and their narratives, was now transformed as though the world had come rushing in, storming the palace so to speak and bringing in with it a riot of language and personal stories that exploded on to the canvas. Resham smiled to herself and shook her head in appreciation. Yes, that was it! Captured in a tiny space was a vast canvas of an intimately articulated personal and political story, a perfect piece of baggage for a nomad, or someone forever in exile.

As though an entire history, say in an eleven volume novel, which churned accepted notions, rules and doctrines inside out and upside down had been condensed into this miniature. And she had bought it! She was satisfied by this knowledge and sure that she had seen a review of the artist's work that had also said something like that. 'Okay Abba, I'll talk to you later…Yes…They're all coming over soon…any moment now…We're having a small get-together…Yes, like a house-warming for me…More like a bathtub warming! Yes, you'll see…it's quite something! That's the only renovation I've really made. You'll see when you visit. Inshallah soon. I hope they like it…we'll find out soon! You should have a floor warming at 43-G! Abba, can you put Bari-ma on the phone, I just remembered something I have something really funny to tell her… Okay, turn on the speaker phone. Bari-ma, are you there? Guess what?

The other night… No, not last night… About a week ago on Saturday evening… I was going down the stairs when I heard someone playing a horn, like, making jazz music sounds… So I come down the stairs and there were these two guys… No, of course not, everything was fine… No, of course it's safe… Bari-ma, I take the stairs all the time. Nothing to worry about… Anyway listen, so there are these two young guys, much younger and one of them has this white horn that he's blowing on…and they're both wearing yamukas…so I ask him what he's playing and he says, 'You've never seen this before?' And I said no and he says it's a sopher! I'm not joking, Bari-ma…No, it was a sopher! White…made of a horn… See! It was. Anyway… And he plays a jazz tune…And then he asks me to give him a song to play and before I could say anything he asked me if I was from India… Of course not, I said, I was from Pakistan… And he said, 'Okay hold on, tell me if you can recognize this.' So Bari-ma, he starts blowing this tune…I swear I could recognize it, a Hindi film tune, but I couldn't remember the words…He was playing a whole filmy tune…What do you mean it can't be done? It was done, I heard it…So he asks me if I know the words, and I said I knew the tune but I couldn't remember it!

So then, unbelievably, this white guy this American kid starts to sing, 'Thum pas aiy, yun muskeray. Abto meray dil, jagey na sota hay. Jane kya hota hai, kya karon hai kuch-kuch hota hai!' And then he turns around and sings it in English for his not-so-thrilled friend, 'You came close to me, smiled that way. Now my heart can sleep or stay awake. What can I do, something is kind of happening to me!' Can you believe it? Only in New York, Bari-ma! He told me he had been in Bombay for a while, like for three months, studying or something… No, I think they were just visiting the building, breaking the Sabbath at someone's house on the third floor. Bari-ma, it's totally safe… I take the staircase all the time, it's good exercise. Don't you like the story? Bari-ma! You're missing the point… Wasn't that something?

Walking in later, Shireen had looked around and declared cheerfully, 'How completely outrageous. How completely in your face! It's so you, Resham. I love it.'

Everyone had gathered in Resham's large, sunny, Soho loft, a few blocks from Amina's apartment.

'Well, I can't believe it! We're all finally here! Imagine that!' Resham exclaimed as she held the apartment door open for her sisters.

Kulsum came in carrying several large paper bags, 'Imagine that! Your schedules are really ridiculous. I mean, just to be able to put together a baby shower for Ana took us so long to organize. We can't seem to manage anything together anymore.'

Amina, coming in right behind Kulsum, said, 'Well, this was sacred. So here we are!'

Ana who had arrived earlier greeted them. 'Isn't this the most amazing space? Come through here guys. Follow me into the bathroom. Have you ever seen anything like this? Just look at this place, you can't even call it a bathroom. Look at this huge cathedral-like space.

Resham: Well not exactly, you do exaggerate a tad bit too much! Ana: But look at these windows. Marvelous! My God, floor to ceiling windows in the bath! Look at the view. Look at this tub!

Copper lined, oh my God! This place has the most amazing bath I've ever seen; it's literally a hamam.

Resham: Well that was the idea when I renovated this place. I wanted a real hamam type of feeling in my bathroom. It's my one fetish and one indulgence!

Ana: I love the peach tones on the walls. I love all this sunshine in here. We love your fetish, dahling. And we love the fact that we can all fit into your fetish. We can all easily fit into it. Thank you for thinking of us when you were doing this renovation.

Resham: Yup. Thank the Google stocks, IPOed at $85 and now it's at $295. The sky's the limit!

Shireen: I'm going to thank your stock market!

Resham: Precisely.

Kulsum: Well, just look at this thing! It could easily hold all of us, that's true. How much did you pay for this extravagance if I may ask?

Resham: You may. Not more than what you must have paid for your home renovations.

Kulsum: Hold on! My home renovations included a whole kitchen the size of your living room and an extra bedroom and bathroom!

Resham: I didn't want all that, all I wanted was this bathtub!

Kulsum: My God Resham, you are extravagant!

Resham: Well, that's what I wanted!

Ana: Kulsum, I hope you've said goodbye to your husband and kids for the weekend. Because we're not going to let you go back to the 'burbs tonight!

Kulsum (laughing): Absolutely, I'm having a sleepover!

Amina: Wow, Resham! You've really gone all out, huh? Look at this place, pink and blue balloons. Matching napkins and flowers, wow!

Resham: Well, you can thank Kelly for that!

Kelly: Well, it's a huge celebration. Ana is having a baby.

Ana (laughing): Indeed I am! Just look at me, as big as...well, name it, 'you're as big as'... But here we are, my baby shower and I'm spending the night too.

Resham asked Amina: You?

Amina: Sure am!

Shireen: Baba, I have to get back to my kids so I can't spend the night!

Ana: Guys I really, really appreciate this.

Kulsum said affectionately giving her a big hug: Ana, we really, really appreciate it too! Good for you! This is so wonderful. I have you all day today and tonight. It's perfect. I haven't spent time in the city in such a long time!! And I've brought all your favorite dishes. Look what I brought! There's haleem, shami kebabs, karhai and nihari.

Ana squealed happily: I think I'm going to faint with happiness.

I've been having such a huge craving for spicy food, it's ridiculous.

This kid is going to want red chili pepper in his milk!

Shireen: My favorite dishes and my favoritest friends. Dishes-elicious! I think I've died and gone to heaven.

Resham: Bless you Kulsum, sweetie.

Amina: Well, I've already done two hours on the treadmill today so bring it all on!!

Kulsum: And guess who cooked all this food, every single dish?

Amina: You're kidding!

Kulsum: No, not at all. She is perfect. She really has the taste in her hands. She's better than me.

Amina: That's amazing. That's fabulous!

Kulsum: I think she really might just succeed in the business if she wants to. I told her the secret to mouth-watering dishes was to think green: fresh coriander, green chilies and limes.

Amina: I love it. Green. My mouth is watering. Bless you, Kulsum.

Resham: And I've got a very special treat for all of us. See these?

Resham held up jars of flowers.

Ana: Are those rose petals? Red roses. Well, that's lovely. For us?

Resham: Yes, but that's just a part of it.

Shireen: Oh. I love treats. What is it, a good Bollywood film?

Amina: I hope it's the Indy film you were talking about, or another exposé on the Iraq war!

Kulsum: Oh no! Nothing depressing, please!

Resham: No, it's something quite different, I learnt about it at a book reading I went to yesterday.

Amina: Oh no! It does sound serious!

Kelly: Sounds mysterious what?

Resham: We're going to indulge in a bit of lustration. Lustrate!

Shireen: A porno flick!! Oh my God, Resham. Even better!

Resham: No! Don't you know what lustration means?

Kelly: Yeah, like Shireen said, pornography!

Kulsum: Actually, I think it means spiritual showers, or like anointing or purification.

Lillian: Very impressive Kulsum, a closet lustrator I see.

Amina: We're going to bathe?

Resham: Yup!! We're all going to bathe in rose petals, mint and sage leaves!

Amina: Excuse me?

Resham: It is a baby shower! So we're all going to bathe with Ana.

Amina: Baby showers are meant for presents, cake and a lot of oooohing and ahhing.

Resham: Nope, I think they're meant for us to bathe with the mother-to-be. I have it all here, roses, sage, mint!!

Kulsum: Bathing?

Resham: Butt naked.

Ana: Ooooooh, I like this, I get to be pregnant and naked with my lovely friends.

Amina: No. You be pregnant and naked. And we be just naked.

Shireen: Well I'm happy to get into hot water with all of you. Just no comments on the cellulite or the sagging breasts.

Ana: Stand in line sister! Okay let's lustrate.

Amina: No way.

Resham: C'mon Amina, it'll be fabulous. And you have to especially after your jailbird experience. Seriously! We could all use a little spiritual cleansing. We're going to fill up this huge thing up with water and with rose petals and sage and we're all going to say prayers to our own personal gods and goddesses and we're going to do this together.

Kulsum: Well why not! Let's bathe!

Amina: No way!

Resham: Way! C'mon Amina, let's do it!

Ana: It's a spiritual bath. Here, look at this lovely book, spiritual baths from all over the world. I thought it would be lovely, it's to cleanse us of all our toxins and bless us and open us up to the universe.

Amina: Give me a break! You went to a book reading for this?

There's a coffee-table book on this? This is news for you! I mean, people do this all the time.

Resham: Really? When was the last time you did this? We know people do it. We know our grandmothers probably did it. But when was the last time you did this?

Amina: Well, last time I was at a majlis or a milad they were sprinkling rose essence all over the place. I got soaked!

Ana: What about baptisms and at church services? Hey, I'm a Catholic, I know about getting soaked!

Resham: When was the last time?

Amina: A couple of light years ago!

Ana: At least!

Kulsum: Well, they do bathe brides in milk and rose essence and what not.

Resham: News for you no brides here!

Ana: And a pregnant person with no husband!!

Amina: Great, so we don't have to do this.

Resham: Yes we do! I insist! It'll be great, just think all of us, together, it'll be so beautiful.

Amina: You're whacked.

Kulsum: And we have the perfect bathtub for this spiritual bath!

Can anyone possibly resist this gigantic bathtub!

Ana: Beware! You'll be sharing my bathwater, I could be contagious.

Kulsum: If only pregnancies were contagious!

Amina: Count me out sister. I'm not getting into a bath with all of you.

Resham: Look I read that Assyrians used to bathe five times a day.

Amina: News flash, not an Assyrian. Twenty-first century, not the first.

Lillian: Look at these beautiful tiles. Resham, where did you get these? Where are they from? Morocco? Turkey? Italy?

Resham: They're a combination. Some are from Hala in Pakistan, some from Florence and most from Turkey and Morocco. And of course that lovely Tuscan shop down in Soho.

Lillian: Absolutely amazing.

Ana: Look at this place. Its heaven with this water, the rose petals, the tiles, this copper lined tub. What decadence.

Kelly: It's sublime.

Resham: The better to bathe in.

Lillian: Amen, dahling. Amen. Just look at us, like flowers in a bowl.

Amina (self consciously): Can people in the building across

the street see us flowers in this bowl?

Resham: And you would care?

Ana: Exactly. The room was filled with the laughter of women and with a peachy glow. Silvery reflections shimmered on to the walls as the sunlight coming in from the wall to ceiling windows struck the water. It was a clear day outside. Inside, it was joyful. Light. The five day forecast on ten-ten winds said the same. On the marble counter, bearing the large eggshell-white urn of a sink sat a photograph, black and white, quite faded, which required closer examination. A photograph in an elaborate frame. This was Zareenabai's mother's family. Resham had picked it out for its old world quality. Closer examination showed eight children of varying ages; two to probably sixteen, gazing out quite earnestly with all the seriousness that they could muster, shoulders straightened out, arms stiffly to their sides, chins thrust forward. They were all arranged against the balustrade of a rooftop. It was obviously a very special occasion, this business of photograph taking, of being arranged just so, with the sunlight just so. The children were dressed in their best clothes. It seemed to be a winter morning because they all had ill-fitting sweaters and jackets over kurtas and pyjamas and shalwar kameezes. The girls' clothes, their dupattas were edged with golden borders. The gold was not obvious in the black and white photograph, but the hint of lightness, as though a glint on the edges of the dupattas from sunlight, made it appear so. Their shoes were new, probably. No, definitely; it was Eid day, and the shoes must be new. And in the background, if you looked carefully, through the morning haze, there emerged the outline of the Taj. This was Agra, circa 1944. The family house of many siblings and their parents. Three years later everything would change. One would die on the way to Pakistan. The rest would go first to Karachi, and from there, over many years of disorientation and discouragement would scatter and leave for Stockholm, Toronto, Boston, London, Gujranwala and Khairpur.

Zareena would marry Razzak and stay in Karachi. And all those held together in this photograph would have offspring, who would variously scatter and work on super computers, lead in psychoanalysis, struggle for a Marxist revolution, make killings on the stock market, join law firms and own very large bathtubs. And in memory, with each passing year, these clothes in black and white would take on color, become more gorgeous, and the winter sunshine would become sweeter, comforting like nowhere else, and the view, closer than it really ever was. The past is always dense, the present not so, or so it is for immigrants. Another framed photograph in color was taken at 43-G: in the foreground sat all five girls, on the sofa behind them sat Hajrabai and Choti-ma. Haji Rueewallah stood behind them. And today in the room, four of these offsprings, each of whom owned their own version of the Taj, sat submerged in it, in a ritual bath in New York City as sunlight danced around them, reflecting off the water and onto the walls.

17

Masks

AMINA got into the subway and sat down near the door. The car was almost empty, the World Series finals were on. The Red Sox against the New York Yankees. It was history in the making for New York. She was on her way to meet Zain for dinner. She settled down for the long ride and thought about her recent escapade, she had lost count, but this must've been like the 112th guy she had met up with. She was tired but determined. Sooner or later Mr Right was going to show up. How hard could this be?

She recalled how she had walked into the restaurant, and there he was Mr Right…Wing. About 15 minutes into the conversation, Amina had made a quick calculation in her head. He said he was here just a couple of weeks ago. 'Did you come here for the RNC?'

Amina had asked him politely if he was here for the protests. He had grinned and said, 'No, not for the protests. Well, not exactly anyway.' She didn't bother to ask anymore. Throughout their conversation, she felt he hadn't really figured Amina out. He didn't really seem to care to find out much about her. He was looking for a good time He looked healthy. Amina liked his blue eyes. And the silvery hair, closely cropped. He could be exactly the thing she was looking for. She didn't know. Amina felt later that she had completely lost her mind and from the moment he told her to sit down, and she had, she had made up her mind that he was getting laid tonight, and that she, Amina, was going to walk away, having done the deed. It had been an impulsive and irrational decision.

Completely like her to deliberate the minutiae and lose it on the big ones! She didn't let their politics get in the way. He seemed to think that she was being arrogant, her reaction to all that talk about baseball and aliens, she had to somehow change that, she had to say something that would make him sympathetic towards her so she had blurted out, 'Look I don't think I'm the right person for you. You need someone very beautiful and very refined, and I just don't fit those categories!' She seemed to have remembered saying, 'Someone more Fox News!' It had worked! He stared at her as though she was a lunatic or something. Then he got red in the face underneath that, no doubt, deep ski and sailing related tan. From that moment on he was apologetic, sweet, gentle. He was the rescuer. And Amina could see that he thought she needed rescuing. She could see it. What was the expression on his face?

Contrite. Her mentioning Fox News seemed to have done the trick. Yes that was it, contrite. Talked about his life, the war he had been in, his college days, how he met his wife. His kids, his church, his commitment to Jesus. His love, his taking it outside one too many times, mano a mano. Mano o mano. The quizzical look on Amina's face made him think that she didn't know what that meant. So he had lunged at her with his fists in a one two punching of the air between them. Amina had ducked. He had laughed. He found that endearing. She was cute, he was cool. He was it, she was the exotic thing. At one point, he actually called her exotic. She almost choked. The Other. He commented on how they fit right in with the city scene. How he had noticed so many mixed couples this time around in New York. Indian girls with white boys, Chinese guys with black girls and so on. She thought him to be so archaic.

The Big Tent. He kept calling the city, and everything about it The Big Tent. Something about the chemistry between Condi Rice and George Bush. Amina thought that she was going to gag. Oh well. He wanted to go for a walk. They walked aimlessly. He held her hand, first looped through his arm, his elbow bent holding her hand tight against him in his hand. That was awkward. Then he held her hand at his side, and she noticed that crossing streets, he leapt onto the street, with her dragging behind slightly. He was the man, she was his woman. Rather, he was the boy and she was his girl. But she played coy and couldn't resist pointing out that here in New York, just looking around at everyone in the Big Tent, she thought that between the two of them, he was more exotic.

After all, grey, white men were an endangered species. He laughed. He was the powerful guy, she was the little girl. Whatever, it was something he did. She could feel this was easy for him, he did this all the time. That was good, it was good. He was good at this, she thought. And she was not, but he was making it very easy. It was reckless, he didn't mention condoms, she didn't care about HIV, though Amina knew he'd been in the army, probably slept his way through the whole damn experience. If she was going to get sick this was going to be the way to do it. But she couldn't care less, her hormones, the whole clock thing was ticking so loud, it was crazy, it was all crazy. He had a strong sweet scent of alcohol and tobacco around him. Amina was someone who didn't even smoke, ate organic food, didn't touch anything unhealthy. She was going to get screwed by a Marine, an ex-Marine, or someone who probably served in Vietnam or something. A war criminal probably. Complete with a red and blue star tattooed on his chest above his heart. 'Red, blue 'n white,' he murmured as she traced her finger around its outline. 'White?' Amina had inquired, not getting it. He grinned. 'Ah yes, of course, I see, of course,' she had mumbled, getting it. The whole nine yards. Could cross-burning be far?

In his free time, he probably patrolled the damn Texan border with his gun in tow as a hobby, keeping the 'wetbacks' at bay. They spent the entire weekend in that room, he made a few phone calls on his cellphone, and she did the same. They ordered up room service. Plate loads of French fries. She even had a vanilla milkshake. She didn't care, they didn't talk much. The sex was great, the best she'd ever had. He returned the compliment. He was slow and sensuous, he loved his body, he loved bodies, it was obvious, he took his time, no hurry. He had told Amina he loved to tinker with the engine of his vintage Chevy, then wash it and wax it down. Amina was getting the full benefit of the great Protestant work ethic. She wasn't going to put up a fight. It took her time to relax to understand that he wanted to go on, focus on her. He kept using this phrase that she had never heard before, that he wanted to 'pleasure' her. It made her cringe until by round two, she figured out that this guy really meant it. Heck that was fine by her. She had been delirious with being pleasured, that's the only explanation she had for her recklessness because there she was later, jumping up and down on the bed. Not something she would do. And naked. Never did that. There she was now jumping on a hotel bed. Naked. Up and down bouncing as he watched her, or her breasts more like it. She had swiped the cover sheet right off of him, and jumped off the edge of the bed with the sheet flying over her head and behind her as though she were superwoman with a green cape. He laughed. When they were finally done and dressed and after the sheets were made up and smoothed down, they had left. He volunteered to pay the hotel bill. She had said no, and that she'd take care of it. He insisted. Got in the way of his manhood or something. She insisted more. He said corporate account. 'Corporate account?' she said. 'Well say no more.' Amina let him win. He won. Then came the question of sharing a cab to the airport. They both decided that wasn't a good idea, big gaps between their flight times. He left Sunday night, held her close before he jumped into the cab, whispered in her ear, 'It was nice visitin' with you! You're beautiful, y'know that, you're beautiful.' Amina felt guilty. He sent her an email or two, wondering if they could 'visit' again. She never wrote back. He had no idea who she was. As far as he knew she was called Rita and she was visiting from Canada.

Raindrops splashed and bounced off the pavement in front of her like thousands of fluttering butterflies just as she stepped out of the subway. She had decided that she would get off at the 72nd street station and walk across to the restaurant on Amsterdam where Zain had said he would meet her at 8 p.m. Her umbrella kept turning inside out because of the strong wind as she fought her way across the avenues to the restaurant on Amsterdam and 84th. She noticed the carcasses of ruined umbrellas, scattered on the sidewalks. It would make a nice photograph, she thought. All of these gathered and piled up. The caption could read, 'Global Warming'. As she stepped into the bar area, she checked her watch: 8.15. She shrugged her shoulders, she had managed to be late again. She spotted Alejandro and Zain at the bar. She laughed, 'Sorry I'm late, the wind and the rain threw me off my scheduled arrival of 8 p.m. sharp.'

'Nada!' Zain said, 'I just got here myself. Shall we go to our table, I went ahead and made reservations.' They waved goodbye to Alejandro who refused to budge from the bar. Zain thumped him on his back, and said, 'Later' But Alejandro was already absorbed in the big game: Yankees vs. Red Sox game seven on the TV above the bar. 'It's going to be a miracle! Not seen in 86 years baby, not in 86 years!'

'Keep dreamin'!' someone at the bar shouted.

'The evil empire is almost over!' shouted Alejandro. Amina raised an eyebrow and looked at Zain for an explanation.

Well, the Red Sox fans keep saying that the Yankees buy their players and that's why they win. Babe Ruth was bought from the Red Sox and all that. And then there's the curse of the Bambino! The fact is that the Red Sox sold the Babe to the Yankees.

'Hey, they got a $180 million team, that's how much they pay their guys so of course they'll always win. They buy off all the best players. Evil Empire! Like Real Madrid, y'know,' Alejandro added.

'Uh huh,' Amina said.

The maître d' led them to a table near the window in the corner of the restaurant. Zain waited for her to be seated, took her coat and set it on the chair on the side. He took off his own and set it on top of hers. The bar area erupted in cheers. Zain jumped up to look at the screen.

He sat down and said, 'Right.'

They stared at each other. And then they burst out laughing.

'What are we going to do about our mothers? This is painful!' he said.

She said, 'You know you have the kindest eyes and the most beautiful smile.'

Zain turned red. 'You seem shy and demonic all at once,' she continued.

'Thanks. But what do we do about our mothers?'

'Awful,' she agreed. 'It's the only way to get them off our backs, isn't it? To go ahead and follow their instructions and report back that it was awful.'

'Absolutely!'

'I mean, why can't they just understand that not everyone is cut out for marriage?'

'Indeed,' she said.

'Well to tell you the truth, I suspect that this is going to be the beginning of an escalating warfare of matchmaking. Now that they've gotten wind of the fact that we actually know each other. I think Yaqub told Sara he met me at your party. She told your mother, who told my mother.'

'Oh, well. We'll just have to ignore them,' Amina said, laughing.

'Indeed. Ignore the instructions from the mother ship.'

'And the interference of well meaning, worrying friends, as well,' Amina said.

'So why do we, I mean mature adults, an investment banker and a lawyer for God's sakes, have to do this?'

'Get pushed around by their mothers?'

'Well yes that, and just this?' Zain said.

'Just this?'

'I mean, why can't we just say no!' Zain said.

'Because we're Pakistanis. Pakistani Americans!'

'First generation,' Zain added.

'And we haven't learned to separate ourselves from the mother ship.'

'Speaking of which, I'm heading there in December of course,' Zain said.

Amina laughed, 'Yeah, me too. Of course.'

A friend of Zain's came over to the table. Zain made the introductions, 'Amina-Dave. Dave-Amina.' Dave was sweating profusely and was red in the face, clearly having had one drink too many. He thumped Zain on the shoulder and asked, 'Hey man, are you going to go to the Halloween parade this year? Wanna be my date?'

Zain said, 'Hi, Dave. Yea, I'm going, but I already have a date.

But I haven't decided on a costume yet. Whoa, watch it there, you're going to fall on top of me with that huge tank of beer.'

Dave steadied himself by leaning on the edge of the booth head-rest. 'You don't need a costume. You're all set!' he said.

'Yeah? How do you mean?' Zain asked.

Dave said, 'Well, just get a beard. Go as Osama or better yet, just take off the mask!'

Zain frowned quizzically, 'What?'

Dave laughed, 'Take that pretty face off and underneath it, bingo, there's Osama!' Dave did the last part like, 'Here's Johnny!'

From the Late Night Carson show. He continued, 'Everyone's betting that he'd show up around now. Just before the election!

Well, take off that mask of yours…'

Amina listened in horror. Zain clenched his fists.

Dave looked surprised, 'What's the matter, sweetie? I'm only kidding. What's the big deal?'

Zain was furious, he had turned red with anger. 'Fuck off, you jerk!' he shouted.

Dave straightened up, put his drink down on the table and raised his hands. 'It's only a joke!'

'A joke?' Zain said, 'After all the time you've spent with me, you think I'd take this as a joke?'

'C'mon, lighten up!' Dave said.

Amina smiled sweetly, 'What are you going as? The Grim Reaper? Because you know that would be totally perfect. Have you seen the report out last week on more than a 100,000 people dead in Iraq? Because of your war! Because of you!'

'Me?' Dave asked. 'What the hell are you talking about?'

'Exactly!' Amina shouted. 'I'm talking about exactly what you're talking about. If his face is a mask, then your face must be one too! You have no problem in saying whatever the hell you want to about him and about us, but when it comes to you, you go all innocent and hurt!'

Dave laughed nervously, 'Hey lighten up!'

'You want us to lighten up!' Amina demanded.

Dave said, 'Yes, I do!'

Zain said, 'No, I think you need to apologize to me!'

Dave put up his hands in protest, 'No, I'm not going to apologize. If you can't take a small joke, okay, a joke in bad taste, but still a joke, man.'

Zain was furious, 'No, I can't take a joke. You need to apologize.'

Dave shook his head and said, resolutely, 'Well, I'm not going to. Take a joke. We can joke with each other. Look at the guys at the bar, man! They're calling each other all kinds of names, just look at what they're calling the Bostonians. Lighten up man. It's all part of the game. You know who I am. You know what I think. I'm no bigot. You've known me for a very long time so don't get all huffed with me. After all these years, you can't take a joke?'

Zain fumed, 'No I can't take a joke. Well there then, your mask is off. No more Mr Politically correct liberal.'

Dave laughed, 'Hey, I'm gay and I'm a liberal. Okay, I'm sorry. I'm sorry. It was a stupid joke. Lighten up. Please just accept the damn apology, okay? Sorry.'

'Zain, he said he's sorry,' Amina interjected.

Zain said, 'OK. Done. Apology accepted. Don't be such a jerk. Now go away, we're trying to have a conversation here.'

Dave swaggered off towards the bar saying, 'Sorry man, didn't mean to get you all hot under the collar.'

Zain watched him go. 'Anyway, all the masks are going to come off in about two days time.'

Amina sighed, 'Yeah... Or go on. I'm afraid the elections will be nothing more than a big fat show. If Kerry gets elected then the mask will never come off. We'll go on with the charade.'

Zain agreed, 'The whole system stinks. Get ready world, it's Halloween!!'

Amina added, 'And the day after that is the day of the dead. And the day after that is the election.'

Zain muttered, 'Same difference.'

Amina said glumly, 'It scares me. I think this country is going to re-elect him. I mean, I think they really are into the blood-letting and looking for pogroms. It's getting pretty fascistic. I mean, that day at Pier 57, the arrest… I really felt I was in a bad movie about fascism, or like a war of the worlds movie where aliens have taken over and they were dressed like us. I mean, just look at that bloody turncoat of a Senator from Georgia, Zell Miller, what he had to say at the Republican National Convention. Man, he sounded exactly like all the Pakistani generals Musharraf, Zia, Yahya and Ayub rolled into one, talking rot, saying that it's the soldier not the agitator or the Press that defends freedom and freedom of speech. And I saw it in action—people protesting, exercising their first amendment rights, being arrested. The first and fifth; you have the right to talk and you have the right not to talk, being violated that way. I mean, I don't know if this place is going to get better. And now look at what your buddy Dave just revealed about himself!

The masks are coming off! And I'm scared.'

Zain took a swig of his beer, 'Yeah, I hear you. I'm pretty scared too.'

Amina snorted, 'I mean, I just had to see that night of speeches at the convention to know that we're done here. If people that we look to as the opposition, I mean, even the so-called liberals were in there, people who are supposed to represent the other side. I mean, even they attended the convention!'

Zain disagreed, 'Yeah, but they were there to comment and protest!'

Amina replied, 'The point is they were there, in there under their Big Tent. I think you need to be outside it if you're going to protest it. You don't need to have a ticket to their party! I mean, it's all so weird. It's hard to tell who is who!'

Zain nodded, 'I know.'

Amina continued, 'And the final straw for me was when that woman wearing a pink slip ran up to Dick Cheney and interrupted his speech. Ha ha ha, a pink slip, you're fired! How cute, how stupid, and a good way to be on national television so that the whole country can see that the protesters are nothing but a bunch of non-serious exhibitionists. It's all so pathetic. Just watch these guys get re-elected. Anyway, I've decided to get out of here.

I've quit my job.'

'What?' Zain exploded. 'One minute we're talking about the Republic National Convention, and the next moment you're telling me you've quit your job! That's a bit impulsive! And risky, don't you think?'

Amina said serenely, 'Yeah. Big decision.'

'What are you going to do?' Zain asked.

Amina sighed, 'Well, I've got some savings. I think I want to take some time off. Go back to Karachi for a while. Sit back and relax, you know. Spend time with my parents…'

Zain whistled, 'Wow! Are you sure? I mean, that's quite a move. You can't just get up and do that! Can you?'

'Sure I can,' Amina said. 'All I have to do is just do it. Like the Nike ad says! And besides, I have my citizenship now. Now that that's not an issue anymore, I can afford to leave. I can always come back. I mean, for the longest time, that was the goal—get the Green Card, get the citizenship. Now I have all that, I'm free. I can do what I want to do, I can go back! I mean, it really is freedom.

So I'm going to take a sabbatical from the whole job thing and chill for a while! Go check out what's up in Karachi.'

Zain said anxiously, 'I don't know. This sounds pretty risky.'

Amina shrugged, 'I've always wanted to do this.'

'Well then, sounds good to me. Go for it!'

Amina looked at Zain and nodded, 'Yeah, maybe I'll get into film making or something, take on a whole new career, go become a talk show host on a cable channel, join Al Jazeera!'

Zain enthused, 'Hey, why not?'

Amina looked at Zain clenching and unclenching his fists.

He seemed still distracted and very angry. 'You okay?' she asked nervously.

Zain said, 'I don't know. What? That jerk? Don't worry about it. Yeah, I'm okay. What can you do? That's just the way it is now.

What can you do, huh?'

18

Meanwhile Back at the Ranch

HAJRA went out on to the balcony and looked out at the busy traffic on Lawrence Road. She had come to air the apartment and have it cleaned. Razia and Jeevan had come along with her for this purpose. She wondered if Amina and Resham would want to live here. Perhaps the thought of returning to Karachi posed the unspoken hurdle for them of being unmarried and being expected to live with their parents. She would ask Amina this when she came home. Amina could easily live here at Lawrence Road independently. Of course they would all visit her regularly from 43-G and she would probably spend most of her time there but at least she would know that she had her own home, perhaps that would make returning more attractive. The thought of independence. The girls had their own portions at 43-G, but that wasn't really being independent. She turned back in from the balcony and called out excitedly to Razia and Jeevan to hurry, they would return to 43-G in an hour. Amina was coming home that night.

Still a good twelve hours to go. The Emirates flight was not due to land till midnight or so. And it was only close to noon. Zareenabai was beside herself with anxiety and ecstasy and had been rushing through the house, from room to room and up to her daughter's freshly aired and mosquito repellent sprayed bedroom, reassuring herself that everything was just so. Just the way her sweet little girl would expect it to be, as it should be, just the way Amina would want it to be. In Amina's room, Zareenabai touched the synthetic, flaxen curls on the blue-eyed doll sitting on the shelf above the bed. Hajrabai had brought it back from London when she had gone to visit Meir. Amina had phoned Hajrabai just a week ago and told her that she had decided to return to Karachi. Just like that. Her mind was made up. She was taking time off from work, she was coming home, maybe for a year, maybe more.

Zareenabai plumped up the stuffed cloth furry dog spread-eagled atop Amina's pillow. Zareenabai looked around her daughter's teenage room, the Red and Black Che Guevera poster, the one of Arafat next to it, and the sign that the teenage Amina had

painted on the back of the bedroom door, with bright colours, 'What if they gave a War and Nobody came?' Seemed as though it was only yesterday when Amina was in high school and this room had been constantly filled with giggling girls. It would be so good to have her back. Zareenabai was certain that home, comfort, luxury, that sense of carefree abandonment, were things that her daughter's small apartment and hectic lifestyle in New York, could not provide. Her beautiful and talented daughter Amina, the successful lawyer in New York, was coming home. Everything had been prepared and then some. Coffee and tea parties had been lined up almost every day, Sara had taken care of that, and there were dinner parties almost every single evening, thanks to Sara, bless her heart, and some very subtly, strategically and carefully planned maneuvers which Amina would not catch on to, or there would be hell to pay, for introducing her to some prospective bridegrooms. She's so lovely, so intelligent, so kind and generous, thought Zareenabai fondly of her daughter, why shouldn't she be married? Zareenabai was still smarting from the recent remarks of a friend who had alluded to the fact that Amina and Resham were now well past marriageable age and that all their talents and high stature in the corporate world were for naught if they were to be left single, unmarried. In short, spinsters. Heaven forbid, a spinster! In fact, in giving her so-called kindly opinion, this vile woman had been quite clear that Amina had misstepped in life. Why there were plenty of girls in Pakistan who had careers and were married, but Amina seemed to be a pitiful exception to all that. Zareenabai shuddered first at the thought of Amina's unbearable fate as a spinster, and then at the thought of her friend. 'Chorrail! That witch!' Zareenabai muttered out loud. The sweeper, scrubbing the mosaic floor of the verandah in which Zareenabai paced looked up in alarm and enquired, 'Hain jee, huh Begum Sahiba, did you call me?'

'Of course not!' hastened Zareenabai in alarm, 'I would never say that to you! Tauba, God forbid.'

At Sara's behest, Zareenabai had recently joined an NGO whose mission was helping destitute women, and the thought of calling the woman on her hands and knees scrubbing the floor before her, a witch, was just too awful and painful a thought to contemplate. Her heart was far too kind, she was far too aware of the social injustices of her society not to feel the acute embarrassment at the thought that the sweeper could have possibly believed that Zareenabai's sudden outburst be directed towards her. And furthermore, God forbid that Jeevan should leave the house today, after this little outburst on her part, and speak of Zareenabai that way to others.

What would people think? As she paced back and forth, Zareenabai held up the skirt of her sari with one hand to avoid contact with the wet floor and passed by Jeevan, bent over on her hands and knees on the wet floor, repeated her thoughts out loud,

'No no, no, I was thinking of Amina Bibi, you know she is coming home tonight, and I just cannot wait!' 'Yes Begum Sahiba, may she have a long life and grow and prosper, may she be married quickly and have ten sons!'

Zareenabai stopped, swung around, released the pleats of her sari, the hem getting wet as it touched the damp floor. She stared at the woman. 'Yes, yes!' she said passionately. 'May your mouth be filled forever with ghee and sugar.' And she walked off hurriedly, suddenly remembering that she had to make a phone call. An essential and important phone call. As she moved away at a rapid pace and shouted back over her shoulder, 'Jeevan, don't forget to take home with you all the food from yesterday's dinner party. And if Amina Bibi gets married soon, I will give you a gold bracelet, you hear!' With an amused smile on her face and a glint in her eye, Jeevan shook her head and watched the corpulent backside of Zareenabai waddle off.

Zareenabai settled herself down in her favorite armchair near the telephone, opened her paandaan and fixed herself a generous paan. While thumping her ample bosom with one hand and fanning herself with the other, she shouted 'Razia! Razia!' to the woman ironing in the laundry room. 'Come quickly, bring me a glass of water and check the speed of this slow poke ceiling fan, I'll die of heat if it doesn't move any faster. I tell you, the air in here is as still as in a grave!' Razia came running down the corridor and checked the fan's regulator switch, 'Begum Sahiba, it can't go any faster, it's already on number one, there must be low voltage!'

'Those low lives! God kill them, who went and detonated those nuclear tests, look what the result is—low voltage! How we have to suffer!' Zareenabai muttered to herself. 'Alright then,' said the profusely perspiring Zareenabai. 'Go tell cook to make me a pot of tea quickly, not in the small teapot, the large one for Hajrabai as well, and bring it upstairs to the terrace.' Zareenabai collected her thoughts as she chewed on her paan and sipped the glass of cool water that Razia had handed to her in a rush. Another order was shot off to Razia to check with Ilyas the driver if there was enough petrol in the car for the drive to the airport tonight, or whether they would need to fill up this afternoon. The response came that there would be a need for a refill and that there were rumors that the drivers' union for the oil tankers were about to go on strike again. Ilyas requested five hundred rupees to fill up the tank. 'Ooofh tauba, the strikes, the price of petrol, the price of everything! The nuclear tests have done us in…' Zareenabai complained as she handed over the funds to Razia to give to the driver to give to the petrolwallah at the station when he went to fill up. All was taken care of, it seemed. Zareenabai, leaned back in her armchair, sighed a deep sigh of contentment and shut her eyes for a few moments, exhausted with anticipation and the fatigue of managing a household. Then she jerked up and rushed up to the terrace where Hajrabai sat reading the day's newspaper. Hajra dipped one corner of the paper to eye Zareena and then lifted it up higher.

'Oh, do put the paper down Hajrabai,' Zareenabai pleaded,

'I can hardly stand it! A few more hours left and they are hard to pass!'

Hajrabai, still holding up the paper, replied, 'Zareena, go away, you're making me nervous! What time is it? She must be somewhere over Europe by now.'

'Yes, I think so too. She must be. Everything is ready. I'll phone Faiza and find out if Zain has arrived.'

Razia brought in the tea and Hajrabai said, 'Can you go and check with Yunis if he has bought the limes that I told him to buy from Friday Bazaar this morning? Amina loves nimbu pani and I want to make sure that she doesn't have to wait a moment for it when she is here. There must always be a large supply of it in the refrigerator for her.' Just that minute, Yunis was coming through to enquire whether he should make an extra amount of shami kebabs to freeze, since Amina Bibi loved shami kebabs with her fried eggs for breakfast. 'Of course, Begum Sahiba,' he said to Hajrabai. 'I've bought the nimbus and I will make Razia squeeze out the juice just as soon as she's done with the ironing.' He winked at Razia, making sure that the older women weren't looking.

After Razia and the cook went off and Hajrabai put up her wall of newspaper, Zareenabai reached for the telephone and slowly pressed the phone numbers of her old college friend, Begum Faridudin. 'Hello Faiza!'

'Zareena! How is everything? Don't tell me the flight will be delayed!'

'No, no, thank God, the flight is on time so far. I just wanted to ask you if Zain is arriving as planned!'

'Zareena, he arrived last night!'

'He's already here, arrived last night,' echoed Zareenabai in an excited squeal to Hajra, who nodded in approval.

'He said his plans had changed and he came in with his best friend. Mashallah both boys are asleep upstairs.'

'He's come with a friend and they're sleeping upstairs,' said Zareenabai.

'I know! I just said that!' Faiza said.

'I'm talking to Hajra!'

'Oh good,' Faiza replied. 'Well, give her my love. I just didn't have the chance to phone you, you know how excited everyone is at his arrival.' She lowered her voice to a whisper. 'And there has been a parade of relatives with a surprising number of young girls in tow!' Begum Faridudin had been entertaining mostly mothers with young daughters who had steadily been streaming through all morning long.

'There's a mob of relatives over there with their young daughters!' Zareenabai said to Hajra in alarm. 'Tell her to keep them away,' said Hajrabai to Zareena.

'Keep them away, keep them away!' Zareenabai said anxiously to Faiza.

'Don't worry darling, he's fast asleep and he is nowhere around them. Jet lag, you know. What a blessing.'

'He's sleeping so he's nowhere near the relatives!' Zareenabai informed Hajra.

'By tomorrow when he has freshened up, we will make sure we keep him away from these hordes, and save him up for Amina!'

Faiza said.

'You are such a dear!'

'No, no, don't say that! Amina is like my own daughter, you know that. I am so fond of her, I cannot think of a better match for Zain than our Amina. They are absolutely a match made in Heaven, if there ever was one! May God give both of them a long happy life.'

'She's saying that Zain and Amina are a match made in Heaven!' Zareena said to Hajra.

'God make it that way!' said Hajra.

'God make it that way!' repeated Zareenabai to Faiza. 'You know how much I worry for her, and I want to see her in a bridal dress and I want to see my grandchildren. Inshallah, this before I die.'

'What nonsense, don't talk like an old woman!' Hajrabai said.

'Don't be so wretchedly dramatic and, not to mention, ungrateful. You have Tahir, Zohra, Zainab, Sakina, Rahul and Kiren!'

Zareenabai ignored Hajrabai's comment, 'Do you think he will be awake this afternoon?' Zareenabai asked Faiza.

'Who knows, but why don't you drop by anyway,' Faiza suggested, trying to soothe her friend's nerves.

'We will, we will. You said he has come with his best friend?'

'Yes.'

'Is he married? His friend?'

'No, but he's an American. Latin, shatin.'

'She's saying the friend who came with him is American,'

Zareenabai informed Hajra and then continued, 'Oh well, acha, then, it doesn't matter. Well, we'll see you in the afternoon. Hajrabai and I are going to stop in after I go to Sara's place. I have had her make a few joras for Amina. I wanted her to be dressed nicely this time.'

'But she is always so well dressed!' Hajrabai protested.

'You know what I mean! She comes here and wears those awful clothes of hers, they are so unbecoming! Her pants and sleeveless shirts, she looks like those horrible creatures on MTV.

I wanted her to be dressed nicely this time. Dupattas, shalwar kameezes, more like Sara.'

'More like Sara?' Faiza asked.

'I hope you mean below the neck!' Hajrabai retorted.

'Anyway dear, don't worry about the way she dresses, all the girls are wearing western things!' Faiza said.

'Not the good girls! Boys still like to marry the sensibly dressed ones.'

'Good point. Good idea.'

'By the way, did you have a chance to talk to him? Did he say anything about his meeting with Amina.'

'Jani, he just came in last night, there were so many people, I haven't had a chance to talk to him about anything, except the humidity, the chaos at the airport, the McDonald's right there which he considers an eyesore and the increase in mosquitoes. Don't worry, and besides we should be very careful about this. Very subtle. You understand? You know how these children are, if they so much as get a whiff of what we're planning, they'll run in the opposite direction.'

'She's saying he was very upset with the mosquitoes and McDonald's.' Zareenabai said to Hajrabai who looked confused.

She continued, 'You are so right, Faiza, so right. I mean, I must be very careful with Amina, you know she'll be very upset if she finds out what I've been planning!'

'Yes, of course. Okay then, I'll see you in the afternoon.'

19

Someone Stole the Taste of Keenoos

THE singsongs and trills of cellphones mixed with the white noise of much frantic small talk by the many guests gathered in Sara's drawing room. Cigar smoke trumped the smell of cigarettes and the scent of perfumes.

Amina had been engaged in conversation with a silver- haired man who puffed on his cigar and blew smoke away from her while he nursed a glass of whiskey soda in one hand. She had been arguing with him about the taste of keenoos. 'Well Bibi, my job is to make money, not preserve nostalgia.'

'But they are all so tasteless now! Someone has stolen the taste of our keenoos!' Amina insisted.

The exporter threw up his arms, 'It's called genetically modified agriculture!'

Amina replied, 'And it's called cold storage! What we're buying in the market here in Karachi is fruit that may have been sitting in cold storage from a season ago, if not more! All the fresh produce, almost all of it now is exported! What a tragedy!'

The exporter chortled and puffed on his cigar, 'You see a tragedy, I see an economic opportunity and markets at work!

That's the problem with you December Pakistanis—you come back looking for a preservation of tragedy! You yourself are an export and an import, but you don't like anything else exported!'

'What?' Amina asked sharply.

'No really, I mean it! You have to justify to yourselves why you left your country and then when you come to visit you have to justify to yourself why you are going to leave again. That's why you see only tragedy here!'

'On the basis of keenoos?' asked Amina.

'Yes, things like this, that keenoos don't taste the same!' He mimicked a woman's voice.

'Come to think of it, chambeli flowers have lost their smell as well, the jasmine at night used for garlands and bracelets, sold by vendors at night on the streets—no scent!' Amina added.

'There you are! My point exactly!' He said mockingly,

'Nothing tastes or smells the same. As though all tastes and smells have vanished all because you left.'

Amina was about to retort but the man's attention was diverted by a beautiful woman who came up behind him and put her arms around his shoulders. He turned away from Amina and she turned to survey the room for someone else to speak to.

The room was abuzz in laughter, a steady bantering mixed with the chimes chirpings and musical rings of Bollywood songs, and symphonies going off as cellphones rang incessantly and simultaneously. Women sat text messaging, presumably to their sons and daughters abroad…or so she gathered from their explanations to each other. All of the available floor space which was covered in Persian carpets and rugs now seemed to be covered in saris and dupatta draped guests. The room seemed layered with them. Guests were seated on the sumptuous variegated upholstered couches, chaise longues, takths, divans, ottomans, sofas and armchairs.

People seemed to have spilled over on to the floor at the

feet of those who occupied all the available furniture. They leaned against knees or sat upright on the ample flouncy throw cushions on the floor. Another layer of guests mostly men, who were standing, were pretending to be in discussion when, as far as Amina could tell, all that they were really doing was gulping down as many whiskeys in as short a time as possible, nodding or shaking their heads rhythmically, checking their watches from time to time. The eyes of almost all of them were gleaming with envy at each other's watches, clothes and jewelry. Those eyes found their partners' pair at different places in the room, signaled to them the number of minutes before they went on to the next event where they could show off and envy some more.

December party-goers in Karachi resembled a frenzied herd moving from one watering hole to the next, as though fleeing from a bush fire. A haze filled the air with cigarillo and cigar smoke. As she walked through the crowd looking for a place to sit, Amina realized that she didn't know anyone here except for Sara.

She overheard someone asking, 'Did you hear about the bomb blast in Peshawar today?'

'Yeah yaar. Awful. God only knows how many people got killed.'

'We'll never know. Just take the official figure and multiply by five.'

And amongst these layers moved the white, uniformed waiters especially procured for the night from the Sind Club, of which of course, Sara and Riaz were members. They moved around in their white livery and white gloves, carrying goblets of white wine and champagne on silver trays, stooping over the seated female guests to serve them. If a guest waved them away, the waiter would look into her eyes and cajole gently, 'Just one small one, madam?' The glint in his eyes and the tone of his voice was perhaps only perceptible to an outsider fresh to these gatherings, such as Amina, who for the moment considered the waiter as important an entity as the other people in the room. A few more weeks perhaps and she would create the hierarchy of insensitivity so vital to survive here.

She would begin, as time went on, to sort through mechanically as to who was to be noticed and who was to be simply cast in the category of 'does not exist'. In a few weeks, she would not notice nor would she care about such discomforting thoughts as she had now: about where this waiter, this underling, lived, or what was meant by the glint in his gaze or the tone of his voice. What it signified. She would not think about the thoughts she was having now about where he would go to after the party finished, or where his home was. And in time even at 43-G, she would stop constantly thanking Jeevan, Razia, Ilyas, Yunis and the rest of them who served her hand and foot.

She would stop praising Iqbal for his wonderful tailoring and his workmanship or Yunis for his incredibly delicious cooking. But for now she was doing just that. She was still fresh. For now, Iqbal, Riaz, Ilyas, Yunis and the rest of them seemed incredibly talented and gifted to her, under-appreciated and under-valued. Soon, they would fade into being equipment for her convenience. The feeling of guilt was much like jet lag, it would wear off in a week and a half of acclimatization. Her gaze left the waiter's white uniformed back and moved on to the other essential symbols of luxury and status.

Costly art. Oil and water color paintings graced the walls and of course, they were all of the well known names. The effect that was sought, and was being achieved had nothing to do with the subject or the substance of the painting, but rather the signature on it. It was an exhibition of the amassing of so many signatures of importance. The names of the artists. Much perhaps like the accumulation of guests that were filling up this room. Stretched along several of the walls were yards of Jamil Naqshes, the usual theme of a fat woman, naked, with pigeons, or fat pigeons minus the naked woman. Paintings conveniently coordinated with the upholstery hues of grey, pinks and green pastels. A couple of Sadequain pencil sketches, again the usual fare; a study of a long necked woman and a man's head, and then, suspiciously as an after thought on the part of the artist, a crow flying out of the man's head. She noticed that her sister and brother-in-law had put up their earlier acquisitions of a few Indian artists as well. There was an M. F. Hussain and a Souza. These paintings had been bought two decades ago but hadn't been deemed as worthy of display in Sara's drawing room till recently. All these images, pigeons, horses, peaches, crows and severed heads peeked at her whenever the wall of inebriated, guzzling and gulping men in front of her shifted their weight, their considerable weights. Then she was able to catch a glimpse of the wall at the other end of the very large drawing room.

This gathering of corpulence signified important names. Everything, from conversation and gestures, to cigars and blackberrys and the paintings on the walls in Sara's drawing room was about amassing names. An intricate web of connections and associations that subtly and not so subtly always based itself on the sources and uses of power. There were a couple of actors from Bombay, part of a troupe visiting Karachi who were here to put on a play and attend the Karachi film festival. Sara had pointed out a couple of guests here on business from China. Important clients of Riaz's. A blonde woman in an ill-fitting and outdated shalwar kameez was the director of some European cultural institute in the city, part of an embassy. And there was the upcoming, young film-maker visiting 'home' from LA for the winter vacation. And over there was the much celebrated Pakistani novelist, just in from London.

And in the corner holding court was the talk show host of BBC Asia. And wasn't that the guy who lost his job on CNN a couple of years back? What was he upto now? And there was the designer, who had just sold a line to a fashion house in Milan. The room was filled with returnees. The power of remittances hung heavy in the air, creating an even brighter and bigger bubble.

'I'm going back to Perth next week. The children don't like it here. What can I do? They've grown up there!'

'Meet Asim, he's just in from Cape Town. He's my first cousin. He's in construction, over there!'

'How's life in Paris treating you, Khurram?'

'C'mon yaar, you must be kidding, you're feeling chilly? Here in Karachi? It's not like December in Toronto!'

'Yeah, but we have central heating over there!'

'Poor thing, they just moved to Moscow you know, posted by their company, the children hate it. They liked Cairo so much better. Still, at least they can continue to come every December to Karachi as usual! Small mercies.'

'The help in Singapore isn't what it used to be!'

'Thank God we still have it good in KL! But how's your Filipina maid working out?'

'Meet my sister-in-law. They've just arrived from Mauritius. Next week, we're going to Bombay and Goa. Intend to spend New Year's there!'

'Great idea, we had a ball there last year. Should've gone again this year but too much happening here. Inshallah, next year. What time is it? I have to go pick up my brother from the airport at 3.00 a.m., he's coming in from LA. Bring him here?

No way, he'll be dead tired! And you know these foreign returns, they have no sense of fun, he'll want to catch up on his sleep!

And I'm in no mood to hear a sermon on disparity and how debauched and irresponsible we all are here in Karachi. Really, we have to find a route in from the airport that doesn't take the car through the slums!'

'Cairo is lovely. You must visit us soon. But nothing like Karachi in December!'

'Yes, I come in every two weeks, it's an easy commute from Dubai. The family didn't want to move, so I decided it was better for me to go back and forth rather than to disrupt the childrens' schooling. And Grammar School admissions are nothing to sneeze at!' Through French windows that covered one side of the room and opened on to the magnificent emerald green lawn, Amina could see the aqua blue water of the swimming pool, shimmering as the lights beneath the surface of the water and above it danced on its waves, tickled by the dewy, cool sea breeze that was beginning to start up as it always did at this time of the evening in Karachi. Elsewhere, outside these walls, there was a shortage of water and of electricity and the idea of a green patch of grass was most definitely a novelty in this parched and sprawling city. The scent of lilies filled the air. Flowers that had been flown in from Dubai this afternoon at a price tag equivalent to the salary of the waiter serving the wine. The wine bottles, which cost two thousand rupees each were being emptied too fast, Sara had complained earlier, while Jeevan had stood by listening. The same amount that Jeevan earned as salary per month. The central air-conditioning, on at this time of the year to justify the wood burning in the fireplace in a tropical climate, was making Amina feel chilly. She decided that she would move towards and perhaps out onto the lawn.

The chatter around Amina made her realize that she had nothing substantial to contribute to the passionate debate on whether the woman named Nichi was the best hair tinter in town or not, whether her masseuse was a lesbian, or for that matter whether the application forms for Grammar School for the coming term would be available from 5 a.m. or 6 a.m. 'You've lost weight, haven't you?' someone nearby said to someone else who clearly hadn't. An incessant question amongst men and women.

Other guests were talking about war 'Dahling, perhaps it's a war of peace? Will they attack? Won't they attack? Keeping us on our toes, that's good, that way there's no war. And we manage to keep the peace. Just a pot shot or two here and there once in a while!'

'You call Kargil pot shots?!'

'Oh for God's sakes, that's old hat now. So much more going on. Don't worry! No more wars with India. They've already conquered us with Bollywood!'

A man laughed, 'Indeed! That's their main army. No need for the 500,000 soldiers of ours, and about 1.2 million of theirs!'

A woman quipped, 'Good Lord! Just imagine how long all this has been going on! The last scare we had was just before Fifi's shaadi last December, no?'

Another added, 'Well actually, it was the same during Kookoo's shaadi the year before. And do you remember the year before that, during basant? Frightful!'

'Poor Faisal had to miss all the events. Poor, frozen, Faisal.'

'Y'know, I read somewhere that the boys are coming back quite impotent, having frozen off their willies on the glaciers, it appears!'

'Terrible situation, this. Really. What's to become of the next generation... We won't have one at this rate.'

'Well, it's not the glaciers anymore, now it's Wana. Not so cold there, no?'

In all this, Sara mingled amongst her guests, dressed in an ankle-length body hugging sheath of black chamois silk, slit up to the thigh under which she wore black ankle length tights. No doubt Amina assessed, that the price of this outfit would easily cover the monthly salary of three of her sister's servants. Sara's head was covered in a black and silver beaded silk hijab.

Just as Amina sat down in a deep sofa seat that she had spotted, she caught sight of Yaqub as he came into the densely filled drawing room. He seemed to stand for a moment looking around as though unsure of himself, getting his bearings. People gathered around him and he was shaking hands and being thumped on the back. She watched him as he stopped and chatted to a few people, and bent his head to listen to others as he smoothened down his bright mustard colored tie. He seemed different from when they had met in New York. Here he had people swarming around him, vying for his attention, whereas there in New York, at her party, he was unknown and lonely. Yet he seemed just as uncomfortable and out of place here as he was there. He looked up and caught her staring at him. He seemed embarrassed and looked away before she did.

Her sister Sara, the gracious hostess of this affair and mistress of the house and all its symbols of access to power, appeared above her and bent down to envelope Amina in a cloud of strong rose scented perfume and in what seemed to be a gigantic bear hug, but turned out to be a well-maneuvered, gingerly executed, reconnaissance of Amina's shoulders instead. Sara swiftly dipped down and lightly, so as not to disturb her blushon, brushed Amina's cheek with her own. Thus, all possibilities of wrinkling each other's clothing, ruffling of hair, smudging of make-up or leaving lipstick traces on each other's cheeks was expertly avoided. It was an art.

Precision pecking. A woman asked Sara, 'Do I look fat?'

'Of course you don't!'

Sara asked Amina, 'Amina dear, have you gained weight?

Come make some room for me on the settee, let me talk to you, I hope you're coming tomorrow for the milad for Chunni's daughter. You know Salma? She's getting married to Kulsum's husband's sister, well—Kulsum's sister-in-law's husband's nephew.'

Amina replied, 'Yes, perhaps we will go, I think you and Chotima have it all charted out, the milads, dinners, lunches, etc.'

Sara listened without looking at her, while keeping an attentive hostess's eye on her guests, 'You've gotten quite dark. You weren't this dark before!'

Amina laughed, 'I know, isn't it great? I spent a week in Antigua, just baking in the sun.'

Sara looked at her sister with irritation, 'Oh God! That's just awful, why would you want to do that?'

Amina raised her eyebrow and asked, 'Go to Antigua or sit in the sun?'

Sara squealed, 'The sun! Weren't there any umbrellas around?

And what about sunblock?' Amina mused at the way Sara had said

'The Sun'. As though Amina had uttered a vile epithet.

'I like the darker look!'

'Are you crazy? You look black!' Sara threw a quick glance at her and then smiled sweetly.

'Great!' Amina said stoutly.

'You are too American!'

'And you're just plain stupid!' Amina said with annoyance and then turned and smiled sweetly at Sara.

'Okay baba, forgive me! You are so over sensitive. I just thought I'd point it out that you could lose a few pounds and perhaps go to a spa. Have you met Zain yet?'

'Well…'

'I think you have in New York, at some party?' said Sara.

'Well…' Sara said, 'He's here, did you know? Of course, you didn't, what a grand coincidence, because Bari-ma and Choti-ma wanted it that way. I'm to introduce you.' Sara jumped up from the sofa excitedly, 'Oh, but look who's here, you simply must meet him. I think you met him in New York as well. Yaqub, Yaqub, come over here for a second.'

Yaqub turned around and made his way through the guests towards Sara. 'Hello Sara, what a successful event, as usual.' He glanced at Amina and quickly looked down at his feet, blushing.

Sara smiled.

'Yaqub darling, you remember Amina, my sister? You met her in New York. Am I right? Raz told me that he had set that up.'

Yaqub seemed embarrassed and at a loss for words. Sara said, 'Why Yaqub, you look like you've just seen a beautiful woman. She put her arms around Amina's shoulders and drew her close. That's the effect we have on men, it's a beautiful family. What can I say?'

Yaqub blushed deeper. Amina squirmed.

'Hello,' Amina said politely. 'How are you?'

Yaqub asked, 'Enjoying yourself?'

'Yes,' Amina replied. 'And you?'

Yaqub said, 'Yes, yes, very much. Although I'm not used to this.'

'You're not? I thought I was the only one.'

Yaqub said, 'What do you mean? You had a huge party at your house, this seems to be a family feature!'

Amina protested, 'That hardly compares to this.'

Yaqub agreed, 'No, I guess it really doesn't, does it? But I haven't really been part of this sort of thing for very long. I really owe it to your sister. She seems to look out for my social life.'

Amina said, 'Ah yes, Sara, she's good at that. You'll have to excuse me, I just saw a friend of my mother's.' With that Amina excused herself and went over to where she had spotted Zain's mother.

Yaqub turned to Sara, his eyes shining, 'I offered her a job when I met her in New York.'

'Don't you think she's lovely?' asked Sara.

Yaqub agreed, 'Of course she is.'

Sara persisted, 'You think so? Lovely? Yes, of course she is.'

She entwined her fingers. 'And we're like that, very close. A job, for what?'

Yaqub said, 'Well, not a patch on you Sara, but still quite lovely! Though she does throw quite a party, like you. I thought she could run my Foundation.'

Sara laughed, 'What a good idea! I want her to come back and settle down here. Well then, I must find ways to have you meet her more often. But I thought you had someone running the Foundation now.'

Yaqub said, 'Yes, Rehana. You know her of course. She's very good, very competent. Hard working. I am so impressed with her coming to work early and leaving late. She has a Ph.D. in cultural heritage and architecture. An amazing person. Very competent. I never even passed class four.'

Sara said, 'Of course I know Rehana, silly! But, you know education isn't everything...'

Yaqub was surveying the room full of guests and said distractedly, 'I never had a chance, you know. Rehana, yes, she's very dedicated. Creative, with many ideas. Supporting her family, she takes public transport, it can't be easy. So many of my staff do. But don't have, well, how should I put it, don't have the...' Sara eyed Yaqub and then looked out towards the other guests, 'Social requirements for the job?'

Yaqub hesitated, 'Well...'

'I understand perfectly,' Sara said. 'You need someone who can raise funds with people like us. Amina would fit the bill. And you want me to make sure that happens?'

'You're an angel!' Yaqub exclaimed. 'By the way, where's your husband?'

Sara smiled, 'Hiding in his study. He should be here any moment.'

Yaqub said, 'Well, you'll have to excuse me. I'm going to follow him there!' And with that, he walked towards the open doors to the lawn.

Amina finally closed in on Faiza, 'Aunty Faiza, where is Zain?'

Faiza explained, 'He's still out. I think he hasn't returned yet, he went for a day trip to Sehwan this morning. I was completely against it, but then I said, chalo, why not. He should see his country, we have so many ethnic things and there is so much history as well, you know. And besides, the weather is so lovely at this time of the year. It would be next to impossible in the summer.

Really, it's marvelous how much history there is here, I never knew until Zain ...'

'Oh no!' Amina proclaimed. 'I wish he had told me. I would've gone along!'

Amina looked about her to see where Yaqub was. He was the only other person that she knew in the room. But he seemed to have left. She sat around listening to the chatter all around her and sipping on the fresh pomegranate juice which had been served to her. She felt betrayed by Zain and Alejandro for not including her in their plans. She could have been with the two of them right now out in the countryside instead of sitting here feeling uncomfortable at her sister's party. And now, to make matters worse, even Yaqub had left her on her own and walked away from her. Barima, Chotima and Abba had declined the invitation, pleading a need for a quiet evening at home and a low tolerance for Sara's massive parties. They had promised Sara and Riaz that they would come to the ghazal session later on in the evening. Suddenly it seemed as though someone had thrown a live wire into a pool of water, a white explosion seemed to have happened, noiseless and silent.

A hush fell over the room just for a brief moment, it seemed as though an electric current seemed to course through the room.

Amina looked at her sister Sara, who seemed to be beside herself with excitement and triumph. Sara scrambled up from the sofa as she squealed under her breath, 'Oh my, he did come after all.

How wonderful! Oh, what a coup! He did make it after all! He has come to my party!'

'Who?' asked Amina in alarm.

'Who do you think?' Sara said, giving Amina a mock salute.

'How could you, Sara!' Amina hissed.

Sara shrugged, 'This is how I see it, this is what I always say. Whoever is in power is going my way!'

A woman seated next to Amina sniggered and said, 'I think the General has just arrived.'

Someone else said, 'Well of course, his wife went to school with Aunty and I think his daughter is married to uncle's brother-in-law's cousin.

Someone said snidely, 'No my dear, Sara met him herself last time she was in Islamabad. I heard he was completely taken by her.'

Amina got up. She was uncomfortable with the remarks she had just overheard about her sister. While the crowd was focused on the General making his entrance, she quickly made her way through the crowd and stepped through the doors leading outside on to the lawn. The lush, newly mowed Dhaka grass was damp with dew and Amina took off her high-heeled shoes to walk barefoot and to feel the blades press against her soles. The air was filled with the scent of night jasmine, raat ki rani, and its perfume mixed with the unmistakable stench of open sewers just on the other side of the high walls of the garden. She could see that the lights were out in Sara's little two-storeyed boutique and in the workshop that was situated further down at the end of the lawn.

The sound of laughter and chatter from the party followed her out here. The sea breeze was cool enough to make Amina shiver.

Amina could see across the vast garden to where the musical event was going to take place later on in the evening, under a canopy where the grass had been covered by carpets strewn with bolsters and cushions. Several braziers had been filled with smoldering coal to warm the guests in the chilly evening, and were being watched over by a servant. Lighting had been strung inside the canopy to give it a soft candlelight effect under which musicians were beginning to set up their tablas, harmoniums, speakers and microphones. Now that the main guest had arrived, Sara would soon be ordering the caterers to have dinner laid out and served. The ghazal singing under the canopy would not begin for another two hours or so.

Closer to where she stood, she gazed past a large magnolia tree into the bookshelf lined study where Riaz and Yaqub sat talking in leather chairs near the desk. The room was lit by a dark green banker's lamp which cast a warm cozy glow. She walked toward them and went in through the glass sliding door. She noted with a smile how handsome her brother-in-law looked as he sat in his leather chair, relaxed. His silver hair gleamed in the lamplight and his eyeglasses reflected the light, giving his face a pleasant sparkle.

Riaz sat behind his desk and puffed on a cigar and Yaqub held a snifter of cognac as he sat opposite Riaz. The room was drenched in the sweet smell of couch leather, Cuban cigars, men's colognes and whiskey. It reminded her of Hank, and to her own surprise, she felt a leap of excitement course through her. 'Come in Amina, are you enjoying yourself or is everyone over there too boring?' Riaz asked. 'Not like New York is it? Not at all exciting!'

Amina laughed and plopped herself down on the dark leather settee, 'C'mon Riaz Bhai, you know exactly what New York is like! Over there I'd have to pay to go to a concert and stand in line with everyone else to get in, but tonight I have it all for free, thanks to you and Sara. A musical evening later on, wow!'

Riaz said, 'Yes! That's an idea, we should promote Pakistan.

Our musical soirées can be referred to as concerts, our mushairas as poetry jams, our servants as chefs, housekeepers and staff and our tailors as designers. It's all a matter of how things are advertised and presented.'

'Why not?' asked Amina. 'Why not indeed! It's all about packaging and marketing. Branding dear old Pakistan as something modern and new. We are masters at doing this, taking the same old and presenting it as something else. We are the masters of prop, stage and set changes, depending on the Director's needs.

If the Director wants, we are moderately extremists, moderately enlightened, or extremely moderately enlightened. We comply. The Director of course, being the US. No need to point out that these so-called concerts are only for the very well off, the ones who keep everyone else worse off and out!'

Riaz beamed at Amina tolerantly, 'I see you haven't changed Amina. Ever the cynic, ever the lecturer! Good for you.' He turned to Yaqub and noticed how Yaqub blushed as he stared at Amina.

Riaz said, 'Come join our conversation Amina, we're talking about your hero. I'm telling this silly man to be sensible. He's like you about that. You're a pair. Yaqub yaar, forget him now for God's sake. It's been ions since he's been dead.'

Amina asked quizzically, 'My hero? Remind me, Riaz Bhai, who that might be? I've had so many.'

Riaz looked at her amused, 'Z. A. Bhutto, of course! Have you changed your mind? Have you forgotten him? Well if you have, then that certainly is a positive change!'

Amina replied, 'Of course I haven't forgotten and I'll never change my mind.'

'What a pity,' said Riaz. 'Because change is a good thing. Never changing is foolish. I hoped that living and working in New York would have made you more pragmatic and wiser.'

Amina said, 'I'm not sure that erasing memory qualifies as a sign of change or wisdom!'

'How can we forget him Riaz?' interjected Yaqub. 'All the time that I was abroad he was that one leader in this country who continued to grow more worthy of respect. I thought of him as my hero. And I feel personally guilty for what happened to him.'

Riaz scoffed at him, 'What guilt? You didn't hang him!'

Yaqub was very serious and said in a low voice, 'We all hanged him. He died for his convictions. And none of us stood up to ours or did anything about it.'

Riaz laughed and protested, 'C'mon yaar, you can't be serious.

That's not true! We don't have any convictions around here, only contradictions and, of course contracts. And, oh yes, the Cold War, and now, we have yet another war that is full of promises of lucrative contracts for ports, pipelines and highways! Contracts that make us forget any convictions we may have ever harbored!'

Yaqub looked at him, his lips pursed, 'Yes, you're right.'

Then he hesitated before speaking, 'Then we are all responsible for Bhutto's hanging.'

Riaz laughed, 'Well, that's not true. The fact that we have no convictions doesn't mean we are responsible for Bhutto's hanging!'

Yaqub said, 'If that's true then, well, there is no way to tell what is true, what is not true, now is there? Because he had convictions and, according to you, we have none. He was hanged.

Everyone else survived because they were more interested in their contracts. They were more interested in being bought by the military. Everyone flourished, went on. A true leader was murdered.

Killed by a ruthless General. A cruel murdering General, in front of whom we all just groveled. And now, we are groveling again under a new version of the same poison.'

Riaz glanced at Amina and nodded in Yaqub's direction, 'See, he's worse than you.'

Amina said, 'What a relief!'

'Yes, it must be,' Riaz said. 'He sounds just like you! Now I have to hear it in stereo. Poor me!'

'I agree with Yaqub,' Amina said resolutely. 'It is our guilt.

Our collective national guilt. Out, out, damn spot! It won't leave you, see. No matter how many mosques we build, how many madrassas, how many prayers we say. We have not reconciled with this yet. It remains there. In place. Firmly in place. The hanging of an elected and beloved Prime Minister.'

Riaz said, 'No doubt the man had charisma. And you are suffering from his charisma—we all are. Had he shown less of it, he may have been alive today and we wouldn't be in the mess we are in now. So what's the solution, for this so-called guilt?'

Yaqub replied, 'Only one solution. The military must go.'

Riaz laughed, 'The military must go? Well, I think it's coming over for dinner tonight.'

Amina said sarcastically, 'Actually, it had just arrived as I left the drawing room. Riaz Bhai, your drawing room is now officially occupied.'

Riaz jumped to his feet, 'He's here! Blast! Well then, I must be on my way. And be good, the two of you and keep your voices down, the man's on the premises, y'know.'

Yaqub shook his head. He seemed quite agitated. 'The military must go back to the barracks. The military has no role as a "ruler" and must be under civil control! Riaz, why do you have that man here, in your house? It is really too bad.'

Riaz laughed and took another puff of his cigar. He spread out his arms and said, 'C'mon yaar, be realistic my good man, you've been away too long. I need to run a business. I'm a family man!'

Yaqub stood up, walked around the room, and turning to Riaz said, 'I am running businesses too.'

Riaz snorted and, taking another puff, replied, 'Please! Yaqub, don't tell me that your businesses are free of the military's cut. I don't think that I can believe that you don't pay some Major or some Colonel or General some huge amount in a personal tax? You have been here now for several years, you know!'

Yaqub laughed, 'Of course I do! Who doesn't? There's no other way to survive here, the army owns everything. I'm not a fool!'

Riaz added, 'You mean the army, navy and the armed forces, Bharia, Fauji and Shaheen! But that aside, I'll still say to you, the army is popular—more popular than the politicians. This country does NOT want the military to be totally subordinated to the civilians. People don't trust all these politicians that they have seen come and go. People consider them to be totally untrustworthy and thieves. Any Chief of Army Staff is better…'

Amina watched the two men arguing and added, 'The acronym for Chief of Army Staff is COAS, chaos indeed.'

Riaz continued, 'Chaos? Without them there would be total chaos. You want charisma. I'd rather have clarity and stability. The military is a reality and a necessity for Pakistan. Do you think we would have survived 9-11 if the General hadn't been at the helm?

We would have been bombed straight to hell. Do you think a civilian leader—say the likes of Benazir or Nawaz Sharif, who had both supported the Taliban, do you think they would have been able to see us through the mess we were in? We would have lost the country and we would have been bombed for sure. The General saved us.

Amina protested vehemently, 'The mess we have always been in has always been the military's making. They were caught in the driver's seat at 9-11, otherwise they would have been in the wings, behind the scenes of a civilian government. They would have been behind the scenes as they always have in the brief periods of civilian rule, letting a civilian government take the responsibility for the mess.

In a way, it was good yes, it was good that the civilian government wasn't in the driving seat on 9-11 and the real culprit was!'

Riaz shrugged, 'There you are! Say what you will. And that is the reality of it. If you want civilian rule, it has to be with the military's agreement. The only solution now is also just that—that the military, from its present position of superiority should voluntarily accept a position as a co-equal in the National Security Council and then eventually as a subordinate.'

Yaqub shook his head in disgust, 'This is why this country is so rotten.'

Riaz was annoyed by the implication but tried to keep his voice calm, 'You've been away too long Yaqub. This is the way things work here. You can't wrap your western sensibilities around it.'

Amina raised her voice, 'Oh my God! This is exactly the ridiculous argument that colonizers use, that usual justification of ground realities. The perverse argument that we don't deserve democracy, and that we deserve US military supported theocracy!

And you're giving me the usual party line; you don't understand the ground realities of uncivilized barbarians.'

Riaz shook his head, stubbed out his cigar in the ashtray and reached for two fresh ones from the open box on his desk, which he then put in his pocket. 'Well my friends, those are the facts.

You don't think there are divisions amongst us? Wow! You don't understand the ground reality.'

Amina replied, 'When my country goes up in flames, as it has done periodically, and will do so again like no other time before, I shall draw little comfort from knowing that the military thought it was the only force keeping the country together and that it thought letting democracy go unfettered was a bad idea.'

Riaz looked at her and said slowly, 'Well, one ground reality is clear, my dear, for your information Amina, this is really not your country!'

Amina stared at Riaz, surprised by his aggressive tone, 'Who decides that?' she asked.

Riaz shrugged, amused, 'Well, for one, your passport does! You decided that!'

Yaqub intervened and said softly, 'You are being very unfair Riaz.'

Riaz shrugged again and made his way towards the door from where Amina had come in, 'Don't take such offence! There was none intended! I'm only pointing out facts.'

Yaqub said, 'A passport is just a travel document for the twenty-first century's work realities. I don't think, Riaz, you should decide this young lady's nationality. Besides, how many passports do you have? How many passports does your General have? How many passports do each of your guests have, who are busy fawning all over him in your drawing room?'

Riaz laughed, 'I see that I've touched a nerve! I better leave before both of you strangle me.'

Yaqub fingered his missing thumbnail and said softly, 'You didn't answer my question!'

Riaz said curtly, 'I'm only pointing out facts.'

Yaqub persisted, 'Still.'

Shaken by the outburst, Amina nodded to Yaqub weakly and stood up. 'Thank you very much for standing up for me Yaqub. What are you saying, Riaz Bhai? That all those who protest are irrelevant and that they should quickly be devalued because they don't live here?'

Yaqub stared at Amina admiringly, 'Good question.'

Riaz asked, 'What is wrong with you two? I can see that you have a lot in common. For heaven's sake! Stop the speeches! What is the alternative? I am talking about a middle ground, can't you see that? A way out is what I'm talking about.'

'What do you mean, a way out?' Yaqub asked. 'Out of what, for whom?'

Riaz pointed towards his drawing room on the other side of the lawn, 'I mean, we should try to put ourselves in the poor General's shoes. How are we to get out of the mess this country is in?'

'Oh my God!' Amina exclaimed. 'You make it sound like the General is some victim, or some unwilling hero! Put ourselves in his shoes!! He's the one who has created this mess. We are almost in another civil war in this country, look at all the sectarian violence, look at all the killings on the border and in Afghanistan, look at all the press that Pakistan gets!'

'Yes. Yes. Yes,' Riaz said, 'but still, we should try to help him save the country.'

Amina was incredulous, 'Save the country? Help him save the country? Who asked him to do what he did? Who asked him to take over the country in the first place?'

Riaz made a motion of a circle in the air with his hand to show that they were now repeating themselves, 'The corrupt politicians, that's who!'

Yaqub shook his head, 'You are going to suggest that the way to help the General is to support his moves to disqualify all of the political leaders as being corrupt?'

'Precisely,' Riaz stated, 'of course. And they are corrupt. Yes, and then to hold local government, provincial and national elections after getting the political parties on board.'

Amina said, 'And who would be in these political parties after we've disqualified all the politicians? Generals or mullahs?'

'Whoever!' Riaz said. 'As long as they are people with spotless reputations.'

'Ah, I see,' mused Yaqub, 'hand picked spotless people, spotted by the General. And then after that, probably you would look to amend the Constitution somehow to make sure that political parties remain spotless.'

'The constitution?' Riaz repeated. 'Surely you are joking, it's a joke! I was thinking about institutionalizing the National Security Council.'

Yaqub said, 'I knew you would say that. Really Riaz, I would have expected you to think differently.'

'Why?' Riaz demanded. 'But I know the reality of this country, there should be a National Security Council as part of the government so that the country's government can be supervised by the army. Then we don't need any constitution.'

'Oh my God!' Amina exclaimed. 'So that is your view of how the army should leave?'

'Yes,' stated Riaz. 'In a nutshell, that's the strategy I would propose.'

'Sounds like you want them to stay forever,' said Yaqub. 'Why not just turn the entire country into one large cantonment and call us all jawans.'

'What a brilliant idea, huh Riaz Bhai?' said Amina. 'We would all join the army and be called jawans. The women in your drawing room at the moment would be all for it. Sara could make all the uniforms.'

Riaz laughed, 'Yes indeed, and damn good looking uniforms they would be. Well say whatever you will, that is my alternative and it's a damn lot better than the fundamentalist alternative.'

'What fundamentalist alternative?' asked Amina, 'There are no fundamentalists here. That is all a fabrication that keeps the military in power and keeps the US foreign policy focused on militarization.

Whatever fundamentalism there is here has been created by the military and its friends in the Pentagon. You keep saying that what you propose is a better alternative to the alternative of fundamentalists because an alternative, no matter what, is so frightening. Believe me that alternative is coming, the alternative forces are probably coming, and they are demanding justice and democracy and a fair shake. But they will not be allowed to get very far and will be mowed down by helicopter gun ships, tear-gas, extra judicial killings, torture and interrogations. And they will be killed and eradicated and suppressed in the name of suppressing sectarian violence. Then we'll be told it's sectarianism between Shias and Sunnis. And on and on. I wonder why you are so afraid of the military being overthrown. I wonder why that is frightening for you. Only because it's not really about religion, is it? It's about class, about equity.'

'Equity?' Riaz said. 'What the hell does that word mean? Jargon! Western jargon!'

Yaqub said, 'That frightens you? I am disappointed.'

'Yes! It frightens me!' exclaimed Riaz. 'And it should frighten you too, Yaqub! How the hell will we get on with business if that happens?'

'Do you really believe that by throwing mud at the political leadership of Pakistan, as if they have been the only ones responsible for the current crises, we will be able to do business??!' demanded Yaqub. 'That we will get on with doing any business? Aren't you suggesting the creation of a puppet democracy? Why are the rules always different for Pakistan?'

Amina continued, 'The generals don't need any encouragement to appoint their chosen pre-screened politicians or to find a permanent role for themselves as the legitimized puppeteers... Really, people like us should be careful.'

Riaz said in a conciliatory tone, 'I'm suggesting a way to finally get elected representatives. We are after all the people who count. We are the thinkers, we are the intelligentsia and we have to think in sensible ways, without emotionalism and sentimentality.

Step by step—not in some revolutionary thinking. The two of you are talking like romantic headed college students.'

Amina glanced at Yaqub and caught his eye. He turned a shade of deep purple.

Amina asked, 'Who said that any of us count for anything? Where did you get that? You think you count? So far you have counted, because you suit the General's purposes, you give him legitimacy. It's exactly this so-called club of people who think they can speak for everyone! Riaz Bhai, you're about to find out how little you count! All of us in our plush drawing rooms and huge villas, count for nothing. We are completely irrelevant.'

Riaz waved his hand at her in protest, 'I'm sorry, I can't indulge in this negative thinking. It's impractical and not at all pragmatic. I'm a pragmatic man. I'm simply saying put yourself in General Musharraf's shoes. You should take into account the real issues of practical governance today. I believe we have a sacred duty to put our best brains, whether in or out of government or in or out of the country, to figure out how to get Pakistan out of the present crisis of rising sectarianism, a threat of civil war and an absolute deterioration of our image and place in the world. We must correct this perception! We all have to pitch in for God's sake!'

'This is ridiculous!' protested Yaqub. 'How can you find a cure without focusing on the causes? How can you even prescribe a cure if you don't acknowledge and remove the cause?'

'Has anyone taken notice of the spotless record of the military?' Amina continued. 'I don't mean just the billionaires who are Generals with money stashed away in the US and Europe.

Money made on arms and drugs and siphoning off of government funds. Every military regime in Pakistan has been embroiled in some lucrative international conflict.'

Riaz complained, 'Oh no, not a lecture on history!'

Amina said sternly, 'Riaz Bhai, those corrupt and awful politicians you speak of, well for your information, no elected civilian government has ever gone to war. So if anyone is wondering what the answers are, or what the reason for having an elected political government rather than a military one is, it is a rather simple—avoiding violence and war.'

'Couldn't agree with you more!' said Riaz. 'This is reason enough to undertake swift measures to revive and sustain democracy but there are several others, and democracy it has to be. But not a western type of system. Our needs are different and the people of Pakistan need to define these differences and illustrate how those should be reflected in our own democratic institutions.'

Amina continued, 'The Pakistan Army is prone to jumping into misadventures, which only result in death and destruction.

Look at the mess we're in! Pakistan and Pakistanis are blamed for 9-11. We are blamed for running training camps for terror, just look at all the scandals about shady arms deals, the selling of nuclear technology to every possible willing buyer and the war in Afghanistan and now the military is fighting our own people in the border regions in Waziristan! Look at the war brewing in Balochistan. Look at all the sectarian killings.'

Yaqub said, 'To blame civilians and democracy for this state of affairs, as some members of the current junta try and do, is ingenious.' 'and you are right Riaz Bhai, it is Pakistan's misfortune that it's elected civilian leaders, whenever they've come in to power, have behaved like military generals. In many ways, this is not surprising. They've only been allowed to take power by the Generals. They've only come to power when the military has completely run down institutions. And then the institutional breakdown has meant that when the civilians come into power, there are no curbs on their excesses. It's a vicious circle!'

'Whatever else you want to say about civilian rulers, they've never taken us to war,' Yaqub raised his voice and said triumphantly.

'No,' Riaz agreed, 'but they've taken us to long periods of military rulers. My friends, civilian leaders have taken us to painfully long periods of martial law.'

Amina said, 'We have a militarized society with an increasingly dangerous and warped ideology based on a warped sense of jihad that's been imported from the Pentagon and Saudi Arabia. And here we are, blaming our politicians for not being able to give us quick fixes in the painfully short periods in which they are allowed to govern!'

Riaz interrupted him, 'I apologize to both of you, I really must go in to the guests. You know Sara will be furious and there will be hell to pay. But the two of you, my God. You guys should take your show on the road, if you could just see yourself right now. You really are a pair! What a lecture. A complete sermon. What speech making.

As though you were both on a debating team!! Lighten up you two, this is a dinner party! Let's enjoy this while it lasts. Anyway, I have to go and welcome my very important guest!'

Amina said, 'Guest? I hope he chokes on his food!'

'Na baba, not in my house! Really you two are a pair. I have to take my leave.' And with that Riaz left to greet the General. Yaqub and Amina got up to walk out as well.

Riaz came up just as one of the General's aide's was saying, 'I've got a very neat system to put the children to sleep. I used to tell them that there is a bogey man who would come to get them, you know, a Kabuliwalla, if they didn't behave. That would work for a while. Then I started to use a neat little mechanism.

Every time the misbehaving got out of hand, I would make my cellphone ring and play for them a taped message from the

Kabuliwalla. Worked every time. That would send them right off to bed. Doctrine followed by proof as reasoning.'

Riaz said, 'Doctrine followed by proof through taped messages! What is all this? Are you discussing some new tape sent out again by OBL?'

Sara turned and grabbed Riaz's arm. 'There you are jaan,' she said. 'No, we aren't discussing Osama. The good gentleman here was giving me advice on how to put the children to bed. I was just telling him how difficult it was to persuade the children to go to bed on a school night nowadays with all the TV channels, video games and movies, not to mention the enormous amount of homework that they have.'

Yaqub and Amina walked back through the lawn towards the drawing room.

Yaqub laughed nervously, 'Well, that was a long discussion on the weather!'

Amina looked at him askance. 'Weather?'

Yaqub said, 'Yes, something Zain said to me at your party in New York—about how Pakistanis discuss politics like the English discuss the weather!'

Amina laughed.

Yaqub continued, 'I was hoping that you had a chance, Amina, to reconsider my proposal?'

'Proposal?' Amina asked.

Yaqub said, 'I meant my request when I visited you in New York. My request for you to come and run my foundation over here. It would be a great deal of help to me and is exactly what my Foundation needs.'

'I really am completely occupied with my current engagements,' said Amina.

'Is there no way that you could do both?' Yaqub asked.

'Do both?' Amina wondered. 'I never thought of that.'

'Well, think about it,' Yaqub said. 'Do come by the office if you can and meet Rehana Mehmood. She is running the show at the moment, very competent young lady.'

'I'm not sure…' said Amina.

Yaqub continued, 'We need to raise funds for these projects. Of course, I have plenty of money for this. But I think if I am to make these projects work it has to have many more people involved. Others have to take ownership. Do you know what I mean?'

Amina said, 'My understanding of what you are doing is very rudimentary. You are trying to restore the older part of the city through a couple of key projects; a museum, a library…'

Yaqub nodded, 'A market, a park, a hotel, all historical sites. Really involves a couple of blocks worth of the city. Actually based on Rehana's doctoral thesis. She documented the entire area. She came to me looking for support and I decided to take it on as a project. The problem is she has the doctoral thesis but not the skills to take this further into a hard-nosed business model.'

'I wouldn't be so quick to say that!' said Amina, 'After all it seems to me she managed to convince you!'

'Yes,' Yaqub conceded, 'but we still need assistance. Rehana needs some mentoring. You could help do that. Well look, can I at least hire you for looking through the legal and financial implications of what we are proposing and perhaps even writing some parts of the proposal for us? We could certainly use the help and we would need this right away and we simply don't have anyone who can do this in a way that would be interesting to donors and financiers.'

'Sounds like a distinct possibility,' said Amina. 'Why don't we set up a time to meet?'

Yaqub said, 'Wonderful!! Sara said you would.'

'Sara?' Amina asked.

Yaqub explained, 'Yes, of course, she thinks the world of you! Always goes on and on about your accomplishments.'

20

Post mortem

'WHAT an utter success!' Sara declared to her husband in blissful satisfaction at about 6.00 a.m., through the open doors as she sat on the terrace outside their bedroom, sipping her morning cup of tea. The sun was just beginning to come up and a strong, cool breeze still continued to blow in from the sea. The azaans from the mosques all around the neighborhood had just tapered off and the birds were coming alive in the surrounding trees. She watched the sun rise, a hazy streak of moisture and dust slicing through its gold-orange disk, making it look like, well, like a McDonald's hamburger. Well there you are. A giant McDonald's rising over the horizon. Yes a Big Mac, thought Sara, giggling to herself, she must tell her children this when they wake up later on.

She could see Riaz in the bedroom beginning to doze off again; it was Sunday, he didn't have to get up till later, he had just finished saying his prayers and had come in from his morning constitutional in the lawn.

'What a success, no?' She called out to him.

'Yes, darling, the General showing up was really something! How did you manage that?' he called out to her.

'I didn't. Apparently he was in town, wanted to do something different, was told that there would be many pretty girls at our party, and here he was. Just wonderful, isn't it?'

'Yes,' said Riaz sleepily. 'But why did Yaqub have to get into that argument with him?'

'I know,' said Sara. 'That was a bit inconvenient. And he went on and on!'

'Rather awkward,' Riaz said.

'Absurd!' Sara exclaimed. 'I mean let the poor man have his drink in peace. Must he always be confronted about his uniform and his coup? Really!'

'Bloody dangerous!' Riaz added.

Sara agreed, 'I know! He could've choked on his whiskey! He certainly puffed up and was so red in the face I was nervous.'

'I mean for Yaqub,' Riaz clarified. 'It won't do him any good.'

'Dangerous for Yaqub?' Sara questioned 'Whatever do you mean?'

'Taking on the General himself, face to face,' Riaz explained.

'He won't take this lying down, you know. He was being gallant in front of the pretty young girls, but he won't let this just pass.'

'Nonsense!' Sara exclaimed. 'It was all in good fun. It wasn't a political jalsa, just my drawing room. No harm, just amongst us.

I wouldn't worry, dahling. And besides, the most important thing to keep in mind is that Yaqub Kishtiwalla is far too powerful to be afraid of the General. And he never does anything that's risky. He must already have the General in his pocket. There's no way he would have spoken to him that way otherwise. I mean, let's face some facts! I mean Yaqub Kishtiwalla is Yaqub Kishtiwalla!'

'I hope you're right,' muttered Riaz. 'But he should be careful.

Oh by the way, Amina and Yaqub. What a pair! You should have seen the two of them, they sounded like a pair of would-be politicians. They have the same point of view. Ridiculous notions of democracy and all that. Must've been trying to impress Amina with that, standing up and talking back to the General! Oh my God.'

Sara sat up and peered into the bedroom, 'Really? Well, that's interesting. A pair you say?'

'Well, what do you think of Amina and Yaqub?' asked Riaz. Sara said, 'You mean as a couple?'

'Yes,' Riaz said. 'What do you think? I mean she has to get married some time, and Yaqub is single and wealthy. Quite a catch! No?'

'She wasn't interested in him when he met her in New York. Remember? Isn't he a bit old for her?' Sara said.

'What do you mean, old?' Riaz asked. 'He's my age! And
Amina isn't exactly young. He could have anyone he wants in this town. With all due respect to your sister, between the two of them, she's not the one who's eligible. I think she should think about it seriously.'

'You do have a point,' Sara conceded. 'But Amina would never agree. He's too boring for her.'

'Boring, nonsense,' said Riaz dismissively. 'It seemed to me that he had her attention this evening.'

Sara said, 'Well for politics maybe, but he's not her type.' Riaz continued, 'What do you mean he's not her type? Did you see her grinning when the General went apoplectic?' Sara got up and came in through the door. 'No I missed that. I was too focused on the General. But it must be obvious to Amina that Yaqub was smitten by her. She could see that written all over his face.'

'Well there you are then,' Riaz said. 'What's the problem? I thought that would be a good thing.'

'What's the problem? That is the problem!' Sara exclaimed.

'Our dear Amina can't possibly accept anyone who likes her.'

Riaz turned over onto his stomach. 'Overly educated women are so stupid.'

Sara said, 'I agree, my dear, I agree.'

'He's a catch!' Riaz repeated.

'Certainly is!' Sara conceded. 'Wealthy beyond belief. Wouldn't be bad to have him join the family. So what if there's no family background?'

Riaz continued, 'He and I are going to go into business soon so he'll have all the background he needs.'

'Is he going to go in with you on the new shipping project?' Sara asked.

'Absolutely, yaar,' Riaz said. 'I've finally been able to convince him. And he's even more loaded than I thought!'

'Well that's good, that's very good,' Sara said thoughtfully.

Riaz said, 'And if I were you, I'd talk some sense into that sister of yours. She's not getting any younger.'

'Well, she may have someone else in mind,' Sara considered.

'Who?' Riaz asked. 'That Zain fellow?'

'Yes!' Sara declared.

Riaz turned over on his back and looked at his wife and laughed. 'Sara my dear, I think you should forget about that.'

Sara replied, 'I know, I know, but there's no reason why he shouldn't get married. Happens all the time.'

Riaz murmured, 'By the way, what's this about an art gallery and art exhibition? Yaqub was talking to me about that. Yaqub was telling me about his art exhibition next week. Now, don't tell me you had something to do with this, Sara?'

Sara purred, 'Jaan, don't breathe a word of it, swear to me!

You know I had something to do with it. Of course I did. And you know those paintings I've been working on. Well I fobbed them off on Yaqub, told him they were from an art dealer friend of mine who went broke. I told Yaqub I had bailed him out just before he died. You know the usual story. Made myself look like a heroine.'

Riaz chuckled, 'Sara, you're evil!'

Sara climbed on top of Riaz and sat straddling him. 'I know. But Riaz, promise me you won't say a single word about it. I told Yaqub that you don't know. I told him that if you found out that I'd used up all my savings to bail out a friend, you'd have my head.

He thinks that you have no clue about these paintings. I swore him to secrecy. Promise Riaz that you're not going to make any jokes at the exhibition next week! Promise?'

Riaz replied drowsily, 'I don't know.'

Sara pouted, 'You know Yaqub is feeling so indebted to me for so selflessly handing over a priceless collection of art, don't for a minute think he didn't think about that when he agreed to go into business with you!'

Riaz laughed. 'So you're taking credit for this? I had nothing to do with it?'

Sara said, 'Of course. Yaqub trusts me completely.'

Riaz teased, 'Ah yes, does he now?'

Sara admonished, 'Riaz! Please promise! It's going to be so much fun!'

Riaz said, 'I don't know.'

Sara whined, 'Please, please, please don't spoil it.'

Riaz laughed, 'I promise okay, baba, whatever you want to do. You're absolutely crazy.'

Sara giggled, 'These ninnies, no? They'll believe anything.'

Riaz said, 'You're really something.' And with that he turned over to sleep. Sara got up off of her husband to go shower and get ready for her morning round of nine holes.

21

Shrining

THE evening air, thick with incense and mosquitoes, stirred into a breeze just as the qawwals began to take their place, clear their throats and harmonize. The early arrivals, a small audience of late worshippers at the mausoleum, settled down to listen. The air smelled of charas, chambeli and incense. Amina, Alejandro and Zain sat towards the back of the courtyard, upon an elevated, concrete podium under a large banyan tree. The two men stretched out their legs while leaning against gaudy purple and red velvet cushions spread out on rugs while Amina sat with her legs tucked under her. In the branches overhead, crows cawed and frequently a bird dropping would come splattering down around them. 'Whoa! Precision shitting,' exclaimed Zain as a splatter of it fell between Amina and Alejandro. Mosquitoes in their vicinity were kept at bay with incense sticks and because of the smoke from the hookah. The flies however, showed a significant resistance and kept landing on Amina's face, much to her irritation. Zain puffed deeply on the hookah that had been placed in front of him and passed it on to Alejandro. Amina looked on. Alejandro moved the spout towards her but she shook her head and said no.

Zain rested his lazy gaze on Amina and drawled, 'C'mon try it. You can't be here and not try it.' Amina wrinkled her nose and shook her head and smiled sheepishly, 'No thanks, not my thing.'

Zain asked with a giggle, 'Why?'

Amina was irritated by his giggling. 'Just not.'

Zain ignored the tone in her voice and persisted, 'Didn't quite see you as a prude.'

Amina shrugged, 'I'm not.'

'But you chug down caiperinas,' Zain continued to push.

'Yes?' Amina made a face as though to say she didn't see the connection.

'Yeah?' Zain said with the same tone as Amina, 'So, why not this?'

Amina was getting annoyed. 'Don't want to. Case closed.'

Alejandro decided to intervene, 'Get off her case Zain!'

Zain smiled and put up his hands, 'Sorry, just wanted you to go native!'

Alejandro said, 'She is a native! And so are you!'

Amina asked, 'Are we? We are just December Pakistanis.

Trying charas in hookahs in these weird and exotic places. And taking photographs and videos of it to show back home!'

Zain added, 'And keeping away from the wine because we don't drink while we're in the land of the pure, even though the pure are drowning in it.'

Amina shrugged again, 'Well, that's me.'

Zain looked at her askance with a raised eyebrow, 'A bit hypocritical, no? And why is this weird and exotic?'

Amina nodded wearily, 'A lot hypocritical, but that's just the way it is. It is weird and exotic for us. That's why we're here. Why else would we be here? We're doing the touristy thing. If we weren't, we'd be sitting with those people on the floor near the qawwals not over here, smoking a hookah, pretending we're in *One Thousand and One Nights*!'

'I'll have to think about that,' Zain said. 'You may just have a point there.'

Amina continued, 'And I don't associate being in Pakistan with drinking wine. I mean my being here, my being in this place. I don't do that.'

'Too western?' offered Zain.

'No!' Amina protested indignantly.

'Are you sure?' asked Alejandro.

Amina looked at him and said, 'Don't know, don't know what it is. Just don't want to let anyone down I guess.'

Alejandro looked confused by her answer, 'Let anyone down? Who is going to be let down?'

Amina waved around her, 'There are people watching, the driver who brought us here for example. I don't want him thinking badly of me.'

Zain snorted, 'Give me a break! He's getting high himself at the moment!'

Amina nodded, 'But doesn't expect me to! And I'm doing the driving on the way back, by the way. I love the way we follow all the rules back home and then we come here and break every single one, like the one about driving while drunk.'

Zain continued, 'Okay, let's stay on that for a moment Ms Prudence while in Pakistan. I think you have these notions, these preconceived notions…'

'Do not!' Amina interjected.

Zain continued, 'Sure you do. These ideas are from Victorian novels, Austen, Bronte, notions of morality that you try to impose on people here and impose on yourself. And one thing is for sure, people here are not stuck in those moralities and notions, they are far less repressed than you are.'

Alejandro laughed, 'Oppressed, definitely. Repressed? No way!'

Zain nodded in agreement, 'The only people around here who are repressed are the people who rule over them.'

They sat watching the crowd gathering and the musicians settling down. Then Zain spoke up again, 'Glad we got out in time, huh? That bomb blast on the main highway today could have spoiled our little party. Got through in the knick of time, I'd say.'

'Hope getting back won't be a problem,' Amina said anxiously.

'It'll have all cleared up in a couple of hours,' Zain said.

'Don't mind the insurgency dear, it's bound to clear up by rush hour!' he giggled.

Alejandro said, 'You guys make bomb blasts sound like bad weather or like a subway breakdown.'

'Smog really. Only less noticeable,' Zain grinned.

Alejandro replied, 'Like the servants.'

'What?' Zain asked.

'Like your servants, man,' Alejandro replied. 'Ever since I've been here, I can't help but notice how you all don't notice all the people that serve you. I mean, this is really a society made up of servants.'

Amina added, 'Servants and masters.'

Alejandro nodded, took a puff of the hookah and continued, 'I mean, if I was designing a stage to explain this country to people, I'd put four sofa chairs upfront and create pigeon holes as the backdrop.'

'Pigeon droppings?' Zain squinted quizzically.

Alejandro laughed, 'Focus, man! You're already high as a bird. On my stage, each of the pigeon holes would be like a mini stage with people, sweepers, cooks, drivers, launderers, gardeners, garbage collectors, farmers, laborers of all kinds. Each pigeon hole would contain these guys toiling away, while up front the four people would be lolling around in their armchairs barking orders to them, ordering them around and at the same time, expounding on Marxism and democracy!'

'Oh, okay,' Zain said slowly. 'You got a good point there. Maybe one of your pigeon holes should be an airport where people are leaving in droves.'

Alejandro continued, 'And the other thing is that you guys are really schizophrenic. I mean, there are two people inside every Pakistani.'

'Yeah,' Zain said appreciatively. 'Yeah. That is so true. I'd say at least three people.'

Alejandro went on, 'Like, I mean total contradictions, actions, words, thoughts, depending on the situation.'

Zain repeated, 'Yeah. That's us!'

'Like that party last night at that factory warehouse. Man, what was that shit? Kids were doing coke and the parents looked proud. I mean, what was that? Same people in a different situation would be a bunch of conservative crazies,' Alejandro said.

Zain laughed, 'People think they're being cool, they think they're behaving like they're Parisians, Londoners or New Yorkers.'

Alejandro snorted, 'But people in those cities don't behave like this. I mean, this is totally whacked! Total contradictions, man. I mean, every single one of them has two, three, four people inside of them. There's the angry, raging Muslim person, there's the party going lunatic, drunk person, there's the democracy spouting Marxist person, and then there's the oppressor, practitioner of bonded slavery, status quo defender person.'

Zain passed the hookah back to Alejandro.

Amina said, 'I'm the pregnant person, good single gal, lawyer, good daughter person.'

'What?' Zain blinked a few times.

Amina tilted her head and said, 'Let's see, come to think of it, at least four in one. The status quo, single, pregnant person.

No, that's three.'

Zain laughed, 'Ok, now I'm really high.'

Alejandro nodded slowly, 'Damn! Me too. I'm so high, I thought you said you were pregnant.'

Amina looked unhappy, 'Yup, that's what I said. Pregnant. By my calculations, probably twelve weeks.'

The two men sat back in a haze of hashish smoke and stared at her.

Zain said, 'What are you going to do?' He started to wave the air around her to clear the smoke and pushed the hookah away.

'I don't know.'

'You can't go through with it?' Zain asked.

Amina asked defiantly, 'Why not?'

Zain laughed, 'On your own?'

'Why not?' Amina asked.

'Have you been inhaling secondary smoke here or what???'

Zain yelled. 'This is Pakistan. Your mother, your mothers, for instance? How are you going to deal with this?'

'He's right,' Alejandro said.

'What happened to all that talk about my being repressed?'

Amina asked. 'This would be the opposite of that, wouldn't it?'

Alejandro said, 'Don't be crazy. This society here isn't ready for that. Your parents aren't going to be able to handle it.'

Zain nodded gloomily, 'He's right.'

Amina had begun to cry, 'I'm not going to …'

Zain moved towards her and patted her arm slowly, 'No one is saying that. Just let's think this through. Let's just clear our heads and think this through. Shit Amina, what a doozy.'

22

Sara and the Military Rescue Amina from her Fall in the Gutter

AMINA, much to Sara's pleasant surprise, had called her, asking whether they could spend the day together, just the two of them. Sara saw Amina practically every day when she went to 43-G but this sounded different. Sara had rushed to make plans and to treat her sister to the luxuries and comforts of her own routine.

She had picked Amina up the next day at ten in the morning and taken her for a brunch at the Boat Club.

She had informed Amina that she was taking her to her favorite spa for the afternoon. Right after they finished eating, they had headed for the salon which was exceptionally crowded that day, although Sara and Amina had shown up promptly at noon. It had been a lazy Saturday, Sara was off for the day. Today her various activities would take a day of rest in Amina's honor.

Although she had informed Amina that golf had been played at 6 a.m., right after her fajr prayers, when she had also offered up to the heavens numerous duas for the well-being of her entire family. Nichi, Sara had gleefully informed Amina in the car, had agreed to do Amina's hair herself. Sara considered this quite an honor and favor bestowed upon them by the city renowned Nichi, the doyenne of hair follicles, waxing and skin pores, the artist celebrant of hair color and bleach creams. This gesture was a public recognition of Sara's importance in the social order and hierarchy of blow-drying appointments. Nichi would have done the whole routine she said, but at 2 p.m. the first of two brides were to show up for their make-up for their wedding functions that evening. 'Baba, I've cut down to two now. I can't handle more than that given this level of business, stress and pressure.' Hearing the tone of Nichi's voice, which verged on hysteria, Sara thought, poor dear sweet Nichi, and then kindly offered to let an apprentice work on herself, while Amina got the full benefit of the maestro. As they sat side by side, fingers and toes being worked upon, cuticles pushed back and dry skin peeled away gently while cucumbers covered their eyes, Sara drawled, 'Amina, I completely forgot to tell you my new discovery!'

Amina asked, with equal ennui, 'What, Sara? A new hair tint?'

Sara said, 'No my dear, remember the painting you were looking for?'

'Yes, I saw it myself,' said Amina.

'So I was right, it was that painting!' Sara exclaimed.

Amina sat up and removed the cucumbers on her eyes. 'Yes. And I want it.'

'The one at Yaqub's new art gallery?'

Amina said, 'Yes. But he won't sell it.'

'Apparently not!' said Sara. 'I asked him as well. I must confess now. I wanted to buy it for you as a birthday present or a home-coming present. I know how much you wanted it. I asked him where he got it and he told me that he's had it for the last twenty years or so. Anyway, he wouldn't even sell it to me!'

'How can that be?' Amina wondered. 'How can he have this painting? I've searched everywhere for it myself.'

'Well, he says he got it from someone before he left the country,' Sara explained. 'It's been in storage since then. Yaqub was waiting to set up his gallery before he took his paintings out of storage.'

'This is so unfair!' Amina exclaimed.

'Well, I can try asking him again,' Sara said.

'Oh Sara, thank you!' Amina said gratefully.

'What thank you?' said Sara. 'He won't sell. Thank me after he agrees to sell it. Anyway, we'll see, maybe he'll agree to part with it for you!'

Amina said glumly, 'I doubt it!'

Sara said, 'We'll see.'

'Maybe if we keep pressuring him,' Amina considered.

'Especially you! He really thinks the world of you!'

Sara said, 'Well he should! I've given him his whole new, glamorous and polished image in Karachi. He says that his collection has a sentimental value to him and he won't sell it.' Amina protested, 'Sentimental value! It has more meaning for us. He must sell.'

Sara said, 'I don't know. I told him the same thing but he said his paintings symbolize home to him and he thought about them sitting in storage all these years while he was away. He says they're his only sense of family. You know, Amina dear, he's an orphan.'

'I don't care!' said Amina. 'What does that have to do with us? The painting belongs in our family.' She covered her eyes with the two cucumbers and slumped back into her seat.

Later, arms, legs, pubic hair waxed, upper lip and eyebrows tweezed and threaded, facials done and blackheads squeezed, hair tinted, highlighted and blow-dried, Amina and Sara stepped out of the salon and onto the sidewalk. Much to Amina's amazement, Sara was busy with her hijab, which she had carefully adjusted over her polished, tinted, glossed and blow-dried hair. Sara had caught

Amina's disapproving stare. 'What? My hair is for my husband!' Amina shook her head and shrugged her shoulders, 'Live and let live, I guess!' With one manicured hand shading her eyes, Amina searched for the car and driver, who was supposed to have been waiting outside the salon with his engine running. Sara had called the driver ahead of time from upstairs, just five minutes before she and Amina stepped out of the air-conditioned sanctuary which was filled with perfumes and hair spray, and out into the searing moisture sucking air of a Karachi afternoon. Amina noticed to her dismay that her beautifully polished, defoliated, and pumiced soles and red lacquered toes were submerged in blackish water, and that she had actually managed to have stepped into a puddle of it, in fact the entire sidewalk and the street seemed to be flooding.

'Oh, oh, a gutter is overflowing,' Sara informed her.

'How disgusting!' Amina shuddered. 'Ew!'

Amina spotted the car, 'Oh well, we'll just have to walk through this...'

'No! Wait, Amina!' Sara shouted, but too late. Amina had already taken a leap, landed a foot ahead of Sara and seemed to have landed on the water covered pavement, and then in a flash her body disappeared right into an open gutter which was submerged under the water. Sara screamed and lunged for her, grabbing Amina's arm just as her head went under. The suction of the gutter was not powerful enough to suck her through because it was filled not only with water, but mercifully with a dense and thickened concoction of Karachi's—as Sara had put it later to everyone— 'putrid, malodorous, fetid and rancid sewage'.

'Help us!' screamed Sara holding on to Amina with all her might, her thin body stretched and arched against the weight of a quickly submerging Amina. Sara kept pulling and screaming for help and managed to drag Amina half out of the open manhole. By the time help arrived from the nearby roundabout where the army had set up barracks, due to the unrest in the city and the bombs, two soldiers had spotted the two women and came running. One grabbed Amina from under her arms and dragged her out. Amina was terrified and shrieking in panic while Sara was screeching orders. Sara shouted to a waiter at a nearby tea-stall to bring water.

Amina was covered in thick grey black filth and she was stinking of it. The tea-boy brought two pitchers of water and threw them at Amina.

'Not that way battameez, what an oaf!' shouted Sara. 'Give me that, and bring more at once! Go!' she ordered the boy, her voice shaking with the fear she had just experienced. She poured the pitcher of water over Amina, and as the boy brought more she stood, still shaking with shock, as she poured pitcher after pitcher of water over Amina's shaking form to clean up as much of the muck as possible.

'Are you alright, jani? Are you alright?' Sara kept repeating in a shaking and teary voice. It had all happened so suddenly, so unexpectedly. It had been just another day, another normal day and such a catastrophe, a near nightmare had struck. Sara felt so exposed, so insecure. She breathed dua after dua under her breath. Amina huddled before her, with her arms wrapped around herself clutching her shoulders, completely disoriented, her muslin shalwar kameez clinging to her body. She was soaked through, her knee was bleeding, and her shoulders and arms hurt. Cars passing by were slowing down to take in the spectacle. Sara was doing her best to shield her frightened and wounded sister. She could hear people laughing, beggars stood nearby, watching, unsure whether they should catcall or beg for money. Guys on motorbikes were not conflicted at all and catcalled and were ogling at Amina's drenched, shivering body. Her undergarments were clearly visible through her soaked clothes and this, in Karachi, was quite a spectacle. One enterprising and quick-thinking beggar actually managed to call out to Sara to give some money as a sadqa, a thanksgiving to God that her sister hadn't drowned in shit! Amina had been saved from her descent into the gutter by Sara and the military.

Sara suddenly realized that they were still outside the salon, a fact she had forgotten in her panic. Sara shoved her back through the door of the salon, the stench of sewage, however, clung to Amina stinking up the salon and overpowered the fragrance of hairsprays and conditioners. Nichi and her clients looked annoyed but Sara managed to convince her 'dear, dahling Nichi' to hand over the bathroom facilities while making a mental note of starting the demise of Nichi as the foremost hairdresser. The look on that woman's face as her sister had walked in, drenched and bleeding, had enraged Sara. Nichi had looked insulted and exasperated, as though she were saying 'Now look what you've gone and done!' Sara decided that Nichi was now a has-been in her books. And if she was a has-been in Sara's books, then the

herd, seated here now under driers with cotton wool stuck between their toes and dyes in their hair, would follow Sara's lead. A thorough clean-up, a deep body cleansing, a soothing massage and a retouch to the manicure and pedicure and a blow-dry were undertaken. Two more hours later, after soothing lemonade and two cups of tea, Sara deemed her sister fit for the car, and ordered the driver to the front of the salon, and this time they managed to make it to the car without incident.

Sara asked worriedly, 'Darling, how are you feeling?'

Amina managed a feeble and shaken, 'Much better now.'

Sara asked, 'Does anything hurt?'

Amina replied, 'Not that I can feel at the moment.'

Sara was unconvinced by the look on her sister's face, 'Are you sure?'

Amina felt faint, 'Yes, I just want to go home.'

Sara said, 'Sweetie, would you mind if we just stop for five minutes at the Sind Club and pick up the smoked salmon sandwiches and the pastries I'd ordered for tea?'

Amina protested, 'Sara!'

'What?' Sara said reassuringly, 'You know you love those sandwiches, I ordered them for you jani, it'll be a waste. It'll take us no more than two minutes, promise. Anyway it's on our way. Actually even a short cut really. Javed Bhai, quickly to Sind Club and then straight home,' Sara ordered the driver. 'Just run in and pick up my order!'

Javed replied, 'Yes Begum Sahib, right away.'

At the Sind Club, the car passed through the awning, past the billiards room with its sign of 'Dogs and Women not Allowed', to the parking lot. Javed ran into the club's bakery to pick up the pastries and sandwiches for tea.

Sara gushed, 'Honestly, they're still the only ones who can put together a decent sandwich for tea.'

Back at Sara's house, a still shaking Amina was beside herself with what had narrowly been averted. Her death, by drowning in Karachi's shit.

'Sara, just imagine! I could have drowned today if you hadn't saved me. I could have drowned in shit, in filth! No one would have even found my body if I had got sucked into the sewerage system. You saved me, you saved me.'

Sara rubbed her own shoulders, which were strained from having pulled out Amina and said in a subdued voice, 'Darling, let's just thank God no one saw you. At least, no one who matters! Thank God, water was available and we were able to go back in without anyone seeing that filth on you. Anyway thank God everything is okay, baba. Nothing terrible happened.' Sara changed her tone to sound like she was talking to a little girl, 'I think, jani, you've put on some weight, huh? My shoulders are killing me from pulling you up.' Then she giggled, 'Just imagine what we would have had to say at your funeral over condolences, people would have been unable to suppress their laughter…Amina drowned in a manhole!'

Amina giggled too and so Sara broke out into laughter.

Amina was still shaking and yellow in the face while they sat in Sara's bedroom. She stared at Sara and swallowed hard, then she burst into tears.

'Oh no,' Sara said, 'I didn't mean to laugh. I wasn't laughing at you! And I didn't mean to call you fat or anything. You know I'm such a maniac, ooofh I can never say the right thing! I'm sorry, jani!'

Amina replied, 'No, that's not it, Sara. Sara, you saved me!' Sara stared at her, bewildered and asked, 'What should I have done...? Don't be silly, just relax now, everything is okay. Don't cry, your eyes will get puffy and what good will that do now? The facial will be totally wasted. You have all the other bruises on your arms to look after, no? No sleeveless shirts for at least a week. What a pity, sleeveless tunics, sleeveless everything is just the thing this season, topped with a delicious shahtoosh. Even a pashmina is okay, personally I like pulkaris as well. And thank God no bruises-shooses on your face. Thank God! That's important, the face is the most important thing. Right there for everyone to see, can't cover that!

And I think I'll call my doctor straightaway, I think you must get a tetanus shot. That's the rule I think! And I think also a cholera, typhoid, meningitis, hepatitis A. And I think B as well!'

Amina whimpered feebly, 'Help me!'

Sara was alarmed by her sister's tone. 'Amina jani, jani the shots don't hurt at all. Now what's the matter?'

Amina was silently sobbing and shaking her head. Sara was beside herself with panic, 'What's the matter, is something hurting? Calm down, everything is alright now. Shall I call the ayah?'

Amina was wailing and rocking back and forth, 'No, don't call anyone. I'm okay. No. No. No, everything is not alright.'

Sara stood up in alarm, 'Oh God help us, do you have pain? I have to call a doctor, I must call Riaz at once. Oh God, I have to call Bari-ma and Choti-ma! They must come over immediately.'

Amina said, 'No don't call anyone. Just listen to me.' Sara asked. 'What is it, Amina jani, what's the matter?' 'I'm pregnant!'

Sara jolted and stood in front of Amina as though thunderstruck. Amina was petrified that she may have caused harm to herself after the fall. There was a knock on the door and Sara shouted, 'Come in! Can't we ever get any peace and quiet around here?' It was the ayah bringing in the tea trolley. She left it next to the chaise longue upon which Amina reclined, then she backed out of the room and shut the door behind her Amina was still badly shaken and couldn't hold back her emotions. She burst out in tears.

Sara lifted her hand, signaling Amina to be quiet. Sara rushed to the door and opened it—no one was there. She peeped into the corridor—all clear. 'Just checking dahling. Servants!'

Amina said, crying, 'I'm pregnant.'

'What are you talking about?' Sara had her hand on her heart. She sat down and then stood up again and started pacing. Sara was stunned.

She tried to compose herself so that she would not frighten Amina. She managed to say, 'But the marriage hasn't even taken place yet.'

'What marriage?' Amina asked.

'Zain and you!' Sara exclaimed breathlessly.

Amina asked, 'What are you talking about?'

Sara explained, 'I thought you and Zain.'

Amina breathed, 'Oh God.'

Sara continued, 'Riaz was totally wrong about Zain and then nowadays of course! Oh my God, oh my God, Amina, what are you going to do? How long has it been? A month? I mean, I can't see anything. Ok. Amina, this is good news. Such good news. I am so happy. Really!'

'What?' Amina asked.

Sara exclaimed, 'You are going to have a child! This is good news. Of course I'm happy.'

Amina was stunned, 'I don't believe what I'm hearing!'

'Why?' Sara asked.

Amina said, 'I don't know. I never thought you would approve of such a ...'

'Now you are having a baby,' Sara said firmly. 'You must be married at once.'

Amina said, 'I know. I agree. Okay.'

Sara's cellphone rang, she glanced at the number and threw an apologetic glance at Amina. 'It's Iqbal.' Then turning on the phone, she said in a stern tone, 'Yes, what is it? Okay, Okay?

Baba, I'll be right there, tell her to wait in my office!' Sara shut the phone and got up quickly. 'Sorry jani, but I have a very important client waiting downstairs. It'll only take half an hour or so. It's a whole trousseau, plus outfits for the entire family for a wedding in Canada. They've come to collect everything today, leaving by the flight tonight. Why don't you come with me and then we can come back up here? Go wash your face, brush your hair, I'll wait.'

Sara punched in a phone number and said, 'Tell them I'll be there in five minutes.'

Amina wiped the tears from her eyes and went into Sara's bathroom. She turned on the water and watched the water spill over from her cupped hands into the white ceramic sink. She splashed her face with the cold water and looked at her reflection in Sara's luxuriously large, gilt mirror lit up by numerous shaded light bulbs. Everything was spinning out of control it seemed, and yet Amina felt strangely at peace and secure. Sara would look after everything, make everything easy. She hadn't told Resham, it was so odd. How strange that Sara should be her confidante. Amina and Resham discussed everything first before they let other people in on whatever was going on in their lives. Having a child on one's own was not an issue that had gone undiscussed with Resham. She had told Resham that she was considering the possibility. Why hadn't she called her? Amina knew that Resham would have had a very clear idea of what Amina needed to do. Resham would have told Amina to come back to New York immediately. Amina was unsure now whether she wanted to do that. She wasn't sure what she wanted to do at all.

Later, Amina sat in a comfortable settee pushed against the wall and wedged between two racks of outfits on hangers and stacks and bundles of cloth waiting their turn to be designed by Sara, cut by Iqbal, and tailored by the artisans upstairs. She watched with admiration as Sara sat at her desk, a marble topped dining table stacked with catalogues and notebooks, and soothed frayed nerves of the three female clients whose orders had not been completed and would need to be FedExed to them next week. Sara reassured them that this would not be an issue at all.

She waved her hand dismissively, the large solitaire diamond of her wedding ring caught the sun's rays and winked as she said cheerfully, 'It's only three or four outfits, all the major outfits are completed, and are with you. You really have nothing to worry about! Have I ever let you down before? How many weddings in your family, Shaila Apa, have I handled, huh?'

The elderly lady who Sara addressed as Shaila Apa nodded worriedly but admitted that Sara had never failed them and that such things were par for the course. Sara had breezed on soothingly that, after all, 'This was a busy season, what with Ramadan just ended and the wedding season upon them. And yes, Moharram just around the corner after that. You know, I'll stop work completely during the first ten days of Moharram so if there is anything else that you are planning to order from me, please do so now and I'll schedule it in for a month from now. Come Moharram, it will be fullstop for me!'

This warning set off a flurry of panic amongst the visitors who were leaving for Canada that evening. They raced through the catalogues on Sara's desk, consulted her on designs and fabrics and then left it all to Sara's discretion to decide on their behalf what outfits they should order from her for the next six months.

Each of them commissioned her to go ahead and make four to six more outfits for them. Sara asked if they wanted a few black shalwar kameezes and black chadors and dupattas as well, considering Moharram was coming. In the last several years, an increasing number of women who attended wore the hijab. Karachi's cloth shops and markets were full of choices for outfits in black and white which were displayed from shop fronts and shop windows. These were all the latest new textiles during the season of Moharram; linens, voiles, muslins and cotton lawns, in black and white prints.

This allowed the newly rich to be piously but fashionably attired.

A practice much frowned on by the pious for its frivolity and veering off course, but embraced by all anyway. Sara's clients agreed immediately and added a few more outfits to their orders.

'Ah Moharram,' said Shaila Apa. 'The fun of Moharram is its own pleasure!'

Sara nodded in agreement and looked over at Amina and said, 'Now Moharram is something you don't get over there in New York, do you? Nothing like Moharram in Karachi!'

Amina laughed, 'I thought the credo was nothing like December in Karachi! But of course we have Moharram in New York.'

Shaila Apa also protested, 'And in Toronto, Moharram is well attended and just as vibrant as anywhere. I am sure we could rival Karachi easily!'

Sara laughed, 'Never! Nothing like Moharram in Karachi.'

Amina said, 'Well, I think the New Jersey Shias say that for

Edison as well. Nothing like Moharram in Edison or LA or Toronto or London!'

Sara looked confused, 'What?'

Amina explained, 'In New York, one has the option to be part of Moharram if one wants to. Do you know there's a procession, a jaloos, on the tenth that goes up Madison Avenue?'

Sara said, 'You keep saying that but is there really anything to it?'

Amina said, 'Absolutely. Zuljana and all. Maatam and alams. The works, baby.'

'Zanjeer ka maatam?' Sara asked. 'What? People actually flagellate themselves on Madison Avenue? Knives, chains and all? I don't believe it!'

Amina said, 'No, of course not, not in the streets of New York, for God's sake! People would freak out. But there's zanjeer ka maatam in the imam bargahs in New York and New Jersey and Washington DC and LA and other places. Perhaps next year you can come to New York for Moharram.'

Sara looked at her sister askance, 'God forbid! Why would we do that and leave our majlises and imam bargahs in Karachi?'

The woman from Canada sighed, 'True, very true.'

'Yes! I can't wait till Moharram begins!' sighed Sara contentedly.

'I live for Moharram.' Sara's attention was drawn by her son playing out on the lawn with some neighborhood friends. She got up, reached for a pulkari shawl draped on the back of her chair which was densely embroidered in yellow silk thread. She flung it around her shoulders, thoroughly aware of the dramatic effect it had on her clients and went to the window, and shouted, 'Tahir, get back to your room and your studies! Exams are in three weeks and all you are doing is playing all the time!' She turned in frustration and looked at her sister and her clients. 'That boy! I'm forever running after him about his studies!'

One of the women exclaimed, 'What a beautiful piece this pulkari is! Sara, could you get me one like this?'

Sara furrowed her brow, 'Hmmmm, let me see. I'll find out what I can do, this is an antique you know, obviously. But let me see what I can do! I've worked miracles before.'

Sara's cellphone rang and she was distracted as she answered it, 'Yes Riaz, don't worry, of course I'll be there! Okay, see you in the lobby at seven.' She turned to her clients, 'My sister-in-law is in the hospital—appendix. They'll operate tomorrow morning, I'm just making sure that I take home-cooked food to her! Riaz insists!'

In the dappled Karachi afternoon as sunlight streamed in through the bamboo blinds, Amina had decided somewhere in the time between her eyebrows being threaded, falling into the gutter, and watching her sister in her various moods and personas, that it would have been cruel to ask Zain to marry her. It would have been absurd to ask him to do so. Instead, she had convinced herself that it would have to be Yaqub. He was the perfect candidate for her to consider. She was convinced that Yaqub was completely in awe of her from the moment he had set eyes on her in New York. He would be perfect. He was single. Sure, he was no match for her in terms of sophistication but he was very, very rich. She thought it would be the perfect thing; she could live like Sara, why not? This life wasn't so bad. Should she choose to, this could be a great life.

She was tired of the drudgery and pressure of work. The rest of her life could very well be lived like a long December in Karachi. Why not? That was perfection. Yes indeed, this felt right, Yaqub could very well become the father of her child.

23

Monkey Act: America Returned

THE beach stretched out in charcoal hues; on its edge the Arabian Sea gently lapped on to the sand on a breezy and cloudy day as Alejandro, Amina and Zain began their stroll.

Alejandro looked in front of him appreciatively and whistled, 'Man look at this gorgeous opportunity! Miles of sandy beach totally undeveloped. This is like Rio, only no one's around. Who would believe this is a city of 15 million people? What's wrong with them? No one out here lying on the beach? Not a single person lying on the beach or swimming!'

Zain replied, 'Take another look at the sand, it's so dirty from the shipwreck out there. Oil slick. Who would possibly want to be out here?'

Amina said in disgust, 'It's amazing; this stupid government missed the opportunity to get money out of this from the shipping company to fix up the mess. It could also get international environmental support to develop this beach by demanding that the shipping company clean it up.'

Zain shook his head and surveyed the landscape. 'Hey look, there's the monkeywallah. Let's call him over!' Zain whistled and waved to the man in the near distance. On seeing Zain wave to him, Mr Chaloo hurried over at a jogging pace with the monkey bouncing on his back like a small child being carried piggy-back.

'Salaam Sahib!' Mr Chaloo greeted Zain.

Zain replied cheerfully, 'Salaam. How's life? Tell us, do you have a new act?'

Mr Chaloo squatted on the sand before the three of them and pulled at the rope tied to the monkey who then climbed down from his back.

'Thank God, life is moving along. Come on, my friend Bandar, tell these good people what's new. What is it? What did you say? Speak to you in English? What? Why should I do that? Why bhai, till yesterday you were Urdu medium only! What? Oh yes, you have just returned from America? Well, isn't that the best thing! Marvelous! Show the people what an America-returned looks like.'

The three friends laughed. Amina shook her head and covered her mouth.

The monkey put on a pair of glasses which Mr Chaloo had tossed at him and a baseball cap as well. Then Mr Chaloo gave the monkey a little miniature suitcase to carry and a toy camera to hang around his neck. The monkey strutted around while his captive audience laughed.

As the monkey swayed about, his keeper shouted, 'Shaabaash, show the people how an America-returned walks. Aisey, wesey, like this, like that, yes! What's that you're saying? Very hot? How does Mr Bandar keep cool?'

The monkey pulled out a fan from the miniature suitcase.

'What? What did you say? Too many flies? Flies!'

Mr Chaloo pulled out a fly swatter and handed it to the monkey. 'Shaabaash, swat the flies, America-returned. What did you say? Too many mosquitoes? Tsk, tsk.'

Mr Chaloo handed over an insect spray. 'Here, shaabaash, spray the mosquitoes. Shaabaash. Mr Bandar, what are you saying? Your stomach is upset? Shaabaash, show the people how you've got the shits. Like this, like that. Aisey, wesey. Oh dear, oh dear!'

The monkey doubled over holding its stomach, and did a somersault and rolled around as if in agony.

'Shaabaash, America-returned, show them how you've got the shits.'

Mr Chaloo handed the monkey a toy lota. The monkey grabbed the water pitcher.

'Wah bhai wah, one two three, bhai show them what you did last night.'

The monkey walked back and forth, to and fro from the audience to his master with the lota in his paw. 'Shaabaash, monkey show them your lota parade. Back to the toilet every five minutes. Shaabaash, now show them how you use the lota. Wah bhai wah' The monkey squatted and with his free hand, stroked his backside.

'Shaabaash! What Monkey, what did you say? Too many flies, too many mosquitoes, you've got the shits and it's too hot? Bye-bye, ta ta you're going back to London. Bhai Monkey show them how you go to USA, to London, to Velayat.' The monkey picked up the suitcase and walked away as far as his leash would let him. Then Mr Chaloo yanked the leash and the monkey strained against it and finally fell back and was dragged closer to his master. 'What Monkey? The memory of home is pulling you back?'

The three giggled and clapped appreciatively and paid Mr Chaloo and walked on. They walked in silence for a while. Alejandro put his arm around Amina's shoulders. Alejandro said, 'Amina listen, Zain and I have been talking.'

Amina replied, 'Yeah?'

Alejandro said, 'We've been talking about marriage.'

Amina said, 'You and Zain are getting married? Wow! Congratulations. But keep it to yourself, okay. It's not going to go down well here!'

Alejandro laughed, 'No, we're not getting married.'

Amina looked at him and asked slowly, 'Then what marriage?'

Alejandro replied, 'About you. You should marry Zain.' Zain jumped in and said hurriedly, 'Yes Amina. We can get married right away. Today in fact. Go announce it to our parents and be done with it!'

Amina hugged Alejandro, and then hugged Zain. She shook her head and said, 'And how will that help? That's really sweet of you but that doesn't work, does it?'

Zain looked at her exasperated, 'Of course it works! It works beautifully. Our parents will be ecstatic. We'll go back to New York. You'll have the baby. And then we'll get divorced. Everyone will be fine.'

Amina said, 'That's really kind but I've made up my mind.

I'm going to stay here. I'm not going back.'

'You're crazy,' said Zain. 'How are you going to stay here and have the baby? I mean, how are you going to stay here, period? This place isn't home for you now. You don't belong here!'

'I'm going to marry Yaqub,' Amina said. 'I can see that's what he wants. I'll make that happen, I know he's getting ready to propose.'

Zain exclaimed, 'Are you crazy? That oaf? No way! What do you guys have in common?'

Amina protested, 'He's not an oaf. I thought you liked him and anyway I don't think you should say that.'

'He's not an oaf, you're right and I do like him,' Zain said hurriedly. 'But he's not for you. He's totally blah.'

'No he isn't!' Amina resisted. 'You should have seen him at Sara's taking on the General himself. I mean that takes guts.'

'Yeah, I heard about it. It doesn't take guts, it takes money and power,' Zain said dismissively.

'I didn't see any other powerful person in the room do that,' Amina challenged.

'Please, Amina, be serious,' Zain pleaded.

Amina said, 'You're right. I know. But even so. We have nothing in common now but that'll happen eventually. I'll make it work.'

'Listen to me, you nutcase!' protested Zain. 'You don't fit in here. Come back with me. It's a perfect plan. We'll get married and we'll go back. We can raise this kid together.'

Amina walked up ahead of the two, 'No, I've decided.'

Zain shouted at her, 'You don't even know this guy and you don't really even like this guy. At least I'm a friend. Friends being parents to a kid is much better, it's much better than a social and economic calculation.'

Amina turned back to look at him, her hair in her face from the sea breeze. She said, 'That's not fair.'

Alejandro shook his head, 'He's right Amina. Listen to him.'

Zain spread his arms out in frustration, 'Of course it's fair! It's totally fair. I don't know what's going on with you. Maybe it's just the hormones kicking in, or maybe it's the whole December scene here, the carnival-circus atmosphere that's gotten to you. Or you're so nuts about suddenly becoming a shark in a minnows' pond and being 'something' in this town that you'd pick him over me! I mean you've got Sara-itis, suddenly!'

Amina said, 'Hey! That's not fair, don't talk about my sister that way. And besides, it's not that!'

Zain refused to back down, 'Oh yeah? Then what is it?'

Amina said, 'I don't want to go back. It's not home anymore.

There's war going on everywhere. I feel like an outsider now.'

'Oh don't give me that shit!' Zain protested. 'There's a war going on? And that effects you? How? In New York?'

'Yeah, in New York!' Amina stated.

Zain laughed, 'You've got to be delusional.'

Amina looked at him, 'Oh yeah? I'm delusional? Don't you feel self-conscious? Don't you feel nervous? Don't forget, I got arrested for nothing! For standing around watching a demonstration against the war! I mean, have you forgotten that? And have you forgotten the whole scene with Dave? And wait till you arrive at the airport after this trip! Oh boy, get ready for the grilling session. Aren't you tired of that? How can you stand it? Like everything you do has to be to demonstrate how wrong they are. That you need to be the anti-stere-otype, the mould breaker. I mean that's how I feel, trying to be the anti-cliché, I am the cliché. I feel suddenly like I know how the blacks must have felt. I feel like a Fuji blimp is watching me all the time!' Zain shouted, 'What? What the hell are you talking about!

Stop exaggerating. It does not effect you one bit.'

Alejandro said, 'Hey, being the new black is a great thing! You're the new black! Come on, that's cool. At least in New York, it's cool.'

Amina shook her head, 'And did you think they would go and elect Bush again! No, you didn't. I did. Well they did, didn't they? You know, it's all been getting to me. Chipping away at me. All the endless hype on TV and in the media, I think people even look at us differently now. I just don't want that. I don't want to spend the rest of my life feeling like I'm under surveillance. Feeling like I'm only being politely tolerated because it's unconstitutional not to let me in through the doors of a restaurant, or in an office, or on a plane.'

Zain laughed, 'You can't be serious.'

Amina said, 'I'm serious. I think it's time to wake up and smell the gas chambers.'

Alejandro snorted, 'Oh God! You're going too far!'

'Oh yeah? Am I?' Amina said defiantly.

'Yeah,' Zain said. 'So what?'

Amina said, 'Isn't that scary?'

Zain said, 'Look Amina, just come home with me.'

Amina stamped her foot, 'No, I don't want it. You can keep it. I matter here. Over there, I don't matter at all!'

'Yeah, but that, over there, is all that matters to you,' Zain pleaded passionately, his tone, wounded. 'You may not matter to it. But you know it matters to you. You love New York. That's your home. You're coming back with me.'

Alejandro said, 'Zain leave her alone.' He turned to Amina,

'Babe, I think you're getting confused between home and childhood. This place was childhood to you. You think by being here, it's all going to be taken care of and that you can be a kid where every-thing was perfect. But it isn't and you know it. Everyone is all grown up here, the people you were around way back then, they're all grown up—and grown up in a totally different direction than you. You don't fit in with them and you're not a kid either. The adult Amina's outgrown this place. And you know it. You know that. You keep saying that every time you come back you're disappointed because you're expecting so much, but whatever it is you're expecting is not here! It's not here. Why's that—because I think you expect to be a kid here and I think so does Zain. The grown up, the adult you, isn't here. She's over there, back home—in New York.'

24

Possibilities

YAQUB looked at his watch, it was 7: 30 in the evening. He walked out of his office and down the corridor and looked into Rehana's office. He cleared his throat and said, 'It's quite late, how are you getting home? Has the car been arranged?'

Rehana jolted and stood up and started to gather the papers on her desk, 'No Sir, the car still hasn't been arranged for. The accounts people are still working out the details. I'll just take the bus.'

Yaqub frowned and said, 'I thought the car had been arranged for you. Please remind me about this tomorrow. I'll call them. It must be done tomorrow. This situation is unacceptable. I'm very sorry. You stay late and I don't want you taking public transportation home at this time of the night. It's so late now. Just look at the time. Things are unsettled in the city today. Anyway, let me drop you home, I'm leaving now for a dinner party. Meet me downstairs in five minutes, I'll just go get my keys.'

Rehana protested, 'No Sir, you don't have to drop me, I can go home.'

Yaqub turned around, 'I insist! Meet me outside in five minutes. That's that, no arguments!'

Twenty minutes later they were stuck in traffic. Yaqub was driving his sports Mercedes this evening and Rehana sat silently next to him, feeling uneasy and out of place. Finally she said, 'Sir, I'm really sorry that you have to take me home tonight. It's a waste of your time.'

Yaqub said, 'Not at all.'

Rehana continued haltingly, 'I have to confess, I'm a bit embarrassed that you're taking me home.'

Yaqub glanced towards her and then back at the traffic. 'Why? Why would I mind?' Rehana sounded apologetic, 'Well, I live in a very poor section of the city, Sir. I don't think you…'

Yaqub said, 'Really, Rehana, I didn't expect this of you. What do you think I am?'

Rehana said quickly, 'Sir, I think you're a wonderful person and I am slightly…Well, I think all this will be new for you, you are used to the posh side of the city.'

Yaqub shook his head, he felt annoyed, 'I didn't expect you to talk like this, Rehana. I think you're a very good human being and frankly more intelligent than that. And I think you are one of the most intelligent and wise people that I have ever met. You must understand that I was not always what I am today. Everything I have, I have earned.'

Rehana said, 'I know that, Sir.'

Yaqub replied, 'No, actually you don't know that. You know what everyone else knows: that I had returned to the city seven years ago after becoming rich abroad. As though I had not known what it was like to not be rich. As though I didn't know what it was like to be very poor and to live in very difficult circumstances.'

Rehana shook her head, 'Sorry, Sir.'

Yaqub said, 'You should know that my return had been for the sole purpose of never leaving again. The work that you are doing for me is very dear to me. It's my ambition, my dream, to become someone who is considered a benefactor, a patron in this city. Do you realize that you are helping me to set the stage for my final days and in fact arranging my final resting place?'

Rehana said incredulously, 'Your final resting place! You're too young to talk like that, Sir!'

Yaqub shook his head, 'No, you don't understand. I wanted to be someone in this place, where I had been a nobody when I left, a poor child working on an oil tanker. Do you know what that means?'

Rehana said, 'I've heard terrible things. I can't imagine…'

Yaqub nodded, 'I don't know what you've heard. But if what you've heard was unimaginably repulsive and horrible then everything you've heard is true. And it's taken me a long time to come to terms with all that has happened to me as a child. Do you know how kids are treated? How kids are treated by those drugged out perverts, the drivers?'

Rehana instinctively reached out to put her hand on Yaqub's arm but stopped half way and checked herself. She withdrew her hand. He continued, looking straight ahead of him. 'I was a child who managed to escape from that life, and managed to become a laborer on the docks by day, and a waiter at a truck driver's restaurant by night.'

He looked at Rehana's face, expecting to see her shocked, but she sat there looking calmly ahead of her.

Yaqub continued, 'I look at these kids on the streets, selling newspapers and cigarettes and flowers and I think these are my family; each and every one is me. I can talk to you this way because I know that I can trust you.'

Rehana said softly, 'You can trust me completely.'

Yaqub looked at her again, 'I want you to know who I am since you've been part of…well, you're literally the architect of my efforts to become somebody in this city.'

Rehana said, 'I'm only too happy to be a part of your life in some way, Sir.'

Yaqub said, 'I have a brief recollection of my childhood, the nightmare of being a "water boy" on an oil tanker. But I never wish to recall it, and have spent a lifetime suppressing the memory. But tonight, your remark about how I would react to where you live has been deeply offensive.'

Rehana looked out of the car window and then at her hands folded in her lap. 'I'm sorry.'

Yaqub agreed, 'At the age of eight I was the companion of a truck driver, on an eighteen-wheeler rig carrying oil from the docks to the hinterlands. That was my beginning. I do not want to dwell on that. There are thousands like me. God only knows how I escaped disease.'

Rehana felt her stomach turn and bile rose in her throat, but

she tried to steady her voice, 'I had no idea.' She panicked, she didn't want him to continue talking.

Yaqub said, 'Yes. And you consider me powerful and able to do anything because of money. Well, I am unable to step out anywhere without averting my gaze from those who care to look at me; I am always afraid of being found out.'

Rehana looked at him, unable to make out his expression in the dark car. 'I don't know what to say. I'm afraid I'll say something stupid.'

Yaqub laughed bitterly, 'No you won't say anything stupid. You are not at all like that. I escaped from that. I ran away to the docks, to a life of back-breaking work and to an existence where rest came at night on a city sidewalk, on the streets. Just like those kids we can see right now, dodging through traffic selling cigarettes and newspapers.'

'I wish they knew your story,' Rehana murmured. Yaqub continued, 'I worked and worked and worked, earning Rs.30 a day, no more than that, maybe even less, lifting bales of cotton onto ships. And finally one day, I got my chance and I hid away on one such ship going to Italy. In the hold of the ship, I remember, there were at least a dozen boys like me, looking for an opportunity to make it. And I did make it. It took years. But

I did. After landing in Italy safely, I stayed there for several years working as a construction worker, a grape-picker and as a stevedore on the dock. After seven years of hard work, selling newspapers, wiping floors, serving in cafés and restaurants, doing manual labor in construction, farming, you name it, anything that I could get, I heard that I could really strike it rich if I could get to Dubai. So I made my way back from Europe to Dubai. One good opportunity after another. That was really the land of opportunity for me. It has taken me close to thirty years to return. But return I did. Wealthy.

The first thing I did was go visit the godown where I used to work and I bought it. An old and crumbling building which had served as a godown for the goods which were loaded into the ships and which I visited regularly every day thirty years ago, to load bales of commodities onto a truck or off it. It had been my wish from the day I left to return and buy this place. I always felt that this godown would be my home some day, the storage, the warehousing of me. I was going to transform my life, and when I returned I would transform the godown. It would become my life. I had hoped that it would survive. And miraculously it had. I returned, purchased it, and had set about the task, the very pleasurable task of restoring it. Thanks to you. Your thesis was a real education for me about the building I had purchased. Thanks to you.'

Rehana said softly, 'Thank you.'

Yaqub said, 'So you see, where you live is a place I would have given anything to have had as a child. You have a home and a family and your neighbors are decent and they respect and care for you.'

Rehana said, 'Yes Sir, I do have that.'

Yaqub said cheerfully, 'And you've done a superlative job in creating a home for me. Rehana, you have designed a space that I only imagined, only imagined in pieces, in disjointed feelings and yearnings. You have gathered everything together. It amazes me how much creativity and talent there is in you.'

Rehana interrupted, 'Sir, I don't think you understand…'

Yaqub continued, 'Please let me say this, you have hurt me today by thinking that your home, the place where you live, is somehow beneath me.'

'Sir, I meant…' Rehana interjected.

Yaqub said, 'No, please listen to me. We don't get a chance to talk like this often. When you say such a thing, that I can sit in judgment of you, then I know that you could sit in judgment of me as well. I think you are better than that. You have managed to turn my simple conversations, the simple conversations of a day laborer, into a work of art. Everything I told you about how I wanted the building to be transformed. You've done it. I am humbled. I cannot tell you how much I love the design of our building! I cherish every detail of it, the sound of trickling water as it reaches all the way up to my apartment on the third floor, and the sound of the sea breeze, swishing through the interior in waves, the sound it creates, of the sea. You were so intelligent in thinking of capturing and using the breeze itself. I would have never thought of that! I know it's an age-old traditional way for cooling, but you actually made it modern again. And the sunlight and how it's used throughout the structure, all of it, is remarkable. You make tradition modern, Rehana. You make tradition modern. That's what you are. I had thought that I had been creating a space for my final days, an ending to my story, and you've actually made it a vital source for my life and made it possible for me to begin my life.'

Rehana was overwhelmed and her eyes had begun to tear. She could have never imagined such a heartfelt tribute from Yaqub.

They had arrived at her house. She got out of the car and leaning in through the window, she asked Yaqub if he would come in and meet her mother. Yaqub hesitated. 'Yes,' he said. 'It's proper that I should meet your mother since I've come all the way to her door.'

He parked the car outside the lane to Rehana's house. Together they walked towards the house. Rehana opened the door to the sehan and they entered. She sighed with relief that her mother was not in the sehan washing clothes. Yaqub stood there for a moment and looked around him. He looked at the tiles on the floor, the flowering plants, the birds and the washing hanging out to dry and smiled to himself. Rehana watched him. He said, 'This is Paradise.' Rehana ushered him into the house and they found Amma in the drawing room watching TV. Amma, who sat curled up in a sofa seat with a cup of tea, was absorbed in a TV drama. She turned when they entered and scrambled hurriedly to stand up.

Rehana walked up to her mother and put her arm around her shoulders, 'Amma this is Yaqub Sahib. He dropped me home and wanted to come in and meet you!'

'Come in come in, beta,' Amma said, one hand smoothing down her hair, ill at ease and embarrassed. She was worried that she was wearing her house clothes which were stained from cooking and crumpled and not at all what she would have liked to have been wearing when meeting her daughter's much talked about boss and now a guest in her house. She smiled self-consciously and gestured towards the sofa. Please sit down. Come in and I'll go make you a cup of tea. She glanced at Rehana as though to confirm that she had said the right thing.

Yaqub protested, 'No, no, please don't move. I won't stay. It's late and I must be going. I wanted to come in and meet you. I want to tell you how much I appreciate your daughter's work and her dedication. I'm very sorry that she has to stay so late at work.' He glanced at the sehan floor and smiled. 'I can see that your daughter has used her talent in the house as well.'

Amma said, 'Yes! I'm very happy that you came to drop her yourself. I worry very much when she comes home so late.'

Rehana said quickly, 'Amma there's really nothing...'

Amma interrupted her daughter, 'I worry, Yaqub Sahib, I worry a lot. The situation in the city…Rehana tells me that there will be an office car soon. I worry when she comes so late by public transport.'

Rehana laughed, 'Amma, please!'

Yaqub stopped her, 'No Rehana, I agree completely with your mother. This is entirely my fault. I should have taken care of that earlier.' Then he turned to Rehana's mother, 'Please don't worry about this any longer. From tomorrow, Rehana will have a car. If we don't have it by tomorrow, then I will make sure Rehana gets home safely; it's my responsibility.'

Rehana's mother was overjoyed. 'Please won't you sit down and have a cup of tea?' Yaqub said, 'Please let me not disturb you this evening. I'll come again another time.' They had moved out into the sehan when the front door burst open and Rahim, Rehana's younger brother, came hurtling in. Upon seeing his sister and mother standing with Yaqub he stopped and tried to suppress his excitement. But it was too much for him and with a nod and a glance at Yaqub he ran up to his mother and gave her a bear hug.

'I have the job! I got the job and the visa! I'm going to Dubai! I'm going to be working at the cargo department at the airport!' Rehana rushed to hug her brother and seemed to have forgotten Yaqub's presence. She looked at her brother's excited young face and said, 'Oh God, that's such wonderful news.'

Amma was crying with happiness and had raised her cupped hands in prayer. 'God heard our prayers.'

Saima came racing down the stairs, 'Oh my God, this is so wonderful!'

Rahim turned to his wife, 'I'm to leave next week as soon as the papers are done.'

Saima suddenly looked worried and unhappy, 'So soon!'

Rahim said, 'Make up your mind! Are you happy or are you sad?'

Saima whined and exclaimed, 'I'm both!'

Amma laughed, 'My manathhas come true. My prayers have been answered!'

Saima said, 'We should have a niaz straightaway this evening before the evening prayers.'

Rehana laughed with happiness, 'Good idea.'

Rahim announced, 'I'll run to the corner store and get mithai.'

Amma said, 'Get enough for us to distribute to the neighbors.'

Rehana added, 'Get the pista and badam mithai and also halwa.'

Saima said, 'Get walnut halwa.'

'And laddoos,' Amma added.

Yaqub cleared his throat and coughed. The entire family turned to look at him. There was a moment of silence, everyone had forgotten him in their excitement. Rehana burst out laughing, 'We forgot! Rahim, Saima, this is Yaqub Sahib.' Rahim and Saima were too happy to be able to put on a pretense of formality and to stand on ceremony. Rahim came forward and shook his hand and Saima nodded and said salaam.

Yaqub laughed happily, 'I'm very happy to meet you and am very happy for you. Please make sure that I get some of the mithai and halwa as well.'

Amma looked at him and said proudly, 'Yaqub Sahib, every member of my family has a job. Every one of us works! We are blessed! Our daily bread is halal!'

Rehana turned to Rahim, 'I have some good news too!'

Rahim asked, 'What is it?'

Rehana said, 'We won't need to get a taxi to take you to the airport! Yaqub Sahib told me that I would be getting a company car for my use! I will start learning how to drive tomorrow!'

Yaqub nodded and looked content with himself, 'That's right. Tomorrow, Rehana will start learning how to drive!'

25

Mass

BY the time Alejandro, Zain, Amina and Jeevan had slipped into the pew, the service was just beginning. Jeevan sat in the pew in front of them.

'Let us read the notices first, dear sisters and brothers. I will begin with the notices of death. Spinster Maria Theresa Francis D'Souza of 21 Preedy Street died last night at 7.00 p.m. at the Civil Hospital. Her funeral will take place on the 28th. The funeral mass will be on the 28th at 11 a.m. at St Joseph's. Spinster Maria Anna D'Silva Pinto of 33 Blessings Homes passed away on Wednesday last at 10 a.m. Funeral services will be held at St Thomas's at 3.00 p.m. on the 26th. Spinster Maria Louisa Elizabeth Lawrence passed away on Tuesday at 4.00 p.m. in her home at Queens Road. Funeral prayers will be at St Andrew's in Saddar tomorrow at 4.00 p.m. Let us say a prayer for the deceased. "Our father who art in heaven, hallowed be thy name."'

Amina leaned in to Zain and shuddered, 'What is all this spinster business?'

'I know,' Zain said, 'pretty grim.' Then he grinned and said, 'See, you need to marry me unless you want to be remembered as Spinster Amina Rueewallah!'

'Give it up,' Amina replied. 'Still, the announcements are kinda sweet. In an old world kinda way.'

'You think?' Zain added. 'I'm not sure Maria Theresa Lawrence would've thought so.'

Amina said, 'Well she'd have known it was coming. Having probably attended hundreds of masses, probably in this church.'

'This is so depressing,' Alejandro interjected.

'I don't know, it's kind of quaint,' Amina said 'So Spinster Amina Rueewallah?' Alejandro teased.

Amina asked, 'Why doesn't the word bachelor have the same connotation?'

'Patriarchal society. No doubt,' Zain offered. 'Absolutely,' Amina stated.

And with these announcements over, Christmas Mass began. Jeevan turned back and looked at Amina. She wore the gold cross

that Amina had given her for her Christmas present this morning, much to her surprise and delight. She had been reluctant to come with Amina to church but Amina had insisted, telling her that Zain and she were taking their friend from America, who was a Christian to the service, and so Jeevan might as well come with them. Jeevan would have preferred to go in the evening, but had come along. She had on the new shalwar kameez that Sara, on behest of Bari-ma and Choti-ma, had bought her for Christmas.

It was a synthetic silk in light blue with white stars on it. A light blue dupatta of tulle was trimmed with a braid of silver beads. Sara had bought the fabric and had it stitched. Jeevan hadn't understood much of the proceeding so far because the Mass was being said in English and Jeevan spoke only Punjabi and Urdu. The Punjabi service was later in the day. Zain and Amina had brought Alejandro and Jeevan to the 7.00 a.m. service at St Thomas's. The church was sparsely attended. People who probably could not speak English nevertheless listened attentively. Little girls in gold embroidered shalwar kameezes made of brocade and with brand new shoes from Bata and English Boot House giggled and shared quiet jokes with each other. Little boys in white shirts and new jeans, with their hair washed and combed, glistening with hair cream, sat up straight and occasionally slouched when drowsy. All in their best Sunday outfits, mothers in their finest shalwar kameezes and wedding jewelry and fathers proudly heading the family. They sat whispering to each other in Punjabi between pauses. On the other side of the isle sat a Portuguese Goan family, set apart from the rest of the congregation by their attire. The women wore hats and gloves and their skin was creamy and pale, unblemished by carefully being concealed from lengthy exposure to the sun. They didn't look at the others, instead they focused on the psalms and readings, trying to ignore the poorer segment of the congregation which, much to their dismay, had grown into the majority over the years.

It seemed, however, that the loudest singers of the hymns were Zain, Amina and Alejandro because the rest, apart from the Goan family, didn't know these verses, at least not in English.

The Christmas decorations in the church, tinsel and paper, hung on strings from the ceiling or were draped across it in the form of a few home-made paper chains. They were distanced from each other, and were criss-crossed above the heads of the worshippers, moving with the breeze and collected a thin film of dust. Two plastic bouquets of flowers, roses in red and pink, graced the altar. There were wrought iron bars on the windows through which swallows and sparrows flew in and out with the cold December early morning sea breeze. Swinging gently in the cool morning breeze were a few cardboard cut-outs of baby Jesus hanging from the ceiling with colored thread. Amina serenely gazed up at them floating overhead. She shivered and snuggled closer to Zain.

26

Beach Luxury Hotel

RAZZAK walked slightly ahead of Hajrabai and Zareenabai, 'What made you think of coming here?' He turned to Hajra and then asked with a chuckle, 'Nostalgia?'

Hajra smiled, 'It was Zareenabai's idea.'

Zareenabai said nervously, 'I thought we'd have tea together on the lawn. It's quiet here and we can have a bit of privacy, no one stopping by constantly to greet us.' And then, referring to the servants, at 43-G she added, 'There are too many ears at home.' The three of them slowly made their way out through the lawn to the pavilion next to the water. It was early in the morning, the gardeners were tending the big lush green lawn and sweepers were cleaning the pathways. At the far end of the large main lawn, a stage had been set up. The hotel was hosting several theatre troupes during the winter season and there were performances every evening. A poster in the entrance advertised a bookfair that was to be held later in the month at the same place. The hotel had always been an affordable oasis in the city for the arts scene to be put up social and cultural activities. As they neared the pavilion, Razzak, Hajra and Zareena could see birds in the mangroves across from them and Razzak said, 'Remember

Hajrabai, how all these birds were once in abundance when we used to come here? Look, hardly any are left.' The mangroves used to be alive with grey herons, purple herons, night herons, flamingos, white pelicans, dalmatian pelicans, brahminy kites, marsh harriers, black shouldered kites, kestrels, Indian sparrow hawks, coucals, purple moorhen and water rails.

Hajrabai said, 'Yes, I do remember. Herons, flamingos, pelicans! So many different varieties of birds, all gone now.'

They sat in silence contemplating the mangroves. A canoe glided and dipped in and out of sight from amongst the mangrove branches. They spotted two fishermen checking their cages and traps for shrimp and other catch.

Razzak said, 'What a perfect idea this was to come here for tea, it's so quiet and peaceful at this time of the morning.'

They sat quietly for a few moments watching the birds across the water. They were the only customers at this time of the day.

The serenity of the place was marked by the noise of heavy traffic in the distance over the bridge leading from the port to the city.

Eventually a waiter from indoors came out and Razzak ordered tea even though he knew this particular hotel restaurant would not be operational till late afternoon.

Hajra said, 'Do you remember Razzak, how we used to come here?' He laughed. Hajrabai laughed as well. Razzak replied,

'Yes, but it's not the same place. It's beyond recognition, almost. Just look at how thinned out the mangroves are. Almost gone, compared to what they were.'

'Yes it is,' Hajra said with a sad note in her voice. 'I thought it would be the same. I don't know why I thought it would be the same. I guess we're not the same either.' Razzak laughed, 'What were you thinking? We would come here and be transformed into eighteen-year-olds!'

Hajra replied, 'Perhaps that's exactly what I was thinking. I guess that's what we think when we think of going back to some place from our youth. It's not the place that we want to go back to, it's our youth that we want to go back to.'

Razzak said, 'Yes, it's true. See those birds over there? They have a lot in common with our daughters!'

Zareenabai said, 'Oh? A lot in common with our children? How?'

'Yes, with our children,' said Razzak. 'For those birds, Karachi means a migration from the freezing cold of Siberia, just like Karachi is in winter to Amina, Resham, Kulsum and Shireen, our December Pakistanis!Our own migratory flock of birds.'

Hajrabai and Zareena laughed.

Razzak continued, 'We're looking at what is part of one of the largest arid climate mangroves on earth, the Avicenna variety which was home to a multitude of life, including migratory birds from Siberia. See how dirty this water is? It's full of all sorts of pollution, ship discharge, oily ballast and bilge water, and cargo tank washings. Oily spills from tankers and general cargo vessels, sewage, waste and washouts from the port area, and industrial water flowing in from Lyari and Malir rivers are all destroying the mangroves. And with the destruction of mangroves, marine life, the shrimp, sardines, crabs and palla and other fish, snakes and the bird life is also being destroyed. There are about sixty species of birds and fourteen species of sea snakes that live in these mangroves. And oil terminals and oil storage facilities operated by various organizations are constant sources of oil pollution. These mangroves are a natural barrier from devastating storms like typhoons and cyclones. And we're destroying them.' Razzak loved to explain things to his wives.

Again they fell into a silence, enjoying the morning sounds. Then Hajra said, 'Razzak, do you remember that painting, the one of the beautiful room opening on to a balcony?'

Razzak said, ‘I think so, I’m not sure. Where did it go anyway? I thought it was no longer in our house.’

Hajrabai laughed, ‘It isn’t. And hasn’t been for a long time. Apparently the painting has materialized suddenly.’

Zareena said, ‘Really? Well, that’s interesting. Where did you find it?’

Hajrabai replied, ‘Yes, it’s very interesting. It’s hanging in Yaqub’s Foundation.’

Razzak said, ‘The painting’s at the old godown?’

‘Yes,’ Hajra said. ‘And that’s quite a miracle.’

Zareenabai replied, ‘It wasn’t a painting of the house, now that I remember it. It was of the drawing room at the apartment on Lawrence Road.’

‘Exactly! The tiled floor in the painting was beautiful,’ Hajra said.

‘Yes,’ Razzak said. ‘All tiles from the Nausherwan Tile Factory. It belonged to Nausherwan Mehta who was also the Mayor of Karachi in 1936.’

Hajra said, ‘Yes, that’s a fact I do know!’ Then she paused for a moment and said, ‘The other fact that I know is that the painting is beautiful, but it’s a fake.’

Zareenabai said, ‘A fake!’

Razzak was surprised too, ‘A fake? How do you know?’

Hajrabai laughed, ‘I know. I should know. Who else but I would know? Meir took the painting with him when he left. The one hanging in the Foundation is not the same painting. And besides, the colours of the tiles in the painting are not the same as I remember them. So someone obviously made a copy of it and Yaqub has the copy.’

Razzak said, ‘Well then, how did this happen? How would, why would, Yaqub have this painting at all, fake or real?’

‘Well Razzak, I don’t know, but I have a strong suspicion that our Sara has something to do with it.’

'Sara! What would Sara have to do with it?' Zareenabai said defensively.

'Zareenabai, I don't know but I am quite sure!'

Razzak said, 'Okay baba, I won't question you, I'm sure she did. The connection between the painting and Yaqub can only be through Sara. Has she seen the pamphlet?'

Hajra said, 'I seem to recall that she had and she may even have a copy of the pamphlet. And we all know how talented she is.'

Zareena interrupted her, 'Hajrabai, Razzak, I also know my daughters well. I am quite sure Hajrabai is right. Sara tends to get into all sorts of unnecessary complications. But that's not so important, is it? I'm worried about Amina. Razzak, that's why I brought you two here.'

Razzak looked alarmed, 'What's wrong with Amina?'

Hajrabai too looked at Zareenabai anxiously. The waiter arrived with their tea and busied himself with setting down the tray, arranging the teacups in front of Razzak, Zareena and Hajra, laying the napkins, placing the tea plates for the chicken sandwiches and meat patties and setting the three-tiered server of sandwiches, patties and kebabs at the center of the table. He was about to pour the tea when Hajra raised her hand impatiently. 'Please leave that to me. We'll call you when we need you.'

The waiter nodded deferentially, set down the teapot, milk jug and sugar pot and left. Hajra poured the tea for Razzak, Zareena and herself. They were silent. Hajra looked across the water. 'Remember Razzak, how we came here? How thrilling that was? How daring? What a risk it was?'

Razzak laughed, 'Yes, of course I remember.'

Zareena said, 'I'm glad that both of you remember that time well. I just wanted to remind you, remind both of you, that such a long time ago the two of you had done what was unheard of—a real taboo.'

Razzak replied uncertainly, 'What is this about? Are you rebuking us, after all these years?'

'Of course not!' Zareena said hurriedly. She looked at Hajra, taking her hand in hers and said, 'I'm just reminding you what a taboo you both broke. And reminding you that I accepted everything.'

Razzak was impatient and uncomfortable. 'But what are you leading up to? You said that something was wrong with Amina.'

'She didn't say something was wrong with her. She just said she was worried.' Hajra corrected him.

Zareena said, 'I am worried, I can hear a very different tone in her voice.'

Razzak said, 'You are worried by a tone in her voice, you are imagining things. Don't we have enough to worry about?'

Zareena said, 'No, no, listen to me. I know my daughters, I know them through the tone in their voices. They're all so far away the only way I can know how they are is to rely on the phone and focus on the tones of their voices. After all these years of being far away from them and having only my ears to rely on, I can tell whether they are happy or sad or if they are not telling me something. Amina's tone has changed! Besides, I'm noticing other changes as well.'

Razzak said, 'What do you mean? I don't follow you.'

Zareena fell silent again, then she heaved a sigh and said,

'Hajrabai remember the fahl? The one we selected when you were at Lawrence Road?'

Hajrabai said, 'I don't remember it clearly.'

Zareena quoted:

I said O fate, when will you awake? The sun is up, it is now dawn-break.

Said fate, you have made many a mistake, Yet keep hope and faith within your breast.

Hajrabai said, 'Yes, now I remember. We were hopeful for her.'

Zareena said, 'I think Amina is pregnant!'

Razzak jumped out of his seat, the tea things on the table rattled and the napkin fell on top of them. 'God forbid! What nonsense, woman! What? What is this nonsense that you are speaking of! Zareena, you are always saying something ridiculous!'

Hajra grabbed his arm, 'Lower your voice Razzak, and sit down. Calm down. Zareena, the ground beneath me is moving, I'm not sure what you are really saying.'

Zareena said, 'You heard me, both of you heard me!'

Hajra said, 'I can't breathe. I feel as though I'm in a dream.'

Zareena said, 'Hajrabai, have some water, now calm down. You are feeling what I've been feeling all of last week. And now I am convinced. I can see a change in her. There is a ring in her voice!'

Razzak snorted, 'A ring in her voice! Is this what you are basing these thoughts of yours on?'

Zareena gently mused, 'Like a little bell almost. She sounds happy.'

Razzak interjected, 'She sounds happy and that's your reason to be worried? She sounds happy, and you think that she is going to have a child!'

Zareena continued, 'But her eyes are anxious!'

Razzak said, 'She sounds happy, her eyes are anxious, her...'

Zareena interrupted him, 'And I can see a slight change in her figure as well. She is pregnant.' They were silent. The three of them sat motionless looking at each other. Then Zareena spoke resolutely, 'So what if she is pregnant? I've brought you here for us to discuss how we can help her. I don't want her to take any rash decisions. We can support her, we can help her. We must make sure that she knows that we are with her. She mustn't think she's alone and that she can't tell us.'

Razzak said, 'This is unacceptable! What a disgrace! But it's not even true, we are sitting here talking about nonsense, basing it all on your conjecturing! On a fahl! This is as usual your stupidity.'

Zareenabai retorted, 'It may be conjecturing and it may not be, I think I know what I know. And it's high time, Razzak, that you respected me for some wisdom. I do not think Amina will disgrace herself or anyone else, no more than you and Hajrabai did, forgive me, Hajrabai. But please try to recall that, Razzak, that you and Hajrabai ran off and eloped. Our families thought that was an unforgivable disgrace. Can you imagine what happened in my household, me already in a nikkah with you! And Hajrabai's father died from the shame and disgrace he felt!'

Razzak replied, 'Calm yourself. There is no comparison, those were different times. The world was gentle, fragile and vulnerable then. Of a different sensibility. And a simple thing like our getting married was considered a big thing, there were traditions then.'

Zareenabai said, 'It was no simple thing, it was catastrophic. We made it seem like it was simple because of our actions. It was our behavior, our attitude that made it fine and not catastrophic.'

Hajra agreed, 'Razzak, you are talking nonsense. Those were not gentle times, they were cruel times, full of bigotry and racism. There was war and there was Partition, there was the Holocaust and there was Hiroshima and Nagasaki. Those were not gentle times. All the opinions and traditions around us—the majority opinion, was not gentle. But you and I rose above that. We acted as individuals and followed our hearts. And yes, it is true, Zareena, it was because of you that we never faced any catastrophe and have only seen happiness. And Razzak, if what Zareena is saying is true, then we must make sure that Amina does what we did, act from the heart and we must do the same. We must help her, Razzak, we must save our child before she assumes that she is expected to do something else.'

Razzak was silent. Tears rolled down his cheeks. 'What is the world coming to?'

Hajra continued in a gentle tone, wringing her hands together and rocking back and forth in her chair, 'And we are good for that! We are good. Our children, our little family is our world, and we are good.' She half stood up and leaned across the table and with her hands and then with the edge of her sari palloo, she wiped the tears that were streaming down Razzak's face.

Razzak sobbed, 'I'm lost. I feel like I'm drowning. I don't know what I can do.'

Hajra said firmly but gently, 'No, Razzak, nothing is lost! This is new ground for us. We will find a solution. The main thing is that we must speak to Amina as soon as possible. We must find out what she wants. There are many things to be done.'

Zareena said, 'Perhaps she can be married quickly, perhaps Zain. Perhaps Yaqub.'

Hajra shook her head, 'I don't know, I don't think so. I don't know, perhaps. We must think we must think.'

27

Zain

ZAIN had woken up early every morning since he had arrived and had watched the sunrise. An upside down golden smile emerging on Karachi's horizon until it turned itself the right side up and became a blinding expression of robust astonishment, a sudden burst of exuberance, diluting and paling as it moved across the sky and the day wore on. He felt that here, each day began with hope and optimism and, as night set in, it began to turn in complexion. Clarity or the desire for it seemed to dilute the most at this time. The things one accepted here or gave in to were unforgivable. The class differences in all their homes, the servants, where they sat, where they ate, who spoke to whom and in what tone. Alejandro kept pointing these details out. Zain too found that this was the hardest thing to deal with and this was probably why he could never live here anymore. Short spurts of being back were all he could manage. Yes Pakistanis deserved better, but things were struggled for and worked for, they were not bequeathed. And here in Pakistan, it seemed everyone was just waiting and practicing lies while they waited. It was unbearable to see poverty living side by side with the unchecked wealth. The acceptance of this was an act of violence in itself. It all seemed to be easy to accept, in fact, the rich constantly gave offerings and sacrifices of living creatures to placate the gods, just to protect themselves from a punishment that they were sure to receive. It was amazing to Zain that people like him spent so much time in the States, accusing everyone else of racism and occupation, while in Pakistan they had no problem with arriving for a vacation to participate in the rituals of apartheid and occupation which is practiced, and is part of almost everything that people do. Strange.

But Zain woke up early this morning because he was preoccupied with thoughts about himself and Alejandro. He could hardly sleep. He felt he had to do something. It had to be done. This dishonesty couldn't go on. He struggled with his own lack of courage and ended up convincing himself that he had to continue the lying. He couldn't tell his family about himself. It was all just too frightening. He hadn't come clean, he knew. And now it was almost time for Alejandro and him to leave and go back to the States. But he knew that his family would never understand. Never.

And it would break their hearts. Zain was terrified that telling his mother would literally kill her.

Amina and Zain had had a good laugh at their families' attempts to get them together. They were both going to be in Karachi in December and they had agreed to spend time together. Zain felt that he would protect her from the endless prospects set up for her, and she would protect him. And besides, he was going to take Alejandro with him to Pakistan, he wanted him to see the country that he had always talked so much about. Amina would provide them with the perfect cover. They had made a pact about it later on. This was cool with her. Then she went and got arrested at the protest march at the convention in late August and that took on a whole new dimension.

She got out, but in Zain's opinion, she was totally screwed up. When Amina told Alejandro and Zain that she was pregnant, Zain knew that there was only one way out. Marry her. Alejandro agreed. Everybody would be happy. They would have a wedding while everyone was still in Pakistan or they could say they had eloped. Be done with it. No fuss. Zain was convinced that their moms would be thrilled. Then shortly after that they would go back, leave. Amina would announce her pregnancy after they left.

Have the baby. Zain would get to be a father. And then a year later, they could get a divorce. Sure their moms would be unhappy with the divorce, but let's face it, they'd be grandmothers and would get over it. Everyone would get what they wanted. Zain's mother would have had him married off, there would be a wedding for everyone to enjoy, Amina would be married. There would be a grandchild for everyone to focus on. No one would need to know anything. And then Zain would be free to live his life and Amina would be free too. It would be perfect. A win-win situation. Amina would be able to get on with her life. It was perfect. What could be more perfect? Then Amina changed her mind and Zain's perfectly thought through plan was about to be foiled.

28

Quite a Brunch

IT was not an unusual Sunday afternoon in the Aziz household. The house was full of people and a brunch was wrapping up. A drowsy atmosphere hung in the air. Outside on the street, the neighborhood children were playing cricket and, as usual, they had blocked the street off for their game. Sara knew that Tahir was out there as well, practicing his fast bowling techniques.

Everyone was in the family room with its French windows opening onto a small brick courtyard. The view of the outside was of ferns, large leafy palms, calaciums and a waterfall which flowed over a rockery in one corner of the courtyard. Inside, the room was warm with afternoon winter light and the sound of people chattering. On the breakfast table in the adjacent room, there were puris and aalloo parathas, basini roti, shami kebab, lehsan ki chutney, omelets, fruit chat, lassi, halwa, cheesecake, orange and pomegranate juice. Everyone had finished eating and were now lazing around in the family room over cups of coffee and tea. The brunch had been part of Sara and Riaz's schedule of family activities for Amina. It was the thing to do while Amina was in town; a chance to have her spend time with Zain and Yaqub. Next week they planned to have a wedding anniversary party for themselves with just the same group to further the feeling of family intimacy. It was the right thing to do for Amina. After all, Sara had been entrusted by her Choti-ma to make sure that Amina had maximum exposure to eligible men.

But now with Amina's condition, Sara felt that she needed to go into high gear. She had to ensure that Amina was put into a social setting with Yaqub at every possible opportunity. Sara was sure that she had taken care of every detail. Yaqub had already told her that he was very impressed with her sister. Why he had even jeopardized his position with the General in his effort to impress her! And it seemed to Sara that Amina was also showing some interest. It was just a matter of time for things to fall into place. Yes, just a matter of time. And all that was required were a few essential encouragements in the right direction. This was just

a cozy brunch to let everyone relax. Provide another home setting with the family for Amina to get used to the idea of Yaqub. Sara surveyed her roomful of guests.

Everything was going as planned. Faiza Auntie and Choti-ma were comfortably engrossed in conversation, seated on the low takht which had been recently reupholstered in the latest tapestry that was all the rage in Lahore this year, and which Sara had bought on her last visit there. Sara looked at Bari-ma and Choti-ma. She searched Faiza Auntie's face. They were undoubtedly thinking along the same lines as Sara. Faiza Auntie was busy cutting chalia with a sarota while Choti-ma was munching a paan contentedly, but kept an eye on Amina. Zain was lounging on a jhoola, similarly upholstered which had a palanquin studded with tiny mirrors, an antique that Sara had bought from a village in the interior of Sindh. An exquisitely carved dark wood panel, a door from a house, undoubtedly from the same village, was up on a side wall and was back lit as an art piece. Sara was known for her appreciation of all things ethnic.

The floor was clay and marble tiled, and was covered judiciously with kilms and other tribal rugs. In this room, Sara had discarded the Persians of previous years in favor of the trendier kilms.

On the wall facing the village door was a large canvas in oils of a reclining woman being kissed by a pigeon. Its colours were green, blue and red. Sara turned to Bari-ma who sat across the room and said, 'I'm on the lookout for a Sadequain, but nowadays a canvas this size would be hard to come by. Do you know anyone who would be willing to sell, Bari-ma?' She had put the word out that she was in the market.

Hajrabai looked at her and replied dryly, 'Not at the moment Sara, but in the meantime, you could copy whichever painting of his that you especially admire and hang it up as a place-saver until you get an original.'

Sara stared at her mother. Zareenabai started to cough as the
paan caught in her throat. Sara replied, 'That's an idea. I could put up a painting of my own.'

'Yes,' said Bari-ma, 'that's an idea.'

Sara was glad that the exchange had gone unnoticed by Yaqub who was in deep conversation with Riaz. As far as Sara could make out, they seemed to be discussing garbage. And Alejandro and Amina were dozing off on the takht.

Yaqub said, 'No really, I'm serious. Don't laugh. I have been doing some research in this and I think this is really a money-making business in this city. A gold mine!'

Riaz was laughing, 'Garbage? You are proposing that I become a jamadar! C'mon yaar, just say you don't want to invest in my business! That's an easier let down than telling me to go collect garbage.' 'My friend, waste is a big business,' Yaqub said. 'Call me a jamadar after you know the facts.'

Riaz said, 'I'm all ears, tell me the facts.'

Yaqub continued, 'Well, our estimates, which are based on various studies already carried out in the city are that approximately 7,000–8,000 metric tonnes of solid waste is generated in Karachi a day, and of this, almost 60 per cent has recyclable commercial value. The saleable items include paper, cardboard, cartons, high density polyethylene/polypropylene bags, plastics, glass, metals, animal bones—yes, animal bones including those of horses, mules, chicken, cattle, goats, fish and offal, by the way. Approximately 3 rupees per kg. The whole thing is worth about 145 million rupees a year.

Riaz whistled, 'You're kidding!'

Yaqub said, 'No, I'm not. And only 1400 tonnes of this is lifted by the municipal authorities while the rest is handled by approximately 40,000 street scavengers, ranging from 10–70 year-olds who make their living off collecting garbage. I mean, there are whole communities of people who do nothing but scavenge. They can earn up to Rs100 rupees a day off 60 kgs of garbage, which they sell to middlemen, who in turn sell it for up to Rs140. Well, according to the research that I've looked at, the district municipal corporations, all five of them together, manage to make about 225 trips per day to the designated dumping grounds. And they also dump at an illegal site in Malir. Now, if someone could get into the act and actually organize the scavenging operation and set up a recycling operation, it could be a very lucrative business.'

Amina, who seemed to be napping, murmured to Alejandro, 'You know what I was just thinking? The history of the US and that of Pakistan has been connected for centuries. I mean, Karachi has always profited from the trouble that has ever come America's way. You know, Karachi made out like a bandit during the US civil war. It was about cotton and war then, and it's about oil and war now. The port is expanding again, and in fact, we're going to have a whole new port in Gwadar. Though back then, the Americans and we were both colonies of the British Empire.

Alejandro yawned and said, 'Well, that's one way to look at it. So the US and Karachi are forever linked because of the Empire's industry and colonial power.' Amina said, 'Only it's a different empire this time.'

Alejandro asked, 'Is it?'

Across the room Zain had suddenly stood up, 'Everyone, I have an announcement to make.'

Amina opened her eyes and looked up at Zain sleepily. She continued her train of thought with Alejandro, 'There's always been empire, nothing has changed.'

Zain said, 'Since we are all family here, Ami, Zareena Khala, Hajra Khala, Razzak Uncle, Sara, Riaz Bhai, I want to tell you something. I can't keep this a secret any longer. I don't know why I thought that I should.'

Amina felt her heart miss a beat. It couldn't be that Zain was coming out. He was making a mistake. No one in this room would be able to digest this information. She sat up and grabbed Alejandro's hand. 'Is he high? Is he out of his mind?' she whispered to Alejandro.

Zain smiled broadly and announced, 'Amina and I are married.'

A gasp went through the room. Amina felt dizzy. Riaz said, 'What? Unbelievable.' He recovered himself and let out a guffaw, 'Well, well, well!'

Sara shrieked, 'Oh, this is wonderful news!! Amina, you little devil, shaitan! You never even breathed a word of this!'

Zareenabai coughed and spluttered, the paan having gone down the wrong way a second time. Faiza sprang forward from the couch and lunged for Zain, drawing him to her bosom. 'Hain beta! What are you saying? Is this true? Oh, my heart is going to explode with happiness!'

Zain said, 'Of course, yes it is true! Please don't explode with happiness though! There are enough explosions in this city without you exploding too! And no doubt, there is some FBI drone flying overhead now and they'll probably call it a terrorist act!'

Amina interrupted, 'Zain!'

Zain continued, 'Now Amina, please. No point in keeping it to ourselves, sweetheart. Everyone, Amina and I, we got married in New York just before coming here.'

Amina shouted, 'Zain, what are you doing?'

Zain said, 'We were going to let you know just before we left. We wanted to avoid the huge wedding scene and tamasha that we were sure both Ami and Khala Jan would insist upon, and you too Sara. So we decided to go ahead and do the deed. Yes, we're married. So let's just treat this brunch like the wedding celebration!'

Sara was shrieking with happiness. Bari-ma was looking at

Razzak. Zareenabai and Faiza were weeping.

Amina said softly, 'Listen, everyone… Please listen to me…'

'And that's not all,' Zain added.

Amina shouted, 'Zain! Don't be a jerk, Zain!'

Zain continued, 'Honey, there's no reason to hide it!'

Amina shouted in disgust, 'Zain, shut up.'

Zareenabai said effusively, 'Oh thank God! Thank God!'

Zain looked at Amina, confused by her rage, 'And that's not all, we're planning on taking you all on our honeymoon!'

Sara said, 'Don't for a moment think you're getting away with this. No way.'

Zain asked in panic, 'What do you mean?'

Sara said, 'Don't look so alarmed! There's going to be a wedding. We're not going to let you get away with this. We are going to have a wedding!'

In all the commotion, the shrieking, weeping, laughing and shouting going on, no one noticed Alejandro. He sat slumped in his chair looking at his feet. Zain had his arms around a squirming, red-faced Amina. Then Alejandro got up with resignation and joined in, and was congratulating them both. Kissing Amina and giving Zain bear hugs.

Sara looked across at Yaqub. 'Poor man,' she thought, 'he's completely distraught. It would take ages to explain it all to him. It might even affect his business deal with Riaz,' she thought nervously. She looked across and caught Riaz's glance. Yaqub avoided meeting her gaze, he was looking down at his hands. Amina felt as though the room was unbearably small suddenly. All this commotion and noise was too loud. Why was Sara shrieking like that? Why was Choti-ma weeping? How could Zain do this? She stood up. She went and stood in front of Yaqub's bowed head.

Amina shouted, 'Listen to me!'

The room went silent. Yaqub looked up.

Amina shouted again, 'I am not married.'

Yaqub, unsure of why she stood in front of him, managed a feeble smile.

Amina said, 'Zain and I are not married. Do you understand me?'

Yaqub nodded, he looked around the room. Hajrabai was looking directly at him, she wore an expression that was hard for him to decipher. She seemed to be asking him for sympathy.

'What are you saying?' Sara said urgently.

Zain pleaded, 'Amina!'

Amina said breathlessly, 'Zain, I'm many things, I could even be pregnant.'

Sara interrupted, 'Amina, stop it! No time for such silly jokes.'

Hajrabai called out her name, 'Amina!'

Amina said, 'I'm not…'

'Amina!' Sara warned.

Amina said, 'I'm not married. Zain, it's up to you to tell them what you are.'

Zain whined, 'Amina, please.'

Amina ploughed ahead, 'Everyone. What does it matter? The rest is detail.'

'What's going on?' Zareenabai asked. 'Someone please tell me what's going on.'

Everyone was silent. Sara had her arms around Choti-ma's shoulders. Hajra was clutching her hands in front of her. Razzak stood up and put his arms around Amina who was still standing near Yaqub. Riaz was trying not to laugh. Alejandro had sat upright and was looking nervously at everyone in the room. Suddenly Zain jumped up from his seat and said, 'I'm gay. I love Alejandro. There, Amina, okay?'

No one spoke, the silence seemed dreadfully long and unending. And then Riaz said, 'Are those really the numbers? I mean of 7,000 metric tonnes of garbage every day. 40,000 scavengers make their living out of recycling waste? Astounding! Sara, did you hear that?'

29

Yaqub

YAQUB knew himself well. He knew exactly who he was. He had no illusions about that, no romantic notions—he was a pragmatic man. He considered himself a man with too much money and many lucrative businesses. He often reminded himself that he could have been viewed as just a shopkeeper in this town. He owed his image, his acceptability into the charmed circles in Karachi, completely to Sara Aziz. He often reminded himself of the time soon after his return, when he had met Sara at a party. A party, where as soon as he had entered, he was made to feel very alone. All because no one there could recognize him as anybody they knew. At the time that he had met Sara and Riaz he could barely speak English. Yaqub knew that he was quite literally not literate. And he was acutely aware that though he had immense worldliness his lack of what was considered sophistication was on display in his outward appearance. He had money and nothing else. It seemed to him that people looked at him and turned away as though he was a beggar amongst them. He could have bought each of them twice over and yet they turned away. Granted, no one at that time knew how wealthy he was. But nor did Sara. Yet she seemed to have spotted him the moment he entered. He felt that she seemed to have seen his plight. Across the room, she had come towards him. She, that pillar and stalwart of the charmed circle, had greeted Yaqub as though he were a long lost friend. 'Where have you been all these years?' she declared in a loud voice so that everyone who was watching them would hear her, as though he, Yaqub, were a long lost friend. And then she had taken him by the arm and steered him to a corner where they had sat down to talk. With that one gesture of hers, she had immediately established him as a member of the inner circle.

She had established Yaqub as her long lost friend. Yet at that time he had no idea who she was. He had only been too grateful to be rescued. To be welcomed. Moments later, she had beckoned her husband to join them and they had all sat there chatting while the party raged on around them. People had stopped to say hello to Sara and Riaz and glanced towards Yaqub inquiringly. Yaqub was introduced to all by Sara by a special emphasis on his surname, 'You know, Yaqub Kishtiwallah!' The way she had declared his name had made the difference between naming an owner of a fisherman's dingy and an aircraft carrier. She didn't tell people who he was or what he did. She simply emphasized the name. She didn't know but she made it sound as though his name was enough, she said it with such flair and emphasis as though people should know who he was.

'Yaqub Kishtiwalla. He's finally decided that we are good enough for him,' she would say with a knowing look, as though the two of them, Yaqub and her, were sharing a secret joke. From then on, the evening passed comfortably for Yaqub in their company, and later they invited Yaqub to their home for coffee. He felt as though he had known them all his life. Sara immediately took Yaqub under her wing when she heard his story. He found that he was able to tell her the broad strokes of his own life with relative ease. He always remembered fondly that she had hired a teacher for him who taught him how to speak English within three months. It was a wonder. He went to practice his English with Sara every afternoon. She was like a mother and a sister to him, in his view. She taught him how to read and write. Never once did she seem taken aback or judgmental about his lack of education. She had never asked him why. All this in six months time. All the things that Yaqub had never had time for, for which he had hired people to do for him, she taught him and opened a whole new world to him. She took a great deal of interest in his project, the reconstruction of the godown as his home and as a gallery. In fact, she introduced Yaqub to the best architect in town. Rehana came to Yaqub through Sara. Yaqub remembered how Sara had shown him the collection of art work that she had quietly been amassing from an art dealer who had died, but who had to sell his collection in a hurry due to a major financial crisis that he was facing. Sara, in her characteristic way of taking everyone on as her cause, bless her heart, had bailed him out, and in return he had left her his collection of paintings. She had told Yaqub that no one, not even her husband, had seen the collection. Yaqub had visited her one afternoon, and she showed him the collection, which she kept stowed away. All in all, she had about eleven pieces of work.

Yaqub had liked them all. He was eager to please her. He knew nothing about art, but it was apparent that Sara knew a lot. Sara had that rare quality of spotting winners, the art work, the godown that Yaqub had bought. She asked him whether he would be willing to house the paintings as part of the collection to be displayed at his gallery. And naturally he had jumped at the offer. Yaqub could not understand why she would do this, and was touched by her reasons. She loved art. She wanted to be able to view the art and see it on display. She could not think of a better place to do so than in Yaqub's gallery, and he had felt that she had paid him a high compliment by saying that she could not think of a better custodian and keeper of this art. Yaqub's art gallery had its first collection waiting for its walls. Thanks to dear Sara. Yes, she had taken him under her wing. It was as simple as that. And lately Sara had been encouraging Yaqub to dabble in politics. What a surprise.

Sara gave Yaqub the social standing that he craved. And Rehana created a place to reflect that. Rehana created that place in which Amina would want to stay and become his life. Yaqub realized through Amina who came to him in her hour of need that he had a bigger role to play. Amina knew that she could count on him because Sara persuaded her to do so. And Yaqub had thought with affection that Sara was truly a guardian angel. Yaqub never wanted to be presumptuous, he considered himself to be an upstart.

He realized he was not about to acquire a background. No, he wanted it to be clear that all that he owned were acquisitions, choices he had made, a matter of taste financed by his considerable fortune. He was nothing but self-made. But he realized and appreciated with all his heart that it was Sara who gave him the finishing touches, who completed him. Without her, he knew that he would never have completed himself. But then the nagging question came back to him: 'Where would he be without Rehana?'

But now he was left with no choice. Begum Rueewallah phoned him unexpectedly one afternoon and asked him whether she could come to have a word with him. It was urgent. Yaqub told her not to trouble herself and that he would come to see her instead. She insisted that she come to the office. She came by at about 3 p.m. and insisted on speaking to Yaqub alone. It was a simple request she had of him. She wanted to know if he would propose for Amina. Marry Amina. Yaqub was astonished. He could see that this wonderful lady was ill at ease asking such a thing, he wanted to ease her discomfort more than anything else. Yaqub told her that she had only said what he had already done. She was confused and embarrassed. Yaqub told her that he had spoken to Sara and had proposed to Amina as well. Yaqub knew that he should have been the happiest man on earth.

Then why didn't he feel that way? Wasn't this what he had always wanted? This stamp of approval. That someone like Amina, beautiful sophisticated, well-established in the social circles of this place and with a place in the world, was going to be his wife? Hadn't he spent all his life acquiring meaning through acquisitions? Possessing in order to be accepted? And now, her entire family it seemed, was asking him to marry her. Even Amina herself had asked him this, and finally everything should have had meaning. Yaqub knew that he should have felt that he was about to be released from an endless quest for acquisitions. He should have understood that life had been good to him and that he had Sara Aziz to thank.

But then what was this that he felt? As if he was betraying someone. He knew that he was causing pain to someone who was fast becoming so dear to him. He could have never imagined that it was so clear and so simple. And yet Amina had asked him for this and Sara had asked him as well and he could not refuse. Yaqub had to do his duty. He was obligated. He could not refuse that dear, kind woman, Sara Aziz or her mother, such a dignified lady. It was his duty in their hour of need. To act honorably. He could not refuse what was asked of him. So one afternoon, when Sara summoned him, he went over to meet her. Amina was there. Sara and Yaqub had spoken earlier. He knew what was coming. Amina and Yaqub had sat alone in silence in Sara's lounge, the afternoon sun peeking in through the blinds, criss-crossing their faces in shadows and lights. 'Go ahead ask me,' Yaqub had said. 'Ask me for anything.

It's yours.'

'Marry me,' Amina whispered.

Yaqub had caressed his missing thumbnail with his index finger and looked at her. 'Of course I will,' he had said softly. The look on Amina's face was that of pure relief.

'So Sara has told you, that I'm...'

'Yes she has. It's okay.'

'Okay?' she said softly. 'That's it? Aren't you going to ask how, who?'

'No, that's irrelevant to me.'

'But will you still marry me?'

'Yes. Are you sure you want to do this, marry me?'

Yaqub hadn't asked her another question. He smiled at her instead.

She looked at him anxiously, 'So the answer is yes?'

Yaqub laughed, 'Yes, it is, yes. But I have something to ask as well.'

She asked fearfully, 'What is it?'

'You'll tell everyone that I'm the father?'

She started to cry, 'Yes. But doesn't it matter to you that I'm asking you to marry me because I'm pregnant?'

'No it doesn't matter. Why are you crying?'

She was sobbing, 'Because you're a very kind man, a very kind and generous man. Thank you very much.'

Amina blew her nose, composed herself and said, 'So we have a deal?'

'We have a deal,' he said.

'And you'll never tell anyone that I asked you to marry me?'

'No, I won't. But there is something you must know.'

'What is it?' Amina had asked without much interest. Yaqub heard himself uttering these words, 'That this means a great deal to me. A great deal for me. A deal.' He couldn't believe that he had uttered these words. There it was.

Amina had looked at him, 'Yes.'

And that's how it happened. It all happened so quickly. The announcement of their engagement was soon all over town. Sara made sure of that. Yaqub was resigned to this. It seemed that so was Amina. A flurry of activity had begun around wedding preparations and Yaqub played his role as best as he could.

Then when Rehana appeared at his doorstep, early one morning just as the sun was coming up over the docks in the distance, he was caught off guard, thrilled that she was there, but astonished. Yaqub had let her in downstairs through the gallery, she immediately walked towards the elevator. She waited there for him to punch in the code, and they had gone upstairs to his apartment.

She told him that she had been waiting outside almost all night waiting for the sun to come up. She had parked the car in front of the building two hours ago waiting for daylight before she rang the bell. She paced in front of Yaqub, constantly entwining and disentangling her fingers. She was breathless, 'I came here,' she said, 'to ask you for myself. I didn't believe it when I heard from others. I sat outside in the dark, waiting for light so that I could ask you.' Yaqub knew what she was going to ask but still he said, 'Go ahead, ask me anything.'

She paced around as though she was casting about in her mind for something to say.

'You know, I saw so many young boys on the street tonight. Coming out of the shadows towards me. Melting back into them when they saw me. I think they were prostitutes.'

'Probably. It's not uncommon,' Yaqub replied nonchalantly. She had stared at him, surprised at his comment.

'Is that what you came to talk to me about?' he had asked, softening his tone.

'The thing is one of them came out of the shadows, and flagged me to stop!'

'What?'

'He wanted a lift.'

'It happens.'

'He looked so young.'

'Yes.'

'How can you be so matter of fact about it?'

'Because I have the right to be.'

'Because of this?' she waved her hand around. 'Because you're rich? Is that why you have the right to be indifferent?' That was the first flash of anger and sarcasm that Yaqub had seen in her.

'No. You know why. Because given a different set of circumstances, I could have been the person you might have turned away from tonight,' Yaqub said.

She looked at him. 'I wouldn't have turned away, I didn't turn away tonight either. I stopped. He backed away and disappeared into the night.' Yaqub considered Rehana standing in front of him defiantly, challenging him. He looked at her and then moved away without taking his eyes off her. He could see that she was struggling with her emotions, her eyes were downcast. She finally looked up and her eyes were filled with tears.

She walked towards him. Yaqub kept moving back until there was nowhere to go, his back was against the wall and Rehana was against him. Her arms encircled his waist, her hands wide open, palms pressed against his back. She was holding on to him and crying.

'Is it true?' she asked him.

'Yes,' he said. 'It is. I'm sorry. I'm very sorry. I am under obligation. If this was my choice, I would have come to your house and asked your mother for your hand.'

'But you did choose, you didn't come to my house. I wasn't the right obligation,' she said.

They stood there that way against the wall, locked together in an embrace. And then she left.

Yaqub sighed to himself, trying to understand what this was. What was this he felt. Was this sadness for Rehana? Sympathy for her? Was he sad because she was disappointed? As the sun rose higher in the Karachi sky and he pressed the remote button to lower the blinds to shield his apartment from its glare, he thought how wrong she was. She had no idea, no idea what she was for him.

30

Planning the Shebang

HAJRA could hear Zareenabai, Sara and Amina's voices out on the verandah as she sat in her bedroom listlessly drumming a tune from a Hindi film on the piano and recalling her visit to Lawrence Road with Amina yesterday.

'You could always live here, you know,' Hajra had said hesitatingly in a soft voice to Amina's back, while seated on the sofa in the small drawing room. The room was dimly lit by the sunlight filtering in through the slats of the wooden shutters on the closed door leading to the balcony. Amina had been peering into a sepia-coloured framed photograph on the wall and chatting with Hajra about the time and occasion of the photograph. It was of Hajra at a college function at St Joseph's in the 1950s. Hearing Bari-ma's suggestion, Amina had turned and smiled at Hajra wistfully.

'You could, you know. I think you would like it here. Why don't you try it now? Stay here a couple of days and see what it's like to live in Karachi on your own. Besides, these old homes and buildings need new blood, otherwise they are all going to be demolished, you know. They are all going to become shopping malls. Come back, stay here. Maybe you'll start a trend.'

Amina had laughed, 'You're so funny, Bari-ma.'

'I mean it,' Hajra had said. 'I often think the reason you girls haven't returned is because you think you have to be married, otherwise you can't live on your own in Pakistan, in Karachi. But you can live here, it'll be perfect. You don't need to be married to stay here. And anyway, I hear that there are lots of girls now who have their own apartments and even their own houses.'

Amina had come over to Hajrabai and sat down next to her, encircling her neck with her arms. 'Bari-ma, jaan. My dearest, loveliest jaan. We will always have this apartment. You'll see, you have nothing to worry about. And I promise that as long as the five of us are alive, Sara, Kulsum, Resham, Shireen and I, we will never change a thing. We won't let anything happen to this building, promise! The sisters Rueewallah!'

Hajra had laughed.

Amina had continued, 'And I think we should come live here sometimes as well. Why not? What do you think, shall we move in here next week for a few days?'

Hajra laughed despite how she felt. 'No, next week we'll all be busy with your wedding preparations. It's better for everyone to stay at 43-G and the girls are all looking forward to it. I'm talking about you, your idea about coming and living in Pakistan. This marriage, this idea that a single woman cannot do what she wants, can't be independent, that you can't live here and get on with life, unless you are married...'

Amina had protested, 'That's not the reason I'm marrying Yaqub.'

'Then what is it Amina? Tell me.'

'I like him. He gives me a sense of security.'

Hajra had sighed. Now this morning she had woken up in her room in 43-G with an uneasy sense as though much of what she had intended had either come undone or had not happened. She had sat playing at her piano trying to understand this feeling. Had she had a bad dream? Not that she could recall. Then what was it? Her conversation with Yaqub had left her uneasy. He had agreed so easily. Hajra had felt as though she had entered into a secret and unnecessary complicity. Yaqub was such a nice man, nice. He was good for getting the job done. Good for selling property, good for asking for assistance on how to set up foundations. But this was too much! Amina had certainly made things difficult for everyone. And all this time Hajra had focused on Sara as the troublemaker! Well, well, well. Hajra's plans for setting up a waqf trust fund in Abbas's name had been set aside for the time being. But Hajra was determined that she would establish a clinic. She had resolved that in the new year, the trust would be established and the clinic would function. Matters had moved forward in this regard when Razzak had bought the shop where the clinic used to be in Soldier Bazaar. That much had been accomplished. She got up and decided to join the discussion on the verandah which, from the sounds of it, seemed like a disagreement between Amina and the others. Hajra went out to the verandah.

'Bari-ma,' said Sara who was stretched out on the chaise longue in the verandah. 'I'm not going to have it any other way!'

'What aren't you going to have any other way?' Hajra asked.

'The wedding! Of course. What else?' Sara exclaimed as though her mother should have known what they were talking about.

Amina interrupted, 'Excuse me! But isn't it me who's getting married?'

Choti-ma said, 'Yes, but you hardly matter. That's just the way it is. There's going to be a wedding and that is that! Sara is right.'

Sara said, 'Thank you Choti-ma!'

Zareenabai smiled indulgently, 'Of course chanda, you're always right.'

Sara laughed, 'And we simply will not be denied, Amina!'

Jeevan who was squatting on the mosaic floor wiping it with a wet cloth chimed, 'Amina Bibi, listen to your sister and mother, we all want a wedding!'

Amina pretended to admonish Jeevan, 'Be quiet Jeevan. At least you should be on my side!'

Sara said with satisfaction, 'There see, Jeevan agrees with me. Now just leave all the details to me. There must be a mayoun, and a mehndi, a nikkah, a shaadi and a valima. And all this would have to be preceded by at least three nights of music and musical evenings.'

Hajrabai said laughing, 'We should have at least, one evening of qawwali, one of ghazal and four nights for singing and dancing till five in the morning.'

Sara said effusively, 'It's going to be so much fun. We won't have had so much fun since my wedding. Do you remember?'

Amina said, 'We definitely had fun. Remember the hideously ugly outfit Riaz Bhai wore?'

Sara shuddered, 'Absolutely. Doomed for divorce from day one. But I reformed him, didn't I?'

Jeevan ventured boldly, 'Bibi, Begum Sahiba has promised me a gold bracelet if you are married. So you make sure I get it.'

Zareenabai said laughing, 'Hai Jeevan, look at you. Do you think I'll go back on my promise? A promise is a promise. Here, take my bracelet, here take this right now.'

Jeevan specified, 'No Begum Sahiba, not your bracelet. I want a new one!'

Hajrabai laughed, 'And so you shall. A dozen.'

'And a new outfit too!' Jeevan quipped.

Zareenabai laughed, 'Jeevan, you shall have five! One for each occasion!'

Amina asked, 'Jeevan I never asked you, are you married?'

Jeevan replied, 'No Bibi, I left home because there was no other choice. I had to support our family. We are from Okara and now we have nothing. We were farmers there.'

Amina asked, 'What happened? Was there a drought or a flood or something?'

Jeevan continued, 'No, there was no drought or flood. Worse. Much worse. There was the army. Worse than locust, worse than floods. We never owned the land but my family has been working on that land since my great-great-grandmother's time. Two years ago, we were told that we couldn't work on the farmlands any longer because it belonged to the army.'

'Only your family?' Amina wanted to know.

Jeevan replied, 'No, there were many others.'

Amina was surprised. 'Didn't anyone protest?'

Jeevan said, 'People did, they did a lot but what can the weak do against the army? They had us surrounded and they even took many of us to jail. Nobody could do anything. Many people came from the city to ask questions and we thought there would be help for us soon but there was nothing. People came from the city to take photos, make films. People tried to help. But nothing. Finally we left as well. My family was thrown out of there by the military. So I came to Karachi with my mother to work. It's better here.'

'Okay, Jeevan now go get me a cup of tea,' Sara sounded impatient. 'Amina, stop wasting time. Jeevan, go tell Razia to make me a cup of tea. Amina, oh I forgot to tell you the most important detail! I'm absolutely over the moon. The American consulate called Riaz. You know, the Consul General is such a good friend of ours.'

Amina said, 'Perhaps he can help out here, on this thing with Jeevan?'

Sara arched a perfect eyebrow, 'What thing with Jeevan?'

Ignoring Sara's tone, Amina replied, 'The lands. Maybe I should help out. I'm a lawyer. I handle human rights cases from time to time!'

Sara said brusquely, 'Stop being so naïve. Are you crazy? No one can do anything around here. Besides, this is an everyday story here. Now listen to me. The Consul just absolutely adores me and loves Riaz. And he had a request.'

'About what?'

Sara said breezily, 'Well, he wondered if he could attend the functions.'

'Well he's a friend of yours so go ahead and invite him, it's your party,' Amina said without much interest.

Sara pouted, 'Don't be like that! He says they always have a few house-guests visiting from the States who stay with them. He says due to security reasons he can't really show them around the country or even the city so he wondered if we would mind letting them come to the wedding and let them see this. Of course I said it's all right. You don't mind, do you, dahling?'

Amina said sarcastically, 'What are we? A circus? The theatre? An opera for God's sake??'

Sara smiled mischievously, 'No, much better than all that. But we are the exotic natives.'

Amina scrunched up her face in disgust, 'Doesn't this return of the Raj sicken you?'

'I wasn't aware that it had ever left!' Sara sniffed. 'Somethings never change. And yes, come to think of it we are theatre, dahling. And why not?'

Amina said disdainfully, 'Sara, are you ever serious?'

'More serious than you seem to be,' Sara shot back.

Amina sighed, 'Do as you please.'

'Look, why not! It's good for all of us,' Sara intoned. 'What do you call it? Networking, no? It builds contacts. We are going to need visas and what not in the future. And you know how difficult all that is, now, even for people like us. You don't understand these things because you're an American citizen. These sort of things only help. Tahir and Zohra will need to go to America, won't they? For college.'

'Whatever!' Amina said.

'Easy for you to say whatever,' Sara continued. 'And just imagine what an honour it'll be. Everyone will see all these people at your wedding. It only increases our stature with everyone.'

'Whatever!' Amina repeated.

'Done then, it's settled,' Sara said. 'Thank you darling, thank you for being so understanding. You'll see, it'll be completely perfect. I'll send them ten cards immediately. As far as they're concerned it's a big production, theatre, a tamasha. Sort of like a Broadway production you know, all the pageantry and colour and everything.'

Amina looked resigned, 'No, I don't mind. What's the difference if we add a few more in the audience. We should probably charge a ticket, don't you think?'

'Hain, let me think about that one,' Sara deftly dealt with her sister's question.

Amina continued, 'What do you think, Jeevan, should we charge a ticket? Recover the costs of all the costumes and lighting? Like at the circus.'

Jeevan responded enthusiastically, 'I've never been to the circus.'

Amina said, 'Well, it's scheduled to start in a week's time. You'll get your first chance. And I promise you'll have first row seats. I'll be the monkey.'

Jeevan giggled.

Sara said, 'And if we don't get you back to a salon soon, you'll look like one. Look, don't be so difficult jaani. Of course everyone wants to come to this wedding, it's the biggest society wedding of the year, if not the decade. After all, I'm hosting and Yaqub is quite the most eligible catch.'

Amina protest, 'And what am I?'

Sara raised an eyebrow. Careful that neither Choti-ma nor Bari-ma were watching her, Sara looked meaningfully at Amina's stomach.

Sucking her breath in, Amina said hurriedly, 'Okay, don't answer that.'

Sara said soothingly, 'Dear, let's be realistic now shall we. Now while we are on that subject, remind me to stop and speak with Ms D'Silva at the Grammar School. You know the waiting list goes into three years backlog. And we must have my dear niece or nephew enrolled immediately. Not to worry dahling, Riaz and I are huge donors for every single event at the school. We're hugely

involved in school activities. We're helping to finance one of the new wings.'

Choti-ma said, 'From your lips to God's ears, Sara. Already thinking of my grandchildren. Bless you my darling child. Well, Jeevan this means you can't take your holiday next week!'

Jeevan replied cheerfully, 'It's okay, Begum Sahiba, I can go home after the wedding.'

Hajrabai said, 'We're going to need everyone here. I've already told everyone else.'

'And, of course, I've told all my servants here as well,' Sara thought out loud. 'Besides, we'll get the caterers. And people from Riaz's factory. Yaqub too is going to send his people. And, of course, we have at least four drivers at our disposal over the next couple of days. There's so much to be done.'

Amina attempted to participate in the planning, 'Well let's make a list of things. Resham, Kulsum, and Shireen are going to come as soon as I tell them to.'

Sara, 'What good to me will all those Americans be? They'll all be in jet-lag and they are all sure to get stomach viruses the moment they get here. And none of them can be trusted to know one thing about where to get anything. No, no, it'll all have to be me. Me, me, me!'

Zareenabai said affectionately, 'Bless you, my darling child! You are so wonderful.'

Sara sighed deeply and said, 'I try Choti-ma, I try!'

Hajrabai uncharacteristically conceded, 'Yes Sara, I don't know what we would have done without you.'

Sara looked at her mother, her eyes filled up. She had never heard her mother acknowledge her for anything before.

Hajrabai said, 'At least you can give us orders and directions and we'll follow.'

Sara said, 'Well yes, that can be done. But not you. You are going to have to sit back and relax.'

Hajrabai shrugged and looked at Amina, 'My dear, are you happy? Is this really what you want?'

Amina looked at her, 'Yes, Bari-ma, I'm happy. This is what I want.'

'You know, don't you, my dear, that you can tell us anything, anything at all, and all of us will do exactly what you want.'

Amina looked at her mother and took a deep breath, 'This is what I want.'

Sara looked at everyone and said quickly, 'Done! End of seriousness!'

31

Intervention

THE car sped towards 43-G from the airport. The plane had been delayed by two hours. Resham, Shireen and Kulsum were crammed in the back seat. Sara drove. Amina sat in the passenger seat up front. The suitcases, a considerable number of them, had been piled into Ilyas's car and sent ahead to 43-G. Razzak, Hajrabai and Zareenabai had stayed back at home waiting for their arrival.

Resham: This is all too weird!

Amina: There is nothing weird, this is great!

Kulsum: No, Amina. There's plenty enough that's weird. This whole tamasha that you've got going! And I can't believe that Bari-ma of all people is playing along with this.

Amina: I thought you of all people, Kulsum, would be thrilled with this!

Kulsum: Well, then you don't know me after all! No, I am not thrilled with this! What has happened to you? Why are you throwing your whole life away?

Amina: I'm not throwing my life away! I'm getting on with it!

Kulsum: By giving up your career and life in New York!

Amina: By building on that and growing and adding to it! And Kulsum, of all the people in this car, I mean you have been pining to come back to Pakistan. You should be overjoyed by this.

Kulsum: I'm not overjoyed. I may be pining but I'm not stupid. And I am who I am, my choosing my life is my doing. My choices are not yours. This is not you. You sound possessed! I'm willing to listen to you and I'm looking forward to meeting Yaqub and everything, but look at this, this is not you!

Resham: Wow Kulsum!

Amina: What is not me?

Kulsum: Well, everything. The way you look, the way you're dressed, the company you're keeping! It's like you've completely forgotten who you are!

Sara: Excuse me? What do you mean by that?

Kulsum: I didn't mean you, of course not, Sara. I meant the man she is about to marry.

Amina: Oh for Pete's sake! And is that so bad?

Kulsum: No, I wasn't putting a value judgment on it. I was just pointing out that you're not exactly how I saw you last time.

Sara: Well, she has changed!

Amina: Anyway, I've got a broader perspective now. And Sara has been absolutely wonderful. She's been a complete gem to me. I owe her big time!

Resham: Uh huh?

Sara: Yes, Resham, we've had a lot on our plate here. It hasn't been easy, okay?

Resham: You've changed Amina? Why?

Amina: I like it here. It's easy!

Resham: Sure it's easy, being waited on hand and foot.

Amina: No, that's not what it's about. It's more than that. It's exciting. Every day is a new experience here for me. I feel so wanted, so relevant.

Kulsum: But you end up giving up so much.

Amina: Like what? Hey, I could get used to it!

Kulsum: Amina! You don't know what you're giving up? Seriously? Can you get used to it, Amina?

Sara: Girls! Please, do we have to discuss all of this right now in this car on the way home from the airport? Please! Now let's all go home. Freshen up. I need you. I plan to press all of you into service immediately. There isn't much time and there is not a moment to waste. And Shireen, what about you? Are you just staying quiet or are you jet-lagged?

Shireen: Baba, I'm happy to be here! Happy to be in the same car with all my sisters! Happy to be driven around and not behind the wheel. Happy that when I get out of this car, I won't have to cook or clean. I am ecstatic. Sara, this was a brilliant idea to come pick us up. You are absolutely brilliant. Marvellous. And yes, Amina, sweetheart, I completely agree with everyone. And we are here to talk to you.

Amina: I can't believe you're home. We are going to have so much fun.

Resham: Get this straight; this is not home. Home is where we live and have our lives. That's not here. It's ten thousand miles from here and light years, centuries away.

Amina: This is the place you came from, Resham. This is where we are all from! This is where our parents live.

Resham: My parents are what is important, not the place. If they lived in Timbuktu I would have gone there this December instead of coming here. Everything I am, everything I believe in, everything that gives me comfort and a sense of home is in them. My parents are my country. This place is not. It's a place for visits in December only. And we, all of us in this car, except for Sara, are December Pakistanis!

Shireen: Okay baba, let's not start an argument. I'm too jet-lagged. It's so bright here. I can barely keep my eyes open. Where are my sunglasses? Just look, I've missed Drigh Road. I just love this wide avenue and those palm trees. Gosh, the sun's so bright, I do need my sunglasses. I can't find them!

Resham: Here take mine. Geez, look at that billboard! No, not that one. Look at the one over there the one for the credit card. I was staring at the same one five traffic lights ago. Just look at it.

Kulsum: Let's see. A pretty girl, a good-looking boy and a waiter. A very good-looking waiter. It's a restaurant. So what? It's a credit card ad.

Resham: Yeah, but look who the girl is looking at.

Amina: The waiter!

Kulsum: So…What do you think it is?

Shireen: Wait! Wait! Me first! Let me take a shot at this. It's this beautiful, poor girl, the waiter is actually her real lover.

The guy paying the bill is the young man back from Canada, a December Pakistani, home to pick up a bride. They're out on this match-making date set up by their families. And she's agreed to do this only because he's rich. And it's his credit card which is the main attraction. That's what gets him the girl. See, she and her boyfriend realize the importance of this poor expat visiting in December to their existence. He's spending money. He's the December Pakistani.

Resham: Oh good Shireen, that's a good one! That would make for a soap opera. Very good.

Shireen: So y'know she's going to go out with him. Make him buy her some pretty expensive stuff. And then she's going to ditch him.

Resham: For the not so rich, but I must admit, better looking and a hunk of a waiter-boyfriend.

Kulsum: I can't believe the two of you! But I think it's your imagination more than the ad.

Resham: I don't know! I think this billboard is saying a lot more than just what meets the eye. It's the subliminal messaging for December and the wedding season in Karachi!

Kulsum: Anyway, getting back to the agenda. Amina, we need to spend time alone with you without Bari-ma and Choti-ma around. We need to talk to you seriously.

Amina: Nothing to talk about! I'm the bride.

Kulsum: Listen to yourself!

Amina: No, this is just the way it is. This would be the way it was even if I was in New York! This makes me very happy.

Kulsum: There you go, look at the things that are already influencing you Amina! This is not you!

Amina: What am I saying that's so out of character? We are all in Karachi. Do you guys want a quick tour around to take a look at what's changed since you were here last?

Resham: Can it, Amina! We're not here for a city tour. And
I've already arranged a city tour for all of us. We're going to the beach, to Chawkandi, to a mosque in Thatta, to Kharadar, to a dhobi ghat, a Hindu temple and to the Quaid's Mazar.

Amina: Oh great, so you've got your fun planned.

Resham: Don't. We're here to knock some sense into you. And look at you! How much weight have you gained here, girl? Do you ever exercise or just chomp on rogni rotis and sheermals?

Amina: I'm pregnant.

Kulsum, Shireen and Resham: WHAT?!?!?!?

Amina: I think the right response is "congratulations".

Resham, wide-eyed and in shock, shook her head incredulously.

Resham: Amina, what's happened to you? You didn't even tell me? I mean, you've really changed. You didn't think you had to call me and tell me? Wow! Okay, now a few things are starting to make some sense. When you first mentioned Yaqub, he didn't sound like the type you would be jumping into bed with, getting knocked up with and throwing caution to the winds.

Amina: It isn't Yaqub. Okay? I was impulsive, I wanted a child. I'm pregnant and I'm not going to be able to handle things on my own.

Shireen: Honey, that's not a good reason to do this! So who's the father?

Amina: I'm not sure, I went to a fertility clinic...

Resham: You go, girl!

Kulsum: Oh my God!

Shireen: You're kidding!

Sara: No, she's not kidding. Not about the pregnancy part at least.

Resham: Shireen's right. Amina, all that you're doing is panicking. You don't need to go through this to have a baby. I say we turn this car right around now and head back to the airport. All of us, we can leave right now. We can go home.

Sara: No, we are not turning the car around, Resham. We are going home. Home to 43-G. Have you forgotten your parents? How anxiously they are waiting for your arrival? How happy they are? We are in the midst of planning a huge wedding. That's that. Get with the program. Rest your throat and stop shouting because you and I have to do a lot of singing!

They turned the corner and Sara drove down the lane alongside the park and pulled up in front of 43-G. She excitedly thumped hard and repeatedly on the horn making a racket. The gate opened instantly, Razzak stood on the side waiting for his daughters to jump out of the car. They piled out and fell upon him, their arms around his neck. Bari-ma and Choti-ma, who had been keeping a look out for the car from the terrace, waved and then disappeared as they made their way down to the driveway. Everyone was hugging and kissing and talking at once. The luggage in the car ahead was being taken out and brought into the house. Resham made her way straight to the dining room to check out the floor, the rest followed. At once remarks began in unison, 'This looks great! I really don't see a change!' and 'Pity the real detail is hidden under the dining-table'. The dining table was moved aside and the centre of the floor was revealed. Everyone gave their resounding approval. Rehana's name was bandied about and praised. The rest of the day was spent with everyone catching up while drinking cups of tea, nimbu-pani and eating kebabs, samosas, cakes and chicken patties on the verandah. One by one, they nodded off because of their jet-lag and were sent to their rooms to sleep it off. Sara left in the early evening to allow her sisters to sleep off their jet-lag. There would be plenty of time in the next couple of weeks to catch up on details.

Having set her alarm for six the next morning, Resham had pulled herself out of bed and made her way to the terrace. The air was damp and cool and the sound of birds chattering and chirping in the trees was delightful. A smoky mist hung over the skies. She looked down on to the garden below at her favourite sight, Choti-ma was reading the Koran and Bari-ma was walking about inspecting the plants. Bari-ma gazed up saw Resham looking down, 'What are you doing up so early my dear?' she called up to her.

'I'm up!' Resham called down. 'I'm too excited to sleep.' She walked around the house, going into the drawing room and dining room and all of the corridors, looking at the familiar paintings and furniture. Nothing had changed since she had last been home, everything was in its place. The dining-room floor was beautiful. Too bad it was covered by the dining table and the chairs. Resham made her way back to the terrace and dozed off on the takht just as Bari-ma was coming upstairs with the morning papers which had just been delivered and brought in by the driver.

Sara arrived in the early afternoon and found them lazing about in their pyjamas up on the verandah. Sara was immaculately dressed as usual, freshly bathed after her golf, her hair blow-dried and tucked under her cream and light pink scarf. She wore a pale pink tunic over cream-coloured capris and a matching pair of three-inch stiletto heels that Resham had brought for her as a gift yesterday. She lifted her feet and showed off her shoes, 'See Resham!' Resham lifted her head sleepily and smiled, 'Very nice! You look fabulous! I want the exact outfit!' Sara smiled happily and said, 'And you shall! I'll make you tons of outfits, sweetheart!' Sara called out to Jeevan to bring her heavy bag out of the car and upstairs. The bag was full of magazines and other assorted items, tape measures, DVDs, fabric cuttings and photographs from other weddings, which would all be needed for the planning this afternoon. 'Why don't you go get it yourself, for heaven's sakes!' Resham said. 'Everyone is constantly shouting out to servants! It's ridiculous!'

Sara lifted one eyebrow and said in a bored tone, 'God, does it always have to be that way when you all get home. One week from now, you'll all be shouting orders!'

Breakfast was in various stages of being served and cleared. Razia had followed Sara up with a tray of fresh tea and nimbu-pani.

After Jeevan arrived with the bag, Sara said, 'Go get the TV trolley, roll it out here on the verandah and plug it in over there. Make sure you bring the DVD player as well.'

Sara pulled up her sunglasses above her head, her scarf got in the way, and she pulled it off, shaking her hair out. 'It's just us family here,' she said looking at her amused audience. Ignoring their winks at each other, she pulled out her notebook and pencil and arranged herself on a wicker ottoman. She looked at her sister Shireen sitting cross-legged on the floor, eating a kebab with toast and asked, 'Have you put on weight, since I last saw you?'

Shireen cast a sidelong sly glance at her and continued to butter the toast, 'No, dahling, I'm still the same. But you seem to have gained a few pounds. Have you?'

Sara smoothed her tunic and held her hands at her waist and asked anxiously, 'Have I? Am I looking fat in this jora? Oh no! No, I don't think I've gained but that's it. If you think I've gained, then that's bad, I must be bloating. It's that time of the month anyway. But that's it. Nothing but papaya and cucumbers till the wedding for me! Razia go make me a glass of sugarless nimbu-pani, this one must be drowning in sugar.'

Then she turned to her sisters and said, 'Oh how wonderful! Just look at us all here together. How wonderful. We haven't had this opportunity since, God I can't even remember when.'

Resham: I can, I think it was your wedding.

Sara: Really?

Resham: Remember?

Sara: That's right!

Resham: And we were so much younger and thinner then.

Sara: Speak for yourself. I am still twenty-nine.

Resham: You're ridiculous Sara, that's what you are.

Sara: Live and let live. To each, her own. And all that.

Kulsum: Why not? I completely agree.

Shireen was munching on a mouthful of kebab and buttered toast: What's with the hijab, Sara?

Sara: Please Shireen, you're not going to lecture me, are you?

Shireen laughed and shrugged.

Shireen: Well, I never questioned all your other phases so why should I question this?

Sara: Times change.

Shireen: And you change with them.

Sara: Of course! Please let's not get into my hijab right now shall we? We have much more important things to discuss. Who wants to do the jewellers? Amina and I have to do a pile of things at the jewellers. Who wants to go and help us pick out the outfit, the jora? And I think we're going to need someone to run over to take care of the caterers and the flowers. We need to start on all of this right away!

Resham: I for one want to do all those things. I intend to get out as much as possible. So definitely count me in on the jewellers and all the clothes shopping.

Razia came back with Yunis, the cook, pushing the trolley with the TV and DVD player. Yunis plugged in the TV, turned it on, flipped through the channels, paused at Al Jazeera and then stopped at Geo. Putting the volume on mute, he left.

Sara clapped her hands twice, sat up and straightened her shoulders. 'Well, the first thing we have to do is to get all of you outfitted for the wedding. Iqbal will be here soon to take all your measurements. So that's one thing we don't have to leave the house to get done. And I've planned for us to go shopping this afternoon to my favourite fabric shops so that you can pick the colours and textiles for your outfits. You can consult with me on how much material we'll need. Now what I need from you is this: do you all know what you want to wear? Here! I've brought along a pile of magazines and catalogues over there and here are four DVDs from a couple of fashion shows this year. Go through them all now. Here, I'll put in the first DVD. See what you like best and we can have those things made for you.'

Shireen laughed, 'Well that's just perfect. How very organized you are! Wow! Look at this number right here! What a dream!'

Sara looked over Shireen's shoulder and said, 'I know, I know. There dear, turn off the news and stick in the tapes. Let's watch the fashion shows. I'm tired of watching the war and the tsunami. Thank God, Karachi wasn't hit. Would've ruined the shaadi season.'

'Sara! Honestly!' Resham drawled sleepily.

Sara said laughing, 'Keep your knickers on, Resham! Only joking!'

Resham yawned and stretched out her legs, 'Really hard to tell.'

Sara giggled, 'Okay, okay yaar. But I'm very impressed with all the charity that the Americans are raising. Not the government, but their people.'

Resham frowned, 'Don't be too impressed Sara, it's less than what they raised for the victims of September 11th—three billion dollars.'

Sara said dismissively, 'That was different. Of course they care about themselves more than anyone else. It's only natural. But it's good to know that they care. After the invasion of Iraq we were beginning to think you Americans were heartless.' Resham yawned and said, 'Oh, don't get carried away. All this outpouring of giving is only a happy convergence of a need to show we're not that awful and of years of treating the weather channel as news.' Then Resham reached for another kebab. 'Okay, enough bashing of my country.'

Sara: Excuse me, dahling! You really are a classic convert.

Resham: What does that mean?

Sara: Y'know, naya, naya musalman, allah allah chilahey. A new convert always shouts Allah the loudest!

Resham: Darling, you're the one in a head-scarf.

Sara retorted: Sweetheart, you're the one smothered in a flag.

Shireen asked: Sara, are you ever going to stop wearing that thing?

Sara: Why? And it's quite the fashion statement! And you know I keep up with fashion. And it's quite convenient for me.

Shireen: Dear, no one could ever fault you for not being conveniently fashionable, always.

Resham laughed: Or fashionably convenient.

Sara: You are so sweet, the two of you. Thank you.

Amina: Please everyone focus!

Resham: Okay. I want to wear saris for all the functions and I've brought along five of my saris. But I'm happy to upgrade my wardrobe.

Sara opened a page in her notebook and titled it 'Resham' and started scribbling. 'Okay, you have your five saris, we'll take a look at them. Then we'll also go to a sari shop and see if you want to pick out new saris. I'll have the blouses and petticoats made for you and will have the falls stitched on to the saris.

Resham: Thank you Sara, I knew I could count on you for this. And I want this exact outfit that you're wearing!

Sara: You'll get this, but certainly not for the wedding events. It's far too plain and informal!

Resham laughed: Informal? I'd wear that to a ball in New York!

Sara sniffed: New York.

Kulsum: I'd like to wear more traditional joras. I really wanted to wear a Hyderabadi for the mehndi. I've brought along my shaadi jora to wear to the wedding.

Sara continued to write, 'Okay, so shaadi jora for the wedding. I'll need to take a look at that, maybe we need to alter it a bit? Well, for all your information, the new thing has been to wear only saris. I mean really, it's not so new anymore, but for the last two seasons everyone has been wearing saris.'

Kulsum: I know. But I prefer the traditional joras. And since its Amina's wedding, I really would like to be decked out.

Sara: I agree. We'll have it your way. But I could also put together incredibly elaborate saris.

Kulsum: Nope.

Sara: Okay. But the wedding won't be the only function. You need to think about the other events as well. What about the nikkah and the mayoun and the dholkis and the ghazal evening. What would you like to wear to those?

Kulsum: Help!

Sara: See! I knew you'd come around to seeing it my way. I know this better than anything else. Kulsum, I think a Hyderabadi would be ideal for the mehndi. How about a classic turquoise and burgundy combination?

Kulsum: I prefer the turquoise and tangerine.

Sara: Perfect. Chiffon dupatta or tulle?

Kulsum: Let's go for the chiffon.

Sara: Perfect. We'll give it the really opulent and heavy look by giving it a very broad dabka border. And cover it in silver and dull gold kamdani. Well, we'll get the cloth this afternoon and see what we can get accomplished, there's so much work to be done. Then for the shaadi, do you want to wear your own shaadiwala jora?

Kulsum: Yes.

Sara: Okay, and for the mayoun?

Kulsum: A shalwar kameez.

Sara: How about a tung pyjama and angarkha?

Kulsum: Okay, I'm agnostic about the mayoun.

Sara: You can wear a shalwar kameez for the nikkah.

Kulsum: Sounds good.

Sara: Girls, how about we all wear shalwar kameezes for the nikkah. (She pinched two fingers together and waved her hand as though she were colouring with crayons in the air.) In sort of muted colours, very light pinks, creams, whites, very plain chiken work, only with some light kamdani and pure cotton? Very, very virginal!!

Resham: Sounds good.

Kulsum: Fine by me.

Resham: Great. A chance to get my virginity back!

Shireen: Me too!

Kulsum: Me three!

Shireen added, 'It all sounds perfect. I've brought plenty of outfits for myself. Last year, one of Amit's cousins got married and I had so many joras made. So I have at least six saris, and Sara, the clothes you sent me are still perfect. I've brought those with me, there's the Hyderabadi you had made for me, in purple, lime green and burgundy, a peshwaz and an angarkha. Really gorgeous stuff.'

Sara nodded, 'Okay, you're all set then. But why don't you go unpack and bring them out here so I can take a look. Are you sure nothing needs alteration or freshening up? Let's take a look. Razia! Razia,' Sara called out. 'Bring the ironing board out here and the iron! Shireen, let's get all your clothes out now and ironed so we can see.'

Shireen said, 'I love this, Sara you're quite the manager. Okay, let me finish my cup of tea and I'll go get my stuff.'

Sara said, 'Resham, you get your saris as well. And Kulsum, go get the shaadi jora of yours. Let's just make sure who's got what and what shape everything is in. Right. There isn't a moment to be wasted. We simply don't have the luxury for that! So you see, ladies, what my life is? This is the way it is every day. People never plan ahead for weddings. It's always in a crisis mode. I always have only one or two weeks to prepare and we always manage to get everything done.'

Shireen remarked appreciatively, 'That's amazing. No way could any of us ever have had all this done in the States.'

Razia came in and announced that Iqbal had arrived. 'Baji, should I bring him upstairs?' she asked Sara.

Sara turned and appraised her sisters who were still in their night clothes. 'Are you all decent? Everyone wearing a bra?'

'What a pain in the ass,' Resham said.

Sara said, 'Well, unless you want to embarrass him and embarrass yourself, you can stay here.'

Everyone scrambled up and went to their rooms to put on their clothes. When they were all back, Sara told Razia to call Iqbal up.

Sara said, 'Ah, here he is. Iqbal, good, you've come just in time. Ladies, Master Sahib is probably the best cutter in all of Karachi. I've taught him everything he knows. Isn't that right, Master Sahib?'

Iqbal scratched his head and shifted his weight from one foot to the next, 'Yes Baji, you're right.'

Sara said, 'Okay, let's start first with Kulsum. You measure, I'll write it down. Come on Kulsum get up.'

Iqbal said, 'Baji, arms out.' Kulsum stretched out her arms. 'Very good.'

Sara turned to her page for Kulsum and instructed, 'Let's get measurements for half sleeve, full sleeve.'

Iqbal measured Kulsum's arm, '6 inches, 22 inches.'

Sara: Bust?

Iqbal: 36 inches.

Sara: Is that a tight 36 inches fitted, or are you holding the inch tape loosely?'

Iqbal showed her: See, Baji?

Sara: Okay. It's 36 inches. Waist?

Iqbal: 32 inches.

Sara: You need to lose weight, Kulsum.

Kulsum wailed: I know.

Sara: Hips?

Iqbal: 40 inches.

Sara: Get on the treadmill, girl! Waist to ankle?

Iqbal: 42 inches.

Sara: Shoulder to knee?

Kulsum: Make it shoulder to calf.

Sara: Yes, it'll look better longer. You're right.

Iqbal: 42 inches.

Sara: Shoulder length?

Iqbal: 22 inches

Sara: Armhole?

Iqbal: 10 inches

Sara: Neckline?

Iqbal: Baji, do you want a low neckline or...

Kulsum: Just normal.

Sara: Iqbal, keep it at 8 inches.

Iqbal measured the neckline and placed the tape from Kulsum's shoulder to eight inches down.

Iqbal: Baji, 8 is too low. See where 8 inches comes on her?

Sara: No that's fine.

Kulsum: It's quite low, Sara.

Sara: Cleavage is good. Shoulder to back?

Iqbal: 15 inches.

Shireen: Sara, do you mind doing the measuring for me!

Everyone looked at her in surprise.

Resham laughed: I guess we're no longer used to it. Don't tell us, Shireen, that you're suddenly bashful. It's only Master Sahib.

Shireen (looking embarrassed): I don't know I guess I've just gotten out of this habit. Living in the States and wearing sweat suits and sneakers half the time....

Iqbal scratched his head and shifted his feet.

32

Dwellings of Safety

HAJRA watched Resham struggle with the clear plastic wrapping around the Peak Freans slim cardboard carton of zeera biscuits. 'Here let me do it,' she said, reaching out to take the box from Resham, who was seated on the floor across the coffee-table from her.

Resham pulled aside stubbornly. 'No, I can do this,' she laughed as she finally managed to pierce the wrapping with her thumbnail. She opened the box and dumped the cookies out in to an empty wooden bowl on the coffee-table. Hajrabai had set out chilli chips and chocolates left over from Meir's visit after the remnants of breakfast had been cleared. Zareenabai had just brought in a tray of teacups and a teapot covered with a red block printed and mirrored tea cosy. Breakfast things had just been cleared up, sooji halwa, puris, nihari and naan bought from Burns Road on the way back from Mewa Shah had been carried into the kitchen by Amina and Kulsum.

At dawn, Zareenabai and the girls had accompanied Hajrabai to the cemetery. The sky had been overcast and a few raindrops had plopped down on the windscreen. Sara had her seat pulled as far forward as it would go to make more room in the back. They drove along a deserted looking Bandar Road at the time before the rush hour began. They had all crammed into one car, Resham and Amina on the front passenger seat and Kulsum, Shireen, Hajrabai and Zareena jammed into the back. It had been a quiet time to go to Mewa Shah, only the caretaker and his family saw them come and go. They had walked amongst the graves reading the headstones. Resham had seen a short film, a homage of sorts, by Asad Rahman on the cemetery and had read an article in the *DAWN* 'Karachi's Own Lost Tribe', by Bahzad Alam Khan on the B'nai Israel graveyard. She quickly found the graves mentioned in it, two inside a mausoleum one whose carved headstone read, 'In loving memory of Sheelo, beloved wife of Mr Solomon David, late municipal surveyor and president of the Jewish Community Karachi, who departed this life on April 27, 1903.' Another beautifully carved headstone with flowers and leaves was for Gershone Solomon Oomerdaker

(1861–1930). Hajrabai said that he was the president of the Magain Shalome synagogue in Karachi. Next to his grave a slab of stone carved in the shape of an open book read, 'Mayest thou find open the gates of heaven and see the city of peace and the dwellings of safety and meet the ministering angels hastening joyfully towards thee and may the high priest stand to receive thee, and go thou to the end, rest in peace and rise again unto life.'

The caretaker and his son, an old man and a teenager wrapped in winter chadors, rushed around them bringing pails of water to clean the graves. The visit was an unexpected and unannounced one. The girls, their heads covered with their shawls, had washed Ibrahimbhai's grave and the grave of Hajrabai's mother, Rahel Daoud. They had marvelled at how clean and well-kept the cemetery was. Raindrops started soon after they arrived and crows began cawing in the surrounding trees at the advent of rain. Zareenabai had said her Fateha hurriedly at the graves and the girls followed her example as Hajrabai looked on.

Now back at Lawrence Road, Hajrabai looked around her at the faces of all her girls. Shireen, Kulsum, Amina, and Resham were seated on the rug around the table. Hajra and Zareena sat on the sofa. Sara stood in the door to the balcony leaning against the scaffold of the door from where a cool early morning breeze was gently blowing into the room. The sound of thunder rolled outside and there was a flash of lightning. The clouds broke and a drizzle had begun. A cold breeze blew in and everyone followed Sara's cue and wrapped their pashminas and shawls closer.

Over the course of the morning, black and white photographs, some faded and most furled at the edges, had been extracted from a photo album and from two shoe-boxes. 'Look at this, Bari-ma! You were so thin! Look at your Dad! He was so small! Where was this one taken?' Resham's face appeared golden, her skin shone in the Karachi light. Amina looked at her sister and wondered whether it was just her imagination, or whether it was true that here, in Karachi, they had a certain alchemy with the very air. They seemed to glow golden here. Shireen's voice had a ring here especially when she laughed. Sara standing in the doorway, her head covered in a pale pistachio green silk was luminously lovely. Kulsum seemed in her element, spread out in her luxurious shalwar kameez with an extra long dupatta draped over one shoulder, flowing down and spreading out on the rug. This would have been an inconvenience in New York. And today, instead of having her hair up in a bun or in a braid down her back, Kulsum had left it undone and it spread around her like a shining sheet of silk.

'I know just the shop for lovely silver frames. What is it called? Beaten metal…tired metal…'

'Stressed? You mean that old look?' Amina offered.

'Is that what it is? Yes!' Sara said, 'You know, very antique-ish…I'll go and pick up a few, put these out.' She gestured towards the pile of photos. 'Put them on the walls here.'

Hajra looked at Sara surprised, and smiled.

Sara shrugged and looked out at the rain, 'No, this won't last. It's just a random winter shower. It better not last, we have so much to do. Can't have the streets flooding.'

Kulsum looked up from a photograph and caught Amina's gaze, 'It's so beautiful here, isn't it?'

'Yes, with the constant breakdowns in electricity, the shortage of water. Remember, we weren't able to take showers this morning. The violence, having to sneak off to the cemetery in the morning, the mosquitoes…'

Hajrabai interjected, 'How I wish all of you would come back to Karachi.'

Resham said, 'We're here.'

'No, I mean forever. If you don't come back, who will take care of everything? This apartment, the house, your father's

business? This apartment will all go after I'm gone and who knows what the other neighbors want to do? What if they all decide to sell? Then this place will be bought by some big drug smuggler who will launder his dirty money and turn this into a shopping mall.'

Resham laughed, 'That will never happen. Never. What would you like to do Bari-ma? Do you want to buy out all the other tenants; do you want to make sure that this building always stays here? Do you want to do that? I can do that. Just say the word, darling. We promise you that this won't change.'

Hajrabai got up and went to the bedroom. She reached under the bed and pulled out a small suitcase the size of a briefcase. Attaché case as they called it. She brought it back to the drawing room.

'Ah the goodies,' Amina exclaimed.

Hajra laughed, 'Yes, I asked your father to go to the bank yesterday and bring it from the locker. He brought it here. I thought it would be better to go through the jewellry here in this apartment without anyone to bother us. We have more privacy here.'

Hajrabai popped open the latches on either side of the gleaming honey-hued leather-bound case and opened its lid. The case was filled with smaller boxes covered in dark blue, red and green velvet and small tin boxes of English biscuits and Quality Street candies from England.

'This type of weather calls for basini rotis and keema!' Kulsum said. 'And lovely songs.'

Sara interrupted her, 'Yes, let's sing. C'mon Resham, sing us a song.'

'Yes,' agreed Shireen enthusiastically. 'Sing the one that you sang at Amina's party. Sing it for Bari-ma and Choti-ma. Bari-ma, you are going to love this. C'mon Resham.'

Resham sang as Hajrabai sorted out her jewellry for Amina's wedding, a dazzling mess of gold bangles and bracelets, long dangling bell-shaped ear-rings, jhumkas, jewellery in solid gold or studded with emeralds, pearls, rubies and turquoise, gold chains to support the ear-rings, saharas, gold necklaces of seven strings of gold beads and seven strings of pearls and rubies. Ankle bracelets and jade studded collars called chokers. Resham's voice rang out in the small apartment and gladdened the hearts of her family. Sara watched her mother and Choti-ma examining each item to see whether it needed repairing or polishing, trying on a bracelet or a ring and then handing it over to her sisters to do the same while Resham sang. Sara, standing at the balcony door, a cold breeze at her back watched the warm scene, distracted by the jewels. She thought to herself that indeed Resham's voice had improved. She cleared her throat and prepared to sing after Resham had finished.

Just as Sara was about to break into song, Hajra interjected as she lifted up a sparkling article from the case, 'Look at this jhumar, isn't this lovely? Amina, would you like to wear it?' The jhumar was a crescent band of round stamps of gold embedded with a surface of pearls. At the center of each was the shape of a six-point star studded with diamonds. Each stamp was held together in a clutch of strands of tiny silvery pearls. Resham exclaimed, 'Oh this is lovely! I'll wear this!'

Hajrabai laughed, 'When you get married!'

Sara smiled, 'Quick Choti-ma, take out a fahl for Resham. Will she get married?'

'Will she get married soon!' Hajrabai corrected her.

'May your mouth be filled with sugar and butter,' Zareenabai said quickly.

'No need for fahls, I'll do it. Get married for the sake of this jhumar. Why not!' Resham laughed.

'Ah what a difference a place makes, you would have never said that in New York!' Shireen said, giggling. 'You're catching Amina's bug.'

'It's that damned bottled water here!' Resham protested.

33

The Costumes

SARA and Amina sat across from Mehreen. Sprawled between them was Mehreen's enormous wood carved and ivory inlaid desk strewn with cloth swatches, magazines, paper receipts, two wads of thousand rupee notes and phones. There were indoor plants in abundance amongst the furniture and rolls upon rolls of silk fabrics of every thickness and colour. Tall windows were draped with bamboo blinds and wooden slated panels through which sunlight peaked in. A large caladium plant in an unusual pink and green hue with veins of a deep red was potted in a huge copper pail and was placed behind the desk. Behind it, a ceiling to floor wood panel of drawers and shelves displayed fabrics. The other walls were similarly adorned with shelves and drawers. Drawers half open revealed their enticing treasures of coloured beads including fresh water pearls. Skeins of silk thread, in every possible imaginable vibrant colour filled drawer after drawer. Each drawer contained the full range of a single colour so that in one a barely pink deepened into shades of fuchsia and magenta, while in another a rose deepened into mauve into reds and burgundy, and still another went from lime to yellows to mustards and so on. Buttons, sequins and beads were in other drawers and containers. Amina felt that an intense expression of opulence enveloped them. Strewn and spread before them on low tables and around them, stacked on the marble floor and piled tightly on shelves all the way to the ceiling were hand-woven silks, brocades, kamqhab, banarsi, chiffon and organzas in heady colours: burnt orange, red, purple, turquoise, moss green, aubergine, and mauve. All the fabrics were densely and intricately worked with gold thread. Plump gold thread embroidered as leafy vines on heavy silk fabrics wound its way around flowers fashioned from tiny pearls and glass beads which vied for space with turquoise, yellow, mustard, red, green, magenta embroidery. These patterns and designs covered the wide borders of chadors and dupattas, gararas, saris, angarkhas, kurtas, peshwazes, sherwanis, ghagras and cholis. Silver stars, full moons and crescents were strewn liberally amongst the gold and gems. Cloth and fabric, if any could be seen, seemed simply a means for holding together every possible shape of fragile and delicate gold and silver detail.

Sara gushed, 'My dear Mehreen Khala, thank you so much for seeing us at such short notice. And this being your busy season, the shaadi season and all.'

Mehreen waved her hand and replied, 'All seasons are busy for me! What will you have, tea or something cold to drink?'

Sara said, 'Let's have tea and I brought you mithai. We have some good news!'

Mehreen picked up an intercom phone, waited for someone to answer and said, 'Three teas, bring us the almond cake as well.' She smiled, 'Someone came from Hyderabad today and brought in a lovely cake from Bombay Bakery this morning. What's the news, beta?'

Sara gestured towards her sister, 'Amina is getting married.'

Mehreen raised an eyebrow and looked at Amina, 'Why?'

Sara asked, 'What do you mean, Mehreen Khala? Why not?'

Mehreen said, 'I thought you of all people, Amina, would have had better sense than that!'

Amina laughed, 'But this is what your work is all about.'

Mehreen shrugged disdainfully, 'All folly and waste. I only contribute to making the folly a bit stylish.'

Amina said, 'And the waste?'

Mehreen laughed, 'Well they're all going to waste anyway. Better that they throw their money in something classic, and in my direction.'

Amina chuckled and winked, 'You're my kind of woman, Mehreen Khala.'

Mehreen said, 'Well, nevertheless one should have a party and one should get dressed up. Always a good excuse to look lovely, that's what a wedding is. That's my part, making the clothes gorgeous. After that, my part is done and then God only knows. It's up to you.'

Amina laughed.

Sara said solicitously, 'Anyway Mehreen Khala, we are going to need at least five joras and we only have two weeks to prepare.'

Mehreen threw up her hands, 'Impossible! I cannot get five wedding joras ready in two weeks!'

Sara spluttered, 'But…'

Mehreen interrupted, 'Sara you should know better than that, you're in the same business. I see that this is as usual, your helter-skelter way of doing things. Unless the joras are just simple plain tailoring, I cannot have them made for you. Do you know how much work goes into the joras? Surely you do! You're in the same line of work. My artisans will need at least five weeks and that too, if they're working day and night. I'm sure you are going to want dabka and kamdani and real gold and silver thread of sacha kaam and embroidery and hand-woven silks. Am I wrong? I thought not. So how do you expect all this to happen in two weeks? How do you expect to have the silk thread dyed in Malir, have the handloom cloth made in Benares Colony, and then embroidered and worked in Malir and Paposhnagar and stitched here in my shop in just two weeks? And don't tell me to have it done somewhere closer to the center, I won't change my artisans just to meet your deadlines. I simply will not compromise my quality and certainly not for one of Hajrabai's daughters.'

Mehreen Khala's cellphone went off in chimes of birds chirping and rainwater. 'Yes?' She put her hand on her heart 'Really? Where? Oh dear! Well where are you? Okay well stay there… I don't know what to say… Oh dear… Oh dear, how gruesome… Okay, be careful, go right home now…No, no need to go do the rest of your errands…go home. Call me when you get home. Okay? Okay beta. Khudahafiz. Khudahafiz.' She got off the phone. 'There's been a bomb blast at the Shell petrol station. They say at least five people have been killed. Limbs everywhere. Somebody's head got blown off. That was Nuzi, my granddaughter, on the phone. She just heard from a friend who was near the station. Apparently the blast could be heard on that side of the city.'

Sara said, worried, 'Every day now, something or the other. Who is doing this? What's this all about? Where are we going? It's like a war out there. Ooff, which Shell station was it? It must be the big one. Oh! We have to go to a dinner near there tonight. I guess we'll just take a different route to the house! Such an inconvenience! We'll probably arrive even later then usual. Oh well.'

Mehreen shook her head, 'God help us. And see now all the workers at the workshop in Korangi will want to take the day off and we have such a backlog of work as it is.'

Sara said, 'Mine too. Oh no.'

Mehreen said, 'So my dear there you are, there's just no way to get your five joras in time. Even if we had fewer bomb blasts.'

Sara whined, 'Mehreen Khala, there's no one in the entire world who makes better joras than you!'

'I know that!' Mehreen smiled. 'You don't need to tell me what's obvious.'

Sara continued, 'Amina must wear one of your outfits on her wedding. There is no other option for our family. You know that. I mean, I could have put her trousseau together, but this is all too special. Surely you have some pieces that are already made and that can be adjusted to her size?'

Mehreen couldn't help but be flattered by the desperation and sincerity in Sara's voice. She replied warmly, 'Well, let me think about it. There are a few combinations that are waiting for delivery in Dubai for a wedding next month.'

Amina interjected enthusiastically, 'Perfect! No one there will even know! Can't we just borrow them for our wedding and then return them?'

Mehreen looked scandalized, 'What an appalling thought. Tauba! That's unheard of!'

Amina shrugged, 'Why not? I could rent them from you?'

Mehreen sounded scandalized, 'Ooof, these American girls! Just listen to her!!'

Sara tilted her head to one side and surveyed her sister. 'It's not such a bad idea. Mehreen Khala, we're desperate. We'll pay full price for them and return them to you right after the wedding.'

Amina said, 'Sounds like a reasonable plan. Very practical. We'll rent them!'

Amina clapped her hands, 'A new business idea! Rentals!'

Mehreen chuckled, 'What do you think I am? The General? Renting out everything?'

Sara played along, 'Why not? Military bases! Airfields and soldiers! Joras! Everything for rent!'

Entertaining the idea, Mehreen shrugged and said, 'Well, let me show you what I have. Come with me upstairs to the house. If we stay down here in the shop we'll be bothered every second and

I certainly don't want anyone else getting ideas. Rent! Unbelievable! Sacrilegious!'

She sighed in resignation and shook her head in feigned sadness. 'But I'll make this one an exception. This is only for you Sara!'

Ringing her hands together, Sara was all gratitude, 'Mehreen Khala, thank you! Thank you so much. I knew you would save us!'

34

A Moment of Reckoning

RAZIA came upstairs to the terrace where Amina and Hajrabai were sorting through a few pieces of jewellery. Zareenabai had taken the rest of the household, Shireen, Kulsum and Resham to the bazaar. Sara was expected to arrive any moment to take Hajrabai and Amina to the jewelers. Razia said, 'Bibi, there's a lady at the gate who says she wants to see you and that she's a friend of yours.'

Amina was surprised, 'I wasn't expecting anyone. Who is it? You don't know her? Who is at the gate?'

Razia said, 'I think she came to the house once, but with Rehana Bibi!'

Amina said, 'Well show her in. Take her to the drawing room. I'll be down there in a moment.'

Hajrabai said, 'Make sure you ask her if she wants tea or something cold to drink.'

Downstairs Noor Afshan had stopped and peeked into the dining room. She had heard about the floor from Rehana and stood admiring it when Amina came in.

'Assalamulaikum Amina Baji!'

Amina said inquiringly, 'Waleykum salam. Please, please won't you come to the drawing room and sit down.' She paused and asked hesitatingly, 'Have we met before?'

Noor Afshan said nervously, 'Why yes, several times, you don't remember me?'

Amina hurriedly apologized, 'Of course I do! Yes, how silly of me. You work at the Foundation. You're...Zilay Huma?'

Noor Afshan shook her head and said, 'Noor Afshan.'

Amina said, 'Of course! Noor Afshan, you must forgive me. I do apologize. My brain is completely confused, there's been so much going on. It's all so hectic that I can't even remember who I am or what my name is!'

Noor Afshan replied, 'Yes, I can imagine.'

Remembering her manners, Amina asked, 'Would you like some tea, or coffee, or something cold to drink? Shall we go to the drawing room?'

Noor Afshan sounded out of breath, 'No, nothing for me, I don't want to take up too much of your time, I'll just say what I came for and then be on my way.'

Amina said, 'You sound so serious and nervous. Please relax. What is it? Is there something wrong? Is there something I can help you with?'

Noor Afshan said stiffly, 'Yes, there is something very wrong. I felt it was my duty to try and do something about it.'

Amina was mystified, 'Please go on.'

Just then the door opened and Hajra came in holding the cellphone. She smiled at Noor Afshan who greeted her. Hajrabai looked at Amina, 'Razia told me you were in here,' she said. 'I was just on the phone with your father, he wants to go with us.' She smiled, 'He will be here in five minutes, he's stuck in traffic just at the roundabout on the main road.' She looked at Noor Afshan inquiringly.

Noor Afshan raised her head high and continued, 'Rehana is my best friend. She is a beautiful, beautiful person. So wise and intelligent and…'

Hajra who was about to leave, stopped and asked, 'Is something wrong with Rehana! Oh no!'

Noor Afshan sounded panicked, 'Yes, there is something wrong and she will never say anything and she would never forgive me if she knew I was here to tell you this.'

Hajra was worried and said anxiously, 'Please tell me what is wrong. Noor Afshan, I care very much for Rehana. She is like a daughter to me. And she has been a good friend to me.'

Noor Afshan raised her voice and pleaded, 'Then how can you do this to her? How can all of you be so cruel?'

Amina was bewildered, 'What am I doing to her? What have I done?'

Taken aback, Hajra stared at Noor Afshan and said, 'Calm down my dear, what are you talking about? There seems to be some misunderstanding. You can't just come here and start accusing us. We don't even know what you are talking about.'

Noor Afshan raised her voice, 'Don't you know? You are stealing her life! Everything that Yaqub Sahib has built in the last five years is because of her ideas and her skills. What would he have done without her?'

Hajra said, 'We all know that, but what is this about stealing? What have we stolen from her?'

Amina turned to Hajrabai, 'I don't understand what I've done.'

Noor Afshan exclaimed, 'Please stop!'

Amina recoiled into herself, 'I don't understand. What is it about?'

Noor Afshan said. 'It's about Yaqub Sahib. It's about you marrying him.'

Hajra and Amina looked at her incredulously and simultaneously said, 'What?!'

Noor Afshan declared resolutely, 'My dear friend Rehana should be his partner in life. Not you! They are meant for each other! Can't you see that? He can't see that. But she lives for him. I know. I know the way she talks about him. Can't you see what you are doing?'

Amina replied haltingly, 'I am not sure what I should say to you.'

Noor Afshan was in anguish, 'Just because we, she, isn't from the same social status as you. Just because she is from a lower income class than you and Yaqub, doesn't mean she is not your equal. She is your superior. Yaqub Sahib is not an equal of hers in any way and yet she cares about him. And now he's marrying you and she is not good enough for him simply because of money.'

Hajrabai was beginning to lose her patience for the young woman who was steadily getting more impassioned, 'Enough! I think you should stop!'

Noor Afshan's voice was shaking, 'Fine, I will stop. I will go away now. And I'm sure that you'll have me fired tomorrow. But I couldn't have lived with myself if I hadn't done this very small thing for my sweet friend Rehana who will never say anything. She just goes on doing what is expected of her. I am not like her. I take what I think is mine. She never does. But I wanted to come here and try to take for her what is hers.'

Hajrabai said quietly, 'I think you should leave now.'

Noor Afshan: 'I am very sorry if I have caused you so much anger.'

Hajrabai said gently, 'I'm not angry. I think you are a good friend.'

Amina said wistfully, 'It seems like a lot of good friends are in the city trying to sort all of us out.'

Hajrabai walked up to Noor Afshan and put her hand on her cheek. 'I think Rehana is very lucky to have you as a friend. It's all too late now.'

Noor Afshan looked beseechingly at Hajrabai and reaching out, took Hajrabai's hand. 'It's never too late. Don't you watch any of the dramas on TV and the films?' She turned to Amina and repeated, 'It's never too late.' Thinking that she hadn't gotten through, she shook her head in frustration and walked out of the house. Hajrabai and Amina sat down at the dining-table, silently staring at each other. 'Well,' Hajrabai began, 'Amina, this is very complicated...' Hajrabai was interrupted by a commotion outside the door. The door opened and Razia came in shouting, 'Hai Allah, Begum Sahiba! There was shooting at the roundabout, Begum Sahiba, just now. Jeevan just came in to tell me. They say someone on a motorcycle shot at a car and killed the people in the car!'

'Hai ma!' Hajrabai screamed, 'Just now? At the roundabout? That's where Razzak called me from, he was stuck in traffic... Where's the phone?'

Hajrabai was still holding the cellphone in her hand. Her fingers trembled as she punched in the number for Razzak's cellphone and waited. 'No one is answering!' she shouted to Amina. 'It's his answering machine. Why is it his answering machine?'

Amina wrung her hands and said, 'Bari-ma, he could be talking to someone else! Dial again, Bari-ma!'

Hajra shook her head and handed the phone to Amina, and while Amina dialed, Hajra sat clutching the edges of the table, her knuckles had turned white from the pressure. Amina's voice was shaking as she waited for her father to answer the phone. 'I'm sure everything will be fine,' she tried to reassure Hajrabai. Amina dialed again and waited. Then she whimpered, 'I didn't even get a ring tone this time, it's just gone into the answering machine. Why doesn't he answer?'

Hajrabai had stood up, her eyes were wide with panic. She couldn't hear anything, everything had gone silent around her. She was deaf to any sound, she saw Amina's mouth moving. She turned and saw Razia and Jeevan standing at the door saying something to her. She couldn't hear a single word they were saying.

Amina shouted, 'Are you sure he called from the car? Bari-ma! Are you sure he called from the car?'

'Hai ma! Razzak, Razzak!' Hajrabai wailed. She rushed out towards the front door, opened it, and ran out of the house and into the driveway, to the gate, which was closed. 'Razzak!' she was wailing as she pulled and pushed the gate and finally managed to open the bolt. Razia and Jeevan were shouting, 'Bari-ma! Bari-ma!' Hajrabai didn't react, she couldn't hear them, and she couldn't hear herself wailing. The gate opened and she ran out onto the eerily quiet street outside. Overhead kites were flying low, the air seemed very clean today, and everything seemed blindingly white. Where was everybody? There was no one in the lane. She could barely see in this bright light. Hajrabai was barefooted, she was out of breath and was stumbling and tripping on the hem of her sari. But she moved as fast as she could towards the main road in the distance where she could see the traffic moving. She heard a few sounds that sounded like gunshots in the distance. She stopped for a second and then hurried forward, breathless and panting. Her heart was beating in her ears and her head was throbbing. She didn't hear Amina who was right behind her telling her to calm down. Amina ran after Hajrabai, caught up with her and grabbed her arm, 'Stop Bari-ma!'

'Let me go!' Hajrabai was sobbing. 'Razzak!' Amina saw a car turning into their lane. It was Sara. She screeched to a stop beside Amina and Hajra and jumped out of the car. 'What are you doing? What's going on? Are you alright?'

Hajrabai had stopped, she sunk to her knees, 'That letter, Sara, that letter!' Hajrabai screamed and wailed.

'What are you talking about? What has happened? Where is Abba?'

Amina was sobbing. Sara screamed, 'Amina, why are you crying? Bari-ma, what's happening? Where are the others? Where is Abba?!!!'

Amina sobbed, 'Abba! Sara, he was at the roundabout. There's been a shooting! He called Bari-ma from the roundabout, now he's not answering his phone!'

Sara grabbed Hajrabai who was moaning and clutching her chest. Sara's voice was cracked as though the sound was caught in her throat, 'No, this can't be true. This can't be true! Maulah madad! Ya Ali Madad!' Sara whispered hoarsely with her eyes shut tightly. She rocked her sobbing mother back and forth with one arm, and with the other hand she dialed Riaz's cellphone. 'Riaz! Riaz! Come to 43-G immediately. Right now… Abba … We don't know what's happened… No! No! I can't calm down… He was at the roundabout, near the house… There was shooting there… Abba hasn't come home yet! He was supposed to be home by now! He's not answering his phone! Come quickly!' Sara jumped back in her car, 'I'm going to the main road.' She reversed the car at a high speed and braked. As the car screeched, dust and the smell of burnt rubber from the tires rose from the road, the car did a U-turn and sped down the lane from which Sara had just come. Sara clutched the steering-wheel with one hand, and with the other on the gear shift, she kept repeating out loud, 'Ya Ali madad, Ya Ali madad, Maulah madad, Ali come to my assistance, come to my assistance, come to my assistance.' Reaching the intersection to the main road, she parked the car on the side of the lane and got out. She hurried to the main road and looked towards the roundabout. The traffic was moving normally. She saw a policeman nearby and hurried up to him. He eyed her from head to toe and grinned. Over the din of honking horns and car engines she shouted, 'Was there a shooting here just now?' The policeman was picking his teeth with a folded piece of tin foil from his cigarette case. 'Why do you want to know?' he asked insolently.

'Answer me!' Sara shouted at him, feeling an uncontrollable anger well up inside of her.

'We don't talk about any criminal activity. We don't have to answer anything,' he replied. 'If you want to find out, you should come to the police station with me!'

'Just answer my question!' Sara tried to calm down, but had raised her voice even more.

'Do you see anything here?' He raised his voice as well and asked her in a menacing tone.

Sara moved away from him and went further down on the side of the main road. Under her breath, she started to recite a prayer for help, 'Nad-e-Ali.' She looked around her, the huge mausoleum for the Father of the Nation was across the road and the large roundabout referred to as the 'Nomaish' had as usual an army checkpoint in the middle of it. A huge poster depicting a stern looking, uniformed General Musharraf saluting out at the traffic loomed at the center of the roundabout and cast a long shadow and shade over the checkpoint. Traffic was moving in its usually frenetic manner, there didn't seem to be any constraints. Then her eyes focused on a burnt out car standing on the side of the road. It was still smoldering and seemed to be a white Toyota, like her father's car. Her legs gave way from under her and she sank to the ground, dizzy and frightened. She managed to get back to her feet, 'Ya Ali madad, Ya Ali madad; Please come to my aid, sweet Maulah!' She waited for a pause in the traffic to cross the street, but that was futile. She would have to inch her way forward into the oncoming traffic, drivers would have to stop for her. She moved forward onto the road, cars honked and screeched around her as she made her way across the busy intersection and around the roundabout. Reaching the other side of the road, and still at least twenty feet from the burnt car she could see that the front passenger seat windows were smashed. There was a small crowd of people around the car, a group of policemen stood idly by. The car was burnt beyond recognition. 'Where are the passengers?' she shouted to a young boy standing near the car. He looked at her and shrugged his shoulders. Another man said, 'What's it to you? Their people came and took them.' Sara stood staring at the car in shock, 'Did you see if they were still alive?' she sobbed.

'Yes, but who knows what happened by the time they got to the hospital!'

'Which hospital?' Sara asked. 'Does anyone here know, did they say?'

'Who knows…probably Civil, it would be the closest. Maybe Jinnah or Aga Khan, or they could have taken them to OMI. That's the closest.'

She heard a voice near her ask, 'Are you alright?' Without answering she walked back across the road, half aware of the noise of cars honking and screeching around her as they braked to avoid hitting her. She stumbled just as she made it to the other side, the heel of her shoe caught in a rut. Sara fell forward and scraped her knee and hands. She stood up quickly, her heel was broken. Her knee had started to bleed. She could see the blood stain come through the fabric of her shalwar. The palms of her hands, now covered in dirt, were threatening to bleed where the skin had broken. She limped back to her car and suddenly realized she didn't have her car keys, she didn't have her bag. Nothing. She had left it in the car. She stared in horror at the locked car. The keys were still in the ignition, her purse, which had her cellphone, was on the floor by the passenger seat. How could she have done this? How could she have been so stupid! She screamed at herself in a tearful rage.

She started crying. 'Maulah, help me!' she sobbed.

She went to the other side of the car, she looked around her on the side of the road. Her eyes rested on a large rock. She picked up the rock with both her hands and threw it at the window of the car door; the glass cracked. She picked up the rock again and hit it against the glass with as much force as she could muster. The glass shattered instantly. She reached in and unlocked the door. Pieces of glass covered the passenger seat. She grabbed her purse, ran around to the other side of the car as she fished for her cellphone. She brushed the glass off the car seat with her purse and got back in. She started the engine just as the phone rang. It was Riaz shouting in panic, 'Sara, I've been calling you and calling you. I'm on my way, where were you? I'm stuck in traffic!'

Sara interrupted him, crying, 'Riaz, please go to Jinnah, I'll go to Civil. I was there at the roundabout, people there told me that they took them to a hospital, but I don't know which one!'

'Sara! Calm down! I've already been to Jinnah, nothing there. I've called Jabbar Bhai at Civil, he checked immediately. Nothing. Same thing at OMI, Asad Bhai checked. And at Aga Khan, Naseem checked immediately. Nothing.'

'What should I do? Riaz! Help me! I have to do something! I have to find Abba!'

'I'm on my way Sara. Just go back to 43-G and wait for me.'

She started the car and turned it around, the Mehfil-e-Khorasan imam bargah came into her view. She drove to it and stopped the car alongside the street and ran to the entrance of the imam bargah. It was locked. She rattled the gate and shouted to the guard inside, 'Open this gate!' He turned away. 'Open this gate!' she roared at him. 'I want to come in. I must come in! I have to pray!' He turned again to look at her. 'Come in the evening at 5:30,' he said. 'We'll open then! It's closed now for security reasons!' Sara started to scream as she thumped her hands on the railings, 'Open

'Did Sara tell you?'

'No, Sara didn't tell me, I didn't even know that Sara knew. She's been very good. No, Choti-ma told Bari-ma and me.'

'Choti-ma? How did she know?'

'She thought she saw a change in you, she was right!'

'I don't know what I was thinking…'

'It's going to be fine. Shall we put a stop to this wedding nonsense?'

'No! We can't! I mean, everything is done! The invitations are all out, we've had one of the dholkis already!'

'We could call it off.'

'Abba, there would be such a scandal!'

'Well, it won't be the first time!'

'No Abba, my mind is made up. I want to be here with you. I want to be here.'

35

Crashing the Party

TINY eight year old Rahim stood in the dark, looking on at the glowing white canopy of the shamiana. People inside appeared to him as shadows dancing on the opaque fabric of the canopy, sending Rahim's imagination spinning about what was going on in there. He could hear the harmonium and tabla sounds of music, the qawwali had begun and he could see the steady stream of guests arriving and leaving... All of them dressed in the finest silks, shawls and suits with jewels sparkling not only on their wrists, necks, hands and ears but on their shoes as well. He could smell the aromatic biryani which he imagined was only one of at least twenty dishes being served tonight. He was here to get the handouts after the meal would be over. He stood amongst a crowd of boys his age and older, shivering in the cold December night air, their feet in rubber chappals, their shalwar kameez clad bodies wrapped in thin cotton shawls. Not enough to keep the cold out. Hunger pangs made Rahim feel faint but he knew that his patience would pay off. He attended such events every night. December was a good month to eat well. He was beginning to recognize the guests, they seemed to all go to the same events as he did. Tonight, this event was part of a wedding and so women were dressed in dazzling clothes and much jewellery. They seemed heavy with wealth. Weighed down by it and floating on it all at once. Other nights, outside of charity balls, he watched women who he thought came half naked, wearing outfits that revealed their backs, waists, shoulders and arms, smelling of jasmine and lemon trees. Their breasts gleamed with glitter, almost completely exposed and resembling the actresses on the TV channels that he saw at roadside cafés. And then his imagination ran amuck following the shadows from outside. Who were these people who had so much and who wore so little? Who were these people for whom he was barely a shadow himself, if even that? They never so much as glanced towards him. What did they do once they were inside the tent? Their actions could only to be guessed at by the shadows they cast. They walked by him and never seemed to notice him, he was as though invisible, standing there, almost standing in

their way. Tonight, he was tired from his day of picking garbage. Competing with insects and maggots for a meal. He watched guests enter the canopy at a brightly lit entrance which was festooned with marigolds and where they were greeted by women holding chambeli garlands. And as he watched, they disappeared through the entrance and seemed to transform into elongated shadows, morphing and merging distortions, sparking his imagination. He felt hungry, cold and unhappy. He looked across at the long line of drivers leaning against the long line of gleaming SUVs, Mercedes, BMWs, Honda Civics and Toyota Corollas. Employees waiting for their employers to be done for the night. When he grew up he wanted to be one of them. A driver of a big car. He listened to two drivers talking to each other about leaving the country. 'Yaar, I've collected enough money to pay the dalal to take me across to Velayat. I'm going to Norway. They say there are plenty of jobs there! I can make enough money in one year to come back here and be one of the guests inside that tent and hire you as my driver!'

Another man said, 'I hear going to Europe is just too dangerous. Better to find a way to get to Dubai instead!'

Tonight was a musical evening. It would go on till at least five in the morning. The long line of servants stood wrapped in chadors and shawls, their faces half hidden as they blew their breath into themselves in an effort to keep warm while they waited patiently, steadily growing colder. And inside Amina felt hot and uncomfortable. The outfit she was wearing was a lime green handloom and embossed silk tunic over tight fitted pants, a churidar, which were embroidered with turquoise and silver thread that was too heavy. She adjusted the voluminous dupatta that she had flung over one shoulder and draped over the other arm and moved away from the coal brazier near her. She looked over to the crowd near the buffet table. It seemed too much of a challenge to go pile food on a plate for herself and keep all of her outfit together. She looked around to see if she could get someone to do it for her. She too had not had anything to eat all day. Bari-ma, Choti-ma and Abba were seated on a sofa near a coal heater. Bari-ma was wearing a dark purple plain silk sari and had a mustard coloured pashmina shawl wrapped around her shoulders and another one flung across her knees to keep her warm. Choti-ma was wearing a deep blue sari, also plain and she had a burgundy coloured shawl wrapped around her shoulders. Her father was dressed in a business suit. Her sisters, all of them wearing saris, were scattered, talking to various guests. Resham was seated near her parents.

She could see Yaqub talking to several men whom she didn't recognize. She figured they must be his guests or maybe they were friends of Sara's and Riaz's. She couldn't hear what they were saying but she could see that it was an argument.

Yaqub: This is preposterous and you know it!

Major Inteqab: No sir, it is not! We have a warrant for your arrest. As we have just explained to you, the National Accountability Bureau has been conducting an investigation into your business dealings for some time and there appear to be gross violations of the law.

Yaqub: I need to speak to my lawyers.

Major Inteqab: You can do so but we have to take you into custody first.

Yaqub: You do realize that I'm getting married tomorrow?

Riaz: What's going on here, Yaqub?

Yaqub: These men are from NAB, they are arresting me. That's what's going on.

Riaz: Hold on here. This is absurd.

Amina could see Yaqub was getting upset with the men. Someone tapped her on the shoulder and she turned to look. She jolted in shock and sputtered. 'What the hell are you doing here?!'

'Well I was in town. Great party you got going here,' Hank drawled sardonically.

Amina looked around her self-consciously, 'What do you mean you were in town? Who are you?'

Hank said: Heard of Homeland Security?

Amina: Oh no!

Hank: Oh yeah! Yup.

Amina: I can't believe it. You said you were retired.

Hank: I said I was retired like you said you were Sri Lankan.

Amina: Not the same thing. But why are you here?

Hank's tone was laconic: Y'know, coalition of the willing!

Amina: Base camp?

Hank: You got it! Your 'old' country, babe, is just one big military base for us. Isn't it great? What do you call this kind of singing? Can't say I really get it.

Amina: It's called a qawwali, of course you don't get it. Oh my God, Homeland Security?

Hank: Oh yeah, sorry, forgot to tell you what I did. Like you forgot to tell me your name. I tracked you down from your lovely photograph taken by the Fuji blimp in NYC. Much better than the mug shot on dating.com version. Or the shot we got of you after your arrest. That Fuji blimp lived up to its name!

'Whoa,' Hank Brown had said to the summer intern. 'Hold on just one sec! What's this we got here?' He had peered over the shoulder of the guy at the computer and looked into the screen in front of him, 'Back up there buddy! Rewind! Well, I'll be…'

Hank grinned at Amina, 'There you were Rita, only your face matched exactly with one of the people briefly detained and photographed, Amina Rueewallah. So I ordered that we track you down and Intel showed that you were traveling overseas. Not Sri Lanka for Christmas. And thank God, safe from that huge tsunami they had over there just now! And so I found out that you were American. First generation. Place of birth, Karachi. And so here I am.'

Amina looked around her again. She could see Yaqub and Riaz talking to the men she didn't recognize, clearly something was wrong. Her father was walking over to them as well. Amina looked at Hank, 'Oh my God. Look, you can't be serious, are you here to arrest me or something?' She felt breathless and giddy.

Hank grinned and leaned over and drawled in a low voice close to her ear, 'Handcuffs would be a nice touch, I think you'd look good in pink furry ones. But no, I'm here to take you back.'

Amina cringed and moved away, 'Take me back?'

Hank: Well I'm here to tell you let's get married.

Amina: To tell me? To tell me? Fuck off.

Hank: Yeah we already did that.

Amina: Well I have news for you. This is my wedding you're crashing. And you're in the gazillionth day of the grand pageant.

Hank: I know, but you're not actually getting married till tomorrow. Your sister clued us in on the festivities. We're invited to that too by the way. By way of getting a cultural immersion. Thanks for the invite. Mighty friendly folk, your sister and her husband. Look, I think you should call this whole thing off! Geez, that guy's hollering! What the hell is that man blabbering. Is that called singing? He sounds like he's in pain!

Amina: He's not blabbering, you jerk! That's singing and he's complaining to God about being betrayed or something. Call it off? You must be crazy. Do you know how much this shebang is costing me, my family? Just this outfit alone, for example!

Hank stepped back and appraised her.

Hank: Is that a fact? Well, you look pretty good. Please Rita, Amina, get real. You said you were in a mess, drowning!

Amina: That was stupid, impulsive. I would've never sent it if I'd known what you were or that you'd actually show up!

Hank: This is my kid and you know it.

Amina: What kid?

Hank: You're pregnant with my child.

Amina: No, I'm not! I've just gained a bit of weight. Not getting much exercise around here.

Hank: You're pregnant!

Amina: How the hell do you know that?

Hank: We pulled up your credit card history and you paid for a pregnancy test.

Amina: You did what?

Hank: Never mind that. You're having my baby. And I'm not letting you stay here and you're not getting married to this guy. You're an American citizen and you're having my baby! Hell, don't I have some rights?

Amina: No, you don't. And you're not the father.

Hank: Yes, I am.

Amina: No, you're not.

Hank: Am.

Amina: Not.

Hank: Am so!

Amina: Am not infinity!

Hank: Okay. Enough. This kid's coming in about four months.

Amina: Yes.

Hank: Well, I'm doin' the math here. Help me out. As I recall four months or so ago, you and I were…

Amina: I know, but this is not yours.

Hank: Whose is it?

Amina: Mine.

Hank: Crap! That's crap and you know it. Listen Rita, I mean Amina, honey, you can't live here.

Amina: Why not?

Hank: This isn't where you belong. You belong back in the States, with me.

Amina: In Texas?

Hank: Maybe. What the hell's wrong with Texas? Okay, maybe not Texas, but in New York, I'm willin' to give that a go. Anywhere, but not here!

Amina: God, please can everyone leave me alone? Listen to me! You didn't pull up credit history enough. I also paid for visits to a fertility clinic. The day I got arrested I was returning from a fertility clinic. Okay?

Hank: I don't believe you!

Amina: Well, figure it out. You pulled up everything on me for that day didn't you? Go figure that out. All those facts about me all in your database, well not everything always matches up, does it? And this kid could be just about anybody's. I told the nurse to mix me a cocktail, so…

Hank: You don't know what ethnicity it is?

Amina: Why should I? You want to racially profile the kid?

Hank: No. But you do! Otherwise why would you have done it that way!

Amina: To break away.

Hank: I don't believe any of this. There was a pedicure and a manicure and couple of visits to an OBGYN, and baby clothes on your credit history.

Amina: I went to a baby shower! I bought a gift!

Hank: Oh God. I still don't believe you.

Amina: Well, I don't care. This is not your child and you don't have any claims over my kid! And I'm going to sue you guys up the wazzoo for infringing on my privacy!

Hank: Boy or girl?

Amina: Who knows? Who cares! This kid is going to be an heir or heiress to a fortune and enrolled at Grammar School.

Hank: What the hell is all this? What's happened to you?

Amina: What's happened to me? Are you serious? You're asking me what's happened to me! You don't know me. You knew some chick called Rita. Who you had a fling with for a weekend.

Hank: Yeah? So? What the hell happened?

Amina: Why don't you ask your fucking database. You happened. You happened. Your Fuji blimp happened. Your spying happened. Now go away.

Hank: You're not coming back?

Amina: That's none of your fucking business.

Hank: And you've sure developed quite a potty mouth. And yes, it is my business.

Amina: It's not your business. And if you can't get over it you can just keep track of me on your system. Keep me under your surveillance. Watch me. Watch over me! Whatever! Do whatever gets you off!

Hank: God, that guy is making a racket. Anyway, you're being unfair.

Amina: It's music you moron. Am I? Being unfair?

Hank: It's a racket. The guy is howling! Yeah, you're being unfair.

Amina: Really? Unfair? All's fair in love and war.

Hank: Is that a grin? Yeah, that's a grin.

Amina: A smirk.

Hank: I'm detecting a grin.

Amina: Moron.

Hank: C'mon. All's fair in love. Right? That's what you meant love.

Amina: All great betrayals, baby, are about love.

Hank laughed: Can't argue with that. By the way who is that cute thing over there.

Amina: Where?

Hank: Over there, by the potted palm tree.

Amina: Who?

Hank: The one over there, the one with the nose ring.

Amina: You mean the one wearing the pink shalwar kameez.

Hank: Yeah, the one in the pink outfit.

Amina: Why do you ask?

Hank: She's stunning. Drop dead beautiful.

Amina: She is?

Hank: Jealous?

Amina: Right. Her name's Jeevan. Wonderful gal.

Hank: Yeah?

Amina: Yeah.

Hank: Well are you going to introduce me?

Amina: No.

Hank: Why not?

Amina: Because… Because…

Hank: Because what?

Amina: Because, uh, she's an incredible woman and you're beneath her. I'm not going to introduce you.

Hank: I wouldn't mind being beneath her, but you're being unfair. I'm a pretty incredible guy.

Amina: Stop smirking. No, I'm not going to introduce you.

Hank: Oooooh, want to keep me all to yourself?

Amina: Because she won't want anything to do with you.

Hank: Wanna bet?

Amina: I want you out of here, now.

Hank: C'mon introduce me. Okay how about that one over there?

Amina: Stop it!

Hank: C'mon, who is that over there? The one in that head gear.

Amina: My sister!!

Hank: No, not her, I've met her. That one over there with the yellow thing on.

Amina: She's a good friend. She's brilliant. An architect. And just stay away.

Hank: She looks like she could use some cheering up. Look at that sad face! Yellow ain't her colour. C'mon wedding girl, introduce me.

Amina: No. Go do it yourself.

Hank: Married?

Amina: No, she's not married.

Hank: Not yet you mean?

Amina: Don't mess with her!

Hank: With whom?

Amina: I mean it! Don't mess with either of them!

Hank: Me? Mess? You know how much I love immersing myself in different cultures. Okay, so enough of this now. Just stop this nonsense. Just c'mon home.

Amina: I am home.

Hank: No, you're not. This doesn't matter to you.

Amina: But I matter to it.

Hank: Detail. C'mon on home. Ah see, there you go again, grinning.

Amina: It's a smirk. And besides, I'm getting married.

Hank: No, you're not. News for you darlin'! Your bridegroom over there is in a shit load of trouble. Those guys over there are about to arrest him.

Amina: What the hell are you talking about!

Hank: Well, it seems to me your Yaqub Kishtiwallah didn't pay all his taxes, and that isn't a good thing.

Amina: Oh my God. Yaqub! You've gone and gotten him into trouble? Don't tell me you have something to do with this?

Hank: Swear to God, nothing. I was just listening in to those two goons over there before I walked up to you. I swear I had nothing to do with it. Though I think your friend pissed off our guy, you know our coalition of the willing partner and dear friend. He's gone and gotten himself into trouble.

Amina: Oh my God.

Hank: So see you in New York? But how about a little motorbike ride later on tonight, after this gig's over, with a boy from back home?

Resham, Shireen and Kulsum had been unable to intervene to stop Amina's marriage, yet all it had taken was the convergence of technology in its many usages, email and surveillance, coupled with the hubris of a dictator.

Outside in the cold, Rahim grew impatient. He was hungry and the dinner inside was still underway. It would be at least another hour before they gave away the leftovers. He walked around in the dark to keep himself warm. He stumbled on a small rock. He bent down and picked it up. He clenched it in the palm of his hands and walked back and forth some more. He was tired, cold and hungry. He looked towards the shadows on the glowing tent. He threw the rock as hard as he could at the tent. It disappeared into the dark and reappeared just as it hit the roof of the tent, noiselessly. Unnoticed.

36

American Shemerican

YAQUB had been arrested and jailed. Though shaken, the business community in Karachi didn't make much of a protest. Instead, they focused on the fact that Yaqub's background was quite unknown to them except for the fact that he had set up a Foundation and a museum and was planning to restore a large portion of old Karachi as a cultural heritage site. It was clear to them that they didn't need to bother too much about his well-being. After all, he had been arrested by the military government which just went to show that he had no real networks or connections and therefore no real power to reckon with, be afraid of or respect. Sara had been forlorn after the débâcle of her carefully laid plans to save Amina from ruin, and because of the sudden ruin of her prodigy, Yaqub. Amina's canceled wedding plans had caused Hajrabai and Razzak a considerable amount of relief. And though Zareenabai had hoped that Amina would be married to Yaqub or to Zain, she was not as upset or disappointed as she had thought she would be. Resham, Kulsum and Shireen had returned to the States shortly after New Year, traveling back on the same flight to spare everyone the misery of prolonged goodbyes. A few weeks later Hajrabai and Zareenabai had accompanied Amina back to New York and had decided to stay on till after Amina had the baby. Razzak had arrived in New York a week after the baby was born and had stayed on.

They had stayed on in New York through the next six months, and were going to return to Karachi on the same flight with Sara next week. Shaadi season was fast approaching again, and the thought of spending December out of Karachi was out of the question for Sara.

Now Amina looked out at a gray November day. Just the way Amina liked it at Thanksgiving. Amina thought looking out of the window, all the buildings, stood out better, against the gray sky and even the details of work on each façade seemed clearer. For example, the fine leafy designs in the molding of the iron cast building opposite hers, the cobblestones in the street below—the etching of a single red flower on the pale blue sign for the Lahore

Café, the yellow of the parked cabs, even the ordinary brown of the paper bag carried by a passerby on the sidewalk below. All seemed more vibrant, the faces of people walking by, all their details too, the Jacquard scarf on that guy with the leather jacket, the silver buckles on that woman's high heel, thigh-high, patent leather boots. This was indeed the best time of the year in New York. All the shop windows were decorated for the holidays. The mannequins were dressed for Santa's arrival and looked as though they were in starved anticipation of sumptuous balls. Christmas trees were on sale on the sidewalk below, and further down at the corner, near the subway exit, were the salvation army's soldiers ringing their bells and begging people for charity. The city was quiet. Everyone had left it or seemed to have gone elsewhere, or were indoors for the feast. It was not windy, but it was cold. Cold enough to wear a coat, but mild enough to have gone for a walk or to the Macy's parade if so inclined. Hot chocolate on such a day was an essential and the smell of chestnuts roasting and warm pretzels made the outdoors seem cozy. Even the outdoors in the city were in reality indoors. Here they were so insulated and safe from all the wars and misery out there in the world outside. Even though New York had become the iconic beginning of the new war, Amina mused, cradling her cup of hot chocolate as she sat in the window seat, the real out there was a horrible reality of human suffering, of wars, earthquakes and tsunamis. The reminder of that out there was on the news stands if anyone cared to glance at them, or on the tickertape at Times Square if anyone really wanted to spoil their holiday. But perversely that moment of reality only served to make things even more cozy here! An incentive to stay home. Ah luxury! Ah what it took to make things cozy! Everyone snug as a bug when there was a war going on!

Amina was in her element. It was hard to believe that almost a whole year had passed. Her entire family was with her: Abba, Bari-ma, Choti-ma, Sara, Resham, Kulsum, Shireen and Sara. She was back in her home in New York and playing the part of the happy hostess. Each detail has been carefully arranged. Her home, freshly painted in pastel bright colours for the walls, was filled with friends and family. Laughter and arguments mingled with the clinking and chinking of champagne and wine glasses, and the crackling of wood burning in the fireplace. The aroma of biryani and kebabs, warming in the oven with the turkey which was on its last hour of roasting filled the air. This year she had made three types of gravy. After all, Thanksgiving was about gravy. She had made one with the turkey drippings and salt and pepper and another spiced up with fresh coriander, ginger, garlic, lemon juice and green chilies. The third was more of a plum chutney with lots of cumin—like the one at weddings in Pakistan. Bowls full of peanuts, walnuts, pistachios and almonds were placed on accent tables. Gruyere, Brie, Rockford, foi gras, caviar, and marzipan were replenished as fast as they were consumed. And Brahms' violin concerto in D opus 77 played in the background. Someone said, 'It's the age of powerful and confused women and of men who know this well.'

'The haleem is to die for! Where do you get it?' A guest asked her.

'I have a fabulous caterer,' she had replied.

'Please give me his name and contact number!'

'It's a she. Her name is Rosario Mirza.'

'Hai, please give me her contact number.'

'No problem. One of her helpers is in the kitchen at the moment and when I get a chance, I'll ask her to come over and speak with you. Or why don't you go talk to her? Be nice to her staff. They're very sensitive and choosy. Rosario is almost impossible to get, she's so busy, you'll be lucky if she agrees to cater for you.'

Amina continued, 'Let me go take a peek at how things are going in the kitchen. I'll be right back.' In the kitchen, standing

amongst the clutter of used dishes and washed wine glasses, Amina checked the messages on her cellphone. Just one, 'Hope it's a good one darlin', thinking about you, wish I could be there, that we could visit with each other some time soon! Sorry about the whole wedding thing! Y'know, if you were ever in the slammer again, I wouldn't come saving you because of your politics. Nope, not because of that. Shit, I'd be there savin' you for you. Comin' to get ya out just because you're you! Think about that for a moment.' She stood for a moment in indecision, holding a glass half full of wine, and gazed out of the window then over her shoulder towards the party which was now winding down in the other room, and then at the sink. She felt dizzy, slightly queasy as well. She put the glass on the counter. 'What a waste. Good wine. Why do people do that?' She put her hands on the edge of the sink to steady herself and then she bent, her left hand reached for the tap and twisted it all the way to the right. She passed her wrists under its freezing flow. She reached into the open dishwasher and picked up a used glass. She rinsed it. She watched the glass filling up with water from the tap and then let the water spill over onto her hand and wrist. Then she drank in big gulps. Water spilled from the side of her mouth down her chin onto her silk wrap. Stone-washed silk. One of Sara's creations. Marred. She looked down at the stain. As the stain spread, she felt it cool her, the wet spot sticking to her skin. She could still hear the guests talking in the next room. They would talk forever, she thought to herself. Talking forever, saying nothing, nothing that mattered. About things in which they had no say. And yet this was all there was. This constant rewinding and repeating argument. Over and over again. Military general, elected governments, military general, elected governments, military general. The repetition and the noise was unbearable. She felt dizzy. There was a burst of oohhs and ahhas from the other room. She hurried back in.

The nanny had just brought in the baby. Fresh from his bath and ready for bedtime. First of course there were to be the kisses and hugs from his mama. Everyone in the room watched as Amina took the baby. There was a stereotypical chorus of goo-goo, ga-ga-ing. What a beautiful baby, just look at those eyes! Takes after his grandfather, you know. No? Well, I think so anyway. Amina, you lucky girl!! Well done. You are a brave girl. Well done. Such a beautiful child. Your chin. Whose eyes? Did you specify or did you leave it to chance? Can you do that? So courageous! I really admire you. I hope everyone's gotten over the stupid social stigma bullshit! Keep your spirits up. I saw the op-ed piece on Yaqub in the *DAWN* online the other day. Very good!'

'Yes, I thought so too.' Sara said. 'I mean the point to make is just that! If businessmen, honest good businessmen, can't be safe in that country, then that's the benchmark right there for the military's performance!'

'Yes,' Amina murmured. 'It was good. I thought so myself.'

'I mean, they keep going on about all the remittances that have flowed back into the country and the tax mobilization... But what's the point when no one is going to invest? I mean, the reason remittances have come into the banking system is because the hawala system's being busted by the anti-terrorism crazies, and people were scared that they would have to come back home to Pakistan. No one's investing!'

'Exactly! Who would invest, when it's clear that the military calls all the shots, and maintains the right to just take over other people's wealth!'

'Poor guy! How's he keeping?'

Before Amina could respond Sara piped up, 'Baba, I try to go and see him at least once a week. I've told everyone, he's my loyal friend and I must be loyal to him. I don't care if he's in jail or what. I think even the General understands that. We haven't had any problem with him. He came to a party of mine recently, y'know. And besides, the amount of money that Yaqub has donated for the earthquake relief has been heroic! He financed thousands of tents, truckloads of blankets, medicines and food. He paid for hundreds of trucks, drivers and the staff to take the supplies up-country and to distribute them. Of course Riaz and I were completely involved with the relief effort, but Yaqub's contribution was truly amazing, everyone knows that! And of course Riaz, Rehana and I went over to the earthquake affected area to supervise the distribution and reported back to Yaqub. We made sure that everyone knew who had made this all possible. Surely that's going to count for something!'

Amina said, 'Rehana writes to me and lets me know what's going on. At least they've given him email. The jail sentence is ridiculous. Fifteen years without bail. But we're fighting it every step of the way. Completely baseless and fabricated charges. And surely all of his involvement with the earthquake relief work will work in his favor!'

Sara said, 'Of course that was not his motivation, but clever of you to think of that. Lucky thing, he's got you for a lawyer!'

Amina replied, 'You better believe it. Thank God. And a very good one too! But good lawyers can only help where there's a rule of law. My only comfort is that he is comfortable, they've given him the VIP wing. So he's got all the comforts of everyday life at least.'

'Still! What a nightmare!' someone interjected.

'Who is handling the Foundation and his business?'

'Riaz Bhai is looking after Yaqub's business interests and Rehana is looking after the Foundation. My mother, of course, helps. And she's got that trust she's set up that's somehow tied to the Foundation, with Rehana's help. It's all good. She's very fond of Rehana. That girl is looking after everything. She's such a godsend for Yaqub. She visits Yaqub everyday. So he has all the company he could ever want. She takes food and books in for him. They're very happy. They're even designing the restoration of an old building which was a covered bazaar or perhaps stables in the nineteenth century and unfortunately has now been reduced to a beat up warehouse and a cowshed. They're planning to turn it into shops for artisans. They really are a pair! What a pair of dreamers. Yaqub trusts her completely. And she thinks he's such a hero. I don't know what I'd do without her. She's coming here to see me next month and we're constantly talking on the phone,' said Sara.

'That is really good.'

'Yes,' Amina agreed. 'Rehana tells me that she and Yaqub are planning to get married soon!'

'Just look at this darling child!'

'I send videos and pictures of him to Rehana on email nearly everyday,' Amina said. 'And we have that little camera thing set up for him as a monitor. It's really quite helpful.'

'Yes technology is marvelous!'

'Really, it makes distances and incarceration so much easier,' Sara said.

'Closes the gap really!'

'Amina, what a doll you've produced!'

Sara smile, 'Isn't he though? I only came here for the sweet little thing's birth! What a doll!'

Amina agreed and smiled into the baby's eyes, 'My sweet child, my little star! Twinkle, twinkle little star, how I wonder where you are!'

In another corner of the drawing room a different sort of pregnancy was being discussed. Zain was saying, 'It was all about hanging and pregnant chads the first time. But this last time round there was no excuse, they elected the creep!'

A woman replied, 'It's shameful, hideous! Just look at the agenda of that awful man!'

Resham agreed, 'Exactly! How many executions are there in his name in Texas?'

Amit said, 'And what I want to know is exactly how many women have partial birth abortions compared to the number of people whose deaths he is responsible for in Afghanistan, Iraq, and in secret and not so secret prisons, Gitmo, and all of those citizens here whose rights he protects for owning AK-47s!'

'Is Gitmo short for Guantanamo or is it short for Get Mohammad, Git-Mo?' Emir drawled in his thick accent.

Resham glared at him as she fiddled with Amina's digital camera. Emir shrugged his shoulders and said, 'Relax, Resham! Darling cousin of mine!'

Sara walked over to them, she put her arms around Emir's shoulders and moved her face close to Emir's so that their cheeks touched. She said to Resham, 'Take a picture of us Resham.' Sara adjusted her hijab edged with a diamanté studded braid, flashed her most charming smile and commanded, 'Now roll! I mean click.'

Emir managed a grin. Resham centered them in the screen of the camera and clicked. 'Again!' said Sara. And Resham took another picture. 'Come Abba, Bari-ma, Choti-ma, get in the picture,' Sara called and gestured towards where Hajra and Zareena were seated. Both of them shook their heads. Sara laughed, 'C'mon Emir, let's go over there. C'mon Resham, take a picture of all of us.' Arranged in front of Razzak, Hajrabai and Zareenabai, Sara and Emir sat on the floor while Resham took another picture.

'There!' Sara declared. 'My cheeweeto little cousin, it's been so lovely to spend some time with you. Now come over often okay?' Sara exclaimed, squeezing Emir's shoulders with affection. 'We'll show this picture to the embassy people, when we go to get our visa for our Ziarats to Jerusalem, no!' Sara moved to another guest just as Resham rolled her eyes. Emir chuckled and shook his head, 'She's a piece of work!'

'The best in the business, and she knows it,' Resham said and noticed that she sounded proud.

The conversation got louder and so did the laughter. There was talk about salsa and tango, technology, stocks that were hot and those that were not, and hedge funds. There was banter about the plays on and off Broadway, the milk boiling over in Remembrance of Things Past, and the longing for the Kiss, the funeral march in Wagner's Ring series that someone had found sublime the year before last, and the similarities of Proust and DeLillo, the baseball in DeLillo's Underworld approximating the Kiss, and garbage as an analogy for history and memory. Then there was some conversation about the delicious little short story by Henry James that someone discovered just the other day, 'The Turn of the Screw!' Oh my! How weird was that? The conversation moved on to a decision that Freud was not a patch on the deep-seated archetypes created by Wagner. And in all this talk there was a steady conversation, almost like background noise, a staple, like a discussion on weather, it was that conversation about politics and war without which such an evening, such a deliciously lit, cozy and comforting evening, it seemed would have been incomplete.

Amina made her way to Tim who was standing alone leaning against the entrance at the foyer, his hands thrust in the pockets of his khaki pants. In the candle-light his auburn hair had a tint of red—he looked quite handsome she thought and then she said, 'Are you leaving us Tim, or simply in need of rescuing?'

Tim grinned at her, his face an expanse of kindness, 'Neither,' he replied putting his arms around her and giving her a hug. 'I'm having a great time. Things have really moved on haven't they since the last time you had everyone over here?'

Amina agreed, 'I'd say! It's the privilege of being a citizen, having it all and getting away with everything! So tell me, how are things with you? Are you and Fatima an item or what?'

Tim smiled ruefully, 'We're thinking about it. But what's the point of ruining a great friendship?'

'I hear you,' Amina sighed.

Tim asked, 'Do you think you'll get involved with civil rights issues, Amina?'

'Oh Tim!' Amina said nonchalantly, 'I don't know! I'm so fatigued with all that I've got going at the moment. There's a lot going on and I simply can't think of anything more!'

Tim suggested, 'Perhaps you should drop some of it, change course completely!'

'I'd love to. But who's going to pay the damn mortgage?'

Tim agreed, 'That does become the final question, doesn't it?'

Amina nodded as she gathered up several empty wine glasses, balancing them between her delicate fingers and picked up a few dishes. She cast a glance at the supply of nuts and chips in the bowls around the room and noted the need for replenishments.

She moved her right shoulder to brush away and push back her shining black hair from her glowing, warm cheek. Amina looked up at Tim, the whites of her eyes startlingly clear, her eyes sparkled as she sighed resignedly. 'I'm afraid so. We're all trapped in mortgages and the good life. And the search for the perfect, organic tomato. And so it goes and so it will go.'